The Midnight Land I
The Flight

E.P. Clark

Helia Press

Newsletter Signup

*Want to keep in touch and be the first to know about offers and new releases? Get the free story collection **Winter of the Gods and Other Stories** and sign up for my newsletter (but only if you want to!) at epclarkauthor.net.*

Epigraph

I've gone over everything very carefully:
There are many contradictions,
But I don't want to correct them...
...In a dark dream
They first appeared to me—
And I had not yet distinguished clearly
Through a magic crystal
The distant prospect of a free novel.
Aleksandr Sergeyevich Pushkin

Chapter One

The sun did not rise on the morning of the trial, and neither did Slava's spirits.

When she looked out the window that morning, all she saw was early-winter snow sifting down onto the courtyard like fine sugar onto cake. Even the clouds were hidden by it. She knew that somewhere far to the South— perhaps on the Middle Sea—the sun was shining down on people who were rising and going about their business with joy in their hearts, but here in Krasnograd there was nothing but snow, both outside on the courtyard and inside of Slava's soul.

Her maids came and dressed her extra-resplendently for the trial. Masha, the older but shyer of the two of them, was sufficiently emboldened by the occasion to ask her, "Aren't you glad he's being judged today, Krasnoslava Tsarinovna?"

"I only wish that it be over quickly," Slava answered.

"I hope he gets what's coming to him!" said Manya, the other maid. She was not quite so shy as Masha, but that was not why she had no fear of speaking her mind in front of Slava. Most people did not. "No punishment could be cruel enough!"

"We always think that about other people," said Slava.

Manya gave her a look that said, "Everyone knows the Empress's little sister is eccentric," and went back to braiding the elaborate headdress onto Slava's head.

Once Slava had been tied, stitched, and braided into her clothing, she was escorted by her guards from her chambers to the Hall of Judgment. For the first time in many years, the sight of their uniforms made her feel ill. She wanted to hang back and delay the moment of arrival, but her guards walked her as quickly as she could manage in her heavy gown. They were so excited by the prospect of the trial that they had a hard time remembering Slava herself.

The Hall of Judgment was packed with people, and therefore hot and close despite the winter air outside. Slava broke out into a sweat as soon as she entered it. Only two places were conspicuously empty: the dock for the prisoner, and the raised dais for the Empress's Wooden Throne.

Slava's guards pushed through the crush of people spilling out into the aisle they had created with their knouts. Everyone whispered and tried to kneel as she walked past, but there was no room for them to reach the floor with their knees. The guards seated her on the edge of the dais, near the foot of the throne.

It was one of the peculiarities of Slava's position that she spent much of her time sitting on the floor, looking at other people's feet. As the Empress's sister, she was allowed to sit in her presence in the Hall of Judgment, but as the junior sister, she could not sit at the same level, which was why she spent so much of her time stationed on the edge of the dais. Well, as much of her time as could be spared from getting dressed and undressed by her maids. Somehow Slava's days were always so full of such meaningless tasks that she never seemed to have a moment to herself, even though she did nothing. Just as she was doing here, perched on her shameful place of honor so that everyone but her could feel as if justice and mercy were being done. There was a cushion for her there, embroidered with the finest silk from the East by her sister's own maids. Only Slava thought this was amusing; everyone else considered it a great honor for her.

When Slava had been settled into place by her guards, there were shouts of "Make way for the prisoner!" and the crowd surged like a stormy sea as half of them tried to rush forward to catch sight of the notorious criminal, and half tried to rush back in fear. There were shrieks as people got caught in the crush, and more shrieks as the guards restored order with their knouts. Only once a wide path had been cleared did the doors open, and the guards try to lead the prisoner up to the dock.

As soon as he appeared in the doorway, though, there was such a scream and a rush towards him that his guards slammed the doors shut, and Slava's guards picked her up under the arms and dragged her across the dais and through a small door to one of the hidden passageways that filled the Krasnograd kremlin, allowing its residents to slip through the walls whenever they wanted to hide from their subjects.

More guards were already waiting for them in the passageway, with a request from the Empress to see Slava as soon as she was extracted safely from the madness that was currently filling the Hall of Judgment. She was led around dark corners to a candlelit open space, where her sister was sitting on a sofa and waiting for her.

Slava wondered if anyone else thought it was odd for the Empress of all of Zem' to be sitting in a hidden passageway in her own kremlin, or for there to be a space for her to do so, comfortably furnished with a sofa and silk cushions. She also wondered how they had gotten the sofa there, and whether it was there all the time or had been brought specially for this occasion, but she knew better than to ask questions like that. No reason to sink herself even lower in her sister's opinion than she was already sunk, especially with all the guards looking on.

"We have called up the regular troops from the barracks to come in and help restore order," said the Empress with a smile. Slava's sister was always smiling whenever the situation called for boldness and good humor, and serious whenever the situation called for seriousness. A riot in the middle of her Hall of Judgment had not shaken her imperturbable confidence, and now she sat on her sofa and waited with absolute certainty that in a very short time her guards and soldiers would beat everyone into submission and remove them from her presence, and she could get on with her day.

And in fact they only had to wait just long enough for Slava to begin feeling even more awkward and pathetic than usual in the face of her sister's serene smile, before Boleslav Vlasiyevich, Captain of the Imperial Guard, came up and reported that the situation in the Hall of Judgment had been pacified and that everyone had been dragged out and dumped onto the street outside the kremlin walls. He advised that the Hall of Judgment be kept empty except for the people involved directly with the trial, and Slava's sister agreed with a smile that said she had perfect faith in herself and everyone under her. She rose from her sofa, and the whole party set off to try to enter the Hall of Judgment for the second time.

"The prisoner has already been brought in and chained to the dock, Tsarina," reported Boleslav Vlasiyevich as they approached the Hall of Judgment. He flicked his eyes Slava's way. "Are you sure you're up to this, Tsarinovna?" he asked, dropping back half a step to fall level with Slava. "I know you find this sort of thing distressing. You are not a woman of fire and steel like your foremothers. You are made of finer, softer stuff. Just give the word, and I will give the Empress some suitable excuse, and allow you to retire to your chambers." He smiled at her the way he often did, as if there were something between them, some secret that bound them and that required him to be more solicitous of her than other people were. For the life of her, Slava could not fathom where he had gotten this idea, but it was clear enough that he was convinced of its truth.

"Thank you, but it is not necessary, Boleslav Vlasiyevich," said Slava, smiling back gratefully. She meant for the gratitude to be feigned, but hungry as she was for any show of kindness and affection, there was a great deal of real gratitude mixed in with it as well, and she knew her smile was much too bright for the circumstances. It would be very wrong of her to give Boleslav Vlasiyevich any encouragement, especially as she had no intention of doing anything more than smile. Although he was certainly not an ill figure of a man...not so large as most of the other guards, but quick and neat, with dark hair, gray eyes, and clever hands...hands that were mostly likely dirty with other people's blood...and, most unusually for her, she could never tell what he was thinking...although she always felt as if she could be sure that his hands would never be dirty with *her* blood, even if he did wear a guard's uniform...well, but she had given up long ago on guessing what men were thinking about her, she had been wrong too many times to be able to trust her judgment on that score...so wrong, so many times...she wrenched her attention back to the sorry matter at hand before she let her thoughts show on her face.

"It is my duty to attend," she told him instead. "I must be ready to give the Empress my council, should she require it."

"As you will, Tsarinovna," said Boleslav Vlasiyevich, with a slight bow and an almost imperceptible brush of Slava's arm. In Slava's current starving state, it was difficult not to brush his arm back...but that would lead to no good...whatever affection men seemed to feel at first always disappeared quick enough...it would be wonderful, so wonderful, though, to have a man stand up for her for once, take care of her for once, instead of putting her down or running away...little chance of that, though...inasmuch as she could tell such a thing, men always seemed to find Slava disgusting...but they found most other women disgusting, too...but Slava especially...and no wonder...Slava sometimes—well, often—found herself disgusting...and no wonder, given the pathetic thoughts currently running through her head...next she would be sniveling in public...which she did fairly often, it had to be admitted...disgusting, disgusting...perhaps Boleslav Vlasiyevich was right, and she should not attend the trial, as she would do no good, no good at all...

"Then we may begin without delay," said Slava's sister, who had not appeared to notice the exchange between Slava and Boleslav Vla-siyevich. He stepped back to his place by the Empress's side, and ordered the guards to let them in. The doors swung open, and Slava's sister marched through them and straight to her throne, looking neither right nor left.

Slava trailed after her and watched her take her seat on the Wooden Throne. It was a simple thing, hardly more than a chair, easily moved from hall to hall as required, and it didn't seem grand enough for its office whenever Slava's sister sat in it. Slava knew she had wanted to decorate it with some jewels and gold, perhaps make it bigger in order to fit her tall frame, but on this one point all her princesses had been unpersuadable. The throne had been built for Miroslava Praskovyevna herself by her own husband, and spells of protection and power were carved into its wooden frame. How much of the original chair remained was uncertain, as it had certainly been repaired many times in the intervening centuries, but it was still, somehow, the same chair, the seat of empresses, and for the right occupant, so it was said, a seat of great power despite its unprepossessing appearance. Unfortunately, Slava's sister was probably not the right occupant. Slava turned her eyes and her thoughts to the rest of the room in order to distract herself from such treasonous thoughts.

This time the Hall of Judgment was almost empty. Pools of blood stood here and there on the floor, from where the guards had had to subdue someone particularly vigorously. Slava looked away from them. Her eyes fell on a group of women that was being held back in a corner by guards. Even before her mind had made the connection, she knew by the pain in her heart that they must be the mothers of previous victims, and she looked away quickly.

Her eyes turned to the prisoner at the dock instead, and then jumped away as if burned. She made her way to the dais and settled on her cushion with her heart racing painfully and her eyes firmly fixed on the floor.

Her dread of this trial had pressed down on her ever since Manya had come to her two days ago and told her gleefully that "This time they had really got him, this time he had been caught in the act and there was no denying it, this time they had really got him and he was to be tried and sentenced immediately."

On the day after Midsummer, a young girl's body, mutilated almost beyond recognition, had been found in a back alley. There had been a great hue and cry, and some young man with a shifty look in his eyes had been caught near the scene and beaten to death by the enraged crowd that very night. Slava had lain awake for several nights after that, alternately picturing herself as the little girl and as the young man. Her only way to find comfort was to remind herself that, however terrible it had been for them, it was over now.

But, while it may have been over for them, it was not over for Krasnograd or for Slava. The next month another body had been found, and once again the parents' grief and horror had caused another crowd to gather together and bring some poor fellow to what they called justice, so that they could tell themselves that they had protected Krasnograd from the menace stalking its streets.

Only they hadn't, and the next month yet another body was discovered. This time the Krasnograd guards stepped in and closed down that area of the city, rounding up all the likely-looking suspects and locking everyone else in their houses. Those whom they deemed suspicious were dragged back to the dungeons and questioned. Those who survived the questioning process were sent off on general principles to do hard labor in distant provinces, and everyone except Slava and the victims' families breathed a huge sigh of relief and started to forget about it.

The next month it happened again, and the month after that. Five little girls had been killed, and at least ten or fifteen—Slava tried not to keep too accurate a count, even though she knew that the best thing she could do for them would be to remember them—at least ten or fifteen people had been killed or sentenced to hard labor on suspicion of being involved. Then this month someone whom everyone claimed was the real culprit had been caught red-handed, and now he was shackled to the dock in front of Slava.

She stared at her knees to avoid looking at him. She knew that as soon as she did, everything that he was feeling would come pouring unstoppably into her. Slava could not bear the miasma of thoughtless cruelty that rose off so many people, and she particularly could not bear that she was helpless before its onslaught. As Boleslav Vlasiyevich had said, she was made of finer, or at least softer, stuff than the rest of her family. Some dreadful taint from the male line, perhaps.

Certainly few of her foremothers were known for their weakness. Fire and steel, almost every one of them. Those who had shown mercy had been the exceptions that proved the rule. Where Slava had come from, no one could say...Her mother was kind enough, that was true, as well as, it was said, Lyubov the Kind, the great-great-great-grandmother who had ended the practice of slavery in Zem', but she had never heard or seen anything that had suggested they were anything like Slava, had possessed anything like Slava's softness...Lyubov must have been a woman of fire and steel, second only to Miroslava Praskovyevna, to bend the princesses to her will and end the slave trade...and Slava's father had been a steppe warrior, renowned for his fearlessness in battle before he had died a hero's death...Slava dragged her mind away from her melancholy musings on the past and back to the unpleasant present.

Yarmila Kseniyevna, the Mistress of Ceremonies, was naming all those involved in the trial. The women pushed back into the corner, whose grief and blind, thoughtless rage had spread out across the room and was already seeping into Slava's skin, were indeed the mothers of the previous victims. A woman standing apart from the others with her arms around a girl of about ten was introduced as the mother of the current victim, and the little girl as the victim herself.

At this Slava peeked up from her knees. She hadn't known that the latest little girl had survived. She and the girl looked at each other, and Slava knew that the girl was terrified of the guards, and of the stern women in their fancy gowns sitting on the dais and staring at her, and of the scary man chained to the dock who had frightened her so badly two days before, and of the angry women in the corner who watched her with such burning resentment, and most of all of her own mother, who had made her life a misery of threats, reproaches, and hysterical, mysterious scenes ever since she had screamed that the strange man was trying to take her away. The girl was heartily sorry now that she had ever said anything, and wished that this could all be over as soon as possible and that her mother and all these strange people would leave her alone.

After the accusers, Yarmila Kseniyevna named the accused and his crimes. Slava's eyes flickered past him as quickly as possible, but not quickly enough to avoid seeing the woman next to him, who was named as his mother. The mother's eyes caught Slava's and held them, and Slava was unable to prevent the other woman's feelings from flooding into her.

In the space of a breath she knew that the other woman was full of resentment that her child was being forced to undergo this ordeal, and an overwhelming, all-engulfing terror that he would not escape from it unscathed, and a willingness to sacrifice a thousand other mothers' children in order for her own to remain healthy, alive, and free. Slava jerked away from her as quickly as she could, but not before she knew that pity for the other woman would torment her for a long time to come.

Various functionaries came up and read statements about the previous murders, the current attempt, the results of the questioning of the prisoner, and every other piece of information they had been able to gather. Slava looked at these women in their dull gray gowns of the Office of Judgment, or the guards in their bright red and blue uniforms and their jingling chainmail, and all she could sense from them was a suppressed excitement at being part of the trial, and a desire to cause as much harm as possible to the prisoner chained to the dock, now that he *was* chained to the dock and therefore offered them no threat. Then the prisoner's mother stepped forward and spoke in his defense.

She argued, trembling and mixing up her words in her fear of the Empress and her terror for her child, that there was no proof that he had done any of the actual murders, and that when he had grabbed the little girl currently standing across the room from him and tried to drag her away, he was only dragging her out of harm's way, because her own mother had been paying no attention to her and a large wagon had been bearing down on her.

"LIAR!" screamed the girl's mother. "There was no wagon!"

"There was a wagon, gracious Tsarina," said one of the women in gray gowns. Slava had heard her speak before, and knew that she was a little sharper than most of the other women her sister had appointed to work in the Office of Judgment, as witnessed by her speaking up now. Slava couldn't remember her name, and felt a twinge of guilt over that, but it was quickly overwhelmed by the misery filling the Hall of Judgment. "All witnesses agree," said the sharp woman in the dull gray gown. "There was a wagon, and the girl's mother did not seem to be aware of it. Nonetheless..."

"He wanted to..." moaned the girl's mother, interrupting the woman from the Office of Judgment. "He wanted to...He deserves to die! Die!"

"DIE!" screamed the women in the corner, and tried to rush past the guards, who had to add to the pools of the blood on the floor in order to restrain them.

The Councilor of Justice, whose gray gown was decorated with a sash of Imperial red, reminded the Empress that a coil of rope and knives "of a sort that are used only for torture" had been found in the prisoner's pockets, all covered with old blood. For a moment Slava was distracted from the horror of the matter at hand by the horror of the thought that knives "of a sort that are used only for torture" even existed.

What, she wondered, had the women who had invented them been thinking as they made them? How could they walk away from their plans and their forges and return to their husbands and children? No doubt their husbands had helped them in the forging; what had they been thinking? Did they think that their wives were the most wonderful women in the world, the beloved mothers of their children? Possibly. At any rate, it was very unlikely that they thought they were evil for making those knives. Probably they thought it was just the way of things, and secretly took pleasure in imagining the use for which the knives had been designed.

"It seems clear enough," said the Empress, interrupting Slava's dreadful reverie. She was no longer smiling, but spoke with a serious dignity perfectly in accord with the current situation. "We pronounce the prisoner guilty on all charges."

The mothers of the victims, both dead and alive, cheered, their faces contorted with a bestial hatred that made Slava want to pronounce the same verdict on them, and see how they liked it. The mothers of dead children, she reflected, unfortunately not for the first time, were normally so broken by their sorrow that they were no more than animals. She might pity them, but it was the pity one would feel for a wounded bear that was rampaging through a village. She wondered how many of them had beaten their daughters when they were alive. Probably most of them. Probably many of them would have gladly thrown their daughters to the wolves when they had been alive, but now that they were dead, they had so handily been given someone else to blame for their failings. The mother of the prisoner threw herself on the floor in front of the dais.

"Mercy," she begged. "Mother, be merciful. You have a child of your own. Be merciful this once, and it will never happen again, I swear it, it will never happen again, it will never..."

"What does my sister say?" asked the Empress, looking at Slava.

"Before I decide on the nature of his sentence, I would hear your opinion. Is he truly guilty, and will he do it again?"

"Dearest, kindest Krasnoslava Tsarinovna," sobbed the prisoner's mother from the floor. "Everyone knows that the gods have gifted you with that greatest gift of all: the ability to feel the pain in the hearts of others. I beg you: let your heart feel the pain of mine, and have mercy on my son. Surely you of all people can be persuaded to have pity on my pain, and..."

"What about mine!" screamed a woman from the corner, and all the other mothers moaned, "and mine!" in chorus. "My pain is greater than yours, and of less cause. You have only yourself to blame for raising a monster that should be destroyed like a mad dog!"

"No!" cried the prisoner's mother, and Slava saw how she tried to ignore those terrible words, because she feared they might be true.

"Silence!" ordered the Empress, and the guards restored order to the room once more. Slava looked at the prisoner.

He had probably been an ordinary-looking man, but it was difficult to tell after the questioning, which had left him badly battered. For a moment Slava was distracted by the sympathetic gaze of Boleslav Vlasiyevich, who was standing next to the prisoner's mother, ready to subdue her if necessary. Slava wondered how much of the prisoner's current condition was Boleslav Vlasiyevich's own doing.

Slava's mother had made him part of her own guard after he, then a young and unknown soldier assigned to protect some distant fourth-sister of the Imperial family, had saved said fourth-sister from an attack by a whole host of bandits, and he was still considered by many to be a great sword and a brave man, but since he had entered her family's service all he seemed to do was question prisoners, hardly the occupation of a hero...once or twice Slava had heard mutterings from the other guards that something had driven him to take up this line of duty, something dreadful had called him to a dreadful vengeance, but they always fell silent or changed the subject when they realized she was listening...and it had led him to rise in her mother's favor, so that her last act as Tsarina had been to make him her Captain...what a terrible way to rise through the ranks...you wouldn't think it to look at him...but he had always been unpredictable, of that everyone who knew him agreed...

Slava wondered if he suffered pangs of conscience because of what he did...she had never been down in the kremlin dungeons, where prisoners such as the one before her were kept and questioned, and most of the time she tried to pretend that they didn't exist, as there was nothing she could do about them and what happened in them. Emptying and ending the dungeons would be tantamount to destroying Krasnograd and its kremlin at their very foundations, for both were built directly upon them, in every sense of the word.

Sometimes, in the dark of night, Slava thought she could feel them down there, a black evil eating away at her mind and at Krasnograd. As far as she knew, no one had dared curse Krasnograd for a long time, probably since its conquest by her family, but no one would need to, in her opinion, since it carried its own curse inside of it, in the form of those dungeons. Neither she nor Krasnograd would ever know peace, she would think darkly on those dark nights, until the dungeons had been torn apart, brick from brick and stone from stone, and nothing was left of them but smoke and ash, but that would never happen. She wished that she did not have to be reminded so horribly of their presence, but that was a selfish thought, and was swept away as soon the prisoner looked back at Slava. She quickly looked away. Then, afraid of making too hasty a judgment, she looked back at him. He had large gray eyes that wanted to swallow her up.

Despite experiencing it many times, Slava was often surprised by how much evil a single human heart could contain, and this time was no different. Even after being starved, and beaten, and probably much worse as well, the one-way gate of the prisoner's mind remained unbroken, allowing nothing but malevolence to pour out and absolutely nothing at all to pour in. Slava could feel the cold fingers of his cruelty slipping through her skin and prying through her mind and body, searching for the best way to cause her pain. And worse, she could feel an answering desire for pain rise up in her own heart. For a moment she, too, wanted to cut others in order to watch them bleed, and feel her own heart race at the sight of the blood. Her mouth watered for the taste of it, and the tips of her fingers itched, as if long claws were waiting to burst free in order to tear into the hearts of others. It would be an ecstatic outpouring, a blessed relief. The desire was as strong as the longing for a lover.

She looked away. She knew that if he were unchained, he would hurt her without a second thought, because for him she didn't exist. He was not a person at all, which meant that other people were not people for him either, and so he could never be trusted with another living being, never, never, because he would always see them only as things. Things to hurt. For a moment she had to bite her tongue in order to quell the urge to hurt someone. Her own pain brought her back to her senses, and she knew that it was all nonsense, that she had been possessed for a moment and that she was not him, not someone who desired the suffering of others. Not very much, anyway, and not strongly enough to act on it. So she told herself.

"He cannot be trusted," she said. Even though she was no longer looking at him—and he was no longer looking at her, but at the floor—she could feel his eyes following her. "He must never be allowed to walk freely amongst others again."

"Then let him die!" cried one of the mothers in the corner.

"Die!" the others wailed.

"He should suffer!" said the mother of the girl who had survived. "He must suffer for what he has done!" A desire for a pain that could blot out their own pain rose from the victims' mothers like a heavy stench, and overwhelmed for a moment the same desire for pain that was coming from the man at the dock.

"Little mother!" The prisoner's mother was still on the floor. "Little mother, have mercy!"

"What mercy did you or your thrice-cursed monster ever have!" screamed one of the mothers in the corner.

"The normal punishment for death is death," said Slava's sister serenely. "And by that reckoning, your son should die many times over. Most would say that there is no torture we could inflict on him that would be cruel enough."

"NO!" Slava's cry surprised even her. The hatred of the mothers was suddenly all focused on her.

"You said yourself he was dangerous, sister," said Slava's sister. "We cannot let such a monster walk free amongst us."

"Send him to the mines," said Slava. "We always have need of more men there. Send him the mines, but do not...you cannot..." Her voice was trembling too much for her to continue.

"NO!" screamed one of the mothers. "I want to see him burned!"

"Flayed alive!" screamed a second one.

"They only knew it was my Masha because of her dress!" screamed a third. "I want to see him boiled, or, or drawn and quartered, or..." She fell on the ground and began rolling around and wailing, but Slava couldn't tell what she was wailing, because the prisoner's mother was beating her head against the floor and screaming in long, gasping screams. The guards moved in and used their knouts to silence both women.

"The mines," repeated Slava.

"Why should he have mercy when he gave his victims none?" asked Slava's sister. She was smiling again, with the mixture of curiosity and condescension that she normally directed towards Slava. For a moment Slava was overwhelmed with the hopelessness of making others act as people, not savage dogs. The desperate need to save him, and the desperate desire to be elsewhere, anywhere else, and not have to cause all these people so much pain, tore in two opposite directions, like wild horses, so that it seemed as if they might tear her in half...If only she could run away from this dreadful place, run away and take him with her, so that he would be safe too—

"Because we are not him!" Slava's voice broke, and the words came out as much more of a shriek than she would have liked. "He...he did what he did because, because he thought that it is acceptable to kill certain people in order to make himself feel better, and if you kill him, it will be because you think it is acceptable to kill certain people in order to make yourself feel better. The thinking is the same. The actions are the same. You will, you will...it will be the same..."

"But we must put a stop to people like him, and we cannot do that by being soft," said Slava's sister, interrupting Slava before she could finish putting voice to her inchoate thoughts. Her voice was full of the same brick-like certainty that surrounded the man at the dock.

"How can you...how can you..." *How can you be so horrible* was what Slava wanted to say, but the words wouldn't come out, partly because she knew they would do no good, and partly because she knew they would cause her sister pain. Slava's sister prided herself, unjustly, on the mercy and justness of her reign, and any just criticism Slava made of it would hurt both of them more than Slava could stand. Slava would have to find some other way of pleading her case. Some way that would work, because her sister and all her retinue were only soft where they needed to be strong. Where they needed to be gentle and yielding they were plated in cast iron.

Once again Slava was overwhelmed by the hopelessness of her own task, and the apparent justness of her sister's words. It would be so easy for Slava to give up, and everyone would say it was the right thing to do. In defending the heartless criminal before her, she was wasting her strength on a cause that would be better not to defend. She should leave him to be burned alive or boiled in oil—no, boiling was only for traitors, that wouldn't happen to him—or broken on the wheel, and once the inhuman screams of agony were over, she and everyone else in Krasnograd could congratulate themselves on a job well done and lie easier at night. Well, everyone else in Krasnograd would. She looked at the floor, in order not to see the others in the Hall of Judgment and all their pain, and gathered her thoughts.

"It has been done before," Slava said, instead of what she was really thinking. That argument, at least, would weigh heavily with her sister, who also prided herself on her connection with Empresses of the past. "Criminals such as him have been sent to the mines before."

"Really?" said Slava's sister, looking at her with a look that was equal parts curiosity, self-satisfaction, and doubt in Slava's abilities. "When? Since you have been spending all your time reading scrolls these past few months instead of assisting me at my duties, I'm sure you have the answer at your fingertips. What is it you're doing with them again?"

"Studying the invasions of the Hordes," said Slava, resisting the desire to point out that she was doing so only in snatches, when her sister had not filled up her days with tasks that were even more meaningless than poring over old scrolls. "But I have also read accounts of mercy such as what I believe is due here," she said instead. "For example, under the reign of our grandmother, Vladislava Svetoslavovna, there was a case similar to this one two years before the last attempted invasion by the Hordes. The man responsible was found guilty, but instead of being killed, he was sent to the mines, at the request of our mother, to atone for his crimes by being of use to the realm."

"But that must have been...Oh, some time ago..." said Slava's sister, waving her hand dismissively.

"Forty-seven years ago," said Slava. "Before either of us was born. Our mother was still barely out of her girlhood at the time. But even then she showed the mercy that was the character of her reign..." Slava stopped, seeing the pained expression that crossed her sister's face.

"Our mother is too kind," said Slava's sister, waving her hand dismissively again. "It is her one flaw. Her character was always more suited to the sanctuary than to the throne. She is better off where she is."

"Even Miroslava Praskovyevna, our esteemed foremother and the founder of our rule, showed mercy from time to time," said Slava desperately. Until that moment she would have laughed if anyone had said such a thing in front of her, but as soon as she said it, she knew that it was, in fact, true. Who would have thought that the words "mercy" and "Miroslava Praskovyevna" would ever be uttered in the same sentence...

"Would that have been before she beheaded the entire Krasnorechivaya family with her own hands, or after?" asked Slava's sister with a little laugh, interrupting her thoughts. "Perhaps while she was subjugating every city along the Krasna with fire and sword? Or perhaps when she broke the backs of the steppe queens' armies and took their territory as her own?"

"She let Ruslan Anastasiyevich live," said Slava. "The Krasnorechiviye's youngest son. And in the third year of her reign, when the dispute between the Stepnaya family and the Malokrasnovy broke out..."

"Meaningless trivia," said Slava's sister, with a third dismissive wave of her hand. "Dead facts about dead women. This is why you were not meant to be Tsarina, Slava: you don't understand what's important. You think that because the scrolls say Miroslava Praskovyevna was once merciful, we should be, too. Sometimes I think our mother was wrong to take a Stepnoy for her second husband: you got all the Stepnaya wildness without any of their courage. If only your father had had a little more of your fearfulness, he might still be alive. As it is you only cower and beg for favors from others, caring for nothing but your selfish pleasure. The gods must be wise, for they made me, who does not flinch away from the responsibilities of ruling, eldest, and you, who can think of nothing but yourself, youngest. It is well you have no need to trouble yourself with the cares of governance, Slava, for your thoughts are too petty, all caught up in your own selfish concerns."

Slava's sister paused for a moment to savor the pleasure of insulting Slava before the assembled crowd. Of late she had taken to needling Slava especially hard about her father, probably because she resented the fact that Slava's father had been a far greater prince than her own had been—Vladislava's father had been a mere Zapadnokrasnov, with more money than either might or magic to his name, while Slava's father had been the son of a great princess, and heir to a long line of feared warriors—and perhaps also because she wanted to remind everyone that Slava had a strong claim to the Stepnaya lands, even as she had no claim at all the throne itself—or so the Empress would like to think.

"But since you seem to care so much, I will do as you ask." Slava's sister turned to the others in the room. "Let it be known that the prisoner's sentence has been changed from death to exile to the mines, in honor of my sister's recent birthday."

"NO!" screamed the mothers of the victims and the mother of the prisoner simultaneously. The guards brought out their knouts again, but that failed to quell them. "He must die!" screamed the victims' mothers.

"He will die there!" screamed the prisoner's mother. She was, Slava knew, most likely correct. The mercy Slava had bought for her son was unlikely to be long-lived, for the mines and the road crews to which prisoners were sent were said to be worse than the dungeons of Krasnograd, and most of that horror was the creation of the prisoners themselves. But it was the only mercy Slava could find.

"I have spoken." Slava's sister rose from her throne. She seemed to be smiling slightly at the chaos she had caused. Her guards surrounded her and escorted her off the dais, across the room, and through the door. Everyone knelt silently as she walked past.

Slava's guards helped her to her feet and began leading her to the doors. The prisoner's mother watched as she went past, full of reproach but too overwhelmed by sobs to voice it. The prisoner glanced at her for a moment. His look made her want to shrink away as she would from a viper that had somehow found its way to her feet, although vipers at least had bright, innocent eyes. The victims' mothers glared at her, all their hatred focused for the moment on her, and spat or whispered threats as she walked by.

Slava followed her guards through the kremlin halls back to her rooms. She felt as if her ears were ringing, even though they were not. Anger and misery had filled the Hall of Judgment as deafeningly as if dozens of drummers had all been in there, each trying to out-drum the other. Each person in the room had been so sure that her pain was the one that should cease, and that everyone else's pain should be increased in order to drown out her own, and somehow the only person who was left unable to breathe was Slava.

Once back in her rooms, Slava lay down on her bed and allowed her limbs to tremble until Manya came in all too quickly and told her it was time to get dressed for the feast her sister was holding in honor of some alliance Miroslava Praskovyevna had made many years ago. Feasts were an important part of kremlin life, and any day that could otherwise have been spent in peace and quiet and worthwhile work—if Slava could even imagine such a thing—was likely to be filled with feasting instead, in honor of something their foremother or her descendants had done.

Slava's sister, like all others of Zerkalitsa blood, and the rest of Zem' as well, worshipped the memory of Miroslava Praskovyevna rather more zealously than she did the gods, and took great pride in every tiny sign that she was descended from such an illustrious foremother. When Slava had particularly displeased her, she would, as she had done at the trial, reproach her with the vast differences between her and the progenitrix of their house.

Slava, however, no matter how painful she found her sister's criticism, could feel nothing but pleasure in being so totally unlike someone she would have liked to deny all connection to. A woman who had put every city between Pristanograd and Krasnograd to the sword! Who had made every princess—and then they had been queens, of course—in Zem' kneel down before her and kiss the tips of her boots, both in deed and in mind! Who had wielded the axe that ended the Krasnorechivaya line with her own hand! They said that gray-haired grandmothers, newly-wed brides, and crying children had all lain down their heads on Miroslava Praskovyevna's block that day, and that she had struck without flinching until there was not a person left alive who could lay claim to Krasnograd, and then she had threatened the same to any family who dared oppose her, before walking off without a backward glance at the bodies of her victims.

The legacy of Miroslava Praskovyevna, in which every other Zerkalitsa took such pride, had always seemed to Slava to be a taint in the blood and a heavy curse. A curse that everyone seemed intent on reviving whenever it was in danger of dying out. Slava was very glad that no one had yet to find a point of resemblance between the two of them. She wished she could be so certain that they had so little in common—but surely, surely, Slava would never act as Miroslava Praskovyevna had, wresting Krasnograd from others with fire and steel. And blood, lots of blood and suffering. Surely, surely Miroslava Praskovyevna had never known what it was to feel sympathy as Slava did. Surely, surely. She was supposed to be the mirror that reflected only reality, but mirrors were cold, unliving things.

Except in my case, Slava said to herself. *I must be some passion-mirror, always seared with hot coals.*

Masha and Manya were fussing at her to get ready for the feast. Slava got out of bed and obediently allowed them to undress her, re-dress her, set her in front of the mirror, undo her hair, and redo it, braiding into it a new and even taller and finer headdress, one that was probably worth two or three of the more miserable villages along the Krasna. Masha and Manya stroked it with loving hands, and murmured over how fine it was, and how fine the Tsarinovna looked in it.

Slava tried not to see herself as they did this, but despite her efforts she still caught sight of her body, which was the skinny but lumpy body of a woman who never did anything; and of her face, which was a funny triangular shape with eyes that were much too large and staring. The bloom of youth was rapidly being rubbed off it, and she feared that in a few years all that would be left would be those terrifying big gray eyes, trapped in an ugly old-woman's face that had been crushed and trampled by other people's passions long before its time.

The problem with mirrors, Slava thought, *is that when you look into them, they look back at you. That's what I do: stare back at other people's souls day in and day out, unable to stop them from reflecting in me. They look at me, and we both see their face in all its glory. I wish I didn't have to go to this feast.*

Masha and Manya brushed and braided her hair with no concern for what was underneath it. Slava knew that to them, she was just a thing to be dressed and undressed at regular intervals, and that they loved her beautiful gowns and magnificent headdresses much more than they could ever love her. They felt the bones of her skull under their fingers, and assumed that there was nothing but bone all the way through, just the way they did about everyone else, just the way they were, it sometimes seemed to Slava, themselves—inches and inches of unfeeling bone, with a tiny soft core in the center that only had room for their own thoughts, and no one else's.

She was aware that such thoughts did her little credit, and only made her unhappy while doing nothing to help others, but she couldn't seem to stop herself. Every day, every hour, she saw fresh proof of the evils of the world of women, and with every piece of this proof she herself sank deeper and deeper into stale brooding.

Sometimes Slava wondered if the gods had created a certain amount of skull material that was supposed to be shared equally, but somehow something had gone wrong, and other people had ended up with hers, so that their heads were thick and unfeeling, while she was left with no protection at all. That was how she felt: as if there were nothing shielding her from the outer world, so that other people's thoughts and feelings could enter into her whether she willed it or no, while her own thoughts and feelings were brushed aside without hesitation, like falling autumn leaves.

Or sometimes she saw herself as carrying a glowing sphere of light where her head should be, while other people were dark lanterns whose shutters could not be opened and whose light could not be released. Only if that were the case, then her light should be able to shine on them, only it seemed as if it never did. They all wore heavy armor, while she had no skin at all. Although, it seemed, plenty of arrogant selfishness...why did she always end up brooding on the flaws of others, when she should be doing something about her own...why, why, why...

Anna Avdotyevna, her sister's personal maid, looked in to check on Masha and Manya's progress, interrupting Slava's thoughts and causing all three of them—Masha, Manya, and Slava herself—to shrink back from the doorframe where Anna Avdotyevna stood, and promise, with much servile bowing on the part of Masha and Manya, that they were almost ready and that Slava would be able to make her way to the feast just as soon as she was summoned.

This was not an unusual response to the presence of Anna Avdotyevna: she was of very noble birth and, aside from being the Tsarina's maid, a formidable figure in her own right. There were rumors of cruelty and dire punishments in her past, and her presence was always greeted with almost the same fear and trembling of that of the Tsarina herself. Anna Avdotyevna gave them a severe look that suggested she found all of them to be a trial and a disappointment, but, after shaking her head as if consigning them to her list of lost causes, she accepted their assurances and swept majestically from the room.

"She makes me go queer all over every time she looks at me," whispered Masha to Manya.

"Me too," Manya whispered back, with a nervous giggle.

"Me too," said Slava, but this sign of solidarity unnerved Masha and Manya so much that Slava was forced to fall back into a dispirited silence and allow them to finish readying her for the evening ahead.

Her guards came when it was time for the feast and escorted her down to the Hall of Celebration. Yarmila Kseniyevna, who ran feasts and executions with equal relish, met her at the doors and told her, "As tonight is supposed to be a night to form new alliances, I've moved you away from your accustomed place at the Empress's side—at her request, of course; she wishes you to have the opportunity of enjoying yourself amongst new friends—and placed you between the two young lovers, which should be very pleasant for you."

"Which two young lovers?" asked Slava, trying to convince herself that the dread Yarmila Kseniyevna's words had occasioned was just ordinary dread, with no particular foundation.

"Serafimiya Svetlanovna and Valery Annovich," Yarmila Kseniyevna told her.

"Ah," said Slava. "Thank you. That *will* be very pleasant, I am sure."

Serafimiya Svetlanovna was the youngest daughter of Princess Malokrasnova, and Valery Annovich was the youngest son of Princess Yuzhnokrasnova. The province of Yuzhnokrasnovskoye adjoined the province of Malokrasnovskoye. The two princesses, carrying on a venerable tradition that had been passed down from mother to daughter for countless generations, had been trying to gain control of each other's territory for some time now, and it had suddenly occurred to both of them that they had a son and daughter of marriageable age.

Admittedly, both Serafimiya Svetlanovna and Valery Annovich had several older siblings, but life and health are such fragile things, especially when one stands in the way of ambitious princesses. Valery Annovich's sister was gravely ill with a mysterious disease, it was said, and his second-sister had met with an unfortunate riding accident and was hovering between life and death. Should the outcomes of those two events prove favorable, there just remained the two older brothers, and once they were removed, the only thing that stood between Princess Malokrasnova and the Yuzhnokrasnova lands were the cunning of Princess Yuzhnokrasnova and the capriciousness of Valery Annovich.

Both were, it was true, formidable obstacles, and so all of Krasnograd had spent the past several months waiting with bated breath to see how the courtship between Serafimiya Svetlanovna and Valery Annovich would turn out. Between the intrigue and the murders, it had been an unusually interesting fall and winter in Krasnograd, and those princesses who had decided to overwinter in the capital had not regretted their decision. Slava wondered, and not for the first time, if Yarmila Kseniyevna were actively malicious or merely monumentally stupid. Then she began to wonder if there were any difference between malevolence and stupidity...probably only in that stupidity was much more common and more difficult to fight...probably it caused a great deal more harm than mere evil...Slava was recalled from her thoughts by her sudden arrival at the table and the need to smile at the others and sit down, which she did with only a minor stumble that no one else seemed to notice, or at least had the good grace not to remark on.

Serafimiya Svetlanovna and Valery Annovich, who, probably due as much to their interesting situation as their mothers' rank, had been granted seats at the Imperial table, although at the very farthest end, both jumped when Slava's guards pulled out the chair between them and sat her down on it. Serafimiya Svetlanovna gave her a strained smile and bowed from a sitting position. Valery Annovich rose to bow, and then returned to his seat, where he sat playing with his knife and fork and pointedly ignoring the two women to his right, especially Serafimiya. An awkward silence settled over that side of the table. Seeing that anything she said would be unwelcome, Slava tried to look around without making it obvious that she was doing everything in her power not to catch her neighbors' gazes.

Her sister was sitting several chairs down, looking extremely pleased with herself, and saying something (probably something of such egregious self-satisfaction that, if Slava were to hear it, she would be forced to leap out of her chair and scream to fill the entire Hall of Celebration and maybe the rest of Krasnograd as well, so it was lucky that she was seated at the far end of the table) to Praskovya Tsarinovna, her heir. The other Tsarinovna in the kremlin. Everyone called Slava "the Tsarinovna," but really there were two of them: herself and her sister's daughter. The "other Tsarinovna" caught Slava's eyes on hers and gave her the sulkiest look a spoiled girl of twelve could summon, which was, Slava had to admit, spectacularly sulky.

She sighed and looked back down at the table. When Prasha was small Slava had often entertained fond thoughts of playing the doting aunt to her, thereby serving at least some useful purpose, but there had never been much mutual sympathy between them, and Slava's sister had done all she could to extinguish whatever small spark of kinship that might have flared up between them otherwise. Slava knew that Prasha bitterly resented being "the other Tsarinovna," and that her mother, Slava's own and only sister, did all she could to fan those flames, especially since she had set Prasha's father aside and left him to languish in some sanctuary somewhere.

Although her sister's husband had often made Slava want to beat her head against the wall with his foolish pronouncements and his self-important way of swanning about the kremlin—something Prasha seemed well on her way to copying—she couldn't help but feel sorry for him after his sudden fall from grace. She had attempted to ensure that his lot in the sanctuary would not be too hard, but he had refused all her offers of help and ordered that the other brothers at the sanctuary deny her any ability to ameliorate his condition.

Prasha, however, had found out about Slava's efforts on her father's behalf and had briefly warmed to her, but only until the Empress had put a stop to that. Sometimes Slava found it very hard to believe that these people were her own flesh and blood. Zem' was said to be the most peaceful and prosperous land in all of the Known World, ruled by the wisest, most capable of rulers...if that were so, then the Known World, and probably the Unknown World too, was in serious, serious trouble...Slava hated to think that the petty scheming and pointless cruelty she saw on a daily basis in Krasnograd was the epitome of what the world could achieve...although by all accounts, things *were* worse beyond Zem''s borders...at least Zem' *was* a country, and not a series of warring tribes...although it often seemed only one step, one tiny step, away from becoming a series of warring tribes...perhaps Miroslava Praskovyevna had done some good after all, difficult as it was for Slava to credit her with any merit at all...perhaps this *was* better than living in huts and yurts and making constant war...at least in Zem' they lived in houses, and the wars were just as often of words as they were of blood...still, all too often they were of blood, even if it was just the blood of a few, rather than outright battle, and even wars of words were hurtful...there had to be some way to make things better, there had to be...

"It was a very kind thing you did today, Krasnoslava Tsarinovna," said Serafimiya Svetlanovna, breaking Slava's train of thought and the awkward silence that went with it. "But then, you are always so kind, everyone knows it."

"Oh," said Slava, who had never been good at responding to compliments. She cast her mind over possible topics of conversation. Everything she could think of was potentially harmful, both to conversation and to their safety in general. Of late Slava had noticed Serafimiya Svetlanovna smiling at her whenever they chanced to meet, in a way that suggested she would like to become better friends. As she had very few friends of any sort, let alone the better one, Slava would have been happy to oblige her, if it were not for the nagging fear of being drawn into the vicious internecine warfare between the Malokrasnova and Yuzhnokrasnova families. If that were to happen, Slava had no illusions that her rank would protect her. More than one Tsarinovna or Tsarina's second-sister had lost her life in these petty battles.

Even if Serafimiya Svetlanovna, who was probably the only person in Krasnograd even more friendless than Slava, were perfectly sincere in her desire to gain Slava's friendship, and had only the purest motives at heart—and Serafimiya, whatever her problems, had always struck Slava as a sincere and pure-hearted girl—any friend of hers would need to be prepared to sleep with a dagger under her pillow, figuratively and literally. Sorry as she was for Serafimiya, and desperate as she was for friends, Slava was neither that sorry nor that desperate yet.

Poor Serafimiya was being led to the killing shed that was a marriage of alliance—Slava would have smiled at her own overwrought tone, except she knew that she was right—and everyone was drawing away from her in horror, even as they patted her arm and gave her encouraging words and told her what a lucky girl she was, and Slava found it very difficult to act any differently from the rest. Standing up for others was so hard, especially when they didn't want to be stood up for. Well, at least she could refrain from telling Serafimiya how happy she was going to be, Slava told herself.

She looked over at Valery Annovich, sulking over his plate. He certainly was very handsome. And, no doubt, would bring any wife of his nothing but trouble. And, Slava was certain, his mother would only encourage him, and Serafimiya's own mother would happily leave her to her fate. Every new wife must learn how to manage her own husband—it was what made a woman out of her, instead of a silly little girl. Slava was no foreseer, but she could already see that pretty, silly, softhearted Serafimiya was going to have the kind of woman made out of her that would make others cringe as she passed. It was what Krasnograd did to people. It was what it was doing to Slava. If only there were a way of leaving Krasnograd, Slava thought to herself. It might not be too late, if only there were a way of escaping it.

"It seems to me that I saw you set out to go riding this afternoon," she said, realizing that the awkward silence had settled back over their end of the table.

"Yes!" said Serafimiya Svetlanovna, seizing gratefully on Slava's words. "I did go riding, as you so observantly noted, Krasnoslava Tsarinovna. I often go riding in the woods behind the kremlin. Do you enjoy riding, Krasnoslava Tsarinovna?"

"Yes, although I go much too rarely." Slava turned to her left. "Do you enjoy riding, Valery Annovich?"

"Valery Annovich is a very accomplished rider, and can ride any mount, I am sure," said Serafimiya Svetlanovna. "I often see him helping his mother's mistress of horse with the training."

"I am glad to meet a young man who occupies himself with something useful, and not merely idleness and dissipation," said Slava, only realizing after she'd said them how condescending the words sounded.

"I prefer horses to people," said Valery Annovich, still concentrating on his knife. "And Zhenya Svetlevna is the only woman whose company I can tolerate for half a day at a stretch."

Serafimiya Svetlanovna flinched so that Slava feared she might burst into tears right there in front of everyone, and the awkward silence regained its iron grip on their end of the table. All three of them sat there with burning cheeks while the servants served them. As soon as Slava's sister toasted the health of the company gathered there and gave her guests leave to enjoy themselves as they saw fit, Valery Annovich jumped up, and, saying that he had had enough of female company and was going to go join his friends at the far table, left.

If Slava had not found his behavior so distressing—and been afraid of distressing Serafimiya Svetlanovna even more—she would have sighed, or rolled her eyes, or laughed, or all three at once. Surliness was currently all the rage amongst the young noblemen of Krasnograd, and it seemed that Valery Annovich had been infected with the latest fashion in spades.

While it had to be said that these young princes were to a certain extent doing no more than aping their sisters' querulousness, there was an undercurrent of hatred to it that Slava found very disturbing. It was as if, underneath the normal dangerous thoughtlessness of youth and manhood, all these foolish, idle, cossetted young men hated their mothers, sisters, wives, and daughters with a virulent hatred that they could barely acknowledge, not even to themselves, and which they could no more stop than a man who has taken to drink could turn away from vodka. Just like the prisoner on the dock that morning.

And yet, instead of earning their place in the world by taking up a man's responsibilities, or leaving the world of women by retiring to a sanctuary, most of them seemed too weak and afraid to do anything about their misery other than sulk and whine, run after other women whenever they crooked their fingers, and occasionally lash out and hit their mothers, sisters, wives, and daughters in the face whenever they thought they could get away with it—which was all too often, as their mothers, sisters, wives, and daughters insisted on treating them as if they were still children of three. Slava could hear the excuses she had heard over and over again, and the exact tone in which they had been said: *Oh, he didn't mean it, it was an accident...life is so much harder for men; their lot is so much harder than ours...I love him, I really do...he loves me, I know it, he really loves me...*Slava could even hear herself say those things from time to time. It was all too often easier than facing

24

the truth.

I am so bitter, Slava said to herself. *Although I suppose my experience has been bitter, too.* But, she could tell whenever she looked around her, no more bitter than any other woman's. It seemed as if the gods had given them men, not as the promised helpmate and strong right arm, but as a terrible trial, or at least so she was forced to conclude after spending an evening in their company. Slava supposed that this was nothing new, or at least everyone around her seemed to think so, but she found it very trying to her patience indeed to see these silly, spoiled princes turn against those to whom they owed everything, with the sure and certain knowledge that all would be forgiven.

And not only that, once they, inspired by the nonsense that was apparently coming out of some of the men's sanctuaries these days (the rumors were that it had been brought over from the West; it certainly sounded like the kind of thing Westerners would do) started going on about their peasant roots—as if any of them had ever spent a day plowing a field or mowing hay in their entire sheltered lives—the true nature of manhood, becoming closer to the gods, and so on and so forth, their talk became so fatuous Slava thought she might be ill. She supposed she should be glad that by his hasty exit Valery Annovich had at least spared them that.

What was most mysterious, at least for Slava, was the way the bored princesses of Krasnograd were in raptures over this new style, and encouraged their brothers and lovers in it without reservation. Slava supposed that it added a bit of a thrill to their tedious lives, as there was more excitement in bringing a surly man to bed than a pleasant one, but it was very hard for her when confronted with this nonsense not to shout, "Then go to sanctuary and be done with it! No one's stopping you! Stop annoying the rest of us!"

Slava often felt a great deal of solidarity with the princes of Krasnograd, whose idle uselessness was so similar to her own, but she had been forced to admit to herself that the solidarity went entirely one way. She might look at them and see kindred spirits, people who thought as she did, felt as she did, lived as she did, but they looked at her—as had been made painfully clear to her—but she mustn't think about that, she mustn't think about it, not if she didn't want to become ill—and saw nothing but the embodiment of everything they hated about themselves and resented about their lot in life.

And this craze for sullenness was more than she could stand. There was nothing so unattractive in a man as childish sulking, she reflected, not for the first time, and, alas, probably not for the last. She tried to turn her thoughts away from the foolishness and ingratitude of men—once anyone of sense embarked on the contemplation of that topic (although embarking on that topic was probably a sign that she was not anyone of sense), she would find enough misery to keep her busy for this lifetime and several others as well, if the gods were in the habit of giving people more than one lifetime, which would be unexpectedly generous of them.

"Why did he leave?" demanded Serafimiya Svetlanovna pitifully. So much, Slava reflected, for her determination not to wallow in melancholy thoughts about faithless lovers.

For the rest of the meal Slava had to listen to Serafimiya Svetlanovna pour out all her fears and feelings about Valery Annovich. By last spring everyone had been saying for months that it was high time she got married, as she was fast approaching her twentieth summer, but she had never seen any young man who caught her fancy, until one day, as she was out riding along the borders of her mother's territory, she had chanced to come across Valery Annovich, who had ridden into Malokrasnovskoye on a bet.

When Serafimiya had asked him what he was doing on Malokrasnova land, he had said, smiling and flashing his white teeth, that his grandmother was a steppewoman and in the steppe, mothers still sent their sons out to capture and bring back the best bride they could find, and asked her if she would like it if he did that to her. Serafimiya had said she would like it very much, if he were man enough to brave her mother's wrath. Valery had said that he had enough manhood to attempt such a feat and still have plenty to spare, and before long they were meeting at midnight in the most secluded groves they could find, where, Serafimiya said with a glint in her eye despite her tears, Valery had proved that he could back up his boasts with deeds.

This had carried on over the summer, and then in early fall the two princesses had both been struck by that stroke of genius that often strikes the selfish and unprincipled, and realized that they could marry their children to each other and then plunder each other's property at will. Princess Malokrasnova had announced her intentions to her daughter, albeit in slightly more self-flattering terms, Slava gathered from Serafimiya's words, in which the phrase "a mother's care for her beloved daughter" had been employed at least a dozen times. Despite the alarms that this should have raised, Serafimiya had agreed without reserve, as she had begun to feel that it was, in fact, high time for her to get married, and her seduction of Valery and its effect on his marriage prospects had been weighing more and more heavily on her mind.

"But imagine my surprise," said Serafimiya, the glint in her eyes now drowned out by a fresh effusion of tears, only partly summoned by vodka, "when, in response to my announcement of this good news at our next tryst, he pushed me away, saying he was tired and should return home. After that he began to find more and more excuses to avoid our meetings. Both our mothers have been pressing him ever more heavily for an agreement to the match, but he keeps putting them off for one trifling reason or another. And I—once he refused me his company, I came to see that I...I lie awake at night now, remembering our trysts and longing for him, not just his caresses but the way he made me laugh, the stories he told, the way he always spoke to his horse so lovingly...And...Why doesn't he love me? Why doesn't he love me? I would do anything for him, anything he asked, give him anything he wanted, spend the rest of my life making him happy, and all he does is put off the day of our betrothal. I know he loved me once, and he loves me still, as far as I can tell, but he spurns the happiness I would give him, he spurns it deliberately! Now all he does is avoid me, and he makes hurtful remarks whenever we are forced to be together, and why? Why? They say you can see what goes on in other people's hearts, so why?"

Serafimiya was now crying in earnest. Slava looked around to see if they were being observed, but everyone who was not too drunk to stand had gotten up and moved to the other end of the room, where musicians were readying themselves for dancing.

"Do you really want to know?" she asked.

"Yes! Anything is better than this torture! Tell me true, Krasnoslava Tsarinovna: has he found another woman, or will he marry me someday, and deliver me from this agony?"

"He wants the happiness that you offer," said Slava, "but he doesn't want to make any of the sacrifices that gaining such happiness would entail."

"Sacrifices! What sacrifices! I would never ask him to make any sacrifices! I just want to make him happy!"

"And for that he would have to be grateful, which would be more sacrifice than he could bear. He longs for what you offer, Serafimiya, and he wants you to force it upon him, just as his mother—well, most likely his mother's serving women—once forced him into swaddling

27

clothes, so that he can blame you for all his troubles and not have to look into his own needy soul. He cannot see other people as people, Serafimiya, and therefore he is hardly a person at all himself."

"But..." Serafimiya's drunken face creased in bewilderment.

"Nevertheless, nature will take its course, and so I have no doubt that soon enough he will consent to the match, although he will resent you for being part of it. Men never seem to enjoy having happiness forced upon them as much as they think they will, no matter how much they seem to demand it."

"Oh!" cried Serafimiya. "Thank you, Krasnoslava Tsarinovna, thank you! I will make him love me, I swear, I will make him love me even more than he does now..."

"I am sure you will," said Slava, "and he will hate you all the more for it. I know you want him to be a man worth loving, but such men are few and far between. Most likely he will turn out to be a monster. But forget what I said. Perhaps I am wrong, or too influenced by my own bitterness and heartbreak..."

"That's true," said Serafimiya, cheering up slightly and losing a lot of her ordinary sweetness. "What do you know about love? You've never been able to keep a man at all, have you? And how could you, with those big eyes staring at him all the time? I must go and find Valery right now."

Slava wondered if she would ever stop wondering at how free and easy all the princesses, including those like Serafimiya who were barely half her age, were in their open disdain of her. It was not just the unkindness of it, even from someone as naturally kind as Serafimiya—although that, too, pained her—it was the foolishness of it that irked her. Of course, her sister encouraged it, and it was true that at the moment Slava had neither power of her own nor powerful defenders, but life and health, as Serafimiya of all people should know all too well, were such fragile things. Slava *was* the Tsarinovna, and should something befall her sister before her sister's daughter came of age, then she, Slava, would be the next to sit the Wooden Throne.

Admittedly, at the moment that seemed very unlikely to happen, but she would certainly not be the first, and probably not the last, Tsarinovna to rule in her sister's stead, should such a thing come to pass. She sometimes wondered why the princesses—normally so good at scheming!—were so impolitic as to ignore that possibility. She supposed that the delight of blaming her for their shortcomings was too great for them to exercise good judgment.

The thought of good judgment, or the lack thereof, brought her attention back to Serafimiya, who, downing another shot of vodka and wiping her face clean, set off in search of Valery Annovich in spite of Slava's earnest advice not to.

The dancing soon started, and Slava made her way over to that end of the hall. She found a seat in a corner she thought would remain deserted, and tried to watch and enjoy herself. But before long a young prince sat down beside her and, turning to make sure that his face was visible to the rest of the floor, set his features in a pronounced sulk. Slava was forced to turn away and start coughing in order to hide her laughter.

At first the young prince attempted to maintain a chilly silence, but before the musicians had even finished the first song, he asked Slava if she had some special reason for sitting by herself. His confiding, "we're-all-boys-together" tone as he asked made holding a straight face even more difficult, and Slava had to bite her lip to keep from smiling at him and his temerity in chatting so familiarly with the Tsarinovna. It would only send him right back into his sulk.

"I tire quickly, especially when there is a great deal of company," she told him. Seeing that he was dying to be asked, she dutifully said, "and you?"

Like Serafimiya, the young Prince, whose name was Vadim Vladislavovich, could not resist pouring out his troubles to Slava. It seemed that he was desperately in love with a certain Marya Dariyevna, and finally, at long last, she had consented to dance with him, as soon as she returned from refreshing herself.

In the brief period between Marya Dariyevna's departure for "that place," and her return to the dance floor, Vadim Vladislavovich had somehow managed to convince himself that Marya Dariyevna cared nothing for him and was only toying with his passions in order to humiliate him as soon as she got the chance. Consequently, when she had taken his hand, he had shaken out of her grasp, demanded to know what had taken her so long, accused her of meeting another lover, and stormed off the dance floor.

"And just look!" he finished indignantly. "I was right! She's already dancing with Praskovich, the heartless hussy! No doubt he lets her dictate her every step! But I...I will not let a woman drag me around like that! I demand constancy!"

"Ah," said Slava, resisting the unkind urge to point out that, when dancing, the woman *did* dictate every step. "Perhaps she might not be dancing with him now if you had not refused to dance with her in the first place," she said instead. "And it is never wise to ask a lady what took her so long in 'that place.'"

Slava could speak her mind to Vadim Vladislavovich, since she could see that he was sunk too deeply into his sulk to hear a word she said. The usual result when talking to a man, she thought sourly: they would rather make a thousand mistakes than hear the truth. I might as well be talking to a wall. Then she chastised herself for her sourness. And tried not to laugh too sourly when Darya Marinovna, widely considered the most beautiful woman in Krasnograd, asked Vadim to dance the very next dance, and he jumped up and eagerly followed her out onto the floor—although only after casting his eyes in the direction of both Slava and his heartless Marya Dariyevna, in order to make sure that they had seen how he had been singled out by the most beautiful woman in Krasnograd.

Slava herself had never been able to grasp the essence of Darya Marinovna's beauty: as far as she could tell, she was noticeably horse-faced and had small, sharp little eyes. But she *said* she was the most beautiful woman in Krasnograd, loudly and often, and Krasnograd seemed more than ready to take her at her word.

Slava often tried to convince herself that it was no concern of hers whether or not Krasnograd worshipped at the feet of Darya Marinovna's supposed beauty, but sometimes that little lie felt like it stood for all the big lies that everyone believed, and Slava couldn't help but think that if she could only expose that one falsehood, she could expose all the others, and then people would see clearly and she would be happier.

But, as usual, she kept her opinion to herself and made little attempt to change anybody's mind. Like as not, she would fail, and if she succeeded, it would only be at the expense of the happiness of Darya Marinovna and all her admirers, and in Slava's mind that was too cruel a price. So she turned her eyes away from Darya Marinovna and her newest conquest, and tried instead to decide how soon she could leave this humiliating spectacle. Soon, she decided, very soon. She could hear a whole group of people coming up behind her, no doubt hoping she would get up so that they could take over the bench she was occupying.

"Women," she overheard a man say behind her. She shifted in her seat slightly in order to see who was talking, and saw that the group coming up on her was composed of the kind of old men who came to feasts in order to eat and drink too much and speak ill of their neighbors while laughing too loudly. Although Slava knew that their coarse manners were the result of ignorance and foolishness, she still found them repellent, especially as they seemed incapable of comprehending just how poor their education, and consequently their behavior, was. She indulged herself for a moment in the hope that they would pass her by and retire to some private room.

She was, as so often happened, punished for her self-indulgence, as the group, after milling about at the other end of the bench and casting her resentful glances, interspersed with whispers about whether or not that really was the Tsarinovna sitting there and whether they dared disturb her, decided to brave her wrath and sit down.

Slava decided to sit a little longer, in order not to appear to be trying to avoid them and therefore shunning them and possibly offending them (which she would regret doing) and any rich and powerful wives they might happen to have (which her sister would make her regret a good deal more), and only turned away from them in order to let them hold their coarse conversation in peace. Unfortunately, the group offered her no such courtesy, and their loud voices drowned out the next song entirely.

Forced as she was to eavesdrop on them, Slava soon gathered that the son of one of them had recently married, and the proud father was sharing the advice he had imparted to his son with the rest of the group, in such overbearing, hectoring tones—the tones of a man whose stock of knowledge was so small that it was impossible for him to comprehend anything, especially the meagerness of his own thoughts—that his words of wisdom traveled to Slava's ears as well, alas. They seemed to be about how to arrange for his son's new wife to bear a son instead of a girl, if that was what he wanted (honey from bees by the horsepond would do the trick, the man claimed), and how to arrange for her to miscarry if it suited him better, loudly praising the efficacy of moldy rye slipped into the wife's porridge.

Slava wondered if moldy rye would still work if it were given in porridge, or if it would perhaps kill its consumer outright. All the midwives and herbwomen she knew said it was a finicky substance, best administered by an experienced hand, and whenever either she or her sister had taken it, half the healers of Krasnograd had hovered over them until all the symptoms had passed.

The other men agreed with their comrade's advice in loud voices, and then added their own remedies for secretly ensuring a wife bore a son, or no child at all—or, conversely, that she bore a child against her will. Slava's regrets at "never being able to hold on to a man," as everyone reproached her for, dwindled into insignificance, as they often did around men.

It was true that she had been spectacularly unsuccessful thus far in attracting and keeping a husband, or even a lover. People kept telling her she just needed to "put her foot down," stop being so critical of the flaws of her potential suitors, and stand up to them when they tried to push her around. How and why she was to ignore their egregious flaws while putting her foot down and standing up to them had not yet been made clear to her, but that advice was not intended to be helpful anyway, just to make the speaker feel better about herself and quiet a little bit of the panic she felt on encountering Slava.

Occasionally Slava had attempted to explain to such non-well-wishers that she preferred dogs whom she could walk on a long leash, horses whom she could ride on a slack rein, and men whom she could set free entirely, so that she could be certain that they would come back to her of their own free will, but, as her non-well-wishers would point out with spiteful truthfulness, they never did come back.

And if that were not annoying enough, Slava knew that everyone who kept telling her that "a woman isn't a woman without taking in a bit of a man"—while patting her shoulder condescendingly and smirking so that she would know, in case it wasn't absolutely clear already, just what they meant by that—was probably right, although probably not in quite the way they meant. She knew that she would most likely benefit from "taking in a bit of a man" in the symbolic, not literal, sense of the words, and that the best way to do so was to keep an actual, literal, man around, but most actual, literal, men she knew were not the kind of people she would like to keep around, even if they would stay in the first place. Which thus far they always hadn't. She wondered whose husbands these men were, and why they hadn't been set aside years ago. More proof, she supposed, that the women of Krasnograd—and presumably the rest of Zem'—preferred stupid men, despite their loud claims to the contrary.

She must truly be bored and useless, Slava thought, if the best thing she could find to fill her thoughts was the foolishness of men. Women who had real concerns, she had always assumed, had better things to do than to dwell on the imperfections of their lovers and other men. It was for the idle, such as Slava, that such things took on such importance.

She knew that she was just as unneeded, and even more unwanted, than most of the princes of Krasnograd, and she supposed that was why she spent so much time agonizing over their stupidity and cruelty. If they, so cosseted and so beloved, were so terrible, how dreadful must she, even more cosseted, if rather less beloved, be? If they were so hopelessly ruined, how could there ever be any hope for her? As with her desire to expose the lie of Darya Marinovna's beauty, Slava often felt that if she could just help at least one or two of the empty-headed princes swaggering around her to stop swaggering so much and start thinking a little, she would somehow fix all the other problems constantly besetting her.

She knew that that was only a tiny bit true, though, and most likely she should better not even attempt such a vain and foolish task. She should find something else to fill her thoughts and her time, something that would bring actual benefit to her land...such as her study of the scrolls in the Imperial library, for example: she should really spend more time at that, if only she could convince others that she should be left in peace and allowed to work on her task...there was much there about the latest invasion of the Hordes that she was sure had never been properly studied and catalogued until now...and if they should ever attack again, which they were almost sure to do, at least Slava would know what they had done last time, and be ready to offer that council if it should be required...

"Now the Hordes, they ride dragons into battle," the loudest of the men was saying with supreme confidence, the conversation having shifted from deceiving one's wife to warfare. Slava would have been surprised at how closely her thoughts paralleled those of the people next to her, except that she had long ago grown used to that sort of thing. "Great giant lizards that breathe fire."

"No, no, no, it's not dragons, it's flying horses," another of the men was saying, with equal conviction. "They breed horses with birds and get flying horses that they fly into battle."

"No, they get them from the sunrise—every time the sun rises, a new one is born," a third man put in, also with impressive certainty.

Slava was, although not for the first time, astonished at the free and easy and unstoppably voluble way so many men (although men were certainly not the only ones guilty of such foolishness) were able to express their opinions, and the blind certainty they had in their rightness, despite all evidence to the contrary. Not a single one of them at the other end of the bench showed so much as a shadow of a doubt about the accuracy of their information or the advisability of their actions, even when any thinking person could see that what they were saying was madness.

There were many unknown things in the world, even the Known World, but the battle tactics of the Hordes was not one of them, not in Zem', anyway. There were many things of which Slava's foremothers had chosen to remain in ignorance, but the methods of their most frequent invaders was not one of those things. There were many, many books and scrolls in the Imperial library devoted to how the Hordes chose to attack, and not one of them mentioned any mount other than horses.

Although most of the men in the group on the other end of the bench had probably never set foot in the Imperial library. Many of them probably could not even read, at least not more than a few words. But surely their fathers had fought against the last invasion...there were more than a few battle-scarred veterans of those bloody days still begging on the streets of Krasnograd...not that any of the men on the other end of the bench would ever stop to speak to a beggar...no more than Slava would...but at least she saw them as she rode by, at least she knew that they were there, even if there was nothing more she could do for them than toss a few coins in their direction...and none of them ever spoke of dragons. Wood-spirits, water-spirits, house-spirits, and gods, yes, but if there were dragons and flying horses out there, they were somewhere beyond the borders of the Known World.

"But how do they ride the flying horses?" asked one of the men, a little younger and sharper than the rest of the group, judging by his voice. Slava wondered how long it would take for him to be as loud-mouthed and thoughtless as the others. Although she couldn't see him, already a vision of him grown coarse and cruel stood out clearly in her mind's eye. Men bloomed and faded so quickly. "Don't the wings get in the way?" he asked, sounding remarkably like a sensible person. The tragedy of his inevitable waste made Slava, already in such a fragile state, fear that tears might start welling up in her eyes. She really needed to spend less time at these feasts, or at least less time lost in thought. "Where do they sit?"

"The wings are on the neck and rump, instead of a mane and tail," said the man who a moment ago had been arguing loudly for the existence of dragons.

"But how do they keep from breaking the horse's tail, then?" asked the sharp young man. "A horse is big. I think if you picked it up by its

34

tail like that, it would break."

All the other men broke into raucous laughter at that thought, and, egging each other on and embellishing the image with more and more suggestions until they lost the power of speech entirely, laughed for quite some time over the picture of a horse dangling from the end of its broken tail, struggling and screaming in pain. Slava wondered what the sharp young man was thinking, and if he found the other men's laughter as painful as she did. She also wondered how long it would be before he started joining in with them. Not long, no doubt.

"It's magic, sonny, magic," said the loudest of the men, once they had recovered their breath somewhat. "It's sorceress secrets is what it is. Don't think you could understand it."

"My wife's sister is a sorceress," said the sharp young man. "Perhaps I should ask her."

"Ah, now wives now, you'll get no sense from them," said the loudest of the men.

There was a loud chorus of agreement. Slava supposed that confidence in one's opinions was easy to come by when one had no actual information on which to base those opinions. She knew that she herself could use a little of that foolhardy arrogance, but it seemed so... so...foolish. If that were the "bit of a man" that she were to take in, she shuddered to think what she would turn into.

The group burst into more raucous laughter over some particularly meanspirited trick one of the men had played on his wife, possibly involving flying scaled horses, and Slava decided she had to leave before she said something more unkind than any of them could bear to hear. Such as that had any of them been *her* husband, she would have sent him to the mines years ago. She tried to squelch that unkind but unfortunately not unjust thought, and failed.

Just as Slava was rising to return to her rooms, Yarmila Kseniyevna came up and, bowing, said that the Empress wished to see her.

"My sister?" said Slava, startled. "Wishes to see me?" Having just been subjected to a display of the ill results of marriage, Slava's first thought was that her sister was attempting to arrange yet another match for Slava with yet another prince who was rich in money and poor in everything else, such as personal charm or common decency. It seemed a little late in the day for her sister to be trying to sell Slava off, though. Normally by this time in the evening the Empress was so intoxicated with vodka and her own success that she had no use, even as a target of her mockery, for Slava, who, as her sister often told her, always brought down the spirits of everyone around her. As the Empress kept reminding her, "No one wants to have those big gray eyes staring at her," and Slava could see whenever she was in company that that was the undeniable truth.

"Just so, Krasnoslava Tsarinovna," said Yarmila Kseniyevna. "Right away, if you please. There is someone she wishes you to meet."

Slava dutifully followed Yarmila Kseniyevna past all the whirling dancers and into a small side room where her sister was sitting with a tall woman with bright red curls covering her shoulders and most of her face.

"Ah, there you are at last, Slava," said the Empress. "Please welcome Olga Vasilisovna, younger daughter of Princess Severnolesnaya, to Krasnograd. Olga Vasilisovna, my younger sister, Krasnoslava Tsarinovna."

Olga Vasilisovna rose and bowed. "An honor, Krasnoslava Tsarinovna," she said, smiling right into Slava's eyes, and Slava saw that Olga Vasilisovna let her hair cover her face not because she was shy, but because she couldn't be bothered to pull it back. She was, Slava saw on closer inspection, much older than Slava had originally guessed, with silver threads running through her hair and her face already covered with lines brought on by lots of smiling and lots of sun.

Everything about her appearance suggested a woman who had just been scrubbed down and pulled into clean clothes with the sole intention of being vaguely presentable when introduced to the Empress. Olga Vasilisovna sat back down without waiting for Slava to be seated and without showing the slightest concern over what Slava would think of that.

"A pleasure," said Slava, sitting down and waiting for the Empress to reveal her design on Slava. Even thrice-blessed as she was with a wild fancy as well as the ability to see into the hearts of others, she was having difficulty imaging what could have brought the younger daughter of Princess Severnolesnaya, who had never had much fondness for Krasnograd, all the way from her Northern forests into the Empress's private chambers.

Inasmuch as Slava had ever heard of Olga Vasilisovna Severnolesnaya at all, she had always heard of her wild ways, her liking for men and lack of liking for her family, and her general aversion to all things that smacked of a city. While Krasnograd had many men and few members of the Severnolesnaya family in it, it was most definitely, undeniably, the biggest and most city-like city in all of Zem', and

36

therefore the last place one would expect to find the woman sitting in front of Slava and, Slava suspected, grinning through her fiery curls.

"Dearest sister," said the Empress, smiling the smile that was supposed to show that Slava was, in fact, dearly beloved, "you will never guess why Olga Vasilisovna has come! She has a request for me."

"Yes, petitioners are rare," said Slava. The Empress paused for a moment, her hurt expression showing that she couldn't tell whether Slava was making fun of her (under their mother's rule, petitioners had haunted the Kremlin night and day), remarking on the current absence of petitioners (due to the Empress's habit of deliberately misconstruing or denying their petitions), or merely making a statement of fact. Slava had in fact intended to make a caustic comment on the Empress's treatment of petitioners, but she was already sorry she had done so, and found herself hastening to soothe her sister's feelings.

"After all, these days your subjects have little need for petitions," she said, and promptly felt ashamed of her lie, since by sparing her sister's feelings, she had only doomed countless others to pointless suffering.

"Of course," agreed the Empress, her face clearing. Slava thought that Olga Vasilisovna was hiding a laugh behind her hair.

"Dearest sister," the Empress began again, "Olga Vasilisovna wishes to make an expedition to the Far North. What do you think of that?"

"Now?" asked Slava. "In winter?"

"Better than summer," said Olga Vasilisovna. "In summer the tundra becomes a sucking mess of mud and mosquitoes, or so I've been told by those who've ventured past the sunline and returned to tell the tale, and when I tried to go there this summer myself, I discovered they were right. It's best done while there's still snow on the ground, so if we are to do it, we should set out immediately."

"What is in the tundra that is of such value?" asked Slava.

"We won't know until we go there," said Olga Vasilisovna. She grinned even more broadly than before. "People once lived there, or so they say, but there's little hope of meeting any of them. All the tales agree they disappeared long ago. But I have high hopes for great magic. Northerners say..."

"Magic is the petty business of sorceresses," interrupted the Empress. "If Krasnograd is to fund this expedition as you ask, it should serve the interests of Krasnograd. Zem' has extended its borders as far as is practically possible to the East and South. We also claim everything to the North, but no one has ever ventured out there on our behest in order to explore the limits of our territory. Olga Vasilisov-na wishes to be that woman. As she says, Zem' is called the Midnight Land, but no one other than a few lawless hunters and trappers has ever visited the truly midnight edge of our country. She has her own group of hand-picked explorers; all she needs is the money and the Imperial mandate. What do you think?"

"Let me come with you," said Slava.

Chapter Two

Slava woke up the next morning well before dawn, although it must be said that in winter dawn comes very late in Krasnograd. She lay in her bed for a moment, wondering why she had the sensation that there was something terribly important that she needed to remember, and then she remembered it. She had asked Olga Vasilisovna to take her with her on the expedition to the Far North, and Olga Vasilisovna had not refused her.

Slava's request to be allowed to accompany the expedition had been met with the broadest of broad grins from Olga Vasilisovna, and stunned silence from the Empress. Slava could not remember ever shocking her sister like that before, and she took a kind of dark pleasure in it.

"Of course, Krasnoslava Tsarinovna," Olga Vasilisovna had told her. "It would be an honor to have a member of the Imperial family on our journey. And I can see your father's blood was not wasted on you: other than a Northerner, only a Stepnaya would have made that request."

"Slava cannot go," the Empress had said. "She has never even been out of Krasnograd. And she's not a Stepnaya. She's a Zerkalitsa and a member of the Imperial family, and her blood is too precious to risk spilling on some wild venture."

"If she's never even been out of Krasnograd, then all the more reason to go now," Olga Vasilisovna had said. "She should see her native land at least once in her lifetime. And she'll be safe enough with us."

"She's too weak; she'll be a burden on your company," Slava's sister had said. "She can barely ski or sit a horse."

"The daughter of a steppe prince!" Olga had cried out in amusement. "Barely able to sit a horse! I refuse to believe it."

"I can ride," Slava had been forced to put in at that point. "I've been riding since childhood. And skiing, too. I may not be as fast as some, but the science is not unknown to me."

"If Krasnoslava Tsarinovna can ride and ski even a little bit, then the rest of us will be able to pick up the slack if she falters," Olga Vasilisovna had said. "Any of my party is strong enough for two. And since she'll have nothing to do for days on end but practice, by the end of the journey she'll be the best horsewoman and skier in Krasnograd, I guarantee it."

"It's just some fancy of hers," Slava's sister had said. "She'll change her mind in the morning."

"Perhaps," Olga Vasilisovna had said, still grinning. "So let's talk about it again in the morning."

Somehow Slava had excused herself and gone to bed, and somehow, and much to her surprise, she had fallen asleep almost immediately, as if the drunken fumes rising off the dance floor had intoxicated her from a distance. She had slept soundly until now, and now, she realized, she must decide whether her impulsive words would bind her to this mad scheme, or not.

She called Masha and Manya, who came in, still rubbing the sleep from their eyes and muttering to each other about the early hour. Slava knew that they would be shocked and hurt if she told them how rude it was to complain of her summons in her presence, and how much it hurt her feelings. Her request to be given her riding clothes and have her horse readied for her was met with surprise, but after a moment Masha and Manya accepted the idea and proceeded to prepare her to go riding.

Talking to each other about last night's feast and the dance that had followed, Masha and Manya dressed Slava in her riding clothes and escorted her to the door of her rooms, where she was met by her guards. They were more taciturn that Masha and Manya, although Slava could see that they, too, were taken aback by this sudden freak of the Empress's younger sister.

The first green glow of dawn was just visible above the kremlin towers when a groom led Slava's horse out to her and her guards legged her up into the saddle.

"Good morning, Rozochka," Slava said, and stroked her neck. Rozochka craned her neck around and gave Slava a doubtful look, but walked forward willingly enough when Slava asked her.

Flanked by guards, Slava and Rozochka made their way out of the kremlin walls and into the park behind it. Sometime during the night the snow had stopped sifting down, and now, after days and days of snow, the first true cold spell of the winter had struck, making Slava's breath freeze to her hat and eyelashes. The horses were wading in snow almost up to their knees, and trees and bushes were no more than indistinct shapes casting very long faint shadows in the predawn light.

"Tsarinovna! Krasnoslava Tsarinovna!"

Slava twisted around in the saddle, lurching slightly as one of the guards reached out and reined Rozochka to a stop without asking her permission. Olga Vasilisovna was trotting up behind them.

Olga Vasilisovna's horse was quite young, and was finding trotting through the snow to be thrilling experience. Every time a clot of snow was flung up onto his belly, he would try to kick at it. As Olga Vasilisovna drew near Slava, her horse gave a particularly vigorous crow hop, causing her red fox-fur hat to go flying off.

One of Slava's guards tried to jump down and hand it to her, but Olga Vasilisovna, laughing, forestalled him, jumping down herself and jamming the hat back on her head, where it clashed horribly with her bright red hair.

"Are you out training, Krasnoslava Tsarinovna?" she asked, stroking her horse's nose and still laughing over having lost her hat. "Accustoming yourself to the cold?"

"Perhaps," said Slava.

"And how do you find it?"

"Cold," said Slava. "Bracing," she added after a moment. "I feel as if with every breath, I am finally clearing the smoky kremlin air out from my lungs, and replacing it with something clean and pure."

"There's no real clean air anywhere in Krasnograd," Olga Vasilisovna told her. "If you want to breathe really clean air, you have to get well out of the city, preferably to the steppe or taiga."

"I wouldn't know," said Slava.

"But will you come find out? Or have you rethought your decision?"

"I don't know. No. Maybe. I don't know. What do you think?"

"Aren't you the one who's supposed to be able to read other people's minds?" asked Olga Vasilisovna with a laugh. Her horse began to prance sideways in frustration at their lack of movement, and she stroked his neck. "Young horses are so wonderful," she said. "Always so eager and willing! It's only after years of bad riders that they get sour and angry. But you have to remember that they are only reflecting the moods of their mistresses. They can't help themselves: it's the way they are."

"Yes," agreed Slava.

"But since you ask me straight out what I think, then I'll tell you I think you should go. Leave Krasnograd and this dark kremlin behind! What do have to keep you here? It may be cold out there, but at least you have room for your own thoughts."

"True," agreed Slava.

"I'll leave you to think it over and make up your own mind. Right now my horse needs to run before he bursts with impatience. Let me know by this evening, for we're setting out at first light tomorrow."

"I will," promised Slava, and watched as Olga Vasilisovna vaulted back up on her fresh young horse and shot away from them in a cloud of new snow.

Slava continued down the path at a more sedate pace, despite her sudden urge to take off after Olga Vasilisovna, for she knew that she had to make her mind up now, while she was relatively alone, and not wait till she was back in the kremlin, where everyone else's feelings would be crowding against her, making it impossible to think.

Truly, she said to herself, *what do I have to keep me here? My sister doesn't need me, not really, and no one else would miss me at all. I'm little better than a ghost, drifting through the kremlin and feeling other people's feelings. I'm already well on my way to becoming too sour to be any use at all, and soon I'll become a danger to everyone around me, like a beaten dog, and then what will become of me? Even freezing to death out in the tundra would be a better fate than that. And they say that freezing is not such a bad death anyway.*

Slava suddenly saw that she—well, Rozochka—had wandered over to a grove of prayer trees during her musings. Ribbons left tied to branches as tokens of previous prayers fluttered all around her, and strange faces peered out at her from the bark.

I wish the gods would speak to me, Slava thought to herself. *What's the point of having prayer trees if prayers are never answered?*

Rozochka suddenly bent down to rub her eye on her foreleg, almost sending Slava tumbling headfirst over her neck and into the snow. All the guards lunged in her direction.

"I'm all right, I'm all right," Slava assured them. Rozochka suddenly raised her head, sending Slava back into the saddle.

42

"She sees something, Tsarinovna," called one of the guards. "Watch yourself in case she spooks...I'll come get you..."

"I'm all right," Slava said again, stroking Rozochka's neck and looking in the direction of where Rozochka's pricked ears were pointing. Two eyes stared out at her from a very old face carved in a very old fir tree. Slava was sure she had never seen it there before. No doubt that was because she had never looked. The face was so old it was almost hidden by all the branches that had grown around the bare place that had been cut for it. Rozochka snorted emphatically and shook her head, making it seem as if the eyes in the tree blinked.

"There must be something in the tree," the guards were saying.

I suppose this is as good a sign as I'm going to get, Slava thought to herself. She turned Rozochka around and headed back to the kremlin.

A groom met them at the stable yard and took Rozochka away. Slava's guards surrounded her and began walking her back to her rooms. On their way there they passed two princesses quarreling in the corridor. Slava had seen them around, but couldn't remember their names—they were some kind of minor nobility who had decided to forsake their gods-forsaken estates for the relatively civilized comforts of Krasnograd.

"You mustn't! I forbid it!" one was shouting. So much for the civilized comforts of Krasnograd, Slava thought. She wished she could blame their behavior on their provincial manners, but she knew many born-and-bred Krasnograders who behaved no better.

"You can't stop me!" the other was shouting in reply, and Slava realized they were mother and daughter. Both stopped in mid-shout and turned to look at Slava as she, helpless to stop herself, drew level with them.

"I apologize, Krasnoslava Tsarinovna," said the mother, embarrassed. "I was only chastising my daughter. You know how young women are!" She laughed awkwardly and tried to put her arm around her daughter's shoulders, but the daughter shrugged out from under her mother's grasp, making her mother's face purse into a sullen frown.

"Oh," said Slava, trying to back away surreptitiously. Being this close to the woman and her daughter and their stench of quarrel-someness was making her want to gag, as if a cloud of unwashed hair and dirty teeth were rising off them.

"Of course, you're still young yourself...well, sort of. Not a moth-er, anyway, so," the older princess's voice filled with resentment and superiority, "you wouldn't understand. Although you always *look* like you do, Tsarinovna." The woman laughed again uncomfortably. "You always *look* so superior—it makes me feel queer all over."

The daughter cheered up at this, until she looked at Slava, and then she, too, cringed away from Slava's gaze. Slava was painfully aware that many of the princesses in Krasnograd liked to strike out at her whenever they were dissatisfied with the Empress's treatment of them or with their own idle, pointless existences, eating and quar-reling and bossing their children and servants around like a pack of querulous old men who had long outlived their usefulness. These princesses were apparently no exception.

"Stand up straight!" ordered the mother. For a moment Slava thought that she had sunk so low that even third-rate nobility from the provinces dared to command her in public, but then she saw that the mother had lost her nerve, or perhaps merely been distracted from Slava's superior gaze by her daughter's latest failure. "You're al-ways slumping and cringing—I can hardly bear to look at you!"

"Then let me leave!" cried the daughter. "Stop keeping me here like a little child!"

"I have to go," said Slava, but neither of them heard her. She made her escape down the corridor unnoticed, pursued by the sound of quarreling voices all the way to her rooms.

She did not begin to feel safe until her guards shut the doors be-hind her, and she was alone. She thought about calling Masha and Manya to help her change out of her riding clothes and into some-thing cleaner, but instead she sat down in front of her fireplace.

I have to leave, she told herself. *I have to leave, I have to leave, I have to leave. I cannot stay a day longer surrounded by these people. They all wear their smooth masks on the surface, but underneath they're no better than wolves. Worse, much worse, because wolves are honest. You know where you are with wolves. Wolves know that they're wolves and see no shame in it. But people are wolves hiding in rotting lambskins.*

And most of the time they don't even know it. That princess in the cor-ridor didn't even know what she was doing, just like the little girl's moth-

44

er yesterday, or everyone else in the Hall of Judgment. They're all so sure they're right, that they are in fact lambs and it's all the fault of others. Only somehow I was made in such a way that when I look at the lambskin, it falls away. Why can I see clearly when no one else can? I wish...I wish I could just place my hands upon their heads, and give my abilities to them. I wish I could give them true seeing with my touch, so that their mind's eye would open and they could perceive what they really are.

For a moment Slava enjoyed the vision of pressing her hands to someone else's head, and watching her scream and writhe in pain as her mind unfolded in new ways and she saw herself clearly for the first time, but she soon had to give up on the fantasy. Even if it were possible, she doubted she could ever do it, because whenever it came down to it, she could never bring herself to cause pain. Even the pain she caused inadvertently seemed to hurt her more than it did others. Other people might seem crippled to her, even if they themselves thought that they stood straight, and she might see when others could not just where the kink, the flaw, the weakness was, and exactly where to push or pull to make it straight, but she was the only one who could see through her eyes, it seemed. No one else seemed to see the crippling of the spirit that affected them all, or how it—unlike mere crippling of the body—hurt people other than themselves, or why they should fix it. So there was little hope of ever getting them to agree to any kind of a cure.

And she couldn't help remembering how Anastasiya Avdotyevna's son had been born with a crumpled hand, and how Anastasiya Avdotyevna's healers had tried to straighten it out gently, over time, but the boy had refused to cooperate and would always manage to take off the braces somehow, and how finally Anastasiya Avdotyevna had lost patience and had her healers try to pull the hand straight in one go, and how the boy had screamed and screamed and screamed, and when they were finished, his hand had been even more broken than before. Such, Slava feared, would be the result if she ever got her wish. This desire to hurt must be the only trace of the taint passed down to her from Miroslava Praskovyevna, the only thing the two of them had in common.

Manya suddenly appeared in her room. "The Empress wishes to see you," she announced.

"Don't you know you're supposed to knock before entering someone's bedchamber?" asked Slava, smiling in order to pretend it was a joke, and that she wasn't annoyed at having her reveries interrupted.

45

Sometimes—well, often—it seemed to her that she did nothing all day except dream fruitless daydreams, and yet on the other hand she was never allowed to finish them in peace. "You never know what you might find if you come bursting in without warning," she added, now smiling in a "we're-all-girls-together-here" smile, in the vain hope of winning Manya's sympathy.

"Oh, there's no danger of coming across anything like that here, Krasnoslava Tsarinovna," said Manya, looking Slava over with an appraising eye. "You're still in your riding clothes! Why didn't you summon me when you got back! And now it's too late: you'll have to meet the Empress in this state."

Slava almost wanted to laugh at the way Manya, who was at least ten years her junior, bossed her around with no consideration of her age or rank, but realized that would probably hurt even Manya's blunt feelings, and so refrained. Guilt at assuming that Manya's feelings were blunt also pricked her conscience: no doubt to Manya her feelings were strong and true. "I am sure my sister will forgive me, or at least not hold you accountable," she said instead. "Let her in."

Slava's sister swept in surrounded by maids and guards, whom she promptly dismissed, saying she wanted to have a nice sisterly chat with her dearest Slava. Soon the two of them were alone together, staring at the crackling fire in the fireplace and suffering from their total lack of any ability to hold a nice sisterly chat.

"Do you really mean to go off on this expedition, Slavochka?" the Empress asked after a while, her features assuming the appropriate air of concern.

"Yes, Vladenka, I do," Slava answered, and watched as her sister tried to ignore the sound of the pet name which Slava had not used in at least fifteen years.

"But why?" asked the Empress, wisely avoiding any further use of names altogether. "Why? It will be cold, and, I may say, rather dangerous as well. The Far North is not a welcoming place even below the sunline, let alone above it. Not only that, but the Severnolesniye are no friends to Krasnograd and our family."

"Which is funny, because they *are* our family," said Slava.

"What?" said her sister, temporarily nonplussed by Slava's unexpected remark.

"They *are* our family," Slava repeated. "The Severnolesniye are our fourth-sisters, or something like that. The descendants of unwanted younger sisters who were sent North to get them out of our hair. And then there was that intermarriage between a younger brother of our great-grandmother and a Severnolesnaya that ended in curses and blood spilled. They have good reason to dislike us, but we're still all of the same blood in the end."

"Oh, we're not so close as that," said the Empress, relieved to see that it was nothing more than another of Slava's mysterious pronouncements. She continued as if Slava hadn't spoken: "Word has it that Olga Vasilisovna and her mother are on no good terms, but that does not mean she would not hesitate to turn against you, should it serve to get her back in her mother's good graces. And she is related by marriage to Princess Primorskaya, who no doubt is itching to do whatever she can to gain the upper hand over the Pristanogradskiye and gain control of Pristanogradskoye. A Zerkalitsa falling into her lap would be like a gift from the gods: she could ransom you for the province and the banishment of the Pristanogradskiye.

"All in all, it seems like a chancy enterprise. And what have you to gain from it? Nothing. And what have you to offer to it? Nothing as well. You will only be a burden to Olga Vasilisovna and the others. They will be constantly occupied with looking after you, because they know that if anything happened to you, their lives would be forfeit. You who claim to care so much for the feelings of others, why would you expose them to that?"

"Is your main objection to my going the inconvenience it would pose to Olga Vasilisovna and her men?" asked Slava.

"No, no, of course not! I need you here, Slava, you need to be here! What would I do without you to advise me?" The Empress's voice was so sincere that Slava was forced to believe that she was saying what she really felt, at least at that moment.

"You have other advisors," Slava said. "You have a whole Council full of Councilors, in fact."

"But none of them are you! None of them have your gifts, Slava! And none of them are my sister, my only sister. Well, my half-sister, but we share the same mother, and that is what matters. All this talk of your Stepnaya blood is nonsense: you're every drop a Zerkalitsa, and my only sister, and I need you here. I want you here."

"You really mean that," said Slava.

"Of course I do! When do I not say what I mean?"

Slava looked at her. The Empress looked back, puzzled and concerned, for all the world as if she really did love Slava as her only, darling, younger sister.

"Krasnograd is killing me," Slava told her after a long pause. "I must leave. I cannot bear to spend another day surrounded by greedy, scheming princesses and sulky, spoiled princes. The air here is like poison to me."

"But why, Slava? Have you not always been the Tsarinovna, the pet of Krasnograd? Have you not always been given everything you ever wanted or needed? How could Krasnograd be so bad?" Triumph at her own powers of logic, laced with a little resentment for Slava's cosseted position, was already replacing concern on the Empress's face.

"How could it not be?" asked Slava, her voice rising. "How could it be anything other than...than...than the most horrible torture chamber? Everywhere I go, other people's feelings force their way into my heart, and I am helpless to prevent it. You spoke of my gift, sister, but it seems that you do not understand it, and how could you? How can the blind person know what green is? Or rather, how can the blind person know what ugliness is? She can't. She goes through life unaware of the hideous shapes that surround her. But I...I was born with something extra, or something missing, so that the veil that was supposed to be over my eyes and the armor that was supposed to be over my heart are not there, and I am defenseless against the world.

"Do you know what that is like, sister? Do you? Do you know what it is like to meet someone, and know that all they are waiting for is for you to shut up so that they can start talking? Do you know what it is like to know that the mothers of the victims at yesterday's trial were no different from the mother of the murderer, and to hate both of them while your heart can't stop bleeding for their pain? Do you? Do you? Do you know what it's like...what it's like..."

"Oh Slava," said the Empress softly. For a moment her heart seemed truly touched, and she looked almost like a person. "Of course I know what it's like. I am your sister, after all. We are the mirror that reflects only reality, just like Miroslava Praskovyevna was said to be. There is no veil over my eyes either. I just don't care."

For an instant Slava thought she was going to blurt out something angry, something about how her sister had resented her and her gifts all those years for nothing, since her sister, it seemed, had exactly the same gifts, she just couldn't be bothered to use them. But she clamped her lips shut long enough for her sister to say, "My blood must be a little bit purer than yours, for my heart, at least, was spared your nakedness."

"Please let me go," said Slava. She had wavered there for just a moment, when her sister had seemed to soften, but her sister's last words had stiffened up her resolve again. She wondered if her sister could ever think of another person without thinking of herself first. Probably not. Probably that was what it meant to be the true heir to Miroslava Praskovyevna and the Wooden Throne. Probably the only way Slava could ever escape from the horror of her own family was to flee Krasnograd entirely.

"Please," she repeated. "I know it will be cold, and unpleasant, and dangerous, and I may even die, but perhaps out there I will be sorry about all those things. Here...here I would welcome..."

"Very well," said the Empress before Slava could finish. After an instant of panic brought on by Slava's unspoken confession, which she had so fortunately managed to forestall and therefore could pretend had never happened, the mask of Imperial certainty was already back in place, and her voice rang with decisiveness. "You are right. You must leave Krasnograd. I will inform Olga Vasilisovna that she will have an Imperial companion, and make sure that she understands the responsibility that entails. Even the Severnolesniye would hesitate before bringing actual harm to the Tsarinovna, I would hope, at least after I impress upon her the consequences of any failure to watch over you properly. Dine with me tonight, and we will discuss the arrangements in more detail then. But now I must go: I have business to attend to." She rose and left the room without saying goodbye.

When her sister left Slava cried for a moment, but there were too many tears locked in her chest for her to cry them all out in the time she had, so she soon stopped. Her soul felt like a limb that had gone dead after being slept on all night, and she knew that it would not be long before the pressure was released and sensation would come flooding painfully back in, and so half her tears were from fear, and half from relief.

Slava got up and, just as one shakes a deadened limb in order to bring back the blood, she began moving aimlessly around her chambers, gathering together things she thought she might need to take with her, but not really sure if what she was gathering was of any use at all. Her teeth were chattering slightly: until this moment, she had not realized how much she hated Krasnograd, and how glad she was to be leaving it.

There was a knock at the door that opened onto the corridor. "Olga Vasilisovna wishes to see you, Krasnoslava Tsarinovna," called a guard.

"Oh…Oh, well, let her in," Slava called back, ashamed to be seen in the state she was in, especially by Olga Vasilisovna, but unable to think of a plausible reason to send her away. She rubbed her face to wipe away any remaining tears, and tried to blow her nose surreptitiously. A glance in the mirror showed that she had only succeeded in making her face even redder and blotchier than before, but Olga Vasilisovna was already coming through the door, so there was nothing to be done but face her.

"The Empress just told me," said Olga Vasilisovna. "Boleslav Vlasiyevich is already discussing the necessary arrangements with my men for ensuring your safety. Not that there's any need: you'll be twice as safe with my men as you would with your own, my head for beheading. And I don't make that oath lightly: your sister has made it clear that I'll answer for your life with my own."

"What if my horse slips on a cobblestone as we are leaving Krasnograd, and crushes me?" asked Slava, trying to speak lightly. "What then? Surely you cannot be blamed for that."

Olga Vasilisovna shrugged. "I doubt your sister would care about my guilt," she said. "I think she'd just want to take her displeasure with fate out on me. But there's no point in worrying about it until it happens." Olga Vasilisovna sounded as if she were not overly concerned about Slava's sister's need for vengeance against fate.

"Oh good: you've already started packing, and without your maids," said Olga Vasilisovna, walking through the sitting room into the bedchamber and looking at the pile of clothing on the bed. "That's wise. I take it you're not planning on bringing a maid with you?"

"No," Slava answered. "I have no desire to bring them with me, and I doubt they would go if I asked."

"Maids are always more trouble than they're worth, in my experience," said Olga Vasilisovna, stirring through Slava's clothing. "You've only got skirts here. You'll probably be better off in trousers, you know."

"Are they comfortable?"

Olga Vasilisovna thought about that for a moment. "They're very convenient for riding," she said. "On the other hand, they're very inconvenient for pissing, especially in cold weather. I always feel so sorry for my men in winter, I'm always sure they're going to freeze their..." Olga Vasilisovna seemed suddenly to remember that she was speaking to the Tsarinovna, and finished the sentence "...well, you know what I mean. But you should probably bring a pair or two. Have your maids sew some up tonight—they can do something useful for once." Olga Vasilisovna continued to stir through Slava's clothing, tossing most of it aside with a contemptuous shake of her head. "Don't you have anything warm and practical?" she asked.

"Not really," said Slava. "Thus far there hasn't been much occasion."

"Where are your maids? Call them in at once!"

Slava called in Masha and Manya, who stared at both Slava and Olga Vasilisovna with frank curiosity. Olga Vasilisovna gave them long and detailed instructions for the kind of clothing she wanted sewn up for Slava by the next morning.

"The Tsarinovna doesn't wear anything like that," Masha protested. "Why..."

Olga Vasilisovna gave her a look that caused the rest of the words to freeze in her mouth.

"I'll inspect everything myself," Olga Vasilisovna informed them, looking down on them in a way that made it clear they would heartily regret any shoddy work.

"Now go! Get to work!" she ordered when they continued to stand there. Masha and Manya retreated, looking severely chastened.

"I don't think even my sister could issue orders like that," said Slava, impressed despite her dislike of the way Olga had spoken to Masha and Manya. As often as they hurt her feelings, she knew she would never forgive herself if she were deliberately to hurt their feelings. Although they might like her better if she did...

"The trick is in not caring what the other person thinks of you," said Olga Vasilisovna with a grin, interrupting Slava's melancholy train of thought. "And I'm surprised at their insolence. I would have expected the maids of the Empress's sister to be better trained."

"I can't train anyone," Slava confessed.

"Oh, nonsense," said Olga Vasilisovna. "One day you'll wake up and discover that everyone is quaking in their shoes at the sight of you. But in the meantime we should inspect your horse and tack. Do you just have one horse? Is she used to much riding?"

"Yes, no...I mean, yes, I only have one horse—although I could ask for more, if I need to—and no, she's not used to much riding," said Slava, becoming ever more embarrassed not only over her lack of fitness for the expedition, but over the growing impression (admittedly, deserved) she was giving of being a nonentity in her own sister's kremlin.

"I'm sure they'll give you two, and fit ones. I'm afraid you'll have to leave your own horse behind, if she's not up for it. Come on, let's go have a look." And Olga Vasilisovna strode off, making Slava and her guards scramble to catch up.

Olga Vasilisovna stroked Rozochka's nose but said, regretfully, that she was much too soft and fat to take with them, and chose two other horses instead. Slava, who was starting to panic about her own abilities or lack thereof now that they were actually about to be put to the test, opened her mouth to ask if the new horses were calm enough for her to ride, then felt ashamed to be asking such a question and so didn't, and then realized she could be putting the whole expedition at risk through her vanity, and so asked the groom if the two horses were well-behaved in groups, hoping in this way to acquire the necessary information without revealing herself.

"Don't worry, Krasnoslava Tsarinovna, they're very well-behaved in general," the groom answered, giving her a look that suggested she had guessed Slava's secret. "You won't have any trouble with them at all, trust me."

"I'm sure you're right," said Olga Vasilisovna, going over both horses one more time with a critical eye before nodding to herself. "Now, tomorrow morning: be sure that Skvorets is saddled for riding, and Ogonyok is ready to be ponied, do you understand? All the Tsarinovna's things will be sent down before first light, and I expect to see them loaded up onto Ogonyok when we come down. And if either of them should get a saddlesore from slipshod saddling...!"

The groom gulped. Olga Vasilisovna slapped her hard on the shoulder, causing her to stagger and clutch at Ogonyok's neck in order to stay upright, and told her she was a good girl, she just needed to learn to stand up for herself a bit.

Having chosen satisfactory horses for Slava, Olga Vasilisovna insisted on being taken to the tack room and given free rein to pick out the tack she wanted Slava to have, and then, still striding energetically, she marched Slava back inside the kremlin and, after looking in on Masha and Manya and impressing on them once again the sovereign importance of finishing all of Slava's clothing on time, she led Slava downstairs to the guest quarters in order to introduce her to her men. It was only then that Slava remembered that there were many more people beside herself on this expedition, and that Olga Vasilisovna should have been helping them instead of her. She voiced her concern to Olga Vasilisovna as they walked down the long corridor to the other end of the kremlin, where Olga Vasilisovna's men were housed.

"Don't worry about it," Olga Vasilisovna told her. "My men aren't the useless sort you get here in Krasnograd: they can pack a saddlebag with supplies as well as a woman—and probably better than most of these soft Krasnograders. And helping you out is fun. In fact, I'm glad you're coming. I've never taken another woman anywhere before. I normally just take men—they're so much better at taking orders than women. I'm sure you'll do well enough, though. Ah, here we are."

Slava stepped into a large room, curious to see her traveling companions. Ten men all looked up from bags they were packing and boots they were greasing, and examined her even more curiously than she was examining them.

"Boys, this is Krasnoslava Tsarinovna, the Empress's younger sister, who'll be joining us like I told you." All the men jumped up and bowed. "Krasnoslava Tsarinovna, this is Dima, Sasha, Vova, Volodya, Vladik, Slanik, Olik, Misha, Grisha, and Zhenya."

Slava nodded to them all, which seemed to please them greatly, especially Slanik, who could not have been over sixteen. He bowed again to Slava, and then became embarrassed and hid his face behind the boots he was greasing.

Olga Vasilisovna went over to Dima, who seemed to be the leader of the rest of the men, and spoke first with him and then with all the others in turn, leaving Slava to her own devices, which was very awkward. She had no bags to pack or boots to grease, and she could tell that any attempts to befriend the men would not only lead to mutual mortification, it would hinder them in their work. So she stood by the door and tried unsuccessfully to look Imperial, commanding, and self-confident until Olga Vasilisovna collected her and took her back to her rooms.

"I'll let you rest now," Olga Vasilisovna told her. "We leave at first light tomorrow, which isn't very early, but we'll have to be up well before that to get ready. Don't worry: everything will be taken care of for you—for now, that is. Once you get used to traveling with us you'll be able to take care of yourself. Now go to bed and try to rest up—it'll be waystations and cabins from here on out—when it's not tents, that is." Olga Vasilisovna slapped Slava on the shoulder and left.

Slava somehow survived an extremely uncomfortable private supper with her sister. Once again the Empress dismissed all her maids and guards—she had four personal maids, as well as a guard whose duty it was to dress her in the gowns and jewels that were too heavy for her maids, not to mention dozens of other maids and guards who were responsible for watching over her comfort and safety—so that they could be alone together, something that, for obvious reasons, happened rarely. But the Empress could make no better use of this rare, and possibly final, private moment with her only sister than to make cold inquiries about the expedition and then fall into a resigned silence upon discovering that Slava knew little more about it, other than it offered her only hope of escape, than she did. Eventually she said that Slava would surely want to retire early to bed, and made her grateful escape back to her retinue of hoverers and hangers-on.

Once free of her sister's scornful presence, Slava allowed Masha and Manya to undress her and put her to bed. She was afraid she would lie awake all night, but in what seemed like no time at all she was being awakened and told it was morning.

Chapter Three

Masha and Manya dressed Slava for the last time, or at least it felt so. Slava knew that in theory she would be back in Krasnograd by spring, but right now that seemed a whole lifetime away, as if she would be a completely different woman when she returned. And she hoped she would be, but at the moment it felt as if she were about to set off on a journey not just to the Midnight Land, but to somewhere much farther than that, right out of this life and into the next. She stood there numbly as Masha and Manya dressed her in her cold-weather gear, not even able to be afraid.

A servant came into the room and announced that the Empress wished for Slava to come down to the Hall of Council for her official farewell before she set off. Sweating profusely in her layers of wool, Slava went out of her rooms for the last time, and was confronted with a multitude of people. What appeared to be all the servants in the kremlin had lined the corridors leading from her rooms to the Hall of Council, and as she walked past they bowed down to the ground and called out, "The gods watch over you, little mother!" Some of them had tears in their eyes. Slava knew that she should acknowledge them, but she was too unnerved by this sudden show of devotion to do more than nod stiffly and hurry past.

The Hall of Council was filled with princesses and princes in their best finery, making Slava even more conspicuous in her plain clothing. She had allowed Masha and Manya to dress her in the trousers they had labored over the night before, and was now acutely aware of the fact that she was standing in front of Zem''s assembled nobility dressed as a man.

Slava's sister stood up from the Wooden Throne, which had been moved from the Hall of Judgment to the Hall of Council for the occasion, and ordered Slava to kneel. Slava was at first taken aback, but then saw by her sister's solemn face that she meant it as an honor, not an insult, and so got down on her knees and bowed down to the ground. Her sister, still with an unusually solemn face, bestowed upon her the Imperial blessing. When Slava rose back to her feet, her sister whispered, "You're sure, Slava?"

"Yes," Slava told her.

"Then be sure to come back safely." Her sister took Slava by the shoulders, kissed her forehead, and said, "The gods watch over you until you are back in my care," and Slava saw that she really meant it, at least at this moment.

Boleslav Vlasiyevich personally escorted Slava out of the Hall of Council to the square in front of the kremlin, where the others were already mounted and ready. Olga Vasilisovna was holding Skvorets and Ogonyok, although not without difficulty, as they were sidling back and forth with excitement. Most of the square was filled with people, who cheered when Slava came out, making all the horses jump and start to sweat in the cold air.

"So many people!" Slava exclaimed.

"All of Krasnograd already knows of your intention, Krasnoslava Tsarinovna, and you have caught their hearts," Boleslav Vlasiyevich told her.

"But why?" she asked.

"You are a great favorite with the people, Krasnoslava Tsarinovna, and with this latest deed of yours, you have proven that you have courage as well as compassion."

"I am? I have?" Slava had never known she was a great favorite with the people. Since she rarely had anything to do with "the people" unless she happened to ride past them, she had always assumed they thought as little of her as the nobility did.

Boleslav Vlasiyevich saw her doubting face, and laughed. "Krasnoslava Tsarinovna! How could it be otherwise? Everyone knows you are the one who tempers the Empress's stern justice with mercy. There is no more attractive trait than mercy, and it seems that all the mercy that is missing in the hard hearts of our princesses is gathered together in you. How could the people not love you? How could anyone not love you? Anyone who is not a fool, that is." He lifted her onto Skvorets's back. "The gods watch over your safety, Krasnoslava Tsarinovna, and may you come back soon," he said quietly, kissing her hand and bowing over it.

"Thank you, Boleslav Vlasiyevich," Slava said, trying to withdraw her hand from his lips without making it apparent that she was doing so. As she often did, she had the uncomfortable feeling that he was playing some deep, duplicitous game, one that was so devious not even he knew what it was. Every day he was at pains to show himself to be the Empress's most loyal servant, while at the same time indicating with subtle signs that there was some special bond between him and Slava, and that he was always watching out for her and solicitous for her wellbeing, unlike everyone else in the kremlin. The riddle of his behavior and the secret he seemed to think they shared was disturbing, and yet so provoking she was almost tempted to try to solve it, foolish and dangerous as she knew that to be. Yet another good reason to be gone.

"All mounted? Everyone ready? Let's be off!" cried Olga Vasilisovna.

Her men all emitted piercing cries. Someone, probably Boleslav Vlasiyevich, pushed Ogonyok's lead rope into Slava's hand, and then they were all galloping as best they could across the snowy square, forcing the crowd to jump back out of their way.

Olga Vasilisovna whistled and her men shrieked as they raced away from the kremlin, eliciting ecstatic cheers from the crowd. Slava clung with one hand to Skvorets's mane, and with the other to Ogonyok's lead rope. She knew she was not so poor a rider that she could not ride a galloping horse and pony another, but at the moment she could not trust herself to tell up from down.

They galloped until they were out of sight of the cheering crowd, and then Olga Vasilisovna reined in her horse and signaled the others to do the same. Soon they were all walking.

"Normally I never let them gallop in town, especially on snowy streets," she told Slava. "It's much too dangerous. But I thought our onlookers needed a spectacle. Dima! Now that she has escaped the confines of the kremlin and become one of us, tell Krasnoslava Tsarinovna our plans. Thus far she has bravely remained in ignorance, trusting us not to lead her astray. With reason, I may add, but it's my rule that everyone has to know what we're doing and where we're going, so tell her."

"With pleasure, Olga Vasilisovna!" Dima, who was riding in front, twisted around in his saddle to face Slava. Like everything else he did, the movement was marked with an easy grace that Slava could not imagine ever possessing herself. The way his lower body continued to follow his horse while his upper body was turned towards Slava spoke of a lifetime spent riding, not sitting around inside a kremlin and sulking over his troubles.

Slava suddenly realized how intently she was looking at Dima, and shifted her gaze in order not to embarrass him and anger Olga Vasilisovna, but neither of them had seemed to notice.

"As you know, Krasnoslava Tsarinovna, no doubt much better than I, Krasnograd lies at the confluence of the Malokrasna and Yuzhnokrasna rivers," he began. "They join together and become the Krasna, which flows North to Pristanograd, the seat of your own Imperial foremother Miroslava Praskovyevna before she conquered Krasnograd and united Zem'. There it empties into the Breathing Sea, sometimes called the Sea of Ice. Pristanogradskoye is the Northernmost province in Zem'. The coast there takes a sharp turn to the North at Vostochnoye Selo, and no one knows how far North our territory extends. The Northernmost settlement in Zem' is Naberezhnoye, which is on the coast. Even hunters rarely travel more than a day's ride North or East of Naberezhnoye.

"Our plan is to cut overland to Vostochnoye Selo, as the Krasna is frozen solid at this time of year, making sailing impossible, and from there we will ride up the coast to Naberezhnoye. There we will gather information from the local hunters, and then set out, probably at first going North up the coast, and deciding where to go from there. Olga Vasilisovna intends to start by mapping the coast North of Naberezhnoye, and then we hope to head inland, although we must wait until we see what the conditions are before deciding. We will probably be gone at least two months, and maybe as many as four, but no more, as we will be unable to travel once the spring muds start, and so must return home before then."

"Oh," said Slava.

"Have you visited Pristanograd or Vostochnoye Selo before, Krasnoslava Tsarinovna?" asked Dima. All the men turned in their saddles and looked at her with interest, making her blush hotly.

"No," she said. She started to explain that she had never been outside of Krasnograd before, became ashamed, and then realized that there was no hiding the fact, and so confessed it anyway. The men greeted the news with polite astonishment.

"Well, you couldn't be in better hands for your first venture outside of the city walls, Krasnoslava Tsarinovna," Dima told her, smiling encouragingly.

And Slava *did* feel encouraged. She kept waiting for Dima and the others to show some signs of duplicity, but thus far everyone had appeared perfectly sincere. Slava was unused to sincere people, and was unsure how to respond to them. In her experience there was a sharp split between people's feelings and actions: either they had base feelings but tried to act nobly in order to gain some kind of advantage, or they had noble feelings but tried to act basely because they thought that to do otherwise would make them appear weak. People who followed their hearts were rare in Slava's experience, especially when their hearts were good.

"There's no need to look so serious, Krasnoslava Tsarinovna," Dima said, still smiling encouragingly. "Setting off on your first expedition can be daunting, but that's no reason not to enjoy it. Look at Slanik here: it's his first time out from under his mother's skirts, and yet you don't see him trembling in fear, do you? No, he's looking around, admiring the sights of Krasnograd. Aren't you, Slanik?"

"Yes, Dmitry Marusyevich." Slanik tried to speak calmly, but just then a princess and her retinue demanded that they make way, and he watched open-mouthed as they rode by.

"Dmitry Marusyevich! Did you see that! She must be very rich, don't you think, Dmitry Marusyevich? With all that gold on the saddles, and the fancy weapons the guards were carrying. Who do you think she was, Dmitry Marusyevich?"

"Some princess," answered Dima with a shrug.

"That was Princess Stepnaya, her son Mstislav Yelizavetovich, her daughter-in-law, and her retinue," Slava said, and then became embarrassed for blurting out the answer, afraid that the men would think she was putting herself above them.

"You know her then, Krasnoslava Tsarinovna?" asked Slanik, impressed but not, apparently, offended. "How do you know such a fine princess, Krasnoslava Tsarinovna?"

Dima laughed. "Did you not just hear the words that came out of your own mouth, Slanik? Who do you think the Tsarinovna is? The daughter of a Tsarina, of course. If Princess Stepnaya had recognized her, she would have had to get out of her fine sleigh, kneel on the snow, and bow down to the ground, ruining all her fine clothing and fine dignity."

Slanik stared at Slava. "Is that true, Krasnoslava Tsarinovna?" he asked. "Why didn't you make her stop, then? Will she get in trouble for not bowing to you? Should we go after her and bring her back?"

"I don't want anyone kneeling on the snow and bowing down to the ground to me," Slava said, squirming at the very idea. "Especially Princess Stepnaya, who has been in poor health these past two years. I'm sure if she had been able, she would have come to see me off at the kremlin, and would have gotten out of her sleigh and greeted me here on the street. She only came to Krasnograd to see me, as I am her closest female heir, though only through my father. She comes to Krasnograd every year for just that purpose, to ensure that she still has an heir who can inherit, but this year she was only able to stay a few days before declaring herself unable to remain here and setting off again for the steppe. I fear this may be her last visit to Krasnograd."

"I could still call for her, Tsarinovna, if you would wish to greet your kinswoman," said Dima, gazing on her with sympathetic eyes.

"No," said Slava. "Princess Stepnaya and I have already said our farewells. Now that I'm with you, I'm no longer the Tsarinovna. Now I'm just another fellow traveler." She thought about pointing out that she was only the younger daughter of a Tsarina, and therefore would forever be only a Tsarinovna and never a Tsarina, unlike her sister's daughter, but a lifetime's ingrained habit of self-protection stopped her from making too much of a spectacle of her own weakness, large as it might loom in her own eyes.

And just for a moment she thought of the steppe army, the most feared army in all of the Known World, and one that was supposedly at her beck and call, and that she might inherit one day. But then she ground those thoughts to powder and blew them away, just as she always did. It was no good having fantasies of strength that wasn't really hers, and never would be. There was nothing of the steppe in her, however much Princess Stepnaya might claim her as kin, and she knew better than to think on it.

"Well enough," said Slanik, who appeared to be of the same mind, if only he had known it, and went back to looking at the buildings lining the street, apparently forgetting all about her and Princess Stepnaya.

Dima's gaze continued to rest on her for a moment longer, and it was full of sympathy, seemingly genuine. Slava could feel herself blushing once again, and was grateful that her face was covered. She was unaccustomed to kindness, and so even the tiniest amount of it made her want to whine and fawn like a beaten dog, but like a beaten dog, she was afraid that the outstretched hand would turn out to be holding a stick, and so she made herself ignore Dima's kindness and look away.

She tried to remember the last time a man had showed her some kindness, and meant it, but she couldn't. Perhaps when her father had been alive...she had some dim memory of him picking her up and calling her his favorite daughter...and she had laughed and said she was his only daughter...and he had said that was because he'd gotten it right the first time, she'd turned out so well he didn't need any other daughters...she'd been so small then, her father's arms had seemed an immense distance above the ground...she couldn't be sure anymore if her memories had actually happened, or if she'd dreamed them in her desperation...ever since then all the men she'd come across had only ever looked at her in order to see themselves...and they hadn't liked what they'd seen nearly as much as they'd thought they would... they'd seen their own hatred and resentment, and they'd fled in horror...no wonder Slava had never been able to hold onto any of them... no one likes to see herself reflected in an unkind mirror, and most men of Slava's acquaintance had only ever seen themselves in the flattering portraits painted by their mothers' loving eyes...why couldn't Slava's eyes paint flattering portraits...although flattering portraits were hardly what most people needed...it would just make them even worse than they already were...most people needed a good hard kick...Slava was not the kicking kind...she would have to find some other way of kicking...

"I can't tell the weather this far South—what do your city-boy senses tell you: will it snow soon, Dmitry Marusyevich?" asked one of the men—Grisha, Slava thought, shaking herself out of her reverie. As far as she could tell under all his sheepskin, he was a rough-looking fellow with a big black beard and a voice that normally would have made her a little bit afraid, but right now she was grateful to him for breaking up her thoughts before her jangling nerves started weeping again.

"Who can tell in this city," said Dima, looking up at the sky and sniffing deeply. "My city-boy senses were trained in Lesnograd; Krasnograd is too much for me. I'll know for sure once we're in the open air again."

"When will we reach the open air, Dmitry Marusyevich?" she asked. "When we pass outside of the city walls?"

"We will have to go several more versts beyond that before we leave the stench of the city behind, Krasnoslava Tsarinovna," he told her. "It's a long walk to the North Gate, and then we must get past Outer Krasnograd, and then through the settlements beyond that. But by tonight you will be breathing clean air, I assure you. There's nothing like it in the world, is there, Grisha?"

"No, Dmitry Marusyevich." Grisha glanced at Slava with what she saw was shyness, and went on ahead to ride with Olga Vasilisovna.

"Grisha is from the deep woods in Severnolesnoye, and gasps like a fish out of water whenever he has to breathe dirty air and talk to the nobility," Dima explained. "He might seem a bit rough, but you can trust him."

"I have every confidence in Olga Vasilisovna's men," said Slava. She cast about for a polite topic of conversation with someone such as Dima. She wasn't sure how to treat him, as he was clearly better educated and traveled than the average guard, but was not, as far as she could tell, the son of a noblewoman. Eventually she settled on more details of their journey, since Dima seemed happy enough to discuss them, and Slava herself was becoming more and more curious about where he had been and where they were all going. "How long does it take to ride from Severnolesnoye to Krasnograd?" she asked.

"Two weeks to a month, Tsarinovna, depending on the roads and where in Severnolesnoye you start. Since it is the North-Easternmost province in Zem', we may return by riding through it, depending on where we find ourselves when we leave the Midnight Land. Do you know Princess Severnolesnaya, Krasnoslava Tsarinovna? Olga Vasilisovna approached her first about money and supplies for our expedition, but she refused, although it seems she hopes our findings will add to her territory. What do you think, Krasnoslava Tsarinovna?"

Dima spoke very innocently, but Slava could tell he was deeply interested in the answer, which frightened her, so she said only, "I met her once, when I was a little girl. I know little about her," and fell silent. Dima gave her an understanding look and turned to talk to Slanik instead, for which she was grateful.

Somehow Slava, who rarely went anywhere even inside of Krasnograd, had imagined that they would leave the kremlin and find themselves immediately in a trackless wilderness, even though she knew that that was not true. In fact, it was not until midday that they even passed outside the gates of Krasnograd. And if it had not been for the gates and the guards Slava might not have guessed that they had left the city, for there were almost as many buildings on this side of the city walls as there were on the other. The road was wider, though, and Olga

The Flight

Vasilisovna called for them to pick up a trot. All the men whooped in delight, and Slava almost felt like joining them, as her seat was numb from a morning spent in the saddle at a walk.

Their quicker pace allowed them to pass through the built-up area around the city in a short time, and in a few versts there were actual fields on either side of the road. This, Slava supposed, must be the countryside. She must have seen it at some point in her life, but she couldn't for the life of her remember when. She looked around with curiosity. The fields stretched flatly away to the horizon, where a birch forest glistened in the winter sun.

"Will we ride through that forest today?" she asked Dima, aware only after she had spoken that she sounded like a small child.

He laughed. "We will," he promised, "and many more forests after that. We have the whole taiga and tundra ahead of us, don't you worry, Krasnoslava Tsarinovna."

"The sun is so bright out here!" she exclaimed. "And the snow so white! And the horizon so wide!" She inhaled deeply. The cold air seemed to penetrate much farther into her lungs than indoor air ever could. "Fresh air!" she cried, feeling a little drunk from the open expanse in front of her.

"Fresh air!" Grisha chimed in.

"Fresh air! Fresh air! Fresh air!" the others shouted, and then broke into a song:

> *Oh air, my air, my dear sweet air,*
> *Why are you so fresh?*
> *Oh sky, my sky, my dear sweet sky,*
> *Why are you so blue?*
> *Oh snow, my snow, my dear sweet snow,*
> *Why are you so white?*
> *My curly-haired love bids me come home,*
> *But I must lay down my wild head*
> *On the wide field,*
> *The field of battle,*
> *And my curly-haired love,*
> *Will look out her window,*
> *Look out her crystal window and sigh:*
> *Oh air, my air, my dear sweet air,*
> *Why are you so fresh?*

This song seemed to please the men greatly, and they sang it over and over again, accompanied by loud yips and cries, until Olga Vasilisovna called for a halt in order to rest the horses and feed themselves.

After a hasty meal of cold pies, eating standing up, they remounted and continued down the road. Soon they were passing through the birches, which inspired the men to sing another song:

> *Ah, you birches, how white you are!*
> *Ah, you birches, how fair you are!*
> *As with my beloved, my curly-headed one,*
> *I slide my hands over your smooth limbs,*
> *Your branches embrace me,*
> *Your bark brushes against me,*
> *And I dream of my beloved, my curly-headed one.*

Slava blushed terribly, but Olga Vasilisovna paid no attention to the song, and the men seemed not the slightest bit embarrassed, even though it was plain that all of them, even Slanik, knew exactly what he was singing. Noblewomen liked to say that soldiers and peasants made much better lovers than princes, and now Slava saw that it could very well be true. Perhaps, she thought, it was because they were free of this current fashion for surliness that had swept through Krasnograd—a sullen lover! Absolutely intolerable, in Slava's experience— or perhaps it was because they were not so strictly raised.

The sons of peasants and tradeswoman were raised much as their daughters were, and had many of the same freedoms, which meant that they were expected to work and gain skills and hold a man's, or even a woman's, responsibilities from an early age, which made them (so it was said, and so Slava was seeing) cheerful and bold. Princes, on the other hand, were notorious for their coy shyness. She certainly couldn't imagine any of the princes she knew even uttering the words "my beloved, my curly-headed one" without becoming speechless with mortification (real or feigned—princes were taught to act even more embarrassed than they really felt, in hopes of capturing some motherly woman's heart), and then collapsing into a protracted fit of sulkiness over his mortification, which would only cease once he had devised a way to blame his mortification on someone else, preferably his curly-headed beloved.

Of course, she thought to herself, it was only natural that men should be shy and difficult when first encountering the world of love—after all, it was women who took in love, in every sense of the word, and men who were taken—but nonetheless, the princes (and all the other men) of Krasnograd were more than Slava could bear.

Now, though, she could see why the princesses of Krasnograd waxed on about the pleasures of a peasant lover...On the other hand, they also said—well, the women of Slava's family, who were notorious for taking peasant husbands (other noblewomen generally preferred to take a lover and then discard him as soon as the first lines of manhood appeared upon his face), said—that all too often they were so brutally violent, like beaten dogs, that they required extensive re-schooling before they could be trusted around women, children, animals, or even each other...

Slava eyed the men around her narrowly. None of them *looked* like rapists or murderers, but who knew better than Slava how easy it was for a meek façade to hide the vicious monster within? She would just have to trust in Olga's ability to control her men...Olga, daughter of her family's most troublesome princess...Her men certainly *looked* very sweet and innocent, though...And not unhandsome...Slava snapped herself out of her reverie, blushing even more terribly than before, and resolved to think no more on such subjects. Olga and her men deserved better than such thoughts, even if they were unaware that Slava was thinking them, and only idle and useless women, which Slava had resolved she no longer was, dwelt day and night upon thoughts of men and love anyway.

They passed out of the birch forest just as the sun was sinking low enough to cast ominous shadows on the snow. Slava looked back at it, glad to see how frightening the forest was becoming as night drew in, and even more glad to be leaving it.

"You see that building, up there on the horizon, Krasnoslava Tsarinovna?" Dima called to her. "That's where we'll be stopping for the night. The first waystation out of Krasnograd. You'll have ridden forty versts from Krasnograd when you dismount there."

"That's thirty versts farther away than I've ever ridden before," she called back.

"And how do you feel, Krasnoslava Tsarinovna?"

"Sore, terribly, terribly sore!" she shouted, laughing with the joy of being terribly, terribly sore.

The joy of being terribly sore stayed with Slava all through supper, which was of the coarsest, most disagreeable food she had ever eaten. Or so she would have thought had she not been riding all day in the cold. But since she had, every crumb of stale black bread was delicious.

After supper Slava had the joy of not sleeping, as she and Olga Vasilisovna lay on a hard lumpy bed and listened to the wind howling under the eaves.

"It will be cold tomorrow, and maybe snow towards evening," Olga Vasilisovna predicted at one point. "You're not asleep, are you, Krasnoslava Tsarinovna?"

"I can't sleep," confessed Slava.

"That's always a problem the first few nights out. It might the worst thing about traveling, Krasnoslava Tsarinovna."

"I don't mind. And..." Slava trailed off shyly.

"What?"

"I was going to say... But I don't want to seem impolite... But anyway, since we're going to be speaking to each other so often... Perhaps you should just call me Slava, and not Krasnoslava Tsarinovna. If you wanted to, that is. Ah, that is, you don't have to if you don't want to, I just...Krasnoslava Tsarinovna is such a mouthful ... But, you know..."

Olga Vasilisovna stopped Slava's flounderings by laughing into her pillow. "Of course I'll call you Slava, if that's what you want. Is that what people normally call you?"

"Well, no. Normally they call me Krasnoslava Tsarinovna. But Slava is what my friends call me. Or they would, if I had...I guess Slava is just what I call myself. But..."

"Very well, Slava. Henceforth you will be called Slava. A very fine name. And you can call me Olga, which is what I call myself."

"Also a fine name," said Slava, beginning to smile into the darkness.

"And I have no doubt that in a few days the boys will be calling you Krasna Tsarina, or something of that nature, and mean it sincerely. They're good boys, but they're not very good at showering noblewomen with fine words. They have better things to concern themselves with."

"Of course," said Slava. "They can call me whatever they like; I won't mind at all. I'm really... Well, you know, I don't care too much about that kind of thing, it doesn't really mean anything to me..."

"Because you know what people are really thinking anyway," said Olga.

"Yes," admitted Slava.

"Well, I'm glad I'm not in the habit of lying, seeing as how we're going to be spending the next several months in bed together. Which reminds me: leave the boys alone."

"I would never...!!" Slava actually sat up, she was so enraged, and then made herself lie back down and pretend not to be offended, in order not to hurt Olga's feelings.

"I didn't think you would, I'm just saying: Dima's mine and the rest of them have mothers who care about them. Not that an affair with the Empress's sister would ruin their value too much, but it might break their hearts when you left them, and I can't be having any of that."

"I wouldn't leave them!" said Slava.

"No? What, you'd give Grisha your hand and heart and parade him around in front of all those princes for the rest of his life?"

"It's a moot point anyway," said Slava, calming back down.

"You're too right it is. Anyway, I think you have someone waiting for you back home already. I saw that scene in the courtyard with what's-his-name, your sister's Captain of the Guard."

"He was just helping me onto my horse. I can't vault into the saddle like you can."

"I'm sure. And when you get back to Krasnograd, I'd recommend you let him 'help you onto your horse' as much as you like. But in the meantime, just let his memory warm your heart."

"Fine," said Slava.

"Besides, he's much more handsome than any of my boys."

"You think so?"

"I do."

"Maybe you're right."

"I know I am."

Slava thought about that for a moment, and then burst out, "But in the end he's my sister's man. Maybe he thinks he's in love with me, but if it came down to it, if he had to choose between me and her, I'm sure he'd choose her. Or actually...I don't know, and that's even more frightening. He has a reputation for being willful and hotheaded, and no one knows which way he might jump."

"Willful and hotheaded? There are worse things in a man. It keeps things interesting."

"Not for me! And I don't know what he wants or why he does what he does, and I'm afraid my sister has been hoping to use him to get to me, which just goes to show what a poor judge of character she is, or maybe he's been hoping to use himself, and besides, you don't get to be Captain of the Imperial Guard without...without putting a lot of terrible things on your conscience, and as everyone keeps remind-ing me, I'm much too squeamish about that kind of thing. So I don't care how gray his eyes or broad his shoulders are, he doesn't stand a chance with me and that's that."

"If you say so," said Olga.

"I do," said Slava, blushing furiously in the dark and wishing she'd been able to keep her mouth shut.

"Good girl, then," said Olga, and turned away from her.

Slava and Olga lay there in silence for a while, not sleeping, un-til Olga said she had to take a piss and got out of the bed. It seemed to Slava that she lay there by herself for a long time. Then somehow she was walking through heavy snow and deep woods, and there were strange men and horses she couldn't quite recognize, and many other confusing images, and then Olga was shaking her shoulder, and she realized it was morning of the second day of her new existence, and she got up and prepared to put as many versts between herself and Krasnograd as she could manage.

Chapter Four

They rode all day that day, and the next, and the next. Slava had known she would be sore, but she had not realized until then how painful riding all day would be. Her sitting bones, which until then had never even entered her consciousness, consumed all her thoughts, except when she thought about her inner thighs. When she sat down to supper the second night out, she had to use her hands to position her legs on the chair, as her knees were unable to open and close on their own.

She tried to hide it from the others, but when she stood up from the table, it was so apparent she was barely able to walk that the innkeeper blurted out, "I'll warm up the bathhouse," before anyone else could say anything. Slava tried to protest, but Olga said everyone should steam in a voice that brooked no argument.

Steaming eased the muscle pain somewhat, but the next morning, when Slava got back in the saddle, a whimper escaped her lips when her sitting bones met the seat. She strangled it as soon as she heard it, but not soon enough to prevent Olga from noticing.

"You'll go numb as soon as we get moving, and by tomorrow the pain will ease off," she said.

Slava was doubtful, but in fact, by midmorning the pain had dulled to the point that she was able to notice her surroundings again. And in truth, there was much for someone as little-traveled as Slava to look at. When, of course, she was not lost in daydreams. Aside from the pain, which did not disappear nearly so quickly as Olga had promised, there was little to distract Slava from her dreaming for hours on end, and when she was not watching the fields and trees go by, she was watching the strange and wondrous visions that crowded behind her eyes whenever she let them. She had not realized until then just how hungry she had been for her own uninterrupted fantasy, and there were times when even the pain and the cold and the new sights were not enough to drag her away from her own inner world.

The first two days they had passed through villages surrounded by fields and small birch woods. On the afternoon of the third day something dark appeared on the horizon.

"Is it more snow?" asked Slava, pointing to the dark mass looming before them.

"There will probably be more snow by nightfall, but that is not what you see," Dima told her. "That is a forest."

"Why is it so dark?" Slava asked.

"Have you never seen a fir forest before, Krasna Tsarina?" As Olga had predicted, all the men had given her that particular shortened version of her name, which they pronounced with obvious delight.

"There are firs in the park behind the kremlin..."

"Those are just firs, not a fir forest. Have you never heard the voice of a fir forest?"

"No."

"Every tree has its own voice," Dima began. All the other men rode closer to hear him speak. "The oak is the old man of the forest, and whenever the wind blows, you can hear it rustling through his beard. Being an old man, he spends most of his time sleeping, and rarely says anything except to grumble at his grandchildren. The birch is the young lady of the forest, and when the wind blows, it fills out her hair and skirts, and you can hear her say, 'How fair I am! How fair!' The pine is the singer of the woods, and lets the wind play its soft songs in her branches. But the fir—the fir is the whisperer of the forest, the keeper of secrets. Whenever the wind whispers through her fingers, she whispers back: 'Be afraid! Be afraid! Be afraid!'"

"Why?" asked Slava, pretending that the hair had not just risen on the back of her neck.

"Everyone fears secrets, Krasna Tsarina. And the secrets of the fir forest are so very dark. But you'll see for yourself when we ride through."

"How long will it take us?"

"This is only a small forest, so we will be through by tomorrow afternoon."

"You mean we must spend the night there?"

"There is a cabin for travelers."

"I've stayed there many times, Krasna Tsarina, don't you worry," said Grisha. "We'll be going much deeper into much darker forests before we pass through the taiga. And don't listen to what Marusich says: he's a city boy and doesn't know how to treat the forest. But I'm from deep Severnolesnoye, where the forest stretches out to the edge of Zem' and beyond, and I tell you: the forest can be as much a home as the city can. Or more so, since the city's full of liars. Wolves and wood-spirits don't lie."

"Have you seen leshiye, then?" asked Slava, who had heard tales of wood-spirits but had a hard time believing in them.

"Oh, many times, Krasna Tsarina."

"And is it true that they look like walking trees?"

"Just like, Krasna Tsarina," said Grisha, whose normal taciturnity seemed to be melting before that pleasure to which men were so susceptible (although Slava had promised herself she would stop dwelling on the imperfections of men, she found that she was doing it quite against her will, perhaps out of habit, and perhaps because there was so much material to dwell upon...but she must stop having those thoughts, she really must), that of holding forth as an expert, although he at least seemed to have some basis for his knowledge.

"I saw my first when I was just a boy and had gone out to gather firewood," he said. "I was in a dark fir wood, where the branches swept down almost to the ground. I was gathering sticks, when I happened to glance up, and I saw two eyes watching me from out of the branches."

"What did you do?" In spite of her amusement at his sudden transformation into a talker, Slava had forgotten to disbelieve Grisha, and now she and all the men were leaning towards him in their saddles, listening with rapt attention.

"At first I thought it was a bear, and I took hold of my knife, in case I had to fight it off, but then it stepped out from behind the branches, and I saw it was a fir tree itself."

"Then what?"

"Then I stared at her, and she stared at me, I don't know for how long, and then she stepped back into the fir trees and disappeared, although I could hear her move through the woods for a long time afterwards. When the sounds of her rustling through the branches had faded into the sound of the wind, I ran home, my heart racing in my throat, and told my mother everything."

"What did she say?"

"She said I was lucky to have seen a leshaya, and even more lucky to come away unharmed. But I have seen more since then, and nothing has ever happened to me. Leshiye are thinking creatures, and they always know how you feel about them—like you, Krasna Tsarina. If you mean them no harm, no harm will come to you."

"I would like to see a leshaya," said Slava. "Although I'm afraid I might be afraid."

"You would have nothing to fear, Krasna Tsarina, for she would know your heart was pure."

"Grigory Marinych speaks the truth, Krasna Tsarina," said Dima. "Even a city boy like me knows that leshiye are nothing to fear, providing you don't provoke them. I hope we encounter one on our journey—it would show the gods mean us no harm."

"The gods mean us no harm, never fear," said Olga, who had also been listening in on the conversation. "But I'd like to see a leshaya too. And I'm curious to see what manner of creature we encounter in the Far North, once we cross the sunline."

"Snow maidens and firebirds," suggested Slanik.

"Snow maidens perhaps, but firebirds only live in the East, beyond the mountains, everyone knows that," said Grisha.

This started off a lively debate amongst the men over different kinds of magical creatures, where they lived, how dangerous they were, and whether or not they even existed at all. The conversation was only brought to an end when a snowflake landed in Olik's eye, and they all realized that it had started to snow.

Soon it was snowing hard enough that Slava could see all the eddies and currents in the air. She had never realized how alive the air was, and watched, enchanted, as the snow swirled around her. She was so taken by the sight that she forgot to watch out for the fir forest, and was startled when it loomed up in front of her.

"How far to the cabin, Dima?" Olga called from the front of the group.

"Fifteen versts, Olga Vasilisovna!"

"We'll be riding in the dark, but only for a little while, then," Olga shouted back at them. "Everyone, have your lanterns or torches ready, but don't light them unless I say so—we don't want to waste supplies, and your night eyes should serve you well enough."

Slava did not even know she had a torch until Dima showed her where it was strapped to Ogonyok's pack. The possibility of riding through the woods in a snowstorm in the dark had never occurred to her before, but when she saw how calm the others were, she decided to try to remain calm as well.

The firs were indeed, as Dima had said, filled with whispers, broken only now and then by the sound of a clump of snow falling from a bough to the ground. Every time that happened, Skvorets, whom Slava was riding that day, would jump and look anxiously at the place where the noise had come from, flicking his ears back and forth and snorting.

"Don't worry, old man: it's only snow," Dima told him. "You'll get used to it soon enough."

"I wish I had skis," said Grisha. "For traveling through the woods in snow you need skis. I made mine myself, and there's nothing smoother or more pleasant than traveling on those skis."

"A horse is still faster," said Misha, starting off another debate between the men over which was faster in winter: skis or horseback. Slava listened and even found herself laughing from time to time.

The mock-argument was interrupted by Olga's sudden stop, forcing everyone else to scramble to rein in their horses in order not to run into her.

"Marusich! Marinych!" she called. "Which way?"

Dima and Grisha rode forward, and Slava saw as the horses parted to let them through that the road forked, and there was no sign indicating where it led.

"Was it like this when you came through last year?" Slanik asked Sasha in a low voice.

"No," Sasha said. "Last time we came through there was only one path; some woodsman or creature must have made the second one. But don't worry: Grisha Marinych will know the way, I'm sure of it."

Grisha did in fact point very confidently in the direction of the right-hand path, and they all set off after him, keeping to a walk. The slow pace allowed Slava to notice that it was almost too dark to see shadows. Olga lit her lantern but told the others not to light theirs, and had Misha ride well in the back in order to keep his night eyes.

When Slava looked ahead, she saw how the snow swirled in the lantern light, and when she looked behind her, the snow seemed to glow in the darkness, making the tall dark trunks of the trees even taller and darker. The horses moved silently through the soft snow, and the air above them was filled with the sound of the wind in the fir needles.

If Slava had been certain that there was nothing out there, and that soon, very soon, they would arrive somewhere full of light and voices, it would have been one of the most beautiful things she had ever witnessed, but as she was certain of no such thing, it was simply eerie. Plus, now that they were walking she had become acutely aware of the pain in her sitting bones, and her hands were so cold she was having a hard time holding the reins.

There was a loud crash off in the trees, and the horses all stopped dead.

"A branch collapsing under the weight of the snow," Olga said firmly. "Keep riding."

They started walking again, but Slava could feel the worry rising off the men like steam. The horses could also feel it, or perhaps they sensed something else, and they started tossing their heads and jigging sideways, jostling into each other on the narrow path.

"I think I hear something moving in the woods," said Volodya. "To the right."

The intensity of everyone's attention to the trees on the right was palpable through the cold air. Slava became convinced that she, too, could hear something moving with slow, dragging steps through the woods.

"A bear?" asked Slanik, his voice trying not to quaver.

"The bears are all asleep for the winter," said Vova, his voice trying not to quaver too.

"Marinych!" said Olga sharply. "How much farther?"

Grisha sniffed deeply. "Not far at all, Olga Vasilisovna," he said. "I can smell the stable from here."

"Then ride on! Trot, everyone!"

The horses sprang forward into a fast trot, their hooves covering the sound of the thing in the woods, if it was really out there. The hairs on the back of Slava's neck told her not to look back, but when she heard Grisha call out, "The cabin!" she glanced behind them for a moment anyway. It seemed to her that something, perhaps two golden eyes, flashed in the light of the lantern, but then they rode into the stockade surrounding the cabin, and barred the gates with a heavy thud.

Once the gates had been barred, the others tried to act as if there were nothing out there beyond them, but Slava was acutely aware of how the trees stood tall behind the stockade fence, their branches hanging over the top, shedding shadows and needles onto the snow inside.

More lanterns were lit, filling the enclosure with their flickering light but not blotting out the immense darkness beyond them, which seemed to hang over Slava's head like storm clouds. She let Slanik take her horses, and Dima take her arm and walk her up the uneven steps into the cabin, which smelled strongly of cold damp wood.

Wanting to appear useful, even though she knew she wasn't, Slava took food out of their packs while Dima lit a fire and Olga toured the cabin, deciding where everyone would sleep and looking to see if previous travelers had left any messages.

"Did you see the eyes?" Slava asked Dima, once Olga was in another room.

"Eyes?"

"There were eyes, two golden eyes, in the trees behind us, I swear it. Could it... And the sounds we heard, as if something were following us... Could it have been a leshaya?"

Dima shrugged, but the set of his shoulders showed he was not as calm as he wished to be. "There are many things in the woods, Krasna Tsarina, but remember: there are fewer causes for fear than our nighttime minds would tell us. And look!" he continued, clearly wanting to change the subject. "A fire! We'll have a hot supper tonight, Krasna Tsarina! What more could we want?"

Soon the rest of the men came in from the stable, and their loud—purposefully loud—voices drowned out the sound of the snowy wind in the firs. But afterwards, when Olga and Slava retired to the bedroom Olga had chosen for them, the whispering rose up again in Slava's ears.

They got into the bed—cold, narrow, and lumpy, of course—and were just settling down to sleep when something scratched against the shutters.

"What was that?" asked Slava, sitting back up and letting in cold air under the covers.

"A branch; lie back down," Olga told her, pulling on the blankets and forcing Slava to lie back down and not let in any more cold air. "We're right up against the stockade on this side of the cabin, and tree branches have grown over the fence and up against the shutters. Go to sleep: tomorrow will be a long day."

Slava lay back down, but did not go to sleep. For the first time she thought about the cost of the fresh air she had been inhaling so greedily. She had been prepared for tiredness, inconvenience, soreness, and all the other things that everyone complained about on a long journey. Thus far they had even been less unpleasant than she had expected. She had also been prepared to face danger, if necessary. She had never thought of herself as a brave person—quite the reverse, in fact—but, never having faced danger, she had assumed that any she happened to come across would at least be obvious and quick to pass—a wolf attack, for instance.

It had never occurred to her that just riding through the woods would be so unnerving, and that one of the most unnerving things about it would be that she would not be able to tell if danger were present, or not. She wanted to talk to Olga about it, but judging by her breathing, Olga was already fast asleep. The branch scratched against the shutter like claws, and in Slava's mind, that was what it looked like: a tree stretching out its claws across the stockade and straight towards Slava.

Think of all the walls around you, she told herself. Both the trees and the walls seemed to press in close around her, while the snow and the sky stretched out above her forever, and the path they had not taken earlier led away into darkness. From behind the snow the stars were watching her, their gaze staring right through the roof, like thousands of tiny, unblinking eyes. The taiga spread out below Slava, and then ice, endless ice...

When Olga shook her shoulder and said, "Wake up!" Slava realized she had been asleep for hours, a sleep filled with clear dreams. Slava dreamt often, but in Krasnograd her dreams always had a frantic quality, as if pressed in from all sides by the dreams of others. Here, though, her dreams had felt spacious, even if it had been the spaciousness of fear, and the image of the snow and the sky, and the trees reaching out for her would, she knew, stay with her for a long time, protected by all the space around it as if encased in crystal.

She sat up quickly, and then wished she hadn't: the worst of her soreness might have already passed, but what was left was still bad enough, especially when it caught her unawares.

"Is it time to leave?" she asked.

"Breakfast first, then leave," said Olga. "We have a long day today."

"How far?" asked Slava.

"Fifty versts, which is nothing in summer, but no joke in the snow. We'll set out before dawn and arrive after dark, but the good news is that we'll be spending the night tonight in Malaya Gora, at the home of Princess Malogornaya, so... well, we'll have a roof over our heads, at any rate. Come: the boys have made breakfast."

They set off immediately after breakfast, when there was still not even the faintest glow in the East. The snow had died out during the night, but heavy clouds remained, blocking out the stars. When they rode out the stockade gate and into the trees, it became completely dark, so that Slava could barely even make out the path.

"This way!" called Olga, and set off confidently.

"How can she know where to go without a lantern?" Slava asked Grisha.

"By the spaces between the trees and the sound of the snow," Grisha told her. "It's easy if you pay attention. Don't worry, Krasna Tsarina! The sun will come up soon enough, and you'll see that we haven't gotten lost."

"I'm not worried," lied Slava.

And it turned out that Grisha was right, for soon enough shadows started appearing on the snow, and then the sun did come up, and they were still on the path. As soon as it was light enough to see more than a horse-length in front, Olga called for them to pick up a trot, and they moved as briskly as was possible in knee-deep snow.

Around midday, or as near as could be reckoned with the heavy clouds, the trees came to an abrupt halt and they found themselves riding through fields again. Slava looked back. She was not sure what she expected to see, but all she saw was a black wall of firs. No eyes, golden or otherwise, looked back at her.

"Do you know Princess Malogornaya, Krasna Tsarina?" asked Slanik, riding up beside her now that the road had become wider.

"No, I believe she rarely comes to Krasnograd. I have heard that she is a strange woman, and that..." Slava stopped, unwilling to finish the sentence she had so carelessly begun.

"What, Krasna Tsarina?"

That she inflicts the most vile cruelties upon her household, Slava had meant to say, but with Slanik's innocent gaze fixed on her face, the words refused to come out. Princess Malogornaya had never, in Slava's memory, deigned to make an appearance in Krasnograd, and the other princesses rarely spoke of her, but when they did, it was always with hushed hints at a dark past, at unspeakable abuses perpetrated on her and by her. But Slava couldn't bring herself to tell Slanik that. "That she can be unpleasant," she said instead.

"I've heard worse of her," said Misha, who was unashamedly eavesdropping. "My second-brother thought of entering her service, but my aunt made him go elsewhere—no son of hers would ever serve Princess Malogornaya."

"She is indeed both unpleasant and dangerous, and no caring mother would ever let her son enter her service," said Dima, twisting around in his saddle to speak to them. "But she always gives Olga Vasilisovna quarters whenever she passes this way, so whatever you see, whatever she says, keep your mouth shut and your eyes down. It's only one night, and then we will be on the road again, rested and fed."

A large group of peasants heading towards the forest to gather firewood interrupted them, and after they had ridden around them, the men broke into song, and sang for several more versts, until they had completely forgotten about Princess Malogornaya.

At first Slava had dreaded their arrival to Malaya Gora, certain that a night with Princess Malogornaya would be a distressing experience, but by midafternoon she was so tired and sore that her only wish was to come to some place where she could get off Skvorets and never get back on again. When they mounted back up after a brief halt, her seat felt as if all the flesh had been stripped from it, leaving her sitting bones to press unprotected against the saddle.

"How much farther?" she asked Dima, trying to sound as if it were a matter of little interest to her.

"At least fifteen more versts, Krasna Tsarina," he said, giving her a sympathetic look. "But it's all through flat fields, so we should make good time. We'll be there shortly after sunset."

"That's not very far at all," she said, smiling. "You know, I think I am growing fitter by the day."

"I'm sure you are, Krasna Tsarina," Dima told her. "By the time you return to Krasnograd, you'll find it more comfortable to sit on a horse than on a chair."

"Oh, I'm sure you're right," she agreed, still smiling. It was astonishing how difficult it was to smile when her mouth wanted to twist into a moan: the strain was making not just her cheeks but her neck and back ache with effort.

"But in the meantime, Krasna Tsarina, try not to fight the pain too much, because you'll never win. But if you outwait it, it will normally go away after a while. Try to think about something else."

"How did you know..." she asked, surprised at having someone else guess her thoughts.

"Don't worry, Krasna Tsarina, I don't have your abilities! But anyone can see by the way you sit that you're in pain. Besides, it's just common sense: you said yourself you're not used to riding, and here we've been doing nothing but ride for days. But it's true, Krasna Tsarina, that soon you won't have any problem at all."

"I'm glad to hear it," she said, and, trying to follow Dima's advice, started looking around at the fields on either side of them. However, there wasn't much to see, just gray snow and gray clouds all the way to the horizon, which was lit by the remnants of sunset.

It was already dark enough that Slava was wondering why they hadn't lit their lanterns, when Misha called out from the front of the group, "Malaya Gora!" and pointed to a slightly blacker mass rising up against the black sky.

"Look, Krasna Tsarina: you can see the lights reflected against the clouds," said Grisha, pointing to a patch of sky above the hill. "The settlement is on the far side of the hill, but it betrays its presence even so."

Once Grisha had pointed it out to her, Slava could see that what she had taken for the remnants of sunset was really the flickering of torches against the clouds.

"How much farther?" she asked, unable by then to hide her desire for their arrival. Not only was she barely able to rise to the trot, but both Skvorets and Ogonyok had grown tired as well, so that she felt guilty forcing them to keep going and to carry her and all her belongings as well. Besides, Skvorets kept stumbling, making her fear she would lose her seat, and Ogonyok hung back on the lead rope, making her right arm sore enough to rival her sitting bones.

"Less than a couple of versts, Krasna Tsarina. We'll be there before you know it."

It wasn't quite that quick, but it was true that it did not take them long to reach the hill and circle around it, arriving at the front gates of the settlement.

"Malaya Gora is something halfway between a village and a fortress, Krasna Tsarina," Dima explained to her. "The whole settlement is surrounded by a stockade fence, and Princess Malogornaya keeps guards posted at the gate day and night."

"What is she afraid of?" asked Slava. "We are hardly out in the middle of the steppe or the taiga here."

"She claims she is protecting herself from wolves and bandits, but some think she is mad with the fear of past wrongs, and some think she is afraid of the Empress's justice for current ones. Princess Malogornaya fancies herself something more like an independent queen than a subject of the Empress—why do you think she never comes to Krasnograd?"

"But her territory is so small," Slava objected. "Malaya Gora is one of the smallest provinces in all of Zem'. And besides, a stockade fence and a few guards are unlikely to stop my sister's soldiers from marching in. My sister...well, there are perhaps some things that she...could do better, but no one doubts the might of her army. Any princess who thinks she can fend it off is most seriously mistaken, I assure you."

"That does not stop Princess Malogornaya from having delusions of grandeur, or from fearing enemies at every turn. But we had better not criticize her in front of her men: they can be fanatically loyal, little as she deserves such loyalty."

The two guards at the gate were rather rough-looking characters, and Slava had a hard time keeping her lip from curling at the sight of them. One of them watched the group with suspicious eyes while the other questioned Olga at length, before reluctantly opening the gate and letting them through.

As best Slava could tell, the buildings lining the unlit streets were mostly falling-down huts. They went around a corner and saw at the top of the hill a long wooden building that, Dima told her, was Princess Malogornaya's palace and kremlin all in one.

"It looks more like a barn from the outside," Slava whispered to him.

"It looks more like a barn from the inside, too, Krasna Tsarina," Dima whispered back. "But it's better than sleeping in the snow, even if it does stink."

And in fact, the streets were filled with the smell of poorly built privies, something that struck Slava particularly forcibly after several days of breathing fresh air. She selfishly hoped that they would leave the smell behind once they rode past the huts and entered the princess's compound, but instead it only grew stronger.

There was another, lower, fence around Princess Malogornaya's building—Slava could not dignify it with the titles "kremlin" or "palace"—with more guards at the gates. They were also less than willing to let in Olga and her group, but after lengthy explanations they grudgingly allowed them entrance. Grooms came out and took their horses from them. Olga, Dima, and Grisha all told the grooms—Olga commandingly, Grisha gruffly, and Dima in a conciliatory tone of voice—that it was essential for the horses to receive the best of care, as they intended to set off first thing the next morning.

The grooms shuffled their feet and promised to look after the horses, but not in a way that filled Slava with confidence. She hoped nothing would happen to either Skvorets or Ogonyok—not only had she grown fond of them over the past few days, but, cold, tired, and sore as she was, she was already looking forward to leaving Malaya Gora and not coming back.

Once the horses had been led away, more guards came up and demanded that everyone turn over their weapons, which Olga did with apparent unconcern and the men did with extreme resentment. When Slava said she had no weapons, the guards favored her with what she realized must be a leer (all the guards in Krasnograd would rather cut off their own hands than leer at the Empress's little sister—except for—No! Don't think of it!—so it was not an expression she was used to seeing) and laughed in a meaningful way.

Once their weapons had been taken, a worn-looking serving woman escorted them inside the main building. The stench of privies, old smoke, and too many people jammed into too little space greeted Slava at the door, and for a moment she stood there, wondering how she was going to be able to go inside without gagging and choking, but then she saw the serving woman staring at her with something that smacked of contempt, and she hurried all the way in.

How do they live like this, she wondered as soon as she was inside and had looked around. The building appeared to be one large room, with tables and benches down the middle, sleeping platforms against the walls, and straw on the floor. There was a hearth and one torch at the far end of the room, where Princess Malogornaya appeared to be sitting, although it was too dark to tell for sure.

The whole company made their way around the benches towards the far end of the room. Slava noticed that the straw was full of old food, and had to suppress a shudder.

The woman sitting in the throne-like chair at the far end of the room was wearing a coarse gray wool dress, like a servant. She was not wearing a headdress, and as best Slava could make out in the dim light, she had a mass of tangled graying hair acting as a hat and shawl. It was difficult to tell in the general reek filling the room, but from close up her hair seemed to be emitting an odor suggesting that it had not been washed in days, perhaps months. Slava had never imagined that a princess could look like that: all the princesses she knew rinsed their hair in rosewater and wore enough gold to finance a small army.

"Olga Vasilisovna Severnolesnaya," said the woman in a harsh voice that spoke of too many years in smoky rooms.

"Princess Malogornaya," said Olga, bowing down to her boot tops. The men all bowed as well, and after a moment Slava realized that she should probably bow too, and did so, although much more awkwardly than the others, as it was not an action she performed often.

"I see you have your harem traveling with you, as usual," said Princess Malogornaya, with a nasty laugh. Slava felt Slanik and Misha, who were standing on either side of her, stiffen in outrage. "You're a braver woman than I, Olenka, traveling with all those men. On deserted roads! You know how men are: if you were lying there in a ditch dying, they'd only stop to steal from you and curse you for their faults, before riding on."

Melancholy a thought as that was, it jibed so well with Slava's own experience that she was unable to come up with any words of defense for Slanik and Misha and all the others, as much as she would like to think more highly of them than that. She glanced at them, and saw that their faces were set with rage. Princess Malogornaya grinned, revealing rotten teeth.

"But I didn't know your taste ran to your sisters as well as your brothers," she went on, looking at Slava. "Who is this proud beauty? Not that she's much of a beauty, at least by this light, but she certainly is proud. Tell me, my proud one, did your mistress never teach you to bow? Or is she still waiting to break you in? If I were you," Princess Malogornaya turned back to Olga, "I'd give her to your men for a day or two, until she learned a little humility. And she'd be all the more grateful for your gentler treatment when you took her back, too."

There was a lengthy pause after this speech. Slava noticed that all of Olga's men had instinctively reached for their weapons, only to discover that they were missing. The sinews on Grisha's neck were all standing out, and she thought Slanik might cry with rage. Sorry as Slava felt for them in their anger, she could not help but be warmed by

The Flight

this show of loyalty and affection towards her. The sight of men showing indignation on someone else's behalf, or anyone showing indignation on her behalf, was so touching that Slava's nose began to prickle
with tears of gratitude. Or maybe that was just the eye-watering stench
rising from the rotting straw.

"I beg your pardon for not introducing my traveling companion
sooner," said Olga, her voice still unruffled. "Krasnoslava Tsarinovna,
younger sister to the Empress."

Chapter Five

An audible gasp rose from all the serving women and guards in the room. There was another very lengthy pause.

"What, did you challenge her or something, and this is your punishment?" Princess Malogornaya asked Slava. "I can't be bothered keeping up with all the tedious intrigue in Krasnograd: one Empress is much the same as another."

Slava was pleased to notice that the news had shaken her, and she was determined to act as if it had not, and that all her brave words were a lie.

"The Tsarina and the Tsarinovna simply wished to show their support for my expedition to the Far North," said Olga smoothly. "And the Tsarinovna wished to survey her sister's territory, meet with her sister's princesses, and generally see what the present state of Zem' is."

"And you think that by riding around with this adventuress you will find out what the present state of Zem' is, little Tsarinovna?" asked Princess Malogornaya.

Although like the others, Slava had been frozen with horror at Princess Malogornaya's initial speech, when she opened her mouth, she suddenly knew what to say.

"Unlike my foremothers, I cannot see from one end of Zem' to the other while sitting in the Krasnograd kremlin," she said. "I have a different gift. I can see into the hearts of women, their innermost thoughts and desires. But to do so I must look upon them with my own two eyes. Olga Vasilisovna has been gracious enough to give me the chance to do so. Thus far it has been most instructive."

"Don't think you can see into my heart, little Tsarinovna," said Princess Malogornaya.

"I am the mirror that reflects only reality, Princess," said Slava, smiling.

"Princess Malogornaya!" interjected Olga, giving Slava a sidelong and surprised glance before smoothing out her face once again and turning back to Princess Malogornaya. "We have ridden long and hard today, and it is, after all, midwinter. Favor us with your hospitality and allow us to rest and eat, if you please."

Princess Malogornaya, Slava could tell, desperately wanted to send Olga and the rest of them back out into the snow, but after chewing on her lip for a while, said, "Oh, very well. But don't think you'll be allowed to keep your men in here with you. I can't be having any of your licentiousness under my roof. They'll have to sleep in the barracks with my guards."

"Of course, Princess."

"In fact, they can go there now. Supper will be served soon, although I don't know if there will be enough. Just remember: your men will be served last. I can't have my own men go hungry because of them."

"Of course, Princess. We have our own supplies, if necessary."

"And have your little spy here send word back to her big sister that I'm destitute? Certainly not! On no account will I allow your men to eat their own rations under my roof. Shurya! Show Olga Vasilisovna's men to their quarters!"

While Slava—and from the looks of it, Olga as well—was trying to figure out whether Princess Malogornaya's words were an offer of hospitality or a threat to force Olga's men to go hungry, a guard whose appearance was almost as disreputable as Princess Malogornaya's stepped forward and started ushering Olga's men towards a side door. Olga gave Dima a meaningful look as he set off, which he returned. Slava didn't know whether to pity the men for being sent off to the barracks, which were probably even nastier than the hall, or envy them for being able to leave Princess Malogornaya's presence.

"You and the little Tsarinovna can pull up a couple of benches to the wall," Princess Malogornaya told them once all the men had been led away. "I don't keep sleeping platforms for guests—no point in encouraging them to come crawling in and eat me out of house and home."

"Thank you, Princess," said Olga, as if Princess Malogornaya had done them a great favor. When it became obvious that Princess Malogornaya had nothing more to say to them, Olga led Slava over to the benches that stood around a long series of tables in the middle of the room.

"These look as good as any, don't you think?" she said, pointing to a couple of benches that looked to be at least as old as Slava.

"Certainly," said Slava, wondering how they were going to sleep on benches without falling off. She and Olga began carrying a bench towards a free spot against the wall. Various women, who were dressed like the cheapest kind of day-workers but for all Slava knew could have been more princesses, stared at them dully from their sleeping platforms without making any move to help.

Between her soreness and the weight of the bench Slava had to scuff through the straw covering the floor, which led her to discover that it was full not only of old food scraps but also old urine. Apparently the inhabitants couldn't be bothered to use chamber pots or go out to the privy. Slava had known horses who were more fastidious.

After hefting two benches over to the wall, Olga opened up her pack—at least they had been allowed to keep their packs—and pulled out a blanket. "There should be another one in your pack," she said.

Slava dug through her pack and discovered that there was, in fact, a blanket down in the bottom. She laid it on the bench that had been designated as hers. It didn't seem like much, either for warmth or for padding.

"We'll use our hats as pillows and sleep in our clothes," Olga said in a low voice, seeing Slava's dubious look.

"Are my accommodations to your liking?" Princess Malogornaya called from her chair.

"A Tsarina couldn't ask for better, let alone a Tsarinovna," said Olga. Princess Malogornaya gave her a nasty look, but Olga kept her face perfectly straight, and Princess Malogornaya decided not to pursue that line of provocation any further.

"I suppose you'll be wanting supper soon after your long ride," she said instead.

"We would be most grateful…"

"Like I said, there might not be enough to go around, but what there is will be ready soon. Actually, now that I think of it, you'll need to move the benches back so we can all fit at the table. We're not so luxurious here as other places you might be used to. Oh, that reminds me, Olga Vasilisovna: have you seen your mother lately?"

Olga froze for a moment, and then said, "No, but perhaps we will pass through Lesnograd on our way back."

"Well, be sure to tell her I haven't forgotten her, and I know what she's up to. Not all sorceresses hold their tongues as well as they hold their spells, at least not the kind she hires, especially if she keeps picking quarrels with them and sending them away. She should pay her servants better if she wants their silence—or make sure to silence them. But seeing the company you're keeping these days, maybe you should try to argue her out of it: I'm sure she'll listen to your advice." Princess Malogornaya pursed her mouth and surveyed the results of her mysterious—to Slava, anyway—pronouncement. Olga was still standing there, frozen, which seemed to please Princess Malogornaya, for she tossed her head triumphantly and said, "What are you standing there for, girl? Move those benches back to the table!"

"Of course, Princess." Olga turned and began repacking her blanket, and Slava saw that an amused smile had come back over her face like a shield. Slava wished that she could find Princess Malogornaya amusing: while she was not blind to the ridiculous side of her appearance and behavior, she had no way of protecting herself from the acrid antagonism rising off of her like smoke from wet wood.

Once Slava and Olga had moved their benches back to the tables, Princess Malogornaya clapped her hands, and more beaten-down looking women in gray wool dresses started carrying in bowls, followed by a vat of cabbage soup and a tray of black bread. Two more serving women came and picked up Princess Malogornaya's chair, with her still in it, and carried it to the table.

"Serve the guests last," she commanded once she had been settled into her place.

"If we are inconveniencing you in any way, Princess, we would be most glad to eat our own rations," said Olga, her face still perfectly straight, except for a hint of an amused smile.

"Certainly not! I won't have it said that I can't treat my guests properly!" A particularly beaten-down looking woman ladled a large portion of soup into the bowl of Princess Malogornaya, who started eating greedily without waiting for anyone else to be served.

The same beaten-down looking woman brought everyone else soup, leaving Slava and Olga for last. Or so Slava thought, until the woman scraped the last bowlful out of the vat and sat down herself at the foot of their table.

"Oh, excuse me, I didn't introduce you," said Princess Malogornaya, gnawing on a crust of black bread rather like a dog gnawing a bone. "My daughter, Zhenya; that is, Yevgeniya Marislavovna."

Slava twitched involuntarily and almost choked on her soup as her stomach heaved in shock and disgust.

"Something you don't like about that, little princess—I mean little Tsarinovna?" Princess Malogornaya demanded.

"I apologize," said Slava. "I had merely forgotten that you bear the same name as my own gracious mother." The horror of seeing Princess Malogornaya's coarse, cruel features under the name Slava associated with her own mother was so great that she forgot to greet Yevgeniya Marislavovna properly. Fortunately, Princess Malogornaya didn't appear to care, or even notice, and Yevgeniya Marislavovna seemed too far gone in misery to feel anything other than relief at being ignored.

"Yes, I was named after her. One of my mother's worthless attempts to curry favor with Krasnograd. I take no pride in it. No good ever comes from Krasnograd. Stand up and bow, Zhenya: we have a Severnolesnaya and even a Tsarinovna eating at our table tonight."

Zhenya stood up and bowed. Somewhere under all the beaten-downness, Slava saw, there was apprehension and even a little curiosity about the fact that she was sharing her supper with a Severnolesnaya and a Tsarinovna, but mostly she was just beaten down. Slava had never met a princess, even the most crazed and selfish, who would allow her own daughter to serve at the table, and she wondered if this were a regular occurrence or a special humiliation. Pity reminded her of her manners and prompted her to stand up and bow too.

"An honor, Yevgeniya Marislavovna," she said. "I do not believe I have ever had the pleasure of seeing you in Krasnograd. When I return, I shall expect to find you there, so that we may continue our acquaintance. Krasnograd is only a few days away, you know; you really must spend more time there."

Slava sat back down under the shocked, and in Princess Malogornaya's case, malevolent, stares of the rest of the company. It was not overly warm in the room, but sweat was dripping down her sides after issuing such a challenge.

"Oh, Zhenya has no business going to Krasnograd and mixing with all those fine princesses," said Princess Malogornaya. "Do you, Zhenya?"

Zhenya gave her head a tiny shake, staring down at her bowl of soup.

"I'm afraid she has no manners, and no mind to learn them," continued Princess Malogornaya, looking down on her daughter with malicious triumph. "And her face and her figure are not exactly the kind of thing you'd want gracing the Imperial kremlin either, now are they, Zhenya? I've always thought I must have got her off that peasant, what was his name?... Well, it doesn't matter, anyway. I needed an heir, so I got one, but a sorry business I made of it, I must say. But there's certainly no call to go inflicting my Zhenya on real noblewomen."

"I am sure Yevgeniya Marislavovna would grace any kremlin, and I hope to see her in Krasnograd upon my return this spring," said Slava, with much more firmness than she would have ever expected from herself.

Princess Malogornaya opened her mouth to argue more, but she was interrupted by a sudden burst of quarrelling coming from behind the far wall, where, Slava realized, the barracks must be located.

"Tell the men to SHUT UP!" she shouted instead.

Even though this was something Slava had longed to say herself, both now and on many previous occasions, she flinched at the harsh sound of Princess Malogornaya's voice and the harsh sight of her coarse, cruel face. Never, Slava promised herself, would she sound or look like that, never, never, never.

One of the serving women—Slava wondered if she were a real serving woman or another noblewoman trapped in the role of a lackey, and if perhaps all lackeys thought they were secretly noblewomen trapped by unkind fate in circumstances beneath them, and if they felt humiliated and degraded by their humiliating and degrading position in life, and if she, Slava, were spending much too much time or perhaps not nearly enough dwelling on this dreadful injustice—went over to the door through which the men had been led away earlier. She shouted at the men, who shouted back at first, but eventually quieted into a sullen silence.

They finished off the meal without further words. Slava didn't know whether to be glad or sorry: she was still hungry, but the food had been so coarse that she doubted she could have forced down more, even after riding all day in the cold. Zhenya went around picking up the dirty bowls, and carried them inside of the empty vat off to what must have been the kitchen. Slava envisioned the hordes of cockroaches that must swarm over everything in the filthy room—or possibly a shed—that they no doubt used as a kitchen, and wished she hadn't.

"Well, let's not waste any more candles or torches," Princess Malogornaya announced, once the table had been cleared. "To bed, everyone!"

Slava was afraid that Princess Malogornaya was going to bed down in the hall with them, perhaps on top of one of the tables, but to her relief she left through a door in the opposite direction of the barracks, and did not return. Slava helped Olga move their benches back to their spot on the wall, and they spread their blankets back out over them.

"It's a little spare, but it's better than being out in the snow," said Olga cheerfully. Now as before, she seemed to be finding the entire ordeal to be a source of great entertainment.

"I've locked the doors for the night, so no one can get out to use the privy," announced one of the serving women. "If you need to, use the straw."

"Ah, the joys of a refined and civilized existence," said Olga in an undertone. "I wonder how often they put down fresh straw? I am not normally shy, but I'm going to wait until all the lights are out and everyone seems to be asleep. With this crowd you can't be too careful. We'd probably be safer in the barracks with those villains our Princess likes to keep around her."

With these words she took off her boots and crawled under her blanket, arranging her hat as a pillow as she had said she would. Slava followed suit. The bench was, as she had suspected, not only extremely uncomfortable but just narrow enough to make her worry about falling off it.

"Olga," Slava whispered. "How far do we have to ride tomorrow? Is it a long day?"

"We'll have to leave well before dawn, never fear," Olga whispered back.

Slightly comforted by the prospect an early rising, Slava resigned herself as best she could to the night before her.

It was, in fact, a very long night. Eventually Slava forced herself to overcome her aversion to "using the straw," which made things slightly better, but did nothing for the hardness and narrowness of the bench nor the thinness of the blanket, not to mention the closeness of the air and the snoring of her companions. When someone started stirring in the kitchen, and Olga whispered, "We can get up now," Slava leaped off the bench with an alacrity rarely seen in someone as sore as she was.

Their actual escape, however, took some time, as the servants were unwilling to return their weapons and allow them into the stable to saddle their horses without Princess Malogornaya's permission, and Princess Malogornaya did not care to rise too early on winter mornings. Only after Olga had spun some lengthy lie about their extreme need for haste, alluding several times to the supposed Imperial mission she was on, were they allowed to gather their things and prepare to depart.

Once the horses were saddled, Olga sent Slava back inside to leave, as she said, "some kind of pretty message that will make Princess Malogornaya feel good about hosting us." Rather fearfully, Slava edged her way back into the main hall and looked around for a servant with whom to leave their parting words. Instead she found Zhenya, who was setting out food for breakfast.

"Yevgeniya Marislavovna!" said Slava, glad to see someone with whom she could legitimately say farewell. "Thank you for your kind hospitality, and please convey our deepest thanks to your mother as well."

"I'm sorry?" said Zhenya, brushing a cockroach off the table and giving Slava a puzzled look. Up close, Slava could see that she did have the clear round blue eyes and rosy face of a Krasna peasant, but it was mostly hidden behind a tangle of filthy hair.

"We must leave now, Yevgeniya Marislavovna, but I repeat my invitation: I hope to see you in Krasnograd this spring."

"Are you really a Tsarinovna?" Zhenya blurted out suddenly.

"Yes, I am the Tsarina's younger sister, Krasnoslava Tsarinovna." Strangely, in these squalid surroundings, Slava for once felt the nobility of her name and blood.

"They'd never let me see a Tsarinovna, if I came to Krasnograd," said Zhenya, looking at the table.

"Here, show them this." Slava pulled a handkerchief out of her pocket and, when Yevgeniya Marislavovna made no move to take it, folded it into her hand. It was silk, and had her name embroidered around the edge in bright thread of Imperial red, which even in the candlelight shone more than anything else in the room. Zhenya gaped at it.

"Keep it, and when you come to the Krasnograd kremlin, if anyone won't let you to me, show them this and tell them you're a friend of mine. They'll have to come get me then, and I'll tell them to let you in right away." Slava closed Zhenya's hand around the handkerchief. "It was a pleasure to meet you, Yevgeniya Marislavovna," she said, and walked away. For a moment she was unsure what the happy feeling rising in her chest was, and then she realized it was pride.

Slava had been afraid that something would prevent them from leaving Malaya Gora, but before the sun had risen they were already outside the settlement gates and trotting swiftly down the road. She had never thought she would be so glad to feel the familiar soreness of settling back into the saddle for another long day of pain. She was also glad to see that the horses, at least, had not suffered from their stay there.

As soon as they were out of earshot of the Malaya Gora guards, the men all burst into vigorous complaints. It seemed that the barracks had been filthy and crowded, the food had been terrible, and the guards had been rude and unpleasant in the extreme.

"All they did was moan, complain, and quarrel!" said Sasha in disgust. "They griped on and on about Princess Malogornaya's treatment of them, but when I asked them why they stayed, they started bad-mouthing other princesses, even Olga Vasilisovna!"

"Was that the cause of the shouting we heard last night?" asked Olga with a laugh.

"Yes, Olga Vasilisovna. We're sorry we caused trouble, but..."

"Well, never mind. I'd like to think your presence would encourage them to leave Princess Malogornaya's service, but I fear not. There are always plenty of people willing to lick the hand that beats them. The fact that her daughter puts up with it says it all, really. If I were her, I'd...Well, let's just say that I wouldn't be serving at table, that's for certain. Of course, Princess Malogornaya's had a hard life. Her own mother for the longest time couldn't find a man to marry her, and after getting a daughter—our dear Marislava, that is—off some mercenary in order to have an heir, married late in life and had two more daughters, very unexpectedly. Her husband was always trying to get his own daughters made heir, and our Marislava led a sort of half-life, caught somewhere between heir and hanger-on. When her mother died her stepfather supposedly handed her over to his guards for a spot of public entertainment—you know how stepfathers can be, always visiting real offenses on their daughters in return for fancied ones from their wives and mothers."

"Did you have a stepfather?" Slava blurted out before she could stop herself. She knew that Olga's mother had been married more than once, but whether she had taken another husband after the one that fathered Olga had escaped her memory. "Was he cruel?" Stepfathers did indeed have a wicked reputation, and from everything Slava had seen and heard, a well-deserved one. She hated to think of high-spirited Olga being subject to any of the indignities stepfathers were said to visit upon their daughters as a matter of course.

"Just a father," said Olga. "He wasn't too bad, either—until he died and left me, that is. But at least my mother had the sense not to remarry. Although it might have done her good—cheered her up, or at least given her something to think about."

"My father died and left me too," said Slava.

"They *will* do that," said Olga. "And then stepfathers step in, like our Marislava's. So he handed her over to his guards, and when they were done with her, he sent her on her way without a grosh. I have to hand it to her: instead of lying down and dying, which many a princess would have done after something like that, she gathered herself a gang of mercenaries, came back, and slaughtered every member of her stepfather's household. Including her two little sisters. Not that they didn't deserve it. They say at first the guards refused to do any harm to Marislava, but then her sisters made them—threatened them, and when that didn't work, egged them on until they were beside themselves. Not that that's too hard, with guards. You know how men are. And the sisters were only little slips of girls at the time, too young to know better—they were no more than ten and twelve, they couldn't've known what they were doing. But they did it anyway.

"And you can see how Princess Malogornaya's lived ever since. They say she's haunted by her sisters' deaths. They say she smashed their heads against the wall with her own hands, and then tried to throw herself on her own sword, but her mercenaries stopped her— she hadn't paid them yet. And so she torments her own daughter as some kind of atonement. She's had a hard life, like I said."

"That doesn't make it better!" said Sasha, still outraged. "They say that she holds floggings as entertainment! She just picks some serving woman or guard, and has the others beat them till she grows bored! And the others go along with it! None of them refuse to take part, even though next time it could be them under the lash!"

"And that's not the worst I've heard of her," said Olga. "They say that often as not, her own daughter is the first victim."

"Some say that Malaya Gora is cursed," said Grisha solemnly. "That the hill itself was cursed by the gods."

"And some say it was cursed when the first Malogornaya murdered her sister for land," said Dima, also solemnly. "And now her ghost haunts the hill, wreaking vengeance on her sister's descendants."

"And some say that the murdered woman's daughter swore fealty to her mother's killer, and served her like a slave. Like I said, there are too many out there who are all too happy to lick the hand that beats them. The only curse ever cast on the Malogorniye was their own stupidity. Let this be a warning to you, and let us not think of it further: we have better things to occupy our minds!"

With that, Olga shook her head vigorously, indicating that the subject was closed to further discussion, and trotted ahead to the front of the group, where she appeared to be consulting with Dima over their route.

The men at the back of the group, where Slava was riding, continued to complain in low voices about their night at Malaya Gora. It seemed that, as well as whining about Princess Malogornaya (which, as Misha pointed out, was particularly stupid since most of the men were mercenaries and therefore free to leave on the first day of spring, but despite that most of them had been there for years) and badmouthing lots of other princesses, they had also had some rather lewd and disgusting conversations that had horrified Olga's men, especially Olik and Slanik, the two youngest.

Slava half wanted to ask what these conversations had been about out of sheer curiosity, but on seeing the look on Slanik's face when they were brought up, decided against it. No doubt it would be better for her not to know, anyway.

"Will it snow again today, do you think?" she asked Grisha instead.

"I think it will clear off by this afternoon, Krasna Tsarina, and become very cold," he said, glad at the change in subject.

"How far are we riding today? Where are we going?"

"It's another long day today, Krasna Tsarina: all the way to Veliky

94

Prud. More than forty versts."

"Veliky Prud? Isn't that the holding of the noblewoman Avdotya Svetliyevna Medvedyeva? And didn't she die a couple of years ago? In childbirth? At least she produced a healthy daughter, thank the gods. A petition about it came before my sister. I think her widower requested permission to govern until the heir comes of age."

"I believe you're right, Krasna Tsarina. They say that Ruslan Praskovyevich runs things now, so we shall see how he's managing. We've been through there a few times before—that's where we picked up our Misha, for example—and he never struck me as the kind of man capable of doing anything more than choose a fine cloak, but perhaps widowhood has agreed with him."

"The only thing that would agree with Ruslan Praskovyevich would be kick in the trousers," said Misha. "I never saw a more useless man in my entire life. My mother is from Veliky Prud, and I did my first service under Avdotya Svetliyevna. All he did was simper and issue pointless commands. When Avdotya Svetliyevna died, may the gods watch over her soul, I quit my service as soon as spring came and signed on with Olga Vasilisovna here. Serving under a man was more than I could stomach, especially a man like Ruslan Praskovyevich. I can't imagine widowhood will be an improvement: quite the opposite, I'd say, since he'll have no wife to keep him in check."

"Poor Ruslan Praskovyevich," Slava found herself saying, but Misha only rolled his eyes and laughed at her words, before riding ahead to see what Olga had decided about their route.

Grisha's weather prediction turned out to be correct. Shortly after midday the clouds started to clear, and by midafternoon a sharp wind rose from the North. It cut through Slava's clothes as if they were made of silk instead of wool, and froze her hands so she could hardly hold the reins. At least she was not alone: everyone else was switching their reins from hand to hand and trying to shake some warmth back into their fingers.

She noticed that the ones who were ponying a second horse, as she was, tucked the lead rope under their legs and held their free hand under their arms or under their scarves, and she did the same. This helped a little, but it also meant that the lead rope was rubbing another hole in her leg, and she had to grip the saddle extra tightly in order to keep from losing the rope, which was almost impossible with her tired legs.

"Not far now," Olga called back to them, as the sun started to set.

"We'll be in Veliky Prud by sunset."

Olga was correct, and they rode into Veliky Prud while there was still a red glow in the sky. Veliky Prud, as might be guessed by the name, was a village built around a large pond. The Medvedyeva house was really nothing more than a peasant hut, but four or five times the size of all the others around it and painted in many bright colors. Still, it looked in better repair than Malaya Gora, which was something.

No guards barred their way as they rode up to the house, but two very sweet-faced serving women opened the gate for them and let them in. The grooms who took their horses were also very handsome, and smiled and bowed very prettily as they welcomed the travelers to Veliky Prud.

"Is Ruslan Praskovyevich at home?" Olga asked one of the serving women.

"Oh yes, noblewoman, and he'll most glad of your company, I'm sure."

The serving women led them into the house, which was the opposite of Princess Malogornaya's in every way. It was warm to the point of stifling, and stuffed seemingly to overflowing with rugs and fine furniture, much of which looked foreign. They wound through several passageways before arriving in the main hall, where Ruslan Praskovyevich was lounging in his chair, waiting for them.

"Welcome, visitors," he said, straightening partway up and making a welcoming gesture that was sort of like a bow. "Whom do I have the pleasure of addressing?"

Olga introduced them all, making Ruslan Praskovyevich sit up rather straighter when he heard Slava's name.

"A real Tsarinovna?" he asked incredulously.

"Indeed, Ruslan Praskovyevich. We hope we do not trespass too much on your hospitality if we ask to stay the night."

"No, no, of course not, you are most welcome," and he jumped to his feet and made another gesture that was supposed to look like a noble command. "My servants will show you to your quarters, and once you have refreshed yourselves, we will have supper. I fear the accommodations will not be as grand as the ones to which you are accustomed, but I hope you will forgive their meanness."

"We are not overly nice, Ruslan Praskovyevich," said Olga. "Especially since we spent last night under the roof of Princess Malogornaya."

Ruslan Praskovyevich shuddered and said that, while his chambers might be small, at least he could vouch that they would not be crawling with vermin, especially of the human kind. After a few more compliments were exchanged between him and Olga, the smiling serving women led them away. As soon as they were out of earshot of their master, they fell into agonized whispering.

"Olga Vasilisovna," said one of them eventually, "we must beg your pardon, but..."

"Yes?" demanded Olga.

"We are most sorry, Olga Vasilisovna, but you see how modest our home is...The fact is, Olga Vasilisovna, that we have few guest chambers, and so if we give you and Krasnoslava Tsarinovna," they both bowed down to their boot tops, "each a chamber, then we will have to pack your men in five to a room. We are most sorry, Olga Vasilisovna, and we hope you will forgive the inconvenience to your men."

"Krasnoslava Tsarinovna and I are used to sharing a room," said Olga. "Put us together, and that'll leave more space for my men."

"As you wish, Olga Vasilisovna," said the serving woman, looking both startled and relieved. "Again, we beg your forgiveness for the inconvenience."

"It's nothing," said Olga, waving her hand impatiently. "Take us to our rooms, and we'll take care of ourselves. There's no need to put yourselves out for us. Just make sure our horses are well cared for."

"Of course, Olga Vasilisovna, of course. Here we are: I hope you find everything to your liking, Olga Vasilisovna." The serving women bowed Olga and Slava into a room, and closed the door behind them. Slava could hear them lead off the men; it sounded as though, rid of her and Olga's oppressive presence, they were engaging in some cheerful banter.

"Is Ruslan Praskovyevich trustworthy?" Slava asked Olga as they surveyed their room. It was overflowing with chairs, wardrobes, and an enormous puffy bed. Their meager baggage huddled together in one chair, looking sad and forlorn. Slava started to feel embarrassed about what she would be wearing at supper: no doubt Ruslan Praskovyevich would be extremely finely dressed, and expect them to be the same.

Olga shrugged. "Probably. He would never plot deliberately against us, as Princess Malogornaya would, but he could no doubt be convinced most easily to take the wrong path. However, I'm sure we're safe here tonight. I suppose we'd better wash ourselves as best we can: Ruslan Praskovyevich runs a much cleaner household than Princess Malogornaya, I'll say that for him."

Olga's remark, and the warm room, made Slava aware that after several days on the road they both, not to put too fine a point on it, stank. She started rummaging rather hopelessly through her things. There was a knock at the door.

The knock proved to be the older and slightly less pretty serving woman, who was bearing an armful of clean gowns. "Dasha"—Slava supposed that Dasha was the other serving woman—"is tending to your men"—Slava assumed that this explained why the older and probably less giddy serving woman was tending her and Olga—"but I thought I'd bring you some clean gowns to wear to supper, and then I'm going to run and start the bathhouse heating, so you can steam after supper. There's nothing like a good steam after traveling."

"Thank you,..."

"Shurya, noblewoman."

"Thank you, Shurya, for your thoughtfulness," said Olga, giving the gowns a sideways glance.

"It's my pleasure, noblewoman," said Shurya, depositing the gowns on the bed, bowing, and leaving the room.

Olga stirred through the gowns with distaste. "Where do they find the time to make all this lace?" she asked. "It's a silly foreign fashion anyway."

"I wonder whose gowns these are," said Slava, holding up a red one and measuring it against her body. The gowns did have a decidedly non-Zemnian appearance. Zemnian gowns tended to fall straight from the shoulders to the floor, and left very little skin exposed, in deference to the Zemnian climate. These gowns, on the other hand, covered very little of the chest, nipped in at the waist, and then had huge skirts that stuck out in all directions. Slava thought they looked very uncomfortable.

"Probably Medvedyeva's," said Olga, pulling out a blue gown and giving it a dark look. "She always liked foolish trifles, as witnessed by her choice of husbands. I wonder how you get into them?"

At the news that the gowns had belonged to a dead woman, Slava gave them a look almost as dark as Olga's, and reluctantly began to struggle into hers. After a considerable amount of pulling, tugging, tangling, and, on Olga's part, cursing, they helped each other into the gowns, which reeked of perfume. At least that would hide the fact that they hadn't bathed for several days. The gowns were, as Slava had suspected, quite uncomfortable, fit neither of them, and also exposed more chest than a peasant would while mowing hay in high summer.

"I wonder if there are any shawls about," muttered Olga, adjusting herself in the too-small gown and staring down at the tops of her breasts, which was not a sight most Zemnian women were accustomed to seeing outside of the bathhouse. "I feel as nervous as a man with his pants down. At the very least, I'm afraid of catching cold."

"There are shawls in this drawer," announced Slava, pulling out two that seemed unlikely to clash with their garish gowns. Hers was too large, but being so stiff, it left a large gap between her breasts and the gown itself, which meant that a taller person would be able to see all the way down the front of the gown to the floor. Covering herself up somehow would be essential for both warmth and modesty.

She and Olga both threw the shawls over their chests and tied them in back, which still left them more naked than they would have desired, but they were at least somewhat protected against drafts and unlikely to expose Ruslan Praskovyevich to the sight of anything his masculine sensibilities would find offensive.

Shurya came and led them back to the room where Ruslan Praskovyevich had originally greeted them, which now had a table that was laid for supper. There were only three place settings.

"We thought your men might be more comfortable in the kitchen," Shurya whispered into Olga's ear as she seated them.

"Ah. Thank you. No doubt you're right," said Olga, settling herself gingerly onto the chair. The gowns had lots of stiff splint-like things in the waist area, and large pads in the back of the skirt, which made them extremely inconvenient for sitting.

Ruslan Praskovyevich, who had been absent when they sat down, now entered the room. Olga and Slava both tried not to stare. His clothing was at least as strange as their own, although Slava had seen something like it on the men who came to Zem' with foreign delegations. Zemnian men normally wore long tunics or blouses over loose trousers and soft boots, which was both warm and comfortable, and also (Slava now realized) attractive, but Ruslan Praskovyevich was dressed in some kind of very strange puffy short jacket, low shoes with turned-up toes, and, most distressingly of all, what looked like stockings that were held together at the join by a leather shield-like...thing.

Slava couldn't help wondering what Ruslan Praskovyevich's men thought of this, and how their own men would react to this outfit. Apparently Olga was troubled by similar thoughts, for her voice was much more choked than usual as she bowed as best she could in her stiffened gown and said, "Thank you again for hosting us, Ruslan

Praskovyevich."

"My pleasure, Tsarinovna, noblewoman," said Ruslan Praskovyev-ich, bowing in return but waving his hands to the side in a very strange way as he did so. This was also something that Slava had seen foreign men do, but the sight of a Zemnian man, one of their own, imitating it, was bizarre to the point of grotesque.

Ruslan asked them about their journey as Dasha and Shurya brought the food in. The dishes were clearly foreign, and once the food was served, it was obvious that the food had been prepared to foreign recipes as well. Neither the pickled cabbage, nor the beet soup, nor the beef, nor the pastries, nor any of the jams and preserves tast-ed the way they should have. None of it was exactly bad, but every mouthful was a shock, much like looking at Ruslan Praskovyevich in his stockings and slippers.

The foreign food was accompanied by a foreign wine, which Olga and Slava drank with caution and Ruslan Praskovyevich imbibed with vigor. After his third glass—the glasses were strange small things on long stems that filled Slava with the fear that she would accidently break one—he began talking about his project of "civilizing" Veliky Prud by importing foreign things from the South and West.

He extolled the virtues of these Southern lands by the Middle Sea, and—after his fifth glass—explained that a large part of his admira-tion of them was founded on the fact that they allowed, even encour-aged, in fact, even required, that their men receive a good education, and even rule. There was also a lot of fatuous talk about the true na-ture of manhood, getting closer to the earth and the gods, throwing off the shackles of convention and over-protective mothering that ham-pered Zemnian men.

Apparently some Western emissary had stopped by Veliky Prud on his way somewhere or another, and filled Ruslan Praskovyevich's head with this kind of thing, so that it was now full to bursting with dreams of running off to this promised land. His words made Slava feel as if she were speaking with herself, but herself from ten, fifteen, maybe twenty years ago, even though she and Ruslan Praskovyevich were of an age. They reminded her of her own dreams of running away to some sunnier clime, down by the Middle Sea, far away from the oppressive clouds and oppressive kremlins of her native land—dreams she had put aside years ago, when she had (unlike, she could see, Ruslan Praskovyevich) read everything she could find on these other, sunnier, supposedly happier places, and met people from there, and realized that they were no better than her own sister Zemnians (at least judging by the men; she had never met any women from there, which boded very ill indeed for it).

Yes, as Ruslan Praskovyevich was saying, there was an empire of sorts down there, and yes, it was currently ruled by a man, as it had been by his father before him, or so it was said, but it was also said that he sat around in nothing but a sheet and some leaves and flowers in his hair (Slava supposed they should be thankful that Ruslan had not decided to borrow *that* particular fashion), and had slaves to oil his skin with scented oils, before joining him, whether they willed or no, in his bed. Slava was willing to accept the flowers and scented oils—she could even see the advantages to them—but she failed to see how keeping slaves and raping them whenever the mood struck was particularly manly, or if it was, how that was something to take pride in and hope to emulate.

And as he went on and on about it Slava saw, to her intense dismay, that behind all his silly finery and foolishness, not to mention his typically masculine confidence in his own lack of information, Ruslan Praskovyevich harbored the same hatred towards women (and men, but especially women), the same desire to smash and hurt them, that she had seen in so many other men, as if they had never grown beyond the tantrums of a two-year-old.

She wondered if this hatred were the result of too much cosseting and spoiling, or something intrinsic to the men themselves, some irremediable taint, and desperately hoped it was the former, because that at least could be fixed, while an irremediable taint meant they were doomed, all doomed...How awful it must be for men like Ruslan Praskovyevich, to be dimly aware of their flaws but unable to escape from them...As sorry as she felt for Ruslan Praskovyevich—and already she could see that he was very, very unhappy, and that the life he had been given here in Zem' was not at all to his liking—she could not help but be glad that he was prevented from ruling here, as she was certain that he would do a terrible job of it, and hurt many people in the process. She wondered at the women in those countries to the West, the ones who allowed their men to rule.

If she had not seen the envoys they occasionally sent to Zem', normally to plead that Zem' open its borders to their slave trading (and while there were many things Slava could find fault with in her native land, at least they did not, as their neighbors to the East and West did, sell their own people into slavery) she would have assumed that their men must be different from Zemnian men, but as far as she could tell, they were not. In fact, they were much worse—even more sulky, self-pitying, and hateful, always glaring at the women around them as if nothing would give them more pleasure than to squeeze their throats till their eyes popped out.

Slava supposed it was possible that foreign rulers used Zem' as a dumping ground for men they otherwise had no use for, but from everything she had read of foreign countries, she rather suspected that that was not the case. She rather suspected that their rulers were of a piece with their vain and thoughtless envoys, men who could in no way be trusted with the fates of others, let alone a whole country. As far as Slava could tell, greater liberty for them had led, not to greater wisdom, but to greater foolishness. Men left to their own devices, unchecked by a steadying female hand, uncontained, as they were supposed to be, by their women, seemed to respond by simply sinking into even worse excess than before.

She supposed they should all be grateful that the constant quarrels between their foreign neighbors over whether or not they had actually fathered their own heirs—such was the price of their foolishness in reckoning their descent exclusively through the male line—meant that they had little attention to give Zem', either in war or diplomacy. What spare time they had was taken up either with repelling the advances of the empire from the Middle Sea, or welcoming it, while what attention they did have to spare for Zem' was tinged with well-justified fear of Zem''s army, made up largely of fearsome (everyone agreed) steppe warriors and their even more fearsome sorceress sisters, and not so-well-justified resentment of Zem''s riches.

Not so well justified because these other lands didn't seem to want to do the things that Zem' had done to gain its wealth, namely unite into one large country that was, despite all the bickering that went on amongst its princesses, stable compared with its neighbors, and then settle down and spend its energies on harvesting and trading, instead of warring.

All its neighbors to both the East and West wanted to steal its wealth, not grow their own. These days the thought of living in such a land, no matter how warm and sunny, made Slava feel ill. Especially since they were, as Ruslan Praskovyevich had said, largely ruled by men, and not sensible, thoughtful men, such as, such as...well, Dima, for example, but warlords and soldiers, which for some strange reason were considered to be the people best suited to rule, despite all evidence to the contrary...the horrors men inflicted on each other in the army and the road crews were well known, and so dreadful that Slava could not see how anyone could fail to cry out against it, denounce it with all of their strength, and yet no one seemed to be able to stop the constant and pointless cruelty, any more than they could fly, and outside of Zem''s borders they even put such people in charge of everyone else.

The thought that half the human race could not even be called human, and the other half barely any better, and that Slava was once again dwelling at length on what she had promised herself she would stop dwelling on, was so depressing that Slava was glad to turn her attention back to Ruslan Praskovyevich, distressing a sight as he was making.

"Over there men can be more than mere men, that's what he told me, but here in backwards Zem' they're nothing but...nothing but..." it took a while for Ruslan Praskovyevich's thick tongue to form the word, "soldiers! Soldiers and guards! And peasants, I suppose. And hunters and sailors. And most men deserve nothing better, of course—stupid fools! Loafing about and living off of handouts! Never developing anything other than their sword arms! Trapped in their manhood! But I ask you, what kind of life is that for a man? For someone who wants to be more than just a man? For someone who wants to be a person?"

Olga and Slava both stared at Ruslan Praskovyevich with horrified pity, but fortunately he was too drunk to notice. Instead, he poured himself another glass—slopping a large amount of wine onto the tablecloth, which was also obviously foreign—and began talking in an incoherent way about music and the life of the mind, both of which were denied Zemnian men.

"Many singers are men, and they live as free as birds," Slava tried to point out kindly. Annoying as she found Ruslan Praskovyevich, and disgusted as she was by his pretensions to an intelligence that, it was becoming ever more apparent, he did not actually possess, she could see no way of dealing with him other than to try to soothe his wounded feelings with flattery. She wondered how much longer he would keep them there.

"And many dancers too. And many princesses—and even the Empress—take council with their men. Why, our own Boleslav Vlasiyevich sits on the Princess Council, as befits the Captain of the Guard," she said, and then, unable to stop herself, continued, "And as for the lower classes, why—you know as well as I do that our men know many trades, and can buy and sell as they will, and keep whatever money they earn. Whereas, if the reports are true, in much of the West—and the East—not only do they keep slaves, both men and women, but *all* their women are little better than slaves. Why, they say in this empire down on the Middle Sea that all women, peasants or nobles, and all slaves, female or male, can't buy or sell or own things, that they can be forced into marriage against their will, and there is no penalty for striking or even raping them, not if the person doing so is their husband or their owner.

"And you compare us to them? You know as well as I do, Ruslan Praskovyevich, that any money you make is yours and yours alone, and if your wife had ever struck you, or taken your money, or, or passed you around to her guards, you could have complained to the Tsarina or taken refuge in a sanctuary, or both. We are many things, Ruslan Praskovyevich, many shameful, terrible things, but we are *not* Westerners, and we should be proud of it! Whatever suffering you think happens here, however bad you think your lot is here, like as not it would be ten times worse outside of Zem''s borders, and even if you *were* one of the lucky ones, that luck would be at the expense of others' misfortune. Would you really purchase a little momentary lift to your vanity at the expense of, of some slave's, or even your mother's—and there would be little difference between the two—fortune and freedom, or even her very liberty and life?"

She stopped, panting a little, her cheeks so hot she thought she could have cooked eggs on them. Olga was staring at her, openmouthed. But she seemed to be the only one affected by Slava's speech. Ruslan Praskovyevich was looking down at the tablecloth. He didn't appear to have actually heard anything that Slava had said at all. "Not the same, not the same at all," he slurred, waving his hand and spilling more wine. He finished what was left in his glass, stared at the tablecloth in bewilderment, and then said, in a carefully pronounced speech, "The bathhouse should be heated by now. I'm sure you wish to steam. I shan't detain you any longer."

Slava and Olga both rose with alacrity, bowed their thanks, and hurried off, desperate to escape their gowns and Ruslan Praskovyevich's peculiarities.

Shurya met them at the door of their room and offered to help them out of their gowns—an offer that was most welcome—and show them the way to the bathhouse.

"I hope you'll be patient and forgive me for having to undress you

one at a time," she said, struggling with the complicated system of lac-
es at the back of Slava's gown. "I'm afraid your men have rather turned
Dasha's head, and she's been spending the evening fussing over them
and bringing them things. We're not used to such fine men as yours."

"Has Ruslan Praskovyevich attempted to introduce his foreign
fashions to his servants?" asked Olga, suppressing what was either a
smile or a shudder at the memory of Ruslan Praskovyevich's clothing.

"He has, the dear little man," said Shurya indulgently, "although
he hasn't been as successful as he'd hoped. But many of the men have
taken to lounging around indoors, wearing soft clothes and gossiping
instead of working. Not that any of that's unusual in a man, of course.
But your men have created quite a stir amongst the girls."

"As long as they keep their hands to themselves," said Olga. "I
promised my boys' mothers I'd watch over them."

"Oh, you needn't worry on that score, Olga Vasilisovna; we'll just
feast our eyes on them and be content. But I'm afraid you won't get
such good service as they will."

"Krasnoslava Tsarinovna and I will probably survive, providing we
can get out of these gowns," said Olga. "I feel like a horse in a henco-
op."

And indeed, Olga looked so out of place in her foreign gown that
it was hard for Slava not to laugh at her. She had only been able to
control herself all evening because she thought that even Olga might
not be able to withstand being laughed at for being forced into such a
ridiculous getup.

Shurya was eventually able to free them from the foreign gowns,
and, after giving them some loose, comfortable robes, she led them to
the bathhouse, which was indeed steaming hot.

"At least Ruslan Praskovyevich has kept his bathhouse," said Slava.
"I have heard that in foreign countries to the South, especially on the
Middle Sea, their bathhouses are completely different."

Olga wrinkled her nose. "Foreigners are so filthy," she said. "I've
heard that they don't use privies down there, but just piss into some
kind of creek they have running through their houses instead."

"I don't think it works quite like that," said Slava. "They say it's very
clean and convenient, although I don't see how we could import it to
Zem': I'm sure it would freeze."

"I think one look at Ruslan Praskovyevich would be all the reason anyone would need not to import things from abroad," said Olga.
"Those shoes! Those stockings! And...well, if I were his mother, I'd die

of shame, that's all I'm saying. Imagine your son going around expos-
ing himself like that all the time!"

"But I can't help feeling sorry for him," said Slava.

"Ruslan Praskovyevich is too foolish to pity," said Olga firmly. "It's
as much a waste as feeling sorry for Princess Malogornaya. I'm going
to throw more water on; you don't mind, do you?"

"Oh no, of course not," said Slava. Olga threw more water on the
hot rocks, filling the bathhouse with such a choking cloud of steam
that Slava was forced to bury her face in her towel, thereby preventing
her from arguing with Olga, not that it would have done any good.

The fact was that she did feel sorry for Ruslan Praskovyevich, almost as sorry as she did for Princess Malogornaya. As a hanger-on
herself, Slava knew just how irritating it could be to depend entirely
on one's mother or sister for everything, although most men accepted
their lot in life much more readily than Slava had. Submitting to necessity seemed to come so much more easily for men than for wom-
en. But even amongst men there were a few malcontents, and Ruslan
Praskovyevich appeared to be one of them.

Unfortunately, his attempts at finding happiness and respect had
only made him unhappy and ridiculous. Slava wished that she could
reconcile him with his lot in life, but she didn't know how, especially
as she herself was so unhappy with her own life and was certainly in
no condition to lecture about happiness. A great wave of misery rolled
over her like another cloud of steam.

"Where are we riding to tomorrow?" she asked Olga, and then regretted opening her mouth, since it let the steam come pouring in to
sear her lungs.

"We have several days of more-or-less wilderness ahead of us,"
Olga told her, throwing on more water and raising yet more steam.
Slava started to fear she might faint. "We'll be mostly staying in cabins, which'll be a welcome change after this. But enjoy the steam while
you can, because we won't see another bathhouse for a while."

"I'll try," gasped Slava, who had been planning to leave the bathhouse, but now resolved to stay for a little longer.

Luckily she managed not to collapse before Olga said they should
go roll in the snow, which they did. Then they went back to the house,
still glowing with warmth despite the cold. They met Shurya in the
hallway outside their room, where she appeared to have been waiting
for them.

"Did you have a good steam?" she asked.

"Yes, and I'm sure my men would like to steam as well," said Olga.

"Oh, of course, Olga Vasilisovna, of course..." Shurya rushed off. They both went into their room and lay down on top of the bed—they were still too hot to get under the covers.

"I think I have steamed out my soreness," said Slava sleepily.

"Oh good," said Olga. "We have a long ride ahead of us. Soon we will ride deep into the taiga. Let's go to sleep..."

Slava closed her eyes. Tall trees seemed to rise up around her, their boughs reaching for her. She flew over them till she saw a vast expanse of white before her, and felt the cold of the tundra seep into her skin... She opened her eyes. She was still in Veliky Prud, but lying on top of the covers rather than under them, which explained why she was so cold. She crawled under the blankets, disturbing Olga enough that she, too, realized she was cold and crawled under the covers.

Chapter Six

The next morning Slava woke up in particularly good humor, a sensation to which she was not at all accustomed. She lay in bed for a little while, wondering at this strange and marvelous occurrence, and finally decided it must be the result of a dream she had had the night before, although she could not actually remember the dream itself. It seemed there had been something about the taiga and the tundra again, but what, exactly, she couldn't quite say…She slipped out of bed and began dressing quietly.

It turned out she needn't have bothered, though, because Olga got up almost immediately and began dressing too. Unlike Slava, Olga was in an unusually poor humor, and answered Slava's morning greeting in a way that was quite surly compared with her usual bouncing good cheer.

"I didn't sleep well last night," she said in what Slava could tell was meant to be an oblique apology for her sullen behavior. "First I was too hot, then I was too cold, and then I had all these strange dreams about our expedition. And about Lesnograd. I kept dreaming about what Princess Malogornaya said."

"Everything Princess Malogornaya said was a nightmare," said Slava with a gentle smile.

"Yes…I just wish she hadn't said anything about my mother. I hate bad dreams. My mother is a big believer in dream divination, and always makes everyone tell her their dreams whenever something important needs to be done or if she's just bored. I don't believe in dream divination at all, but every time I have a bad dream, I can hear my mother's voice nagging me in the back of my head, and, well, there's no point worrying about it, is there?"

"Of course not," agreed Slava soothingly, hoping that Olga would come out of her bad mood before their next encounter with Ruslan Praskovyevich, as he was sure to set her off.

Just as they had finished dressing, Shurya came to them and said that Ruslan Praskovyevich had requested that they join him for breakfast before departing.

"Sure, as long as we don't have to wear those gowns again," said Olga.

"I'm sure Ruslan Praskovyevich will understand if you come dressed in your own clothes," said Shurya. "He is a very kind and understanding host, and is most sorry that you will be leaving us so soon. As are the rest of us. We rarely have visitors in Veliky Prud, especially in winter, especially such interesting ones."

"Perhaps we shall stop by on the way back," said Slava, filled with sudden pity at the thought of what boring lives everyone here must lead. The princesses who came to Krasnograd for the winter always complained of the tedium of life on their estates—not that they seemed to shake its clutches in Krasnograd—but Slava had never really realized what that meant. Krasnograd had always seemed like such a hothouse of other people's feelings that life out in the country had always sounded like a wonderful escape to her.

Now, though, she saw that these provincial estates and villages must be even worse than Krasnograd, since you would spend month after month speaking only to yourself and to the same four or five people, until it seemed like the outside world no longer existed and the only thing that mattered were your own petty problems. At least in Krasnograd you could look out the window and watch the passers-by.

"Yes, we may stop here if we return the same way," said Olga guardedly, shaking Slava out of her reverie and making her realize that she had no authority to speak on behalf of the group, and that it would be better to avoid such pronouncements in the future, especially with Olga in her touchy state.

"Why does Ruslan Praskovyevich not come to Krasnograd?" she asked in order to cover up the awkward moment. "Many in his position would."

"Oh, Ruslan Praskovyevich is happy enough here," said Shurya, smiling indulgently as she always did when pronouncing his name. It was clear that she viewed his foibles much as a fond mother would the mischievous behavior of a youngest son. "Sometimes he talks about leaving, but we all know that's just nonsense. His place is here, and all that talk about going off to strange lands is just idle dreaming. You know how men can get sometimes, especially with no wife to keep them in check. He'll get used to it in time, the dear little man, and stop all this foolishness."

"Mm-hmm," said Olga. "We have another long day ahead of us, so breakfast..."

"Is already on the table. I'll take you there now." And Shurya, who had apparently taken to treating Olga and Slava with the same indulgent fondness she lavished on Ruslan Praskovyevich, led them back to the room in which they had eaten supper the night before. The table was laid with another foreign tablecloth, and there was more foreign food waiting for them in more foreign dishes. Apparently Ruslan Praskovyevich had a fondness for table settings as well as indoor furnishings. Slava wondered how much of his wife's money he had spent on such fripperies.

Ruslan Praskovyevich came in while they were still surveying the table, wondering what it was they were going to be eating. He was dressed in another foreign costume, although not as outlandish as the one from supper—the trousers were at least more or less Zemnian in cut—and showed no ill effects from all his wine the night before. Slava guessed he was long used to over-indulgence.

"I trust you slept well?" he asked, gesturing for them to be seated and taking a seat himself.

"Very well, thank you," said Slava, as Olga still appeared to be in a bad mood.

"And I can't convince you to stay another day or two?" he continued, gazing at them both wistfully, almost like a love-struck little boy.

"We're supposed to be traveling North, not sitting around comforting lonely widowers with too much time on their hands!" said Olga.

Ruslan Praskovyevich's face filled with so much hurt Slava was afraid he might burst into tears. They both gave Olga reproachful looks, Ruslan Praskovyevich directly and Slava out of the corner of her eye in order to soften it.

"I'm going to go check on the boys and the horses!" Olga announced, standing up abruptly from the table and striding off, a roll of foreign design clutched in her hand as if she were afraid it would run off if she didn't squeeze it within an inch of its life.

"So that's what you think of me," said Ruslan Praskovyevich, once Olga was gone.

"No, of course not," said Slava reassuringly. "She's just in a bad mood this morning... So many cares, you know, with the expedition..."

"She's right, you know," said Ruslan Praskovyevich, looking down at the tablecloth. For the first time he began to look like a real man. "I am a lonely widower. My wife is dead and our daughter is off living with her aunt, learning how to manage an estate and all the other things that women learn how to do. They let me keep Veliky Prud until our daughter comes of age, and then I'll be a hanger-on in my own house."

"I'm sure your daughter..."

"I'm sure my daughter will be exactly the same kind of loud, forceful woman as her mother and her aunt," Ruslan Praskovyevich said. "They're all excellent managers, reasonably fair with their servants, reasonably loyal to their betters, reasonably kind to their husbands—no, there's nothing wrong with them, nothing you could criticize. But I...I always wanted more.

"When I was a boy I wanted to be a singer, you know. I would sit in the shade of the birch trees and sing songs of my own composition. But then my mother married me to Avdotya Svetliyevna and I had to give all that up, even though there was nothing really that needed to replace it. I mean that I wasn't needed to help run Veliky Prud, or anything of that sort. I just sat around with my arms folded, looking the part of Avdotya Svetliyevna's husband. She was much richer than my family, and married me in order to get a handsome daughter—I know this because she told me so herself. Much good that handsome daughter did her, in the end—she died before her heir took her first breath.

"I suppose it just goes to show that you should be careful what you ask for. Look at me: I wanted to be more than just a man, and I took to reading—she taught me how to read—and, well, you see the result. I've become...I don't know what I've become. A laughingstock, for sure. Unfit to be a real man, but unable to be a woman. So I sit here and pretend to myself that things would have been better if I had only been born a thousand versts away."

Ruslan Praskovyevich fell silent, staring at the tablecloth and running his fingers over his foreign silverware. He looked much more like a person than he had before.

"I'm sorry," said Slava. "I'm sure many of us like to believe that things would have been better if only we'd been born a thousand versts away, or if we'd been men instead of women or women instead of men, or not had a brother or a sister, or, who knows, had blue eyes instead of gray. I...I also often wish that I weren't myself. But there doesn't seem to be any cure for that. You can't run away from yourself."

"You're trying," said Ruslan Praskovyevich, raising his eyes momentarily from the tablecloth and giving her a shrewder look than she would have expected from him.

"Yes, and...it might even be working, not because..." Slava had to wait for a moment for her new thoughts to coalesce into coherent form, "not because I'm escaping from myself, but because I'm, I don't know, transforming, I guess. Back home I was constantly being hammered into all kinds of strange shapes, like hot iron on an anvil. But eventually you have to get out from between the hammer and the anvil, and go live your life, whatever kind of tool you happen to have been turned into."

"So tell me, Tsarinovna: how can I get off of this anvil? Is there any escape for me? Because I don't see it. I have to manage this estate as best I can, equipped only with a feeble male mind, as my wife's sister is so fond of reminding me, until my daughter comes of age, and then I have to hand it over to her without a quibble."

"Do you want to keep it?" asked Slava. "Do you enjoy running the estate?"

"By all the gods, no! It's nothing but constant tedium. But at least it gives me something to do. Once my daughter comes of age, I won't even have that. And don't tell me I'm a bad father for wanting to keep something that belongs rightfully to my daughter," he added, his voice taking on an unpleasantly self-righteous whine, "I know that already. I suppose I can't be as selfless as you women, devoting yourselves to the line: selfishness just seems to come naturally to me."

"I know many selfish women, and even some selfless men," said Slava, although Ruslan Praskovyevich could most certainly not be counted amongst that small number of selfless men. No wonder he was so unhappy, dependent as he was on his own pleasure, and independent of everyone else's, for his happiness. It gave him very little to lean upon.

Once again, she could see hatred rising up inside him, and she knew, no matter how unpleasant a thought it might be, that his wife's sister had been right to take her niece away from him, because he certainly couldn't be trusted with her. She was surprised that he had been allowed to keep the estate—she supposed that his wife's sister thought it a worthwhile sacrifice, in order to keep him away from her. "And there is always the choice of the sanctuary, either now or when your daughter comes of age," she said, trying to say something helpful and comforting instead of all the cruel things she was really thinking. "Many men have made that choice, upon losing their wives. There you will not be a hanger-on, most certainly."

"Why is it that women always suggest the sanctuary, as if that were a good choice, Tsarinovna?" demanded Ruslan Praskovyevich, pouting unattractively.

Slava resisted the desire to point out how silly he looked. Before, for a moment, she had seen that he did in fact possess a soul. Now, though, she could no longer see it. She supposed it slipped away whenever he was feeling sorry for himself. As with most men of her acquaintance. And women too.

"Why is it that women always assume men have nothing better to do than go to a sanctuary, if their wives don't need them?" he continued. The whine in his voice made Slava's skin crawl. "A sanctuary isn't a choice, it's a sentence! I'd rather be dead than go to a sanctuary!" His face twisted up as if he were about to cry, and Slava, annoying as she found his overflowing emotions, took pity on him and tried to think of something helpful to say instead.

"Why not leave, then?" she said. "When your daughter comes of age, that is. Why not run off to the Middle Sea, or wherever it is you want to go?"

"What?" said Ruslan Praskovyevich, startled for a moment out of his self-pity.

"Go to the Middle Sea, or wherever it is you want to go," Slava repeated patiently. "When your daughter comes of age and takes control of the estate. Stop hanging around here, feeling miserable, and go do something that you want to do."

For a moment she thought Ruslan Praskovyevich was going to complain about how women always tried to fix things for other people, without ever actually listening to them or showing any sympathy for their plight, but it seemed he was too unhappy even for that. "I'll never be able to," he said instead, sinking into gloom. "They'll never let me. They'll never give me the money."

"Who has to 'let' you?" demanded Slava. "Who has to 'give' you the money? You manage an estate, Ruslan Praskovyevich! So manage it well, and save up enough money through your economy to pay for your travel to the South. You say you envy men who are given the chance to develop themselves, to rule—but you have been given that chance! You rule Veliky Prud! So be a ruler!"

As she said it, she wondered if she were saying the right thing—

Ruslan Praskovyevich had hardly impressed her with his ability to rule, so encouraging him to do so was a dangerous step—but then she consoled herself with the thought that it might work, and if it didn't, the most likely outcome would be for Ruslan Praskovyevich to ignore her or welter in his own incompetence. It was unlikely that he would do any more harm than he was actually already doing.

"You truly think I should go to the South, Tsarinovna?" asked Ruslan Praskovyevich slowly.

"Yes! I think you will find your existence here much more bearable, and handing over the estate when your daughter comes of age much less painful, if you have a plan to look forward to. Stop moping around your estate, wasting your time on ill-fitting and foolish clothing, and start living your life as you wish it to be lived! That is not how a ruler behaves! A ruler commands instead of blaming her troubles on others! You have no one to blame for your misery but yourself!"

For a moment Slava had a vision of Ruslan Praskovyevich heeding her words, turning over a new leaf, and becoming a good leader and a worthy person, and she truly believed what she was saying. Then she saw his face, which was a mask of so much fear and self-doubt that she knew there was very little hope for him, very little hope at all. Better, a hundred times better, because a hundred times more familiar and less frightening, to sit here and curse fate than to do something to change it.

"Tsarinovna!" Shurya came bustling into the room. "Olga Vasilisovna is calling for you, Tsarinovna," she said with a bow, "and bids you to come as quickly as possible, for the rest are all already mounted and anxious to depart."

Slava rose from the table. Ruslan Praskovyevich rose with her.

"I forgot for a moment that you were a Tsarinovna," he said. "My apologies if I said anything untoward." He sounded, not embarrassed, but sincerely sorry that he might have inconvenienced her. His face had smoothed out, and was filled for the first time with thought.

"Of course not," said Slava. She smiled at him. "Everyone always reveals their secrets to me, even if they don't mean to or wish not to. I hope you find happiness, Ruslan Praskovyevich. I hope you find happiness by your own hands."

"Thank you, Tsarinovna." He bowed. "May your expedition find success, of one kind or another." Slava could feel his eyes following her out the room as she left, but they were so bewildered she couldn't tell which feeling was uppermost. She wished she could have more confidence that the good feelings would prevail.

After they had left Veliky Prud the men broke into a spirited discussion of their stay, in which it was difficult to tell whether disgust for Ruslan Praskovyevich or admiration for the treatment they had received was uppermost.

"Whatever else, he did feed and house us, so we shouldn't judge him too harshly," Olga said, ending the discussion. Slava could tell that she was still in a bad mood, and ashamed of herself for it, which was putting her in an even worse mood.

"Yes, we won't be so comfortable for the next few days," said Dima.

"We're not judging him, Olga Vasilisovna, we just think he's funny," said Misha.

"Perhaps we should pity him instead of laughing at him," said Dima.

"How could anyone pity him!?" exclaimed Misha, laughing and shaking his head at the thought. "Just looking at him makes my fists itch. He's an embarrassment to all of us real men."

Dima glanced at Slava's face and said, "I'll bet our Krasna Tsarina does."

Misha and the other men turned to look at her curiously. "You do, Krasna Tsarina?" Misha asked, straining not to appear incredulous.

"I do," she admitted.

"Really? You do? Do you feel sorry for everyone?" he asked.

"More or less, yes," she answered.

"But why, Krasna Tsarina? Why waste your time feeling sorry for fools like Ruslan Praskovyevich? It's not like it will help them any."

"I can't help myself," she told him. "I just do. I always know what the person next to me is feeling, and I always feel it with her."

"You should stop that, Krasna Tsarina," said Misha. "You'll only make yourself sad if you keep that up. Surely you have better things to do. Why, that must be completely exhausting! How could anyone live like that, always feeling other people's feelings? Really, Krasna Tsarina, you ought to learn how to stop it."

"Enough, Misha," said Dima, looking at Slava's face. "You've over-stepped your bounds. Apologize to Krasnoslava Tsarinovna."

"Really?" asked Misha, looking startled. "I'm sorry, Krasna Tsarina, I didn't mean anything by it, it was just…"

"Think nothing of it," said Slava hastily. "I'm sure you're right, anyway."

"And I'm sure you're not," said Dima, still watching Slava's face. "Go ride on ahead, Misha, and see if you can find us a good place to stop for midday."

"With pleasure, Marusich!" Misha rode ahead, whistling cheerfully and seeming unaffected by Dima's displeasure.

"Ignore Misha, Krasna Tsarina, he's just a silly young boy," Dima told her once Misha had left the group.

"Yes, but he only says what others are thinking," said Slava. She dropped back to the rear of the group, where Grisha was riding along silently, looking out over the horizon as if it might tell him something of importance. He nodded to her when she joined him, but, to Slava's relief, said nothing.

Slava tried to gather information from the horizon too, but soon started staring at the ground directly in front of her horse's ears, consumed by her own thoughts. What *was* the point, she asked herself, as she had asked herself so many times before, of feeling what other people were feeling? What good did it do? None at all, as far as she could tell, because it only went one way.

If only, she thought for the many-hundredth time, she could make people hear her as she heard them. That would be genuinely useful. But as it was, not only was she constantly miserable herself, she made everyone around her miserable as well.

Had she ever, she asked herself, made anyone really happy in her entire life? She ran through all the people she could think of whom she might have made happy at one time or another: her sister; various princesses who were supposed to be her friends; past lovers, back from when she was still hopeful enough to take lovers…In the end they had all gotten nervous around her and revealed such monumental selfishness that she had driven them away, only to realize afterwards that she had behaved as least as cruelly as they had…more so, in fact, since she was aware of what she was doing, and they were not…She suddenly saw Zhenya's round face rise up in front of her, and felt that here there was some kind of answer, something she had done right, that she needed to do again…

"Look, Krasna Tsarina, the forest," said Grisha.

Slava looked up, startled at how deeply she had sunk into her reverie. A dark mass had appeared before them on the horizon.

"How big is it?" she asked.

"Big, Krasna Tsarina, very big," he told her. "We shall be riding through it for at least three days before we reach the other side. Do you know what it is called, Krasna Tsarina?"

"No, what?"

"The wood-spirits' woods. It borders Pristanogradskoye and Severnolesnoye, and is a small outcropping of the vast forests there."

"Have you ridden through it before?"

"Oh yes, many times, Krasna Tsarina, never fear. But it is different each time; although there is a road through it, travelers are so few—most prefer to keep along the Krasna—and its inhabitants so many, that the paths shift all the time. There are cabins to stay in, at least, but it seems the track from one to the next changes every time you take it. Some even claim that the cabins themselves also change their location, but that's just nonsense. It's just elk-tracks that make the paths move about from season to season."

"How do you find your way, then?" asked Slava, trying to sound curious rather than afraid.

"By the sun and the stars, and many other signs as well. Don't look so troubled, Krasna Tsarina! We shall make our way through it safely, I promise you."

They reached the edge of the forest just as the sun was sinking down to the horizon. The trees were large firs, whose boughs reached out onto the path and hid whatever was beneath or behind them.

"The fir is the mother of the forest, Krasna Tsarina," said Grisha as they entered the woods. "See how her arms reach out to embrace us!"

"It's very dark in here," said Slava. The sun was close to setting, and the dark fir needles were blocking out what light was left in the sky.

"Your eyes will adjust, don't worry, Krasna Tsarina."

Slava supposed that her eyes were adjusting, but the light was fading even faster, so that it did little good. However, the path was broad and straight, and the people in the front of the group seemed to be having no trouble making it out.

"We'll ride for a few more versts, Krasna Tsarina, and then come to a cabin, so we'll have soft warm beds tonight," Grisha told her.

"I'm glad," said Slava, who thought it unlikely that the beds would actually be soft and warm, but at least they would be beds.

They rode the rest of the way in silence. As the woods grew darker, Slava became more and more aware, as she never had when riding in the parks in Krasnograd, that their road was just a thin strip through a vast stand of trees, and that beyond the branches blocking their view, the woods were teeming with countless creatures, oblivious to the passers-by. The forest seemed filled with the unbroken hush of winter, but Slava was sure it was deceptive, and that, should they stray even a few feet off the path, they would see that many eyes were watching them.

It was dark enough that Slava was having a hard time seeing the tail of the horse in front of her by the time they reached the cabin. Like the last one they had stayed in, this one was surrounded by a stockade. They rode in, and Grisha closed and barred the gate. The sound of the slamming bar seemed to Slava to focus the forest's attention on them, and make it clear that they were intruders here, determined to shut the forest out.

For a moment she wanted to protest and say they should leave the gate open, it would be safer that way, but then she looked up at the treetops leaning over the fence, and it seemed to her that they had taken on a menacing look. She closed her mouth without saying anything.

This cabin was even smaller and less comfortable than the previous one, but no one complained, least of all Slava, who realized partway through supper that her soreness was almost gone, and was too delighted by this to complain about anything.

They went to bed immediately after eating. According to Olga and Grisha, they would not be riding that far tomorrow, but it might be slow going, and they would need their rest. Besides, there were no candles in the cabin, and Olga did not want to waste supplies.

That night Slava dreamed that something was trying to get in, something large, something that needed to speak with her, and it was imperative that she listen...She awoke in the middle of the night, certain that something was scratching against the shutters, but there was nothing, not even the wind. She went back to sleep, but only plunged back into the same dream yet again.

Chapter Seven

The next morning it was completely still and silent, and when they looked up at the sky, it seemed to press directly down on the treetops, as if it were muffling the forest and everything in it. The horses moved slowly and carefully through the snow, and even the men were subdued. Slava wanted to ask if there were a particular reason for all this, but the words could not seem to leave her head.

Sometime around midmorning—it was hard to tell under the heavy clouds and tall trees—Grisha, who was riding in front, threw up his hand and pulled his horse to a halt, forcing the rest of them to halt their horses quickly too.

"Tracks," he announced, breaking the silence for the first time that day. "Fresh elk tracks, crossing the path. A young female, I'd say by the size."

The other men all rode forward to examine the elk tracks. There was a discussion about whether or not to go after the elk in order to supplement their supplies with fresh meat. Some of the men had clearly been filled with hunting zeal by the sight of the elk tracks, and tried to persuade Dima and then Olga with various arguments that a quick hunting party was essential. Olga, however, said that they needed to keep moving, to Slava's intense relief. She had never been hunting, and the idea of going now filled her with so much instinctive revulsion she was afraid she might have cried, had Olga given her permission. They carried on without investigating the elk tracks further.

Half a verst down the road the horses all stopped and looked to the right. After a moment the people could hear the sound of something moving through the trees too. Grisha cocked his head towards the noise like a dog.

"The elk," he whispered. "Coming towards us."

"Everyone stay still," Dima whispered in response.

Slava, who was next to Grisha, saw with horror that he was slowly, silently, stringing his bow. She had noticed it hanging from his saddle, but never given a thought as to why he would be carrying it. Hunting was so far out of her experience that before this morning it had never occurred to her that anyone from their party would ever even consider doing it, but now she realized that had been foolish. Of course they were all keen hunters. She wanted to knock the arrow that Grisha was carefully pulling from his quiver out of his hands, but was chained in place by the thought of how the others would react if she did so.

Let the elk turn away, she prayed to whatever gods might be listening. *Let her pass us by.*

But the footsteps grew closer. Slava kept waiting for someone to sneeze, or one of the horses to neigh, or for something to happen that would warn the elk they were there, but everyone seemed frozen by the same immobility that was affecting her.

You don't want to come here, elk. Go away, go away, go away. Slava tried to send out her thoughts harder than she had ever tried before, but to absolutely no effect. The elk was now so close she thought she could hear it breathing.

Smell us, why can't you smell us, she asked the elk with anguish, but the elk seemed oblivious to the danger ahead of it.

Misha pointed. A dark shape could just be made out, moving through the trees. Grisha nocked his arrow and raised his bow.

Stay, stay behind that tree, Slava implored the elk, but her head appeared from behind the large fir tree that was shielding her from Grisha's aim. Slava could feel everyone else's thoughts focusing on the elk, like snakes about to strike...The elk took another step from behind the tree...Grisha drew back on his bow...The elk took another step, presenting Grisha with the target he needed, and suddenly stopped, her head turned towards them, her eyes bright with non-human intelligence. She seemed surprised, but not afraid, not afraid enough...Grisha was about to let fly his arrow, Slava could tell, and the elk wasn't going to run...Grisha's fingers were already letting go of the arrow...

"NO!" she screamed.

For a moment there was too much confusion to see what had happened. All the horses shied, especially Slava's, so that she had to hang on to Ogonyok's mane to keep from losing her seat. When she looked back up, the elk was gone, and Grisha's arrow was quivering in the snow. Everyone was staring at her, and she knew they couldn't decide what to feel: shock or anger.

"Krasna Tsarina..." said Grisha eventually, and then fell silent. Olga was wearing a very peculiar expression, as if she had placed a bet but couldn't tell yet if she had won or lost.

"I'm sorry," said Slava. "I don't know...I just couldn't...I'm sorry..."

"We need to keep riding," said Olga, still wearing that very peculiar expression. For once, Slava couldn't tell whether she was angry or glad, maybe because she was neither. "We wouldn't have had time for it anyway."

They started moving again down the road. Slava let herself fall to the back of the group. She could see the men's bewilderment rising off of them with the steam of their breath. It had never occurred to them, she could tell, that anyone would ever have any objection to hunting, or that someone would stop them from bringing in fresh meat, and they didn't know how to respond to her action. Some of them, she was sure, wanted to be angry with her, but her behavior had been so strange, and she herself was still in some ways such a mysterious figure, that they ended up puzzled and uncertain rather than angry.

Slava herself didn't quite understand what she had done, or why she had done it. Did she not eat the products of other people's hunting and slaughtering every night? But somehow she had been unable to stand idly by while the elk was killed. Doing so would have been a terrible mistake, she was somehow certain of it.

The rest of the day was passed in the same strange silence as the morning. They arrived at another cabin just as night was falling. Once again Slava had the very odd feeling that they were doing something wrong when the gates slammed shut, but she didn't know what else they could have done; she certainly didn't want to sleep out in the snow.

Supper was a quiet affair, especially in the part of the room where Slava was sitting. The men had apparently decided not to be angry with her, choosing to fear her instead. Slava was glad to be able to disappear into the tiny bedroom—barely more than a closet—that she would be sharing with Olga, and slide under the covers as if behind a shield.

That night she dreamed that the elk was trying to get into the bedroom, which left her feeling moody and withdrawn in the morning. The men treated her slightly more normally at breakfast than they had at supper, but were still nervous in her presence, as if she might suddenly start screaming and rolling around on the floor.

"It's snowing heavily," Dima announced as they went outside. "We'll have to travel slowly today."

"As long as we make it to shelter," Olga said. "I'd hoped to leave the woods by tonight, but if not, there's another cabin only twenty or so versts from here. We can spend the night there if we have to."

It was indeed snowing so heavily it was hard for Slava to keep her eyes open; snowflakes kept falling in them. In the time it had taken them to step out of the cabin and over to the horses, enough snow had built up on her saddle that she had to brush it off before she mounted—although she couldn't vault into the saddle like the rest of them, she could at least mount without a leg-up now, something of which she was extremely proud, even though she didn't want to brag about it in front of the others. It seemed like such a small accomplishment. And she wasn't quick enough to keep snow from building up again between when she put her foot in the stirrup and when she landed in the seat of her saddle, so that she knew she would end up spending the day riding in wet trousers.

They rode out of the stockade and started down the path. Slava hoped that the snow would lighten up soon, but instead it began to fall even more heavily, so that she had the sensation that she was drowning in thickly-falling snow. She rode as closely as she dared to Misha's side, and thanked the gods and whomever had bred and trained Skvorets that he was docile and didn't try to pick fights.

Slava's sense of distance was still very poor in comparison with the others, but she thought they couldn't have gone more than a couple of versts when they came to a sudden stop. She strained to see what was happening through the snow.

"I think there's a fork in the road, and they don't know which way to go, Krasna Tsarina," Misha told her, having apparently forgotten about yesterday's incident in the face of this new trouble.

Snow-shrouded figures that might have been Olga, Dima, and Grisha huddled together in consultation for a long time, before starting very uncertainly down the left-hand path. The rest of them followed, moving at a slow walk.

After what seemed like only a few hundred feet they came to a stop again. This time they were all bunched so closely together that Slava could hear Olga saying to Dima, "This isn't a path at all, just an opening in the trees. We have to go back."

"At least we still have our tracks to follow," he replied. They all turned around and started backtracking. Slava was now in front, and the space between the trees was too narrow for the others to pass her.

"What do I do?" she called back to Misha, who was directly behind her.

"Just follow the tracks, Krasna Tsarina—it'll be easy," he called back.

At first following the tracks of twenty horses was easy, just as he had said. But they walked for what seemed like much longer than they had come, and still they didn't rejoin the real road.

"We should be there by now," Slava could hear the others muttering behind her back. "But we can't have missed it."

Just when Slava had begun to be really afraid, they rode into a larger opening. "The road!" Misha exclaimed in relief.

But it wasn't the road, only a snow-filled glade that they certainly hadn't passed through earlier. They all stopped.

"How could we have gotten lost?" Slanik asked, looking around. "We followed our own tracks, I'm sure."

"I'm sure too," said Grisha, also looking around, much more grimly than Slanik. "We've been led astray."

"By what?"

Grisha only shrugged and continued looking around, as did the rest of the party, including Slava. The firs rose around them, refusing to explain how they had followed their own tracks to a place they had never been before. There was no sign of the road, or of anything that might lead them to it, nothing...

"Look!" cried Slava. "Over there!"

Everyone turned in the direction she was pointing, where a flash of gray was disappearing between two dark trees.

"What..." asked Slanik.

"The elk!" said Slava. "She went that way!"

Everyone gave her a puzzled and distrustful look. "Even if it was an elk, Krasnoslava Tsarinovna, I don't think..." began Dima.

"No, no, we have to follow her!" insisted Slava. "I'm sure of it. Come on!" She urged Skvorets forward, pulling Ogonyok after them. They squeezed awkwardly through a break in the trees. Slava thought she saw another flash of gray.

"Come on!" she called again. Looking back, she saw that the others were still standing there, staring at her in frank bewilderment mixed with growing alarm.

"It's a sign!" she shouted at them, continuing to ride on. "We're supposed to follow it, I'm sure!" The others exchanged looks, and then set off hesitantly after her.

Slava couldn't say why she was so sure, but as soon as she had caught sight of the flash of gray, she had been instantly certain that it was the elk from yesterday, and that she was leading them in the right direction. She urged Skvorets on, and he broke into an eager trot, with Ogonyok following closely behind.

"Krasnoslava Tsarinovna!" someone shouted from behind her. "At least wait for us, Krasnoslava!"

"Keep up! Keep up!" she called back. She gave Skvorets his head, and he moved with surprising ease through the snow and trees, snorting with eagerness and breaking into a canter anywhere he could find space.

"Krasnoslava...!" The voices were falling farther and farther behind her, but she didn't even try to rein Skvorets in, afraid to break his concentration. Both he and Ogonyok broke into something that was as close to a gallop as they could manage in the heavy snow and narrow, twisting passage between the trees.

Slava grabbed Skvorets's mane with one hand and held onto Ogonyok's lead rope as tightly as she could with the other. A wall of trees rose up before them, but Slava didn't even try to stop or turn Skvorets, who seemed to know what he was doing. He flicked his ears this way and that, and headed for a narrow gap, blocked only by waist-high branches. Slava thought there might a clearing on the other side.

She felt Skvorets gather himself, and then they jumped over the branches and slid to a halt, so that Slava fell forward onto Skvorets's neck, almost smashing her nose. Ogonyok crashed into them from behind, and both horses stumbled and almost fell over before righting themselves. Slava pushed herself upright, and looked around. They were standing in the middle of the road, in front of the fork where they had taken the wrong turning earlier. The elk was standing only a few feet away from them.

"Hello, little sister," Slava said to her softly. She turned her head and looked straight at Slava, her eyes bright with the same non-human intelligence of the day before.

"Thank you for saving us," Slava told her. She had never been this close to an elk before, and was astonished at how large she was, even though, according to Grisha, she was not yet full grown.

The elk snorted and walked up to Skvorets, who, instead of shying away, pricked his ears at her and stretched out his head in her direction. Ogonyok also surged forward, pushing Skvorets slightly to the side so that he could reach the elk as well. All three animals stretched out their heads as far as possible, and sniffed each other's muzzles, snorting and waving their ears.

This went on for several heartbeats, until the elk suddenly withdrew her head, fixed Slava with another bright gaze, and took off down the right-hand path. Both horses watched her until she was well out of sight, their heads up and ears pricked. Then they both simultaneously shook their heads, as if they had gotten water in their ears, looked at each other, and then turned to look behind them, where, Slava realized, the others were coming through the trees.

"Krasnoslava Tsarinovna!" Dima cried, his horse forcing her way through the fir branches to the road with difficulty. "Are you all right? What happened?"

"The elk," said Slava, feeling light-headed. "She led me back to the road, and then she spoke to the horses, and then she left."

"Spoke to the horses?" asked Olga, stopping to break some fir branches and widen the passage. "You mean she talked?"

"No, no, of course not, I mean she came up to us and sniffed at them, and then she took off that way, telling us which way to go." Slava pointed down the right-hand path, where the elk's hoof prints could be seen clearly in the snow.

The others were now bursting through the branches and looking around. "The road!" several of them cried. "You found the road, Krasna Tsarina!"

"It was the elk," Slava explained, still feeling breathless, as if her chest weren't opening and closing properly. She didn't know if it was from the sudden gallop, or the encounter with the elk. "She showed me."

"The elk?" Everyone was staring at her with a variant of the same bemused look they had been giving her since yesterday.

"Yes, yes, the elk," Slava repeated. "She went that way." She pointed again in the direction the elk had gone. Grisha started riding down the road.

"Elk tracks," he called back. "Leading down the right-hand path. And they do look like the same ones as yesterday."

"She wants us to follow her," Slava said with conviction.

"Well, we know going left was a mistake," said Olga, giving Slava another peculiar look and riding to the front of the group. "So right seems like the only option. Grisha, take the lead and make sure we don't go astray again. Slava, you ride in the middle, between Misha and Dima: I want them to keep an eye on you. You look flushed."

Slava obediently allowed Misha and Dima to ride up on either side of her, and the group set off, this time taking the right-hand path. Slava was still having a hard time breathing, and, now that Olga had pointed it out to her, she could tell that she was indeed flushed. She felt as if she had just taken a large quantity of vodka on an empty stomach.

"I just knew," she told Dima, gasping slightly as she spoke but too excited to remain silent. "I don't know how I knew, but I just knew... and so did the horses, they took right off after her, and then when we all stopped on the road, she came right up to us and sniffed them, and she looked at me, it was as if she were talking to me, her eyes were so bright, so bright..." Slava trailed off as her teeth started to chatter. She saw that Dima and Misha were exchanging worried glances above her head, but it didn't seem to matter, everything seemed very far away, as if she were watching it through wavy glass, or deep water...

"Krasnoslava!" someone shouted, and she felt hands grabbing her arms, and she realized she had slumped onto Skvorets's neck. There was a jumble of shouting, and then somehow she was sitting on the snow, and people were holding up her head and trying to pour vodka into her mouth, and swearing violently as she coughed and choked on it. She looked up, and saw Misha's blue eyes looking straight back into hers, and it was as if she were inside his head, and Dima's, and Olga's, and Slanik's, and inside all the men and horses too, and spreading out over the entire forest, filling every tree and creature there...

Chapter Eight

"What happened? What's wrong with her?"
"What will the Empress say?"
"Is she breathing?"
"Wake up, Krasnoslava, wake up!"
"I think she's breathing."
"What will the Empress say?!"
"She's definitely breathing. Help me lift her out of the snow, Dima."
"What will the Empress say!?!!"
"Wait...I think she's trying to say something..."

Slava realized that she was moaning something incoherent, and that the reason she couldn't see anything was because her eyes were closed. She stopped moaning and opened her eyes. Eleven anxious faces were staring down at her. Olga and Dima had their arms around her, as if they were about to pick her up from where she had slumped into the snow.

"Krasnoslava Tsarinovna!" they both cried, as soon as they saw her open eyes.

"What..." Slava's mouth felt strangely weak, like the rest of her body. "What happened?" she managed on the second try.

"You just...fainted, Krasnoslava Tsarinovna," said Dima, his face still wearing a very frightened look. Olga was staring down at Slava with the same peculiar expression she had been giving her ever since yesterday.

"Misha! Olik! Lay out some blankets on the snow! Dima, help her over to the blankets."

By clutching Dima's shoulders, Slava was able to pull herself to her feet and stagger over to where Misha and Olik had laid out blankets on the snow. She collapsed down onto them as soon as she reached them, but managed to maintain a sitting position.

"Do you faint often, Krasnoslava Tsarinovna?" asked Olga, as soon as Slava was sitting back down.

"No...I don't think so...never before..." Slava wanted to shake her head to clear it, but was afraid the movement would make her sick.

"Have you been feeling unwell lately?"

"No..." Slava closed her eyes again, and visions wheeled before them, making her dizzy. She hastily opened her eyes.

"I saw..." she began.

"Yes?"

"I saw...I saw everything."

"What do you mean, 'everything'?"

"I saw you, and the horses, and the forest, and everything in it...It was as if my mind reached out to everything at once..."

"I see," said Olga, although she clearly did not.

This time Slava was able to shake her head, which did seem to help. "The elk," she said. "It was the elk, I'm sure. She looked at me, and it was as if she could see inside of me, as if she opened my mind, and then it...then it...it spread out," she finished awkwardly, rapidly becoming aware of how crazy she sounded and how impossible it would be to explain to the others what had happened. Saying that her mind had "spread out" was not quite right; it was as if it had engulfed the entire forest and everything in it, like embers that had suddenly been fanned into wildfire.

"The elk?" said Olga, bringing Slava back to herself.

"Yes, it was the elk, I'm sure of it. She looked at me, and...anyway, here we are." Slava stood back up, her strength returning to her as quickly as it had disappeared. Her head was still fuzzy, as if her mind had been wrapped in many shawls, but she no longer felt in any danger of fainting.

Olga and Dima exchanged glances, and Slava knew that they didn't believe any part of her story. "Are you sure you don't want to rest a little more, Krasnoslava Tsarinovna?" asked Olga.

"No, no, I think we should carry on. I feel fine now."

"Are you sure?"

"Yes, yes, very sure," Slava assured them.

Olga and Dima exchanged glances once again, but allowed Slava to return to her horses. She stroked Skvorets's nose, noticing as if for the first time—although it was not—how alert and intelligent his eyes were, just like the elk's. Ogonyok sniffed at her shoulder, and she felt his curiosity even more strongly than she did the bewilderment of everyone else in the group.

Misha and Olik gathered up their blankets and shook the snow off them and packed them back in their packs, and then they all mounted up and continued down the road. They moved at a slow walk, with Slava in the middle, and everyone else watching her with concern. She wanted to tell them that she was fine, better than fine, but she knew that they would not believe her, and if she had been them, she wouldn't have believed her either.

The gasping, breathless feeling was gone, and Slava took large, deep breaths of the cold air, feeling it go deep into her lungs. She looked at the passing trees with interest, now seeing them each as individual beings, alien perhaps to humans, but beings nonetheless, each special and separate from the one next to it. She thought she could sense more elk somewhere deep in the woods, and even deeper in, so distant that she couldn't be sure, she thought that wolves were lying in wait, hoping to catch something to keep them going through the cold lean months of winter.

For the first time in her life, she felt as if her mind were reaching out beyond itself, trying to touch others, instead of crouching down, trying to defend itself from the relentless assault that others were making on it. She looked at the rest of the group, and they seemed somehow both much closer and much farther away than they had before, as if she could sense them or not at will. She ran her hand down Skvorets's neck, and marveled at the change that had been wrought upon her.

Between getting lost and Slava's incident, they only made it as far as the next cabin by nightfall. Slava rode inside the now-familiar stockade—they were all built to the same pattern—but this time, the clang of the gates being barred shut did not invoke the same feeling of unease that it had before. Why worry about shutting the forest out, when it was right there, on the other side of a thin wall of wood?

Still feeling as if her mind were wrapped in many shawls, and at the same time more naked than ever before, Slava let the others take away her horses, guide her into the cabin, sit her down, and prepare her supper. Then Olga led her into the bedroom and put her to bed like a small child, but Slava didn't care at all. She was a little worried— although the sensation was pleasantly cushioned by all the wrappings around her mind—that she wouldn't be able to sleep, but in fact she dropped almost instantly into a deep well of dreams.

The elk was cantering through the forest, brushing through the snow-covered branches. "Thank you for saving me," she told Slava. "Now I have saved you in return."

"Was the second path a trap?" Slava asked her. "Were we being tested, led astray for some purpose?"

"Humans are so arrogant," said the elk, "always assuming that everything is about them. The second path was there because it was there, and you happened to go down it by mistake, and then go astray when you attempted to find your away back from the leshiye's clearing. Keeping to your course is much harder than is often believed. But when you did go astray, we decided to guide you back to safety."

"Who are 'we'?" asked Slava.

"We are 'we'," said a voice in Slava's ear. She turned to see where it was coming from. Two golden eyes were staring out from the trunk of a tree.

"Why did you save our sister the elk?" the tree asked Slava.

"I don't know. I just did. I do that sometimes," Slava confessed. "I can't help myself."

"Can't help yourself?" repeated the tree.

"I feel...I feel pity for every living thing that comes before me. If my worst enemy were standing in front of me, and I knew that she had committed a thousand terrible crimes, and would go on to commit a thousand more, I would still feel pity for her. For me, the barrier between 'me' and 'them' is as thin as silk, so that often I feel more for 'them' than I do for 'me,' and I can't help myself. Others say it is my gift."

"But you do not," stated the tree.

"It would be a gift if others had also been given it. But as it is, it is as if they are all drinking my blood, and giving none of theirs in return. I do not want to give up my gift, even if I could, but I wish...if I had one wish, it would be that others could share it. Then I would not be so alone."

"Alone?" said the tree. "When the hearts of others are open to you?"

"Yes, alone!" said Slava. "Because the hearts of others are open to me! They show themselves to me, and I see little that I recognize in myself, even in the deepest and darkest parts of my soul, the parts that I keep under lock and key so that they never, ever come out to rule over me. But when I look into others, all I see is selfishness, sometimes with a little cruelty mixed in. That's if there's anything there at all. Many people, when I look inside them, are nothing but hollow dolls and dead souls.

"And I hate myself for seeing that, but I cannot help myself. I wish I saw goodness and kindness, but I don't. I am...I think I am the harshest judge anyone will ever face, because I see what no one else will even admit is there, even though I wish I didn't. And yet, even as I am so cruel, I am overcome with pity for the same people I cannot help but despise. Sometimes—more and more often—I feel like I am being torn apart between hatred and pity. There is not enough room for both of them inside me, and yet I must carry them both."

"These are human problems," said the tree. "Other creatures do not suffer your strange troubles."

"So you cannot help me?" asked Slava. "Even after I saved the elk?"

"You think that one deed was enough?" asked the tree.

"Well, no," Slava admitted. "It was nothing, especially since I didn't even know I was going to do it until I did it. There was no special merit in it at all."

"Precisely," said the tree.

"But then how?" asked Slava. "How can I stop this? How can I save myself from myself?"

"You will have to stop being yourself, then," said the tree. "Become one of us."

"No!" cried Slava. "That is not the answer! What I mean is, how can I save myself from myself without losing myself?"

"Only you can answer that," said the tree. "Such problems are certainly beyond my power to solve." A cold wind sighed through its branches. To Slava's ears, it sounded like laughter.

When Slava woke up, she couldn't tell whether she had seen a vision or just a dream.

But does it matter? she asked herself.

Of course it does, she answered herself. *If it was a vision, then it was the truth. If it was just a dream, it was just a dream.*

Either way, it was true and you know it, she told herself. Olga stirred beside her in the bed.

"How do you feel?" she asked groggily.

"Fine," Slava told her. "Completely fine."

"You don't feel faint? Weak? Sick? Will you be able to ride today?"

"I feel fine," Slava assured her again. "What happened yesterday... it was nothing for you to worry about."

"That's easy for you to say," Olga mumbled, still not quite awake. "*You* weren't thinking about what would happen when we dragged your lifeless body back to your sister in Krasnograd." She opened her eyes and smiled at Slava. "I thought some of the boys were going to join you in your faint, they were so worried about what the Empress would say."

"It was nothing for you to worry about," Slava repeated. "It was just...It was...I had a vision, I guess."

"A vision?" Olga sat up in bed and stared at Slava. "And I thought you were just raving yesterday! Do you have them often?"

Slava shook her head. "Many of my foremothers had the ability to farsee or to foresee, but I never have. But ever since we have set off, I have been having strange dreams, even stranger than usual, and then yesterday...it was as if I saw all the forest at once."

"Dreams? What kind of dreams?" Olga's voice had grown suddenly sharp.

"I kept dreaming of the forest, and that I could see where we were going...but I thought they were just dreams...until yesterday, that is. Now I think..."

"Yes?" Olga was staring intently at Slava, as if she were the card that would win or lose the game, and Olga was still waiting for her to be turned over.

"I think my 'gift,' as people call it, is growing. I think..." Slava was embarrassed to admit what she was thinking, in case Olga thought she was bragging, but at Olga's impatient head gesture, she went on. "I think that back there, in Krasnograd, I was under such a constant attack from all sides that there was no room for my abilities to flourish, but here, out in the open air, away from too many people, they are

132

spreading out, flexing their wings."

"Does it hurt?" asked Olga curiously, and then looked sorry she had said it.

"No."

"Except when you faint," said Olga. "Do you think you'll be doing much more of that?"

"I don't know," said Slava. "I wouldn't think so, but I can't be sure. But you shouldn't worry about me too much."

"As long as you're sure," said Olga, getting out of bed. "Frankly speaking, we can't go back very easily at this point anyway, so we might as well go on. But in the future, try to warn us if you're about to have a vision or a fainting spell or anything of that sort."

"I will," promised Slava, smiling back at Olga's smile.

The men all treated Slava as if she were some kind of fragile glass object, bringing her food at breakfast, helping her onto her horse, and watching her solicitously when they thought she wasn't looking. Several times Grisha told her he had a flask of vodka under his coat, and she should just say the word if she felt she needed some, and Slanik rode so close to her side she was afraid of getting tangled in his stirrups, while Olik insisted on ponying Skvorets for her.

Slava submitted to all this with good grace, careful not to laugh when Misha insisted on helping her down from her saddle when they stopped to eat at midday. Sasha demanded the honor of being allowed to hold her horses for her while she ate, while Vova dug through their supplies, searching for the choicest delicacies to offer her. They were, Slava thought, much more concerned about taking care of her now that she seemed frail and special to them than when she had just been the Empress's younger sister. This made it hard not to pat their heads as they hovered around her.

Slava didn't know what she had been hoping for, but she had certainly expected something to happen when she left the stockade and rode out again into the forest. However, they rode along as they always did, and Slava was visited by no visions, nor any animals or anything else unusual or interesting, somewhat to her disappointment.

"We'll be leaving the forest shortly, Krasna Tsarina," Misha told her at one point.

"So soon?" she asked. "Somehow I thought it was much larger than that."

"This was just a tiny finger of the great taiga above us, Krasna Tsarina," he told her. "Wait until we pass Vostochnoye Selo: then you'll see forests more vast than you can possibly imagine. And if Olga Vas-ilisovna succeeds in her plans, we'll pass beyond the taiga entirely and venture out into the tundra. I know she's hoping to trade in our horses for dogs at Naberezhnoye, so we can leave the settled lands behind entirely."

"She is?" asked Slava, startled. Of course she had known more or less of the plan, but for some reason the details kept escaping her, and she had either not known, or forgotten, that she would have to give up her horses.

"But never fear, Krasna Tsarina, you'll get Skvorets and Ogonyok back," Misha told her confidently, correctly interpreting the reason behind her silence. "We certainly won't let anything happen to them! Have you ever traveled by dogsled before? I can't wait. My older broth-er served for a time in the North—in the North of Severnolesnoye, I mean, where they use dogsleds all the time, and his descriptions when I was a boy always made me so envious..."

And Misha, as confident of Slava's interest as he was of everything else he did, went into a lengthy story about his childhood, which Sla-va found fascinating. Before this journey she had never in her life spoken at length to common soldiers (not, she supposed, that Olga's men could really be called common soldiers, being in fact much su-perior, but they were not of the nobility, which made them fascinat-ingly foreign in Slava's eyes), and knew nothing about how they lived or thought. Misha, like all the other men with Olga, and in fact like Olga herself to a certain extent, lived and thought with a combination of charming simplicity and horrifying brutality that was constantly catching Slava off guard.

"Look, Krasna Tsarina, the edge of the forest," said Misha sudden-ly, interrupting himself in the middle of a story about bear hunting, much to Slava's relief, as she had no stomach for lengthy descriptions of skinning techniques and the knives that went with them, something to which Misha was blithely oblivious.

The forest ended in an abrupt line, the firs rising up forbiddingly and then giving away to snow-covered fields that presented an even bleaker picture than the dark woods.

"In another fifteen versts or so we'll come to a crossroads and a waystation, Krasna Tsarina," Misha told her cheerfully. "And then for the next few nights we'll be staying with various noblewomen who know Olga Vasilisovna, and then we'll reach Vostochnoye Selo and we'll be in the true North, isn't that grand?"

"Yes," said Slava, forgetting the bleakness of the gray fields and gray sky at the prospect of being in the true North in only a few days' time.

"Then we'll have to rough it, I'm afraid, Krasna Tsarina, but don't you worry: we'll take care of you like you were in your own kremlin," Misha promised, apparently sincerely.

"I'm sure you will," Slava told him kindly, trying to picture how that would be possible and holding back a smile in order not to hurt his feelings. "I'm sure you all will do an excellent job."

The next week went by as ordinarily as it was possible for a week of travel to go by, in a procession of waystations and the houses of minor nobility, where they were treated with a respect bordering on terror as soon as Slava's name was announced. This bothered Slava, even though the men all told her that they were being treated much better than usual because of her presence.

"They should treat you like that anyway!" she told Dima indignantly as he was praising the hospitality they had been given at the house of a very minor princess, known for her parsimony and lack of welcome for travelers.

"And my mother always said I should be taller, Krasna Tsarina," he replied, laughing. "We should all be different than we are, I dare say. But I'm glad that the fear you inspire in them, this far from Krasnograd, is making soft beds for the rest of us."

"I wish they weren't so afraid of me," Slava said. "It's annoying. Of course, it's also annoying that the princesses closer to Krasnograd ignore me as much as possible, but I still can't stand all this kneeling and forehead-beating that the noblewomen up here do. Especially since they don't actually like any of us one bit; they're just terrified of the name 'Zerkalitsa,' no matter who bears it."

"Well, we are in Pristanogradskoye now, Krasna Tsarina," he pointed out. "The original home of your family. Fear of the name Zerkalitsa, especially when coupled with Tsarinovna, has been bred into these people until it goes bone-deep. They aren't like your Krasna or your steppe princesses, who can look back to a time when their foremothers were once queens. These noblewomen drop to their knees as soon as they so much as hear your family being mentioned, they can't help themselves."

Slava knew he was right and so stopped arguing, even though she found the behavior of the Pristanogradskoye nobility highly irritating. She knew, of course, that behind the fear there was nothing but dislike for her for making them feel the fear, and so she wanted to leave their presence as soon as possible, even as they fawned over her, trying to get her to stay.

After a week of this, though, and just when Slava was beginning to despair of ever escaping the tedium of each identical day, Olga announced that if they rode as hard as they could that day, they could reach Vostochnoye Selo that evening.

A huge cheer went up amongst the men, which Slava almost found herself joining. Vostochnoye Selo was one of the last outposts of Zem' and of civilization in general, and the thought of riding into it that evening was thrilling.

She noted that Olga did not seem to share their enthusiasm, but perhaps, she thought, she considered it beneath her dignity. That seemed very out of character for Olga, but it was evident that she was not pleased at the idea of spending the night at Vostochnoye Selo, even as she encouraged the rest of them to keep up a good pace in order to ensure their arrival. Given her connection to Princess Primorskaya—Slava couldn't remember exactly what it was; she knew Olga had been briefly married to a Primorsky son or nephew or some such person, but beyond that she wasn't sure, and Olga herself never spoke of it at all—Slava would have expected her to be, if not riding joyously towards open arms, at least looking forward to being kept in comfort by her kin. Perhaps, Slava told herself, she had had another bad dream.

Slava didn't know if she could actually sense a change, or if it was just the knowledge that Vostochnoye Selo and the seashore were ahead of them, but she thought there was something different in the air that day, something she had never breathed before, that must be the scent of the sea. She was not sure if she liked it or not, but she kept drawing the air in as deeply as possible in order to taste it more fully. Slava had only the haziest conception of what the sea might be, and it seemed to her that if she could just capture the essence of this elusive scent, she would know what to expect when they arrived at Vostochnoye Selo.

Chapter Nine

A fine snow sifted down all day, but not enough to prevent them from making good time. The men chattered exuberantly about the soft treatment they would be receiving at Vostochnoye Selo, and Slava listened in eagerly, although in truth she was eager to reach their destination more out of curiosity than a desire to finish their day's journey. She was now fit enough that, while riding was not yet quite as comfortable as sitting in a soft chair, she could ride all day without being in extreme pain, and it was in fact even enjoyable at times. The day had a kind of holiday atmosphere that made Slava sorry to think of it ending, despite her keen anticipation of their arrival and her first sight of the fabled Vostochnoye Selo. Only Olga appeared to grow ever more morose as the day wore on. Every now and then she would clutch her right arm to her chest, and then drop it to her side and shake her head angrily.

They trotted through more and more villages, drawing admiring cries from the children playing on the road. As darkness set in, Slava thought she could see the sunset glowing before them, but then realized that she was looking North—she had also learned how to tell direction since she had been on the road—and that the glow must be the fires of Vostochnoye Selo.

"Is that it?" she asked Grisha, pointing.

"It is, Krasna Tsarina," he told her, his nose wrinkling. "I can smell its stink from here."

"Vostochnoye Selo does have a nasty stink," said Olga, wrinkling her nose with a force all out of proportion to the actual strength of the odor, especially considering all the odors coming from closer by. Although Slava would never say so to Grisha, the sheepskin jacket he wore emitted a very powerful smell, which made his complaints of the stink of cities somewhat amusing to her, although after more than two weeks away from Krasnograd, she, too, had grown accustomed to breathing fresh air, and always felt as though she were choking whenever she rode into a settlement. Now she could also smell the privies and stables the town was full of, but even that was overpowered by the mysterious sea-scent that had been growing in the air all day.

Vostochnoye Selo was, Slava saw as they drew nearer and the town's fires became brighter, a small kremlin on a bluff overlooking the sea, surrounded by a sprawling collection of buildings apparently built at random, connected by winding streets. Princess Primorskaya was a fairly minor princess who had a small piece of territory carved out of Pristanogradskoye, the province from which Slava's own family had originally come before Miroslava Praskovyevna had captured Krasnograd and united Zem'.

Vostochnoye Selo was, as its name suggested, little more than a village on the Eastern shore of the Breathing Sea, and its kremlin was really more of a large house or a small palace than a true fortress. There was a stockade around it that was no more impressive than the stockades around the cabins in the woods. Thus far, Slava had to admit, Vostochnoye Selo had not lived up to her expectations, especially as, after one brief glimpse, they rode out of sight of the sea.

Two rather shabby-looking guards were sitting at the gate, checking travelers with a minimum of enthusiasm. They livened up a little at the sight of such a large party, accompanied by two noblewomen, and when Olga told them, in answer to their question about their reasons for coming to Vostochnoye Selo, that they were going to visit Princess Primorskaya, they stood up in something that almost resembled attention.

"Just follow the main street, it'll take you right up to the kremlin, noblewoman," said the more senior-looking of the two guards. "It winds around a bit, but just keep going uphill and you'll find it." Both guards bowed deeply as they opened the gate to let them through, although Slava saw them both slump back down into their previous poses of indifference once they had closed the gate behind them. Now that she thought about it, she supposed being a gate guard would be one of the more tedious occupations a person could have, and sitting out all day or night in the cold would not be pleasant either.

She suddenly wondered how many gate guards there were in Krasnograd, and what their lives were like. Perhaps, she told herself, she should find out once she returned, although what she would do if she didn't like what she found, she didn't know. One of the reasons Slava did so little in Krasnograd was because there was so little she had the power to do, and so even starting something was rarely worth the effort. She should try to find something useful, some worthwhile endeavor, once she returned, she told herself, so that all this newfound strength she had gained on her journey would not go to waste. Then she realized she was daydreaming instead of seeing the sights of Vostochnoye Selo, and trained her gaze outwards, rather than inwards, as firmly as she could.

As the guard had said, the main street wound around a bit, but Olga led them confidently through each turn. When Slava remarked on her knowledge of Vostochnoye Selo, Olga said shortly that she had been there many times before, and left it at that.

The kremlin itself was guarded by much more alert-looking guards than the town had been. They questioned Olga about her reasons for coming there and then told the party to wait while they made sure that Princess Primorskaya was, in fact, ready to welcome Olga Vasilisovna Severnolesnaya, although they bowed very deeply as they pronounced Olga's name. Slava couldn't tell whether their respect was for Olga Vasilisovna, as kin by marriage, in particular, or for the Severnolesnaya name in general. The Severnolesniye were much greater princesses than the Primorskiye, not that the Primorskiye would ever admit it. Olga did not, Slava noticed, explain who she, Slava, was, other than to call her "my traveling companion, the noblewoman Krasnoslava."

They received permission to come in much more quickly than Slava had been expecting, and at least a dozen very attentive grooms came and relieved them of their horses, while half-a-dozen more attentive servants came and showed them into Princess Primorskaya's palace, the first building they had stayed at since they left Krasnograd that, despite its small size compared with many of the palaces in Krasnograd, could legitimately be given that title.

Once inside, the men were led off down one corridor, presumably towards the barracks, while Slava and Olga were taken by two serving women up a flight of stairs and down another corridor to what must have been the guest quarters.

"If you will follow me, noblewoman," said the serving woman who had apparently taken personal charge of Slava, bowing and opening a door for her.

Slava stopped and looked questioningly at Olga, taken aback at being separated like this.

"Princess Primorskaya's palace is fine enough to allow each guest her own bedroom," said Olga, although she sounded grimmer than Slava would have expected as she said it. As soon as they had stepped through the doors into the palace, her face had pinched shut, and it was still pinched shut, as if she expected attack to come at any moment from some unexpected quarter, possibly within.

"Indeed it is, Olga Vasilisovna," said the other serving woman, with a small bow. Slava allowed her own serving woman to lead her into her bedroom, while Olga carried on down the hall.

"Olga Vasilisovna will be in the next room, noblewoman," the servant assured Slava, bustling around the room and checking that everything was in order.

Slava looked around. Although not nearly so fine as her own rooms back home in Krasnograd, of course, it was still much nicer than any place she had stayed since leaving, and she felt rather awkward and out of place in her dirty traveling clothes. This must have been apparent from her face, for the serving woman said, "They have already started heating the bathhouse, noblewoman, and there are clean clothes in that wardrobe there. Shall I unpack for you?"

"No, thank you," said Slava, who had no desire for a serving woman to go rummaging through the dirty, jumbled mess that her travel bags had become. "I can do it myself. How do I get to the bathhouse from here?"

"I'll show you myself, noblewoman, for it's quite twisty," said the serving woman. "Would you like to go down now?"

"Very much," said Slava, who was becoming ever more aware of how dirty and tired she was with every passing breath she spent in civilized surroundings.

"Follow me, then, noblewoman," said the serving woman, and, gathering up clean clothes for Slava, led her out of her room and down several corridors and staircases that were in fact quite twisty, through a covered passageway across the courtyard, and into the steaming bathhouse.

"Olga Vasilisovna is already here, noblewoman," Slava was told as she was led into the antechamber of the bathhouse. "Enjoy your steam, and call me when you are finished."

Olga was indeed already naked and in the bath, although she had thrown so much water on the rocks that she was almost impossible to make out through all the billowing clouds of steam. Slava stumbled to the bench and lay down, hiding her face in a towel in order to be able to breathe.

"Too hot?" asked Olga after a while, as if she had not noticed Slava coming in at first.

"Oh no," gasped Slava.

"Good," said Olga, and went back to contemplating the clouds of steam. Every now and then she would rub her right arm as if it pained her, although Slava had never seen her favor it before today, and she knew of no accident that would cause it to pain her.

Slava was glad not to be forced to talk, and therefore inhale more steam, but she was a little surprised at Olga's taciturn behavior. Was it really all just because of another bad dream? Had Slava in some way angered her in her absence? Slava could not think how she might have done that. Then she remembered Olga's grimness on the ride there, and the respectful treatment they had received from the guards, and decided that Olga's kinship with the family was not a happy one. Slava thought about waiting for the steam to clear a little, and then asking Olga tactfully about it, but before she could do so, Olga murmured, "I'm leaving," and left.

Between the stories about bath-spirits and the possibility of fainting, Slava had never liked steaming by herself, so she left the bathhouse shortly after Olga, even though she would have liked to have steamed longer, now that the bathhouse air had cooled to a breathable temperature. She also suspected, though, that supper would be served shortly, and that she would not be allowed to tarry too long there in any case.

The serving woman, she discovered, had indeed been waiting for her in the antechamber, anxious for Slava to finish her steam and allow herself to be dressed in time for supper. She helped Slava into several very thick robes before permitting her to return to her room. Once there she insisted on dressing Slava for dinner herself, and did so with a skill Slava had not at all expected to find in an out-of-the-way place like Vostochnoye Selo. Apparently Princess Primorskaya expected her maids to be as skilled as those in the capital. Having dressed her, the well-trained maid escorted Slava down to where supper was being served.

Slava was impressed by the care exerted by Princess Primorskaya's servants, but she also noted that she had never been allowed to be by herself since she had arrived. She couldn't tell from the serving woman's demeanor if this was out of concern for her safety or in order to prevent her from spying.

The serving woman led Slava through what must have been the palace's great hall and into a side-room, almost entirely filled by a small table set for three. Olga was already sitting there, looking stony-faced.

"Did you have a nice steam?" she asked Slava when she came into the room, without looking up from her plate.

"Yes," said Slava, not wanting to complain that it had been cut short.

"Good," said Olga, and went back to staring at her plate in silence.

There was a sudden bustle outside the door, and then two serving women escorted an extremely imperious-looking woman who must have been Princess Primorskaya to the third seat at the table. Olga and Slava both rose and bowed to her, which she answered by a brief nod of the head before sitting down.

"Is supper ready?" she demanded of the serving women.

"Momentarily, Princess," said one.

"Well, bring it out. I don't feel like waiting!"

The two serving women bowed and retreated, looking deeply impressed by their mistress's dislike of waiting. Only once they were gone did Princess Primorskaya turn her attention to Olga and Slava.

"So, Olga, off adventuring again," she said, in a voice that made it clear she had known Olga since she had learned to walk.

"Yes, Vladislava Vladislavovna," answered Olga in a flat voice that made it clear she did not appreciate being known since she had learned to walk. Her usual shield of good humor had slipped off, revealing a much harder and angrier person than Slava had seen before. She clutched for a moment at her right arm, and then, with an angry shake of her head, forced herself to let go.

"And what does Princess Severnolesnaya think of this?"

"I am no longer a little girl," said Olga, not looking at Princess Primorskaya directly. "I have no need of my mother's approval for my every action."

"Well, at least she already has an heir," said Princess Primorskaya. "But if you were my daughter, even a younger daughter, I wouldn't let you go regardless. What if something happened to your sister? You should keep that in mind, the next time you're tempted to go chasing after white bears or wood-spirits or the gods know what. And tell me, how fares Vasilisa Olgovna?"

"Well," answered Olga, and shut her mouth firmly. Slava tried to guess who Vasilisa Olgovna was. Surely not...

"And how would you know that?" demanded Princess Primorskaya. "Since you spend all your time running around with your lovers instead of watching over your only daughter?"

"Vasilisa Olgovna is a woman grown, and well cared for besides," said Olga, while Slava tried to grapple with the fact that Olga had a grown daughter.

"Only because your mother has taken charge of her," said Princess Primorskaya. "Of course, if I were her, I would have done the same. But I'm surprised she hasn't insisted on more where she came from, considering your sister's weakness in body and spirit."

"My sister has an heir," said Olga. It was hard to tell in the candlelight, but Slava thought that red patches were appearing on her neck and face. She moved as if she wanted to rub her right arm again, but thought better of it.

"Well yes, one sickly little girl in between four dead boys."

"My sister is not sickly, and neither is my niece."

"Well, given her father, it's only a matter of time before she loses her wits entirely. They say your sister set aside her halfwit husband after the last stillbirth and took a soldier as a lover in hopes of getting another heir; is that true?"

"Unfortunately not," said Olga, her eyes firmly fixed on the tablecloth.

"Yes, I suppose if she had, you would have had something in common to talk about. Tell me, how is our Andrey Vladislavovich these days? Is your mother still keeping him as a pet?"

"Andrey Vladislavovich will always have a home with her, as you well know," said Olga.

"Well, it's not uncommon for a mother to prefer her son-in-law to her daughter," said Princess Primorskaya, nodding sagely. "And with Vasilisa Vasilisovna's husband in such a sad state, perhaps your sister prefers to keep a real man around the kremlin, too. Tell me, Olga: what does your mother think of—what's his name? Dima, is it not? One of the men currently eating supper in my barracks? What does she think of him? Especially since he has yet to provide her with another granddaughter."

To Slava's profound relief, since it seemed very possible that Olga was going to leap up and strangle Princess Primorskaya across the table, at that moment supper was brought in. However, the relief was short-lived, for as soon as the dishes had been set out, Princess Primorskaya ordered the servants to leave, saying she was perfectly capable of serving such a small number of guests herself, especially as they were used to rough living, and then went back to needling Olga.

Over the course of the supper, of which no one ate very much—Olga and Princess Primorskaya were too caught up in their battle to pay any heed to the food, and Slava, even though she had no stake in this fight, felt too ill from the hateful air around them to do more than pick miserably at her food—she implied in as many ways as she could possibly manage that Olga was a thoughtless, ungrateful daughter and a selfish, irresponsible mother, so that it was no wonder that her mother preferred her son-in-law to her own daughter, and that Dima was certain to be unfaithful to Olga—in fact, that he was probably in the arms of some serving girl at this very moment.

After a while both Princess Primorskaya and Olga gave up any pretense at being polite, so that Princess Primorskaya's insults became more and more open, and Olga's refusal to respond to them became more and more pointed, until in the end Olga was ignoring Princess Primorskaya completely, while Princess Primorskaya shouted at her, "I told your mother she should have had you beaten more often, I even offered to do it myself, but she wouldn't listen, and now see how you've turned out! She should have whipped you until you couldn't walk, I told her a thousand times, but she always turned a blind eye to your blatant misbehavior, you insufferable girl! Well, I hope she's happy! I hope she knows she got what she deserved! No daughter of mine...!"

"But you have no daughters," said Olga, standing up abruptly. "If you will excuse us, we should go to bed. We must depart early tomorrow. Come, Slava." And she took Slava's arm and marched out of the room before Princess Primorskaya could utter another word.

Olga didn't let go of Slava's arm until they had arrived in Slava's bedroom, where Olga sat her down on the bed and shut the door behind them. Then she paced around the room several times while Slava watched, bewildered but also burning with curiosity.

"I suppose you wonder what that was all about," said Olga eventually.

"Yes," admitted Slava. "Although I guessed some of it," she added.

"Well...Well, I suppose I should tell you the whole sorry tale, so you know what you've landed yourself in here. I'm sorry, Slava, not to have warned you beforehand. I know I should have, but...most people in the North know, and it isn't something I like to talk about."

"If it pains you...and I knew that you were kin by marriage with Princess Primorskaya, I had just assumed that you had set your husband aside, and it was all ancient history. But if speaking of it pains you..."

"It shouldn't," said Olga, shaking her shoulders angrily and rubbing her right arm. "It's all ancient history, like you said yourself, and shouldn't affect me at all. It's just...Well, I'll tell you, and you can judge for yourself.

"As you probably already knew, I have an older sister, so I was never much more than a hanger-on in Lesnograd...But no matter. The fact is that my sister has never been very strong, whereas I...Well, you've traveled with me. My sister's father died shortly after she was born, and my mother took a lover to get another heir. She even married him, so that there wouldn't be even a shadow of a doubt on her intention to acknowledge me as heir, should the rule of Lesnograd need to pass to me or my daughters.

"I only knew him when I was quite young," continued Olga after a short pause. "My father, that is. He was a hunter, and one day he didn't come back from the hunt. But they say I'm just like him in every way.

"My sister and I've always been complete opposites, so that you'd never guess we were even of the same family, let alone sisters. We both took strongly after our fathers, something I think irritated our mother, although she's an irritable woman in general, so I can't say for certain.

"My mother and Princess Primorskaya were girlhood friends—Princess Primorskaya was fostered at Lesnograd—and they married two brothers, both of whom died young. Instead of bringing them closer together, however, this has been a source of constant strife between them ever since. They both claim to have been extremely attached to these husbands, and they quarreled bitterly over what to do once they had been widowed.

"My mother, as I said, had only one daughter at the time, who was not strong, and Princess Primorskaya had only a son, who was also not strong. Even so, Princess Primorskaya was vehemently opposed to dishonoring her husband's memory by remarrying or taking a lover. She proposed marrying her son to my sister in order to keep the lands and title within the family, but my mother refused, as they were brother and sister, even if only through their fathers. In the end she decided to have me, despite Princess Primorskaya's protests.

"Once I was born, though, Princess Primorskaya became reconciled to my existence when they agreed to marry me off to her son. She even wanted to raise me herself, in order to bring up a better daughter-in-law, but my mother for once in her life did something for my benefit, and refused.

"I was," Olga smiled, "as you might guess, a very rowdy and difficult child, and grew up into a willful and difficult young woman. But for once in *my* life I did something for my mother's benefit, and when I was sixteen I did indeed marry Andrey Vladislavovich, and less than a year later produced a granddaughter, who at the time was heir not only to Princess Primorskaya but to my own mother as well."

Olga stopped and stared at the wall for a long time, before shaking her head and continuing, her right arm pressed against her chest as if it ached fiercely.

"Since then my sister has managed to produce an heir, to everyone's immense relief." Olga stopped again and swallowed. Slava was about to reach out and tell her not to go on if it caused her such pain, when Olga squared her shoulders and began speaking again. "But as soon as my daughter was weaned, my mother took her away from me, saying that I could not be trusted to care for something so precious.

"Frankly speaking, I never took much to motherhood, and I didn't protest too much. Think of me what you will. I also had nothing but contempt for Andrey Vladislavovich. He is," Olga made a pained face, trying to describe her husband.

"I realize I have no right to criticize him," she said eventually. "After all, I left him for no reason other than I despise him, and I acknowledge that I am in the wrong before him and before his mother. Nevertheless, I cannot describe him as anything other than exactly the wrong kind of husband for me. Whenever anyone does anything," and Slava could hear irritation rising in Olga's voice at the mere thought of her husband's behavior, despite her best efforts to suppress it, "he demands that he be included in it, that he be consulted and his opinion respected, no matter how foolish his thoughts on the subject are. He thinks only of himself and his own pleasure, and never of how much he might be inconveniencing others.

"And if anyone should try to leave him out, he sulks and moans and cries and...Well, I'm sure you've seen similar behavior in other men. He's so afraid of being ignored that he always has to be in the center of everything, and can never bear the thought that others might act without him, that others might have some duties or other business that doesn't include him. He can never leave anyone in peace for a moment, nor can he obey any command without a thousand cries, complaints, arguments, and objections. Frankly, I'm astonished he ever managed to marry me: he must have been desperate to get out from under his mother's thumb, that's all I can say.

"Anyway, less than two years after we were married I had, in effect, no daughter to occupy me, and no duties as the heir either, leaving me with nothing to do but dwell on my husband's imperfections, which were many.

"As you might have noticed," Olga smiled at the thought of her own imperfections, "I don't suffer foolishness gladly, or at all, really, and so in a very short time my husband and I were completely separated, and in a very short time after that I was already eyeing other men. And then my mother needed someone to ride to the edge of her territory in order to deal with some trouble on the border, and I forced the party to take me with them.

"And I have been off 'adventuring,' as Princess Primorskaya calls it, ever since, more than twenty years now. Andrey Vladislavovich still lives with my mother, where he is, as Princess Primorskaya says, her beloved 'pet.' There are also rumors of a connection between him and my sister, but I don't know what to think of that...Both of them are so finicky, I have a hard time imagining them nerving themselves up for something like that, but who's to say...My daughter is being raised as the spare heir in case something should happen to my sickly sister or her sickly daughter. Actually, neither of them is really sickly, but my sister has always been prone to hysteria, and her daughter's father is a half-wit, so everyone is always waiting with bated breath to see if she will manifest her father's weakness.

"But you can see why I cannot shun Princess Primorskaya, much as I would like to, whenever I come near Vostochnoye Selo, and why she treats me the way she does. Both she and my mother are women of very difficult character, I'm afraid to say, and neither of them has known what to do with me since the day I was born. When they are not deploring my admittedly deplorable behavior, they like to bemoan my lack of obedience and compare it unfavorably to the behavior of their husbands and my sister and husband, all of whom were and are models of meekness and obedience, at least according to them. Well, all I can say is: look what it has brought them! My mother took my father because she wanted a strong child, and she got what she wanted, for all the joy it has brought her. But I hope you see why I concealed your name, now—I couldn't stand to have you dragged into this family quarrel. I'd like to think my mother and my mother-in-law aren't dangerous, just annoying, but I can't trust them in anything that concerns me."

Olga finished the recital of her family history, looking almost as flushed as she had while being criticized by Princess Primorskaya, and gave Slava a look that Slava saw was both defiant and pleading.

"We can none of us choose our mothers or our sisters, unfortunately," Slava said. Although she had learned that sharing what she thought of someone was often a poor idea, as honesty was rarely as welcome as people claimed it to be, she decided to venture it in this case, and continued, "and Princess Primorskaya is a very unpleasant person, and I am sure her son is equally as bad, and so who can blame you for how things have turned out? When you find yourself a tool in the hands of bad people, sometimes you have no choice but to rebel."

"What do you know of rebelling?" said Olga, almost, despite her sad story, laughing at the idea.

"When I was not much older than you were when you were married, my mother...became concerned that I would never produce an heir, or even...warm up to men, and at my sister's instigation she plied me with vodka until I was well-nigh insensible to my surroundings, and locked me in a room with someone—some guard who had been chosen for the sorry task. I have often wondered who he was, and how he was chosen, and how he felt about it, and if I will ever be able to forgive him, but thus far I have never received an answer to any of those questions. I remember very little of it, thank the gods. Just, well...I saw his uniform when he came in the room and thought he must have come to take me to my mother..."—Slava choked on a sob for a moment, hating herself for wanting to cry over something that had happened so many years ago, and that she barely remembered in the first place—"I'm not even sure I would know him again if I saw him, and I know I've never seen anyone I took to be him.

"When I regained my senses, he was gone, but I knew what had happened...I ran, somehow I slipped away and I ran to an herbwoman I knew, who gave me moldy rye just in case and kept me until my mother came and got down on her knees and begged for my forgiveness, with tears coursing down her face...I never gave it to her, of course, but I consented to return with her and not to expose her terrible deed to the world, and after that I knew...I knew that not even those closest to us can be trusted to see to our interests...and after that no one dared try such a trick again. Even my sister, who keeps nagging me to get a child, hasn't dared it, and neither of them have ever spoken of it since, nor, as far as I know, shared our secret with anyone else.

"Not that most of the princesses would care much one way or the other, except to say that I had brought it upon myself, most likely—after all, if they could tell themselves that, they could tell themselves that nothing of the sort would ever happen to them or their daughters—but my father's kin, the steppe...I swore that day that if any of them ever even thought such thoughts about me again, I would run to my father's family and raise the steppe against them and never rest until there was nothing left of Krasnograd but smoke and ash, and they knew I spoke truly. The steppe is always restless, and if Princess Stepnaya ever learned that such a cruelty had been visited upon her beloved brother's only daughter, she would rise from her sickbed and set fire to the kremlin herself. Even Krasnograd fears the steppe, and rightly so. So you see, sometimes it pays to rebel—even I can attest to that."

"I wish *I* had thought of that," said Olga, sounding impressed at Slava's temerity, and not in the least compassionate for her suffering. "But your mother! I thought she was supposed to be good!"

"Even good mothers may do bad things, when they think they are acting for the best," said Slava. "And there was always something in me that she was afraid of, something more of spirit than of flesh, that she desperately wanted to drive out, and she would stoop to any cruelty to do so, even though all the things she professed to dislike about me, that she wished to expel from my mind and body, were all the things that I had inherited from her...she loved my sister for not resembling her, and sometimes she hated me for being so much like her.

"Sometimes I think what she really wanted was a son, someone she could love as her creation without being forced to confront what she had created in her own image—reminding her of all the things she hated about herself. But mothers are always afraid their daughters will make the same mistakes they have, and so they lead them at all speed straight to the same thorn thicket that their mothers led them to, and abandon them there to suffer with the same sense of a deed well done."

"Well, at least I can't blame myself for that," said Olga, brightening up even more. "At least I haven't forced some man upon my daughter—other than her own father, that is, and I can't seem to get rid of him, and she doesn't even seem to want to, as poorly as he treats her. Home is a sorry place, especially when there's family there, and the less said about it, the better, that's what I say."

"Well, you got away in the end," said Slava. She wasn't sure whether to be sorry or glad that she could recite her story without hardly even a quaver in her voice by now.

"I did, true enough," agreed Olga. "I suppose we all get away in the end!"

Slava's words seemed to cheer Olga up even more than she had expected, and after a few more bracing comments about escape from bad situations, she left Slava's room in an almost calm frame of mind.

The next morning Olga came into Slava's room very early, saying that they needed to pack up and leave as soon as possible, as they had another long day ahead of them. Slava had barely even gotten out of bed when a serving woman came with the message that Princess Primorskaya was unwell and would be unable to join them for breakfast.

"Send her our regrets," said Olga, dismissing the serving woman. "Probably just wants our sympathy," she said to Slava as soon as the serving woman had left. "That's the way she is," she added. "I wasn't contrite enough last night, and I didn't let her torture me enough, so now she's trying to make me feel guilty about going off so soon."

Olga looked so angry that Slava would have liked to tell her she was mistaken, but judging by what she had seen of Princess Primorskaya the night before, she was probably right. Slava decided the best way to show her sympathy would be by packing as quickly as she could.

Before she had finished, however, the serving woman returned with another message, this time for Slava, in the form of a note, which said only:

Come see me at your earliest convenience. Primorskaya

Slava read the note and showed it to Olga, who shrugged and said, "You'd probably better go. I'll finish your packing—I'll do a better job anyway."

Since this was true, Slava let the serving woman lead her down several winding corridors to Princess Primorskaya's private quarters.

The serving woman brought Slava into a sitting room, poured her tea, and left her by herself.

The tea was still much too hot to drink, so Slava spent the time that Princess Primorskaya kept her waiting by looking around. The room was paneled with bright birch wood, the floor was covered with the skins of white bears, and the roaring fire in the fireplace was making it almost uncomfortably hot. Everything was spotlessly clean. It was exactly the kind of Northern splendor Slava would have imagined someone living in Vostochnoye Selo to have, while still being attractive. Slava was forced to admit that, whatever other flaws she might have, Princess Primorskaya had good taste.

"Ah, you're here? Good." Princess Primorskaya came sweeping into the room. Now that Slava was able to look at her objectively, instead of being transfixed by her rudeness, she saw that Princess Primorskaya had once been beautiful, but that years of bitterness and brooding had cut ugly-looking grooves across her handsome features, so that now all anyone could see was her bad temper. Slava promptly resolved to spend less time frowning and more time smiling.

"I don't think we were ever properly introduced," continued Princess Primorskaya, walking over to the tea table. Even the way she poured herself tea held an air of command. "Olga, silly girl that she is, didn't bother with trifles like that."

Slava rose and bowed slightly. "Krasnoslava," she said.

"They say"—Princess Primorskaya fixed Slava with a look that on a less impressive woman would have been greedy—"all the servants are abuzz with the rumor that has leaked from the barracks and taken over the entire kremlin—that you are not just any Krasnoslava, but in fact Krasnoslava Tsarinovna, younger sister to the Empress herself. Is that true?"

"It is, Princess."

"And Olga somehow failed to mention this?"

"She didn't want me to be drawn into her family troubles," said Slava.

"You don't look much like a Tsarinovna," said Princess Primorskaya, apparently not hearing a word that Slava had said. "Although... Come closer."

Slava obediently walked over to Princess Primorskaya, who leaned in towards her and examined her face carefully.

"Yes," she said after a while. "You have the Zerkalitsa eyes, there's no doubt about it. Wolf eyes. With a slant from the steppe. Tell me, little Tsarinovna, is it true what they say about you? About why you are so feared back in Krasnograd? Can you truly read other people's minds?"

"Not their minds, only their hearts," Slava told her.

"Really? Have any of your foremothers ever had that gift? I have never heard of it before."

"I don't know," said Slava. "And..." She didn't know why she was telling Princess Primorskaya this, but she went ahead anyway. "I don't know if it is a gift like farseeing or foreseeing, or any of the other talents my foremothers had. It doesn't seem like magic to me. I just see more clearly than anyone else."

"Really? How so?" To Slava's surprise, Princess Primorskaya looked interested.

"I know what other people are feeling when I am standing next to them," explained Slava, "but there doesn't seem to me to be anything magical about it. If you were to ask me how I knew that someone was feeling something, I would tell you that her eyes made a certain shape, and then her shoulders sat in a certain way, and her voice had a certain sound, and then my eyes made the same shape, and my shoulders sat in the same way, and my voice had the same sound, and then she and I were feeling the same thing. But it only lasts as long as we're standing next to each other, which is why people still surprise me all the time: they feel one thing when they're next to me, and then as soon as they go away they feel something else entirely and do something completely unexpected. And it doesn't seem to me like there's anything magical about what I can do; after all, dogs and horses can do exactly the same thing."

"True," said Princess Primorskaya. "Tell me, little Tsarinovna, do you enjoy your gift? For magical or not, a gift it is. I doubt there is one woman in a thousand who could do as you do. So do you feel gifted?"

"It's horrible," said Slava. "Like being possessed by every person who happens to walk by. And they're all...I'm sorry to say this, but they're all so much nastier than I am—not so much more evil, exactly, but just so petty and stupid, or, I don't know...I hate myself so much for the evil I cause others, but they cause me and everyone else around them so much evil themselves that I cannot...I cannot imagine how much they must hate themselves, so much more than I do. I can feel their terror, their constant terror of being found out by anyone, including themselves, and...and I cannot imagine what it must be like to be them. How awful it must be to be them."

"I can," said Princess Primorskaya dryly. She gave Slava a look that was equal parts pity and scorn: pity for her suffering, and scorn for the softness that caused her to suffer.

"So that it makes me feel dirty on the inside even to be in the same room with them, and full of rage at myself for feeling that way, and drowning in pity for them, even if they seem to have so little pity for me," Slava continued. "But I don't know if I would give it up. If you lived in a dungeon, would you give up the use of your eyes?"

Slava realized she was looking up at Princess Primorskaya, who was much taller than she was, with a pleading look in her eyes, like someone trying to persuade a lover, and made herself stop.

"They also say," said Princess Primorskaya, "that, despite your claims not to be magical, you had an...encounter in the woods with what might have been wood-spirits. Is this true?"

"Yes," admitted Slava.

Princess Primorskaya paced around the room a few times. "Well, I suppose it matters not," she said eventually. "Tell me, little Tsarinovna: why did you come on this expedition? What did my dear daughter-in-law do to make you join in this rash venture?"

"Well," said Slava, "it's good to travel across the motherland, to meet with princesses and noblewomen and judge the state of Zem'."

"And this is something you can do better than your sister, the Empress?"

"Oh yes," said Slava. "After all, wherever my sister goes, everyone kneels at her feet and calls her 'Empress' and dares not speak the truth, whereas wherever I go, princesses of Northern backwaters such as Vostochnoye Selo summon me summarily to their chambers and call me 'little Tsarinovna.' I say I see a much clearer picture of our motherland than my sister ever will."

Princess Primorskaya looked like she had just bitten into rotten cabbage, but only for a moment. "I can see why no one really likes you, little Tsarinovna," she said, once she had regained the use of her voice.

"Yes, so can I," agreed Slava.

"And I don't think that was really why you chose to go off on my daughter-in-law's harebrained journey."

"Well, that's none of your business anyway," said Slava. Princess Primorskaya's behavior was having a remarkably bracing effect on her. Part of her couldn't believe she was doing what she was doing, while another part of her felt as if it had just stretched out newfound wings. This, she thought, must have been what her sister had been talking about: to be able to see what other people thought about you but not to care.

"You *are* a Tsarinovna after all," said Princess Primorskaya, sounding impressed. Slava found it difficult not to roll her eyes at how easy it had been to impress Princess Primorskaya with a little rudeness, when kindness and good manners had had so little effect. "So tell me, little Tsarinovna who can see into the hearts of others: what can you tell me about my daughter-in-law?" Princess Primorskaya went on. "How much hope should my son have that she will drop this disgusting... companion and return to the man who is lawfully hers?"

"Very little," Slava told her.

"But there is still some? Or were you just being kind?"

"I was just being kind," said Slava.

"Olga has always been a thorn in everyone's sides," said Princess Primorskaya. "I told her mother not to take that peasant boy as her husband, but did she listen? No she did not. And then she got a daughter off of him who was even worse than he was himself. This is why you need to be careful in choosing men. A husband or a lover you can set aside, but any daughter you get off of them is yours for life. And Olga lived up to my predictions: willful, stubborn, unfaithful..."

"Probably waiting for me impatiently," Slava interrupted her.

"What?"

"Olga is probably waiting for me impatiently," Slava repeated. "We have a long day ahead of us, and we need to set off." She rose and made as if to leave the room.

"Wait!" cried Princess Primorskaya.

Slava stopped.

"I called you here for a reason, and not to question you about my daughter-in-law, feckless and irritating as she is. Since it cannot possibly be her good heart that has brought you on this journey, tell me truthfully: why have you come?"

"Why?" asked Slava.

"Why?" repeated Princess Primorskaya, puzzled.

"Why do you want to know? And why should I tell you?"

"Tell me, little Tsarinovna: what do you know of Princess Severnolesnaya?"

"Olga's mother?" asked Slava, now puzzled herself.

"That's right, Olga's mother and my sister-in-law. Well, former sister-in-law, before she chose to dishonor our husbands' memories and take that brash peasant into her home and her bed and bloodline...

but no matter. What do you know of her? Are you frequently in contact with her?"

"No," said Slava, growing ever more puzzled. She could tell that Princess Primorskaya was deeply interested in her connection with Princess Severnolesnaya, but she couldn't tell why. She remembered Dima quizzing her on their first day out about Princess Severnolesnaya. He had never explained why he had wanted to know. Slava would have assumed it was simply because of his connection to Olga, except that now Princess Primorskaya, who, it seemed, was Princess Severnolesnaya's oldest and closest friend, was also asking questions about her. And Princess Malogornaya had made strange, cryptic remarks as well...Slava had never been very adept at playing political games, but a lifetime in Krasnograd had taught her to sense one within a few heartbeats, and unless she was greatly mistaken, a very deep one was being played here.

"I really must leave," she said.

"And your...incident in the forest?" asked Princess Primorskaya. Her cheeks were flushed, and her movements were those of a woman clutching at any support. "The sudden increase in your abilities, as soon as you are out of your sister's sight? What about that? Very suspicious, I would call it. Don't tell me that had nothing to do with it!"

"With what?" asked Slava. "What could that have anything to do with Olga's mother?"

"You don't mean to claim you have no ambitions of your own! You don't mean to claim that you are only acting out of loyalty to your sister!"

"Of course," said Slava, still mystified, although feeling sicker and sicker from the underhanded scheming she could feel looming over her. "How else would I act? And what has that to do with Princess Severnolesnaya?"

Princess Primorskaya shook her head, but in answer to her own thoughts, not anything Slava had said. "You must be right," she said. "That had nothing to do with anything. Princess Severnolesnaya has never been a friend to your family, and I thought...You would not be the first Tsarinovna to hanker for the title of Tsarina...Forgive a mother's care, Krasnoslava Tsarinovna: I am only trying to find out as much as I can about the woman who is supposed to be taking care of my son. Please, let me see you out."

She took Slava's arm and steered her solicitously towards the door, but Slava could see that she was still deeply suspicious, and was certain that Slava had been lying. Slava thought about asking her straight out what schemes she thought Slava and Princess Severnolesnaya had been hatching together, but she could see by Princess Primorskaya's face that such a question would be a waste of time.

Everyone else had in fact already been long ready to leave, and so all Slava had to do was put on her outer clothes and go down to where the horses were waiting. Princess Primorskaya walked her right up to her stirrup, watching her closely all the while. Slava could still feel her eyes on them as they rode out of the kremlin and into the town.

Chapter Ten

They were a silent party as they walked down the winding streets to the town gates. The raw salt-smelling wind coming off the sea would have been reason enough to keep quiet, but Slava could see that everyone was bursting to talk but didn't dare until they were clear of Vostochnoye Selo.

The guards bowed respectfully as they let them out, and they immediately picked up a brisk trot, still not talking. Slava was glad, as she was still savoring the sensation of speaking her mind to someone, and the silence allowed her to do it more fully. She wondered if her sudden boldness with Princess Primorskaya had been an aberration, or if she were indeed growing braver. She hoped it was the latter, although the thought of being a brave person was such a strange one that she could hardly take it in.

It was not until the town walls were almost out of sight that the men started abusing the hospitality they had received, with only Dima, Olga, and Slava remaining silent. It seemed that the servants had been slow and unwilling, and every time they had done anything, they had reminded Olga's men of the transgression Olga had committed against the Primorskaya family, with such hostility that half the men had been afraid to eat the food they had been served, and they had been forced to brag of having a Tsarinovna in the party in order to be certain that they would not be poisoned with their tea.

"I'm sorry, boys," Olga said. "You shouldn't have had to suffer because of my guilt."

This brought on a bout of the most vehement swearing Slava had ever heard, the gist of which being that the people of Vostochnoye Selo, and Princess Primorskaya in particular, were the kind of dirt that

Olga shouldn't even have to clean off her boots, and if she should ever want to put the Primorskiye and Vostochnoye Selo in their place, she knew whom to ask. Misha also offered to introduce her husband's face to "a real man's fists," an offer everyone other than Dima all loudly seconded, so that quarreling broke out over who would have the honor of kicking him from here to Krasnograd and back, until he learned not to go sniveling to his mother because he wasn't man enough to satisfy a woman like Olga Vasilisovna.

Slava watched with a mixture of amusement, admiration, and horror. She was impressed by the men's show of devotion to Olga, which she knew was genuine, and horrified at their obvious willingness to beat Olga's husband to a pulp just because he had had the misfortune to have an unfaithful wife. Despite being Olga's friend, Slava could not, of course, help being sorry for her husband, and the men's extravagant plans for violence against him left her rather sickened. She supposed that she had not, in fact, changed all that much, her conversation with Princess Primorskaya notwithstanding. She was both disappointed and relieved: disappointed because for a moment she had thought that the terrible burden of always feeling more for the other person had been lifted, and relieved because she doubted she would like the person she would become if that were ever to happen.

Eventually the men's bloodlust abated, and they started singing, even though the cold wind off the sea whipped all the words out of their mouths. This allowed Slava to ride up to Olga and speak to her without being overheard.

"I was very surprised when Princess Primorskaya asked to speak with me this morning," she began.

"Never be surprised by anything she does," said Olga, who was now in a very good mood after the loud show of support she had just received.

"Well, I was even more surprised by the questions she asked me," Slava continued.

"Really? What did she want to know?"

"Oh, she asked me if I really was who I am, and things like that, and then she wanted to know what I knew about Princess Severnolesnaya, and if I was in contact with her."

"My mother?" asked Olga, frowning. "Why would you be in contact with her? And why would Princess Primorskaya be asking you questions about her? They may have their differences, but in the end they'll always be as close as two petals from the same flower."

"That's why I was so surprised," said Slava. "And then I remembered that Dima had asked me questions about her on our first day out."

"He did?"

"Yes. He wanted to know," said Slava, remembering, "how well I knew her. At the time I thought nothing of it, but now that others have asked the same questions, more or less, I am beginning to wonder..." Slava did not in fact know what she was beginning to wonder, except that there seemed to be a hint of treason in the air whenever her name was paired with that of Princess Severnolesnaya, which was too frightening even to contemplate, and so she trailed off suggestively instead of finishing her sentence.

"Dima's never actually met my mother because I've always kept them apart—against their wishes, I might add," Olga said. "I'm not surprised he's curious, although of course he'd never complain about it to me. As for Princess Primorskaya, who knows what she's thinking? Probably she and my mother've had another disagreement and aren't speaking, so she has to go getting her information second-hand, or she was just looking for some weapon to use against me. I wouldn't worry overmuch about it if I were you: trying to figure out what these princesses are up to will drive you out of your mind. Thank the gods I'm a younger daughter! Now, enough about such tedious topics: let's think of the journey ahead of us. We have several days' ride from here to Naberezhnoye, but as hunters frequently travel back and forth on this road there'll be waystations every night. You know once we arrive in Naberezhnoye I'm planning to leave the horses behind and acquire sled-dogs: what do you think?"

"What happens to the horses?" asked Slava, alarmed at being asked her opinion on such a foreign topic, and also, despite previous assurances that she had nothing to worry about, she was concerned by the idea of giving up Skvorets and Ogonyok. She had grown quite attached to them, and she also did not want to be responsible for losing horses that were not actually hers.

"That's what some of the money your sister gave us is for," Olga told her with a smile. "You have horses belonging to the Imperial stable, and the rest of us have spent a long time finding and training our own good horses, so we don't want to give them up. But once we leave the roads behind dogs will be more use. So we'll stable the horses in Naberezhnoye and hire dogs, and, I hope, a guide as well. Although I intend to venture out much farther than any guide has gone before.

But still, it would be good to have a native to advise us, especially since some of us have never slept in the snow before. I still haven't decided what direction to strike out in once we leave Naberezhnoye, so that'll depend on what the guide says too."

"We will be..." *sleeping in the snow*, Slava meant to say, but then realized how silly the question was: of course, if they were going to be exploring unmapped territory, there would be no waystations where they could spend the night. She had known that all along—she just hadn't realized what it really meant before. "We still don't know which way we'll be going from Naberezhnoye?" she asked instead.

Olga shook her head. "It all depends on what the guides say," she said. "We could either continue up the coast or turn inland. Frankly speaking, I'm of two minds: on the one hand, continuing up the coast will take us farther North, and allow us to map the coastline, or at least start mapping the coastline, which would be a useful thing to do, but on the other hand, by turning inland we would be entering truly unexplored territory very quickly, and who knows what we might find there. What do you think?"

"What do *I* think?" asked Slava.

"Yes, what do *you* think? Your advice would be most welcome."

"Why?" asked Slava. "What advice could I possibly give?"

Olga laughed. "Slava! You have gifts the rest of us do not! How could your advice not be extremely valuable?"

"But I know nothing about anything," Slava protested. "Least of all exploring."

"But you claim to have spoken to animals and leshiye! If this is so, then you're the most valuable member of our party!"

"That was days ago," said Slava. "And it was only one time. Who knows if it will happen again? And it wasn't very useful when it did happen. I didn't do anything to help the rest of us, I just fainted."

Olga gave Slava a sideways look, still laughing. "True," she agreed, "but perhaps you will improve with practice. In the meantime, if you think of anything that seems to you I should know, tell me immediately."

"I promise," said Slava, hoping that there would be nothing to tell.

As Olga had said, the next few days of travel were quite easy, even though they started early and finished late, traveling much longer days than they had at the beginning of their journey. It occurred to Slava that what she now realized was their slow pace at first had probably been for her benefit, but she decided not to ask: either the others would deny everything, or insist that it had been their pleasure, and either way it would be embarrassing.

The men reveled in their quicker pace, whistling and singing all day long, except when the wind was too strong. Then they complained at least as loudly and fluently as they sang when the weather was fine. The only one who seemed unable to join in the merriment was Olga.

Ever since they had left Vostochnoye Selo she had been in a dark mood more often than not, despite what Slava could see was a constant struggle on her part to remain cheerful. Occasionally she even snapped at the others, became ashamed, became ashamed of being ashamed, and retreated into shame-faced silence.

Slava, who had come to think of Olga as a veritable fount of courage and good cheer, found this new Olga to be a particularly pitiable sight—what could be worse than a cheerful soul fallen into sadness?—but could think of no way of restoring her spirits, other than to count on the efficacy of time and exertion. Apparently Olga's family troubles were much more painful than she would like to admit, even to herself, and she was troubled by them much more than she cared to confess. Slava tried to distract her as much as possible by talking of other things, which worked for a time, but in the end she always ran out of things to say, and Olga would sink back into ill humor and melancholy, a most incongruous sight.

Despite Olga's poor spirits, the journey North from Vostochnoye Selo was not unpleasant. They rode for the most part in sight of the sea, except on the rare occasions when the road strayed away from it in order to pass through some village or noblewoman's holdings. Slava stared at it in unceasing fascination for the first day, and after that grew used to the sight of the vast expanse of frozen water opening out to the North—and then, as they followed the bend of the coastline, to the West—and no longer paid it any attention, unless she happened to think that she was riding along the Breathing Sea in complete indifference. Then she smiled at the ease with which she had become accustomed to something that a month ago would have seemed the height of strangeness. She was a little disappointed that the sea was not currently breathing, but that, she knew, only happened in the spring and fall, when the ice moved and melted and released sprays of water.

By this time Slava had started losing track of how long they had been on the road, and could no longer reckon the days accurately, which was both frightening and freeing. Frightening because she felt she was losing touch ever more quickly with her life back in Krasnograd, and soon she would be a completely different person, and freeing for exactly the same reasons. Although, she knew, she was still little more than a helpless burden to the others, she *felt* a hundred times braver and more capable than when she had left Krasnograd. The farther North she went, the more she felt as if she were opening up, like some strange winter-blooming flower that recklessly surrendered its petals to the snow.

A careful review of waystations one morning told Slava that they were six days out from Vostochnoye Selo. When Grisha told her they would be arriving at Naberezhnoye that afternoon, a delicious tingle of excitement ran all over Slava's body: to think that she, who before this had never been out of Krasnograd, would be spending that very night in the Northernmost settlement in Zem'! She watched the horizon with keen anticipation, anxious for her first glimpse of this fabled place. She imagined it several different ways, but forced herself to give up in order not to be disappointed.

And when they first rode in, she *was* a little bit disappointed. Naberezhnoye was no more than a collection of huts by the frozen shore. Somehow Slava had been expecting more: a kremlin at least, even though no princess lived here.

After the initial letdown, though, she realized that Naberezhnoye was even better than she had hoped. For someone who had spent her whole life in a kremlin, the huts were exotic, especially when she realized that they were occupied by hunters and traders. She looked around as they rode down the dirty street, wondering who lived in each weathered wooden building and what secrets of the Far North they knew.

People turned and stared as they went by, and Slava saw that even though everyone in their party was wearing what to her seemed coarse, heavy clothing, by Naberezhnoye standards they were all extremely well dressed, and that no one would ever take them to be anything other than travelers. The local inhabitants were all in head-to-toe fur cloaks that would have driven the princesses of Krasnograd wild with envy, if only they had been better made. As it was, the people looked like walking fur bales, poorly strung together with coarse thread.

Olga led them to a large building in the middle of the town, where she stopped and dismounted. Two serving men came out, bowed, and said, "Welcome to our waystation, noblewoman. Can we take your horses?"

Slava realized just then that this was, of course, the last waystation in Zem', and another delicious tingle of excitement ran over her. The two servants and the men took the horses off to the stable, and Slava followed Olga inside.

It looked just like any other waystation, only bigger, with benches and a bar to the right of the door, and enormous piles of furs to the left.

"Hunters bring their furs here to trade," Olga explained, seeing Slava look at the furs filling the room from floor to ceiling. "There must be more furs in Naberezhnoye than anywhere outside of Krasnograd."

Looking at what must have been hundreds if not thousands of furs, Slava had to agree. She had a sudden gruesome image of all the bloody carcasses that such a collection of furs must have left behind, and tried to think of something else.

Olga turned away from the furs and went over to the bar. Slava followed close behind her, feeling a bit nervous. She had grown used to staying at waystations, even those, like this one, that were no more than glorified taverns, but this one was particularly disreputable. The Imperial mark over the bar, showing that this was one of the Empress's waystations, seemed comically out of place.

She tried to look around without drawing too much attention to herself, but unsuccessfully: many of the benches and stools were full, mostly with rough-looking women and a few even rougher-looking men, all of whom stared at Slava with undisguised interest. She supposed that despite her traveling clothes, she didn't look much like a hunter at all. She could feel herself shrinking inside from the pressure of the stares, and found herself looking at the floor instead of at her surroundings.

It sounded as though Olga was arguing with the woman behind the bar about whether or not they could stay there for the night, and Slava's heart sank even further—if they couldn't stay here, where would they go? To sleep in some hunter's hut? The people of Naberezhnoye did not look like they would welcome strangers with open arms, even if they were capable of providing them with hospitality at all, which most of them probably weren't. Slava began to wonder if they would end up sleeping on benches like they had at Princess Malogornaya's.

"Fimya, this is Krasnoslava Tsarinovna," said Olga's voice, making her look up.

The rather weathered-looking woman behind the bar stopped what she was doing—counting coins, Slava saw—and stared at her open-mouthed. Slava gave her a small bow and said, "A pleasure to meet you…"

"Serafimiya Radislavovna," supplied Olga.

"Serafimiya Radislavovna," finished Slava.

"Tsarinovna?" croaked Serafimiya Radislavovna, backing slightly away from Slava as if she were a potentially dangerous beast.

"Tsarinovna," confirmed Olga. "Krasnoslava. My traveling companion on this expedition."

Serafimiya Radislavovna shook her head in disbelief. "How…I mean, Olga Vasilisovna…How did you…"

"I wished to see the country, and Olga Vasilisovna was kind enough to bring me along," said Slava, hoping to smooth over the awkward moment. "I am most gratified finally to have reached fabled Naberezhnoye."

Serafimiya Radislavovna stared wildly at Olga. Meanwhile, the occupants of the benches and stools had grasped that something unusual had happened, and were getting up and moving closer, hoping to find out who the strange arrival was.

"We…we have no accommodations fit for a Tsarinovna," said Serafimiya Radislavovna.

"Oh, nonsense," said Olga, amused. "Slava's been sharing my room ever since we left Krasnograd, and she hasn't complained once. She's a woman just like the rest of us."

Serafimiya Radislavovna looked as if she couldn't possibly believe that. A man with a long beard and worn furs that spoke of a lengthy absence from civilization came up to Slava and asked, bowing down to his boot tops with every other word, "Did I hear right? Tsarinovna? Krasnoslava Tsarinovna?"

"Yes," Slava told him. She was about to say more, something to put everyone at ease, but the man forestalled her by dropping to his knees.

"Little mother!" he cried. "Merciful Krasnoslava! Allow me to kiss the hem of your clothes!"

"There's no need," said Slava, embarrassed.

"No need! Little mother! After you poured your generous mercy upon my second-brother! Our family is forever in your debt!"

"Who is your second-brother?" asked Slava, trying to remember ever having poured any generous mercy on anyone from Naberezhnoye.

"Vasily Vasilisych, little mother! Shukshin! He was brought before the Empress for poaching, and because of your merciful intercession, he was only flogged!"

The rest of the room dropped to its knees too, except for Olga, who was watching with amusement.

"Of course," said Slava, trying to bring up her vague memories of Vasily Shukshin and the other poachers, who had come before the Empress more than two years ago. They had been undeniably guilty of wide-scale poaching, and the Empress's councilors had wanted to execute them in some particularly brutal fashion—they had been unable to settle on the details—as an example, but Slava had—she winced as she remembered her part in the affair—burst into hysterical tears and begged on her knees for mercy, which her sister had finally granted out of exasperation. Slava tried not to think about the incident too much, as it had been then that her character had been definitively sunk in Krasnograd. After that princesses edged away from her as if she had a bad smell, and princes had started turning away from her before she could ask them to dance.

"Eh..." said Slava, while a room full of people stared up at her as if she were a raincloud in a time of drought, "What happened to Vasily Vasilisovich afterwards?"

"He lived, gracious Tsarinovna, he lived!"

"As did my second-brother Pyotr Liliyich, noble Tsarinovna!" shouted a woman with tangled gray hair and a frightening scar down her face. Her one good eye appeared to be filling with tears of joy.

"And mine, little mother, and mine! They all lived!" cried a man who strongly resembled a bear.

"They all lived!" shouted the room, and bowed down to the ground.

"I am most glad to hear it," said Slava.

"You rescued us, little mother! You are our benefactress! Naberezhnoye will never, ever forget your kindness!" cried various people.

"We will of course find you and your party room, gracious Tsarinovna," said Serafimiya Radislavovna, who seemed at last to have regained the power of speech.

A lively discussion broke out, in which it was decided that everyone else at the waystation could crowd into one room or find a bed with one of the locals, thereby freeing up enough space for Slava and the others. Before Slava or Olga could even give their assent to this plan, they were being led, with many bows, down a narrow corridor and into a bedroom. The previous occupant, the woman with the frightening scar, was hastily shoving her things into a pack. She stopped when she saw Slava come in, and smiled in an apologetic way that looked very strange on her wild features.

"I'll just be a moment, Tsarinovna," she said, bowing down to her boottops before continuing to stuff the damp clothing she had been drying into her pack.

"There is no hurry,...?" said Slava.

"Anastasiya Mariyevna, Tsarinovna," said the wild-looking woman, bowing down again to her boot tops and smiling even more apologetically. Slava saw that she was not nearly as wild as she had first appeared, only shy and awkward around strangers.

"We are most grateful, Anastasiya Mariyevna," said Slava. "I hope we are not inconveniencing you too much."

"Oh no, Tsarinovna, of course not," answered Anastasiya Mariyevna hastily. "I can go stay with my daughters. I was only staying here because my oldest daughter had another child, and her house is very crowded...but it will be no trouble at all, Tsarinovna," she assured Slava, bowing yet again.

Olga's interest in Anastasiya Mariyevna sharpened appreciably at the news that she had daughters in Naberezhnoye. "Are you familiar with the locals, Anastasiya Mariyevna?" she asked.

"I *am* a local, noblewoman," Anastasiya Mariyevna told her proudly. "I just spend so much time in the woods that my daughters have taken over my house as their own. Of course, they need it more: they've got husbands and children. Well, the oldest two do. The youngest takes more after me: always in the woods."

"Really," said Olga, looking at her with even more interest. "Would you be willing to work as a guide, by any chance, Anastasiya Mariyevna?"

"A guide?" Anastasiya Mariyevna stopped packing and stared at Olga. "Where are you going, noblewoman? I thought you were here to trade."

"Oh no, I am exploring," Olga told her proudly, and Slava saw, more clearly than she ever had before, how much Olga cared about what she did. In Krasnograd she had been careful not to appear too strange, and with her men there was no need to say anything, but here, with Anastasiya Mariyevna, she could reveal her true feelings. "The map of Zem' is distressingly blank around the edges. We must fill in those blank areas as best we can."

"Eh, and where are you going, noblewoman?" Anastasiya Mariyevna asked again, looking puzzled by Olga's grand statements.

"Beyond the edges of the map," Olga explained.

"In which direction, noblewoman?"

"That would depend on the guide, Anastasiya Mariyevna."

Anastasiya Mariyevna looked even more puzzled. "You don't know which direction you want to go in, noblewoman?"

"Anywhere the map is blank, Anastasiya Mariyevna."

"Well...well...this sounds like a young woman's venture, noblewoman. But perhaps my youngest daughter would do for you. She's a great tracker, hardly ever leaves the woods, in fact. She's only here for her sister's baby. But I can tell she's itching to leave town again."

"When can we meet her, Anastasiya Mariyevna?" asked Olga, her eyes gleaming.

"Well...whenever you like, noblewoman."

"Now?"

"Well...they're not expecting you...the house is hardly fit...a new baby and everything, you know..."

"Oh, we don't care about any of that," Olga interrupted her. "I'm looking for a guide, not a maid."

Anastasiya Mariyevna almost smiled in the midst of her confusion. "Well, in that case, noblewoman, we can go now, if you wish."

"I'll inform my men." Olga rushed off. She seemed to have shed the gloom that had been hanging on her ever since Vostochnoye Selo, and was now twice as alive as she had been before, like a racehorse finally given free rein.

Anastasiya Mariyevna moved as if to finish her packing, then looked up awkwardly at Slava.

"Please finish your packing, Anastasiya Mariyevna," Slava told her. "I don't wish to inconvenience you any more than I already have, and besides, Olga Vasilisovna might burst if we keep her waiting."

Anastasiya Mariyevna almost smiled through her uncertainty again. "You're too kind, Tsarinovna," she said with a bow. "But everyone knows you're the kindest woman in Zem'."

Slava felt a strange burning sensation creeping up her neck and cheeks, and realized she was blushing like a girl receiving her first compliment from a lover. She was so embarrassed she could not even think what to do: deny it? Argue with Anastasiya Mariyevna? She did not think of herself as particularly kind, but on the other hand, most women were even less kind than she was. But that was not the kind of thing that Slava liked to say. Only when she saw that her silence was making Anastasiya Mariyevna uncomfortable did she manage to say, "Thank you, Anastasiya Mariyevna."

"I'm sorry if I overstepped my place, Tsarinovna," said Anastasiya Mariyevna, looking mortified at the possibility.

"No, no...you were merely too kind to me, that is all," Slava assured her, and watched as a relieved smile spread across her face.

"I will let you finish your packing in peace," Slava told her, and made to open the door.

"Where are you going, Tsarinovna!" Anastasiya Mariyevna cried.

"Out into the corridor, so as not to disturb you," Slava told her.

"Without a guard?! Where is your escort, Tsarinovna?"

"I brought no special guard," Slava explained.

Anastasiya Mariyevna gave her a horrified look and insisted that she stay in the room rather than wait unguarded in the corridor, and Slava acquiesced in order to spare her feelings.

Anastasiya Mariyevna finished her packing, fumbling with her things in her nervousness over Slava's presence, so that Slava considered going out despite her objections. Fortunately Olga's return, with Dima in tow, saved Slava from her dilemma.

"Is everyone ready?" asked Olga brightly.

"Yes, noblewoman," said Anastasiya Mariyevna, bowing so deeply she almost dropped her bundle, and then clutching it to her chest in embarrassment.

"Let's set off, then!" said Olga. "Lead the way, Anastasiya Mariyevna!"

Anastasiya Mariyevna did so very nervously, shrinking under everyone's curious stares as they walked back into the front room of the waystation and out onto the street.

The incredible cold of the nighttime air made Slava sneeze violently as soon as they were outside, but Olga only inhaled deeply and, taking Dima's arm for the first time that Slava could remember, practically skipped down the street in her impatience to meet with Anastasiya Mariyevna's daughter, and quizzed Anastasiya Mariyevna about the current winter and how it was affecting hunting and trade.

They walked deeper into Naberezhnoye, down several hut-lined streets, until they came to an old but well-cared-for little house with brightly shining windows. Anastasiya Mariyevna led them through the gate and onto the porch, and then said, shuffling her feet, "Just, if you don't mind, let me warn them first..."

"Of course," Slava and Olga answered simultaneously. Anastasiya Mariyevna bowed gratefully and stepped into the house, leaving them out in the snow.

"It's so cold," Slava said, hugging herself. It had been cold all along, of course, but the cold of Naberezhnoye seemed to be a special, deeper kind of cold, that she was only appreciating now that she was walking around after dark.

"Look up," Dima said suddenly, pointing at the sky. Olga and Slava both looked up.

The sharp wind that was cutting through Slava's body as if she were made of straw had also blown away all the clouds, leaving behind a brilliantly black sky covered with a thousand thickly clustered stars. It seemed impossible to Slava that this was the same dull sky that hung over Krasnograd. She felt as if she must have ridden into some other world, one that had no smoky kremlins and stifling palaces. For a moment the cold was no longer an assault upon her body, but something delicious and wild that filled her up like the most potent of vodkas, and she wanted to run out into it and become a wild thing, some wolf or elk.

"Please come in, Tsarinovna, noblewoman," said Anastasiya Mariyevna, opening her door and looking out at them. "I hope you aren't too frozen."

"Oh no," Olga assured her, while Slava hugged her body tightly, more aware now than before she had seen the stars that she was under attack from the cold.

When she stepped into the house, the heat hit her from all sides, so that she started coughing as it forced open her lungs. When she saw that Anastasiya Mariyevna was watching her anxiously, she made herself stop coughing while she let Anastasiya Mariyevna take her hat, coat, shawl, and gloves, and offer her house slippers in place of her boots. Two little girls also hovered around, carelessly helping Olga and Dima with their things, which they dropped in their hurry to obey Anastasiya Mariyevna's command to bow to the Tsarinovna and show her to the stove room.

Three women were standing up in the middle of the room when Slava was led in. They all bowed down to their boot tops, even the oldest, who was holding a newborn baby, and the large group of men and children who were filling the room behind them bowed down as well. The room felt very full of bowing people.

"My daughters, Tsarinovna," Anastasiya Mariyevna introduced

them. "Yevgeniya, Yevpraksiya, and Yevdoksiya Anastasiyevna."

The three women dropped to their knees and bowed again, this time to the ground, as did everyone behind them.

"You do us great honor, Tsarinovna," said Yevgeniya Anastasiyevna. "No one among us will ever forget your kindness to the people of Naberezhnoye."

"I thank you for your hospitality," Slava told her. "Truly, you do me too much honor."

At this the kneeling people bowed down to the ground again, making Slava distinctly uncomfortable. "Please, get up," she told them.

Everyone stared up at her, Yevdoksiya Anastasiyevna with interest and the others in disbelief.

"Please, get up," she repeated. "Truly, I have no desire to inconvenience you."

Yevdoksiya Anastasiyevna got to her feet and looked Slava right in the face with a bold stare. In spite of being thin as a rail and not much taller than Slava, she reminded Slava of the steppe warriors in her sister's army. She had the same assured look of a person who had spent her whole short life becoming good at one thing, and now she was very good at that one thing. Yevdoksiya's older sisters rose hesitantly, and then the rest of the family stood up as well, looking even more nervous.

"A chair! A chair for the Tsarinovna!" cried Anastasiya Mariyevna, and there was a tremendous bustle as the assorted family members attempted to push forward a chair for Slava while also getting out of her way. After a moment of painful confusion, Slava found herself seated in what must have been the best chair in the house, while everyone else gathered around her respectfully. Olga and Dima had not been offered chairs, and stood in the back of the group, Dima looking good-natured and Olga looking amused.

"I hope the chair is comfortable, Tsarinovna," said Anastasiya Mariyevna, wringing her hands in agitation. "I'm sure you're used to much finer furniture, but I fear we are simple folks and this is the best we can offer. No doubt a chair such as this one would not be allowed in the servants' quarters in your kremlin, but..."

"The chair is extremely comfortable and fine; we would be lucky to have such fine chairs in Krasnograd," Slava lied, which gratified Anastasiya Mariyevna exceedingly. She fluttered—if a scarred and grizzled peasant woman in shabby men's clothes could be said to flutter—off to see about offering the Tsarinovna some refreshments, leaving behind an awkward silence as her children and grandchildren stared at Slava in mingled fear and fascination. Slava cast about for something that would put them at ease.

"That's a very fine-looking child," she observed to Yevgeniya Anastasiyevna. "When was it born?"

"Four days ago, Tsarinovna," Yevgeniya answered in a faint voice. "A girl, thank the gods, after three boys."

"My congratulations, Yevgeniya Anastasiyevna. Is the father here?"

Yevgeniya gestured to one of the men standing against the wall, who took a halfstep forward, along with three small boys. "My husband, Yury Kseniyevich, Tsarinovna, and our three sons: Ruslan, Oleg, and Vladimir."

Yury Kseniyevich and the three boys bowed to Slava again, although Vladimir was so small he stumbled and wobbled into his brothers as he did so.

"A very fine-looking family, Yevgeniya Anastasiyevna," Slava told her. "They must be a great source of pride for you."

"Oh, indeed, Tsarinovna," Yevgeniya agreed eagerly. She paused for a moment, and then blurted out, breathless with nervousness, "Tsarinovna! Please...If I may ask a great favor..."

"By all means," Slava told her.

"Please, Tsarinovna...if it won't offend you...can I name my daughter after you? Look, Tsarinovna:"—Yevgeniya held the baby up towards Slava—"she's a fine, healthy girl, and I'm sure she'll live to her nameday. I'd count it a great, great honor, and teach her to honor you above all others as well."

"It would be my pleasure," said Slava, causing Yevgeniya to gasp with joy and hug her daughter to her chest. "And here," said Slava, digging through her pockets. "A handkerchief for my little namesake, and a grosh for each of the boys."

Everyone stood for a moment in stunned immobility, and then Yevgeniya snatched up the kerchief, weeping with happiness, and the three little boys stumbled forward and each took their coins from Slava's hand, staring at her in frank curiosity as they did so. The three sisters embraced, and the men all slapped each other's backs and exclaimed, "Ai-da Tsarinovna!"

Anastasiya Mariyevna returned from the kitchen, bearing a tray of food, which she almost dropped upon being shown the gifts the Tsarinovna had given her grandchildren. Luckily she set it down, as she certainly would have dropped it when Slava handed out more coins to

Yevpraksiya's two children as well. Her generosity caused such an out-break of joy that it was some time before the room was quiet enough for conversation.

Once Yevgeniya had gone to put the baby to bed, and the children had run off to admire their coins, Slava motioned Olga and Dima to come join her, and reminded Anastasiya Mariyevna of the purpose of their visit.

"Ah yes," said Anastasiya Mariyevna, pressing more smoky, dirty tea on Slava. "You are looking for a guide. Allow me to recommend...I mean, you might consider my daughter Dunya. Dunechka, come here."

Yevdoksiya stepped forward from where she had been standing and watching the proceedings with the same expression of self-contained observation she had been wearing ever since Slava had entered the house.

"I know she's very young—not yet twenty—and not much to look at," said Anastasiya Mariyevna apologetically, "but she's the best track-er in Naberezhnoye, even if I say it myself. There was a time when I held that honor, but my daughter has far outdone me."

Olga and Slava both examined Dunya with interest. Slava didn't know what Olga saw in her, but for herself she noticed that Dunya had appeared unmoved by both her mother's criticism of her appear-ance and praise of her abilities. Slava supposed that she was, in fact, rather plain, being so thin she was almost drawn, with a nondescript little face and colorless eyes and hair, but all that was rendered unim-portant by her expression, which said she was so entirely self-suffi-cient that she was completely indifferent to the opinions of everyone around her.

"How long have you been tracking, Yevdoksiya Anastasiyevna?" asked Olga.

"Call me Dunya," said Dunya. "All my life. Since I could walk. I've gone the farthest out from Naberezhnoye of anyone here. My mother says you want to go out beyond the map?"

"Yes," said Olga. "It's time to fill in some empty edges."

Dunya shrugged. "Which way do you want to go?" she asked.

"Which way do you advise?" asked Olga.

Dunya gave Olga, Dima, and Slava a considering look. "Come..."

"Olga Vasilisovna," Slava supplied.

Dunya nodded once in Slava's direction in thanks. "Come, Olga Vasilisovna, let's go for a walk," she said. "Your companions can come

172

too, if they want."

Anastasiya Mariyevna looked as if she wanted to protest, but then thought better of it and helped Slava into her outer clothes as the others dressed themselves. Soon they were out again in the freezing air. Slava looked up at the stars, and caught Dunya doing the same. Dunya gave her another considering look, this time with more respect, and motioned for them to follow her.

They walked down the snowy streets as Dunya questioned Olga about her men, her supplies, and her intentions. Olga appeared not at all offended at being questioned closely by a girl half her age, but instead answered all Dunya's questions willingly, which seemed to raise her in Dunya's estimation. Slava walked in the back of the group, trying not to interfere or show how cold she felt.

Even though she had been looking around keenly, Slava had not in fact been paying attention to what she had been seeing, and was therefore surprised to find herself out of the town and on the edge of a snowy field, beyond which lay a forest.

"The end of the Known World," said Dunya, as casually as if she were announcing the outskirts of town—which of course, she was. "Naberezhnoye is behind us, and all maps end at this forest. If you travel North, you'll reach the end of the taiga itself and enter the tundra, a land few see and even fewer return to tell of. Or you can journey East through the taiga as far as you wish—I doubt it ends before the Great Eastern Mountains. Both those directions lie beyond the knowledge of mapmakers. So which will it be, Olga Vasilisovna: tundra or taiga?"

"Have you made it to the tundra?" asked Olga, her eyes gleaming in the starlight.

"Twice. I'm the only one now in Naberezhnoye who's gone out and come back twice, once in summer and once in winter."

"And what's it like?"

"Empty, and cold, and more majestic than any Southern city-dweller could possibly imagine. People once lived there, or so they say, but there's no sign of them now. In the summer the sun never sets, and in the winter it never rises, and so if we were to go out there now we would be traveling in constant darkness."

"Do you think you could take us there? Now, I mean? I've heard it's better to travel there in winter than in summer, despite the darkness."

"You've heard true," said Dunya. "Less mud, fewer mosquitoes. With dogs you have little need of light. But midwinter is almost over:

the sun is due to rise there in about two weeks."

"So you think you could guide us there?"

"I can guide you," said Dunya, "if you are able to be guided. It's not a journey for the weak." Slava thought Dunya's eyes might have flickered in her direction as she said that, but she told herself it was probably her imagination, and then almost smiled at her lie.

"There are no weaklings among us," said Olga, pulling herself up proudly. "If you can guide us, we can follow. When can we set out?"

"Look up," said Dunya, pointing at the sky.

Surprised, they all looked up. Curtains of glowing green were hanging in the sky.

"The Northern Lights!" cried Dima. "I haven't seen them in years! It's a good omen."

"Yes," said Dunya. "If you rely on omens. I think we should set out soon. I'll come to you tomorrow, and you can show me your men and make arrangements."

"Of course," said Olga absently, still staring up at the lights with her mouth open in wonder.

"We should go back before you freeze," said Dunya. "You're not dressed for the true Northern night."

"Of course," agreed Olga, still staring up at the lights. Dima had to take her arm and start leading her back towards town, and even then they stumbled often, as their gazes were both fastened on the sky.

They took their leave of Anastasiya Mariyevna and returned to the waystation, by which time the lights had disappeared. Olga was still wrapped up in her own thoughts, and said good night to Slava in a distracted way, before going to bed and lying there in silence, clearly not sleeping but not tossing and turning in frustration either.

Dunya spent much of the next couple of days talking to Olga and her men, looking over their equipment, and discussing where to quarter their horses, how many dogs they needed, and where best to acquire them. Every now and then she would give Slava a sideways glance, as if questioning her fitness for such a journey, but she never voiced her opinion out loud, at least not in front of Slava.

As she could contribute little to the preparations, Slava spent the time visiting with her horses, whom she dreaded leaving, and skiing around Naberezhnoye, accompanied by one of Olga's men and an ever-growing crowd of locals.

Slava chose to do all this skiing both to see Naberezhnoye and to prepare herself as best she could for the coming journey, which, she knew, would be much harder than the one she had just undertaken. Dunya had told them that they would probably have to ski or run next to the dogs much of the time, and Slava wanted to be as ready as possible, although she knew she would still be by far the weakest and slowest member of the group. When she went into the bathhouse she was astonished by the new body she had acquired in her travels, one that looked as if it could be counted on to make a hard journey, but one glance at Olga and Dunya's bodies had shown that she still had no chance of keeping up with them, if she had ever happened to entertain such an idea.

The people who came to see her at the waystation, or followed her as she skied, or leaned out their doors to shout blessings and praise as she went by, bothered her less than she would have expected. Although their constant joy in her presence could be a little tiring at times, like the company of a too-loyal dog, the experience of pleasing people was such a novel one to Slava that she could hardly tire from it so quickly.

She was unused to being greeted with unfeigned happiness, but here, where the memory of her intercession on behalf of the poachers was still fresh even two years later, her name was pronounced with the same reverence normally preserved for spirits and gods. Slava was accustomed to fighting off the waves of hostility that rose from most people in Krasnograd at the sight of her, and so to be praised for the same traits that in Krasnograd normally provoked mockery was a disorienting but exhilarating experience.

After two days of adulation for her every action, Slava discovered that she actually took pleasure in performing acts of kindness and charity. When she could make people cry with joy just by giving a coin to a little girl or telling a mother she had a handsome son, it was difficult not to indulge in such acts as often as possible, and Slava gave herself free rein, marveling as she did so at the new sensation welling up inside her.

This sensation, she guessed, must be happiness or something very like it. Always before Slava's mercy and kindness had been wrenched from her by force, as the suffering of one person temporarily overwhelmed the misery of others, and Slava was helpless to stop herself from alleviating the pain that was most acutely felt at that moment. But as soon as she rescued one person, she was attacked by the pain of the others, who were plunged into misery on being deprived of their prey, and would turn their anger onto Slava.

Now, though, she was able to make one person happy without stealing that happiness from another, and as a consequence, she became happier herself. She was sure that the people here had their own strong undercurrent of cruelty, and she would soon be drawn down into it if she were to try to swim against the stream, but for the moment she gave with a liberal hand, and took pleasure in the pleasure of others, her one unfailing source of delight, if only she would be allowed unhindered access to it.

Slava was so caught up in her newfound talent for spreading joy that she paid little attention to Olga's preparations—although she was sure to nod attentively while Olga spoke of them—and so she was caught by surprise when Olga announced one evening at supper that they would be setting off the next morning.

"We are?" she blurted out, and then added quickly, "At last! How marvelous! But what about the horses?"

"The next party to Krasnograd will take them back, just as promised," said Dima, with a kind smile. "I arranged it myself, and made it clear that they will be rewarded handsomely...for the delivery of the horses safe and sound to their home stable."

"Oh good," said Slava. "I'd feared someone would be tempted to take the money and sell the horses on."

"So did I, Tsarinovna, but I believe the party I have chosen is trustworthy."

"Then I suppose everything is...is ready for us to set off," said Slava, wishing that she had thought to bring carrots to the horses when she had visited them that afternoon, and that she wasn't suddenly full of wretched doubts about the wisdom of this enterprise.

"Yes," said Olga, her eyes bright. "We'll be meeting with Dunya and the dogs at the crack of dawn—well, actually well before dawn, of course—and will be heading North. Dunya said with fair weather we will be in the tundra within a week."

"And then what?" asked Slava.

"Then it is in the hands of the gods," Olga said, sounding as if she had complete faith that the gods would dispose of them kindly.

Olga ordered them all off to bed as soon as they had finished their supper, saying, with barely suppressed glee, that they had a long hard day ahead of them and needed their sleep. Slava obediently went to their room and lay down on their bed. After a couple of nights of deep, dreamless rest, she was afraid sleep would abandon her at this critical juncture, but almost as soon as her head had touched the pillow, and in spite of her fears, she could feel oblivion rising up from the corners of the room and overtaking her.

Chapter Eleven

The great snowy plain stretched out before her all the way to the horizon, where a pale sun was rising. Everything glittered so that it hurt the eyes, and the wind seemed to catch her breath and fly off with it before she could draw it back in.

"You humans," said a voice behind her. "So ill-made for this place. Why do you come?"

Slava turned around, and saw a fat fluffy white fox watching her with an expression of keen interest.

"Are you speaking to me?" she asked.

"Is there someone else I could be speaking to?" asked the fox, cocking its head at her.

"Where are we?" she asked.

"Where do you think?" said the fox, cocking its head the other way and looking amused.

"I have always heard that foxes are sly, but I've never had any proof before," said Slava.

"Oh, we are sly," agreed the fox. "And cunning, too, which is why you rarely see us venturing out where we're not wanted. Humans, on the other hand, blunder all over the place. So why are you blundering around here, human?"

"Is this the tundra?" asked Slava.

"I don't see what else it could be," said the fox. "Which begs the question: what are humans doing here? Foxes, yes, we were created to live here, but humans rarely survive more than a day or two. Some tried, but it went ill for them. Oh!"

The fox bounded off to a hillock, stopped, looked at the ground with each eye in turn, and suddenly began to dig furiously in the snow.

Her paw darted into the hole and dragged out something that wriggled and squeaked. Slava flinched and looked away before she could stop herself. As soon as she did, she knew she had done something wrong, but before she could look back, the squeaking stopped. When she turned around again, the fox was trotting back towards her, still gnawing on the little creature she had caught. She stopped on seeing Slava's face, and laughed.

"This is one reason why humans last so little time out here," she said. "Squeamishness. You need to learn to be tougher, like me." She lifted up her head and sniffed.

"You must fly," she said.

Slava started to ask what she meant, but before she could get the words out, an extra-strong gust of wind picked her up and blew her away from the fox. She skimmed over the snow, marveling as little hillocks rose and fwell beneath her, faster than a galloping horse, and then a great line of tees reared up, and she knew she would crash into their trunks.

"Wake up, Slava!" screamed an elk, and her eyes snapped open in the darkness.

Slava could not help feeling that her dream had had some special significance, but whatever it was, it eluded her. She thought about it as she dressed and ate breakfast, but came to no conclusions. The fox had seemed so incredibly real, but dreams always did.

The men were excited at breakfast, talking in loud voices about their upcoming journey and the thrill of traveling by dog sled. Olga was also smiling and talking unceasingly about her preparations and plans, to which Slava responded with polite nods.

When Dunya walked into the waystation, she was greeted with loud cheers and whistles from the men. For a moment she almost smiled, and then her face resumed its usual expression of quiet confidence.

"Are you ready?" she asked, provoking another round of cheers.

"The dogs are outside," she announced, once the cheering had died down.

All the men jumped up and ran out onto the porch to see the dogs. Even Dima forgot himself for a moment and followed them. They then all retired hastily in order to put on their outer clothes, shivering uncontrollably and singing the praises of the dogs as they did so.

"I did not know they were all such dog lovers," said Slava, watching them and feeling tempted to rush out and look at the dogs herself.

"Grisha and Sasha are the only ones who have driven dogs before," Olga told her. "The rest are just excited at the prospect."

Getting dressed took even longer than usual, as everyone was anxious to get outside but afraid of leaving behind anything important, and so they all milled around in the front room, struggling into their coats and hats and checking and rechecking to make sure they hadn't forgotten anything. Meanwhile, a crowd was gathering to admire the dogs and wish them farewell. The dogs—Slava thought there were at least thirty, hitched to three sleds piled high with supplies—had been infected with the humans' excitement and were barking and wrestling with each other as best they could in their harnesses, making it seem as if the street were filled with an enormous dog fight. Many people added to the confusion by kneeling in the snow and shouting, "The gods watch over you, Tsarinovna! Come back safe!"

At last, though, they were ready. With piercing cries, Dunya, Grisha, and Sasha ordered the dogs forward, and they took off. The rest of them followed on their skis.

As Slava had feared, by the time they had reached the outskirts of Naberezhnoye she was gasping for breath and wondering how she was going to manage the next several weeks. She looked back with fondness on the horrible soreness she had experienced on their ride up to Naberezhnoye; that might have been unpleasant, but at least her shame was less apparent to the others.

They reached the field where they had seen the Northern Lights, and Dunya stopped her dogs.

"We'll follow this road today," she said, pointing at a track in the snow that Slava had not noticed before. "About sixty versts from here it stops at a hunting cabin. We'll spend the night there and carry on the next day in whichever direction you choose, since we'll no longer be held back by roads."

Slava heard what Dunya had said, but she was so horrified at the idea of traveling another sixty versts that she could not understand the rest of it. For the first time since she had left Krasnograd she considered giving up and going home, as her complete inability to be anything other than a burden to others became perfectly clear to her. Before she could say anything, though, Dunya called several of the party forward, including her.

"The skiers will take turns being pulled by the sleds," she said. "You're first."

Being pulled by the sled, while not pain-free, was much easier than trying to keep up with the rest of the party using her own strength. Every few versts they would switch off at Dunya's orders, although, Slava was quick to see, she spent much more time being pulled than anyone else, while some of the others, like Olga, could keep pace with the sleds for versts without hardly getting out of breath. Her pride told her she should offer to give the others more time in her place, but her common sense told her that by attempting to do the noble thing, she would only slow them down even more, and so she allowed herself to be towed along like another piece of baggage.

The day was so short this far North—according to Dunya, up in the tundra the sun had not risen for weeks—that they continued traveling well past nightfall, even though Dunya said they were making such exceptionally good time that she was tempted to carry on past the cabin. A groan of cheerful protest arose from the men at this suggestion, and she took it back, almost smiling for the second time that day.

"Well, one night under a roof won't kill us," she said. "I'm sure we'll get tired of each other's company in the tents soon enough."

This reminded Slava yet again that they were going to be sleeping in tents, as there were of course no cabins in the trackless wilderness to which they were heading, and she tried to imagine what that would be like. She wanted to ask Dunya how many tents they had and what they were like, but shyness in the face of Dunya's serious expression, and embarrassment at admitting her own ignorance, stopped her. She supposed she would find out the next day, anyway.

The hunting cabin was truly little more than a hut, with an even smaller hut attached to it for dogs. The cabin itself had only one room, which served as a kitchen, dining room, and bedroom. It was cold and dark when they arrived, and lighting the fire and laying out their bedclothes made it only slightly more habitable. They gulped down their supper—everyone was ravenously hungry after their day on skis—and lay down on the floor, where the men went over the day's events in loud voices for some time before suddenly falling asleep and allowing

Slava to fall asleep too.

It was decided to continue up the coast until they left the taiga behind, in the hopes that the going would be slightly easier there rather than deep in the forest. Everyone was in great spirits as they packed up their things the next morning, excited about going beyond the Northernmost building in Zem', and when they set off, many of them, including Slava, kept turning around to look at it as best they could in the darkness. A chill that had nothing to do with the piercing wind ran over her when it disappeared behind the trees: now she was really, truly on a great expedition, something she could legitimately brag of when she returned to Krasnograd.

"Goodbye, house! Farewell!" called Olik when it went out of sight. This inspired the men to burst into song, and they sang:

> *Farewell, farewell, to all my dear ones,*
> *Farewell to my mother, my dear old mother,*
> *Farewell to my father, my dear old father,*
> *Farewell to my sister, my kind pretty sister,*
> *Farewell to my brother, my brave bold brother,*
> *Farewell to my beloved, my black-browed beauty,*
> *Who waits for me by her window, her crystal window,*
> *Who sits and spins for me,*
> *Spins spells and songs of magic,*
> *Who watches over me till I return.*
> *Watch over me, black-browed beauty,*
> *Watch and wait till I return,*
> *Bearing gifts,*
> *Bearing many fine things,*
> *Fine things from distant lands,*
> *To lay at your feet, your slender feet,*
> *So that you say to me:*
> *"He is the one I prefer, prefer above all others,"*
> *And give me your hand and heart,*

> Your slender hand and kind heart,
> And I'll kiss your brows, your beautiful black brows,
> And say farewell no more!

The men sang this song with great enthusiasm several times, and then Sasha and Vova began teasing Slanik about some black-browed beauty they were sure he had left behind, making him so angry he almost cried and forcing Olga to reprimand them. They looked abashed for a moment, but then demanded a song from her, starting a general cry of "A song! A song from Olga Vasilisovna!"

Olga protested at first, but then gave in and sang, grinning broadly as she did so:

> Oh my lad, my bonny black-browed lad,
> My curly-headed beloved,
> Why did you leave me, leave me at my crystal window?
> Why did our princess, our cruel cruel princess,
> Call you away to war?
> I sat and spun, spun spells and songs of magic,
> I watched over you, watched and waited,
> While you preferred another,
> Another girl, some heartless girl,
> And so I've set down my wheel, my spinning wheel,
> And taken up my sword, my dear father's sword,
> And set off into the world, the wide wide world,
> To find someone new.
> His hair will be curlier,
> His heart will be bolder,
> His head will be wiser,
> And to him I'll give my hand and heart,
> And never let him go!

This song elicited wild cheers and fervent applause from the men. They then sang several more songs, with Olga joining in from time to time, still grinning broadly every time she did so, as her words always contradicted theirs, making them laugh heartily and shout, "Ai-da Olga, Olga Vasilisovna!"

Once they had run out of breath they demanded a song from

Dunya, and to Slava's surprise, she complied. Her song was a long one about the forest in winter, which she sang to a slow, eerie melody very different from the jaunty tune the others had used. When she was finished, the men thanked her with grave faces, and there was no more singing that day.

Although they traveled longer—as best Slava could tell from the sun's brief appearance followed by many hours of twilight—that day than they had the day before, according to Dunya they made much less progress, as they had to pick their way carefully through the soft snow and tall trees. Slava could tell that Olga was impatient with their slow pace, even though there was nothing she could do about it, but she herself was grateful, as she had much less trouble keeping up with the others and felt like less of a burden when they were all creeping along.

They stopped for the night in a small clearing, where Slava discovered that there were three tents: one for them, one for the men, and one for the dogs. As they were setting up camp, Dunya started to give her a command, and then stopped and gave her an uncharacteristically uncertain look.

"What can I do to help?" asked Slava, hoping to be given a task and not just left there to stand around with her arms folded.

At first Dunya asked her to help set up the tents, but then changed her mind and set her to feeding the dogs instead, probably because she was so inept at handling the tents. At least if she dropped any of the dog meat, the dogs would just snatch it up and eat it anyway. They all watched Slava with bright eyes as she set out their food, and she felt a great rush of affection for them: there was no good reason for them to go bounding across the snow, pulling their sleds, but they did anyway, and seemed extremely cheerful about it, too.

The tent, while by no stretch of the imagination as comfortable as a nice bed, was less uncomfortable than Slava had expected, even though it was small enough that she was pressed up against Olga, who was pressed up against Dunya, who explained that the cramped quarters helped preserve warmth.

"Once we get out into the tundra it might even be a bit warmer than down here in the taiga," she said, "but the wind will be even fiercer, with no trees to stop it, and so we'll be glad to have each other. When it was just me, I slept with the dogs. So if you get too cold, let me know and I'll bring some in."

"Thank you for your kind offer," said Slava, trying not to laugh at the picture of the Tsarinovna of all of Zem' bedding down with a pack of dogs.

"Mmm," said Dunya, and rolled over and went to sleep.

The next day was much the same, as was the next and the next. Every morning the men, with the exception of Dima and Grisha, would sing a few songs and then dash off on their skis, outstripping the more cautious pace that Dunya and Olga insisted on setting. By the time the sun rose, the group would be back together, though, and by evening those who had raced ahead would be lagging behind or begging rides on the sleds.

After it happened the first time, Slava assumed they had learned their lesson and would be more frugal with their strength in the future—but there was nothing of the sort. After several days of this nonsense, she even asked Olga and Dima why they didn't put a stop to it, but Dima only laughed indulgently, with the air of a man remembering his own wild youth, while Olga rolled her eyes and said that some kinds of folly were too deeply ingrained to be rooted out by anything other than time. So Slava tried as best she could to ignore this obvious stupidity and concentrate on keeping pace herself.

From time to time she would think about how vast and trackless the taiga really was, and then she would marvel at how surely Dunya guided them through it, and then she would feel a shiver of fear at the thought of losing Dunya and being left alone there, the only person in hundreds of versts of trees, but most of the time she just tried to keep up with the others and to stay as warm as possible.

One day it warmed up slightly and snowed heavily, making it almost impossible to move. The next day the sun came out for a few moments—although its pale light was barely visible through the trees—and brought with it a cutting wind that blew in their faces as they slogged through the piles of fresh snow. Even the most foolhardy of the men was forced to keep to a walking pace. As for Slava, she could do nothing more than keep her head down and tell herself, *one more step, one more step, one more step* over and over again, and remind herself that eventually they would stop, and she would know that they were closer to their goal. She was vaguely aware that Olga was measuring the distance they were traveling and making notes about the forest they were traveling through, for inclusion in the map she was drawing, but all Slava could think about was the cold and the journey. Except for the pain and exhaustion, it was almost restful.

Then one day—she supposed they had been out of Naberezhnoye

for about a week, although, helpless traveler that she was, she had lost count of the days already—the trees started to shrink.

"We'll be in the tundra soon," Dunya announced that night. "Tomorrow or the next day."

Several of the men cheered, and several of them nursed their frozen fingers and grimaced at the thought of being out in the wind.

"We'll be able to travel faster once we leave the trees behind," she continued. "Maybe it will help stave off frostbite.

This seemed to cheer up more members of the party, although some of them still looked skeptical. Everyone was still in reasonably good spirits, but the long days of travel with little progress, along with sleeping in the crowded tents at night, were taking their toll, and a certain grimness had settled over the group.

The next day was a bright clear day with a sharp wind that whistled through the branches, filling the forest with a faintly ominous sound. As they traveled, the trees continued to shrink with every verst, and the sun sank disconcertingly swiftly. The men muttered about this, until Dunya told them that this was because they were approaching the sunline, and that today or tomorrow they would enter an endless night.

This cheered up the bolder members of the group, especially Grisha and Sasha, who were from the Far North and had always wanted to cross the sunline, but Slava thought that Slanik and Olik looked a little frightened at the prospect, now that it had finally arrived. Who knew, she could see them thinking, what lay beyond the fabled sunline? They said people used to live up there long ago, but now they were gone, and who knew what had driven them away? And they had not even been proper Zemnians, but something else entirely; who knew what kind of ghosts they had left behind?

At this point Slava began to suspect that those were more her thoughts than Slanik and Olik's, but she could tell nonetheless that they were haunted by thoughts more or less along those lines, even if they had neither the knowledge nor the words to populate them with the same fancies that Slava did.

Shortly past midday the sun sank out of the sky completely, and the trees were no more than knee-high. As Dunya had said, despite the darkness they were able to make better time without the trees, and as the long Northern twilight turned to true night, they left the trees behind entirely and entered into an eerie snow-covered plain, which glowed faintly blue under the moonlight.

"Look at the stars!" cried Dima, pointing up at the sky with his ski pole.

"So many," said Sasha, shaking his head in wonderment. "I've never seen so many! Where do they come from? Why are they here? What do you think they are?"

"What do the people of the Far North say, Dunya?" asked Dima.

"What do the people of the South say?" countered Dunya.

"Some say that a beautiful maiden caught her rival's reflection in a pool of water and splashed it into the sky in her rage, and some say that each star is home to a god..." began Dima, but stopped when Dunya shook her head.

"People call Zem' the Midnight Land, but the true Midnight Land only starts above the sunline, where the sun and the moon and the stars were born," she said.

"Once upon a time there was nothing but the Great Sky, arching over what is now the Midnight Land, but it grew lonely. So it gave birth to the sun and the moon, and sent them South. But they grew lonely, and gave birth to the stars, and sent them all over the sky, but they prefer the North, the home of their grandmother. And then they too wanted to give birth to something, and they blew down a great cold wind, and made the earth and all the gods who walk upon it.

"The gods, like the stars, are cold, but even cold things grow lonely, and so they too made children—the leshiye. But the leshiye were strange and wild, and so they made women, who were warm and kind. But women, being warm and kind, demanded the privilege of children, something they could love and watch over as they grew. And so the gods agreed to help their granddaughters, but being gods, and having no care for their children except as sport, they made women pay a price for their gift. For until then, women did not grow old and die as they do now, but lived for many lifespans, like the trees of the forest.

"And, they say, they were not so closely tied to their bodies as they are now, but could roam at will in spirit form. Perhaps it was then that people lived in the Midnight Land. But with the gift of children the gods tied women to their short, earthly form. And they also gave women a companion, man, to help make the children and watch over them. But they, being gods, made man a double-edged sword, vain, fickle, and dangerous, as likely to cause harm as to help"—here the younger men started laughing in shame-faced pride, until Olga looked at them and they fell silent.

"Some say that men have more of that cold wind than women— that they are more like the stars and the moon—cruel, changeable and uncaring," said Dunya, once the men had stopped laughing. "But some say otherwise, and that it is women who are cold. Be that as it may, it is the stars who watch over us—not as a mother watches over her children, but as a hunter watches over her prey. And yet we are all their granddaughters, and they cluster thickly overhead."

Dunya's story was greeted at first with silence, but then the men broke out in an argument over how it differed from what was said in the South—not very much when you got right down to it, as far as Slava could tell—and whether or not it was true, and this kept them occupied for some time.

As she was completely incapable of keeping up with the others now that they were no longer hampered by trees, Slava was being towed by Dunya's sled, which left her free to snatch glances at the sky. It did seem very close, and at the same time, the stars seemed to stretch up away from her forever, as if the sky were an ocean and she was standing on its bed, looking up towards the light.

"Dunya?" she asked tentatively.

"Yes, Tsarinovna?"

"What about the Northern Lights? What do you Northerners say makes them?"

"Some say it is a sign from the gods," Dunya told her, "and some say it is the stars giving birth to more sisters, and some say all kinds of nonsense."

"What do you believe, Dunya?"

"What do I believe, Tsarinovna?"

"Yes, Dunya: what do you believe?"

Dunya thought about the question for a moment, and when she answered she spoke very slowly, as if she were unused to being asked such questions and didn't know how she wished to reply. "It doesn't really matter, Tsarinovna," she said in the end. "Gods, stars, old stories: who knows the real truth? What I just told you is what I learned from my mother, and what she learned from hers, and what every mother in Naberezhnoye teaches her children, but how true it really is I can't say, nor do I care. What are gods and old stories to me? I believe in what I can see and hear, taste and smell, and what else do I need?"

"Isn't that lonely?" Slava asked.

"Lonely?"

"I mean, isn't it lonely not to depend on others like that? Not to believe in what others believe? Don't you feel by yourself, even when you're around others?"

Dunya turned back her head and gave her an appraising look. "Lonely?" she repeated. "Perhaps, but no more than anything else. Tell me, Tsarinovna, are you not lonely? I see how you're always by yourself, even when you're surrounded by people. They say that you know the hearts of others; does that make you any less lonely? Do you see anything comforting when you look into their souls?"

"No," confessed Slava. "Of course I am alone even when I am in a crowd: how many Tsarinovnas are there? Not many, and my title shields me like armor—the only armor I have ever had—so that all who do not bear it are repelled. But as for what I sense from other people—sense, I should point out, not see"—Slava realized she was being irritatingly pedantic, and forced herself to stop—"what I sense from other people does make me feel even more alone. I feel what they feel, and I wonder how anyone could stand to feel that even for an instant.

"Most people have such base and dirty hearts that I wonder: how do they live? How can they tolerate it, not just for a moment, but day after day, year after year? No wonder people are so unhappy! Sometimes they make an effort to change, to become better, but so often that effort is a sham. Most people prefer to pretend to have a clear conscience, rather than actually keeping it clean. But why do I have to be tainted by their filth? Why do I have to feel it too? Why can I not be left in peace? And I wonder...sometimes I wonder: is there anyone else like me? Or am I some kind of freak, a monster that should have been stillborn? Am I the only one of my kind out there?"

Slava stopped, embarrassed at her outburst and afraid that she had hurt Dunya's feelings by implying that she, too, was base and dirty, but Dunya only rode along in silence. Eventually she asked, "What do you sense of me, Tsarinovna?"

"Of you, Dunya?"

"Yes, of me."

"Very little," Slava told her. "You are very contained, and so I sense almost nothing, even when I am standing right next to you."

"Does that bother you?" asked Dunya.

"No, not at all. It's restful, like entering into the silence of the forest after the bustle of the city."

It was hard to tell, but Slava thought Dunya might have been pleased by her answer. "Then you should stay near me, Tsarinovna," she said. "If it's restful to you."

"You won't mind?" asked Slava. "I'm so helpless; I don't want to be a burden…"

"I'm capable enough for two, Tsarinovna," Dunya assured her. "Besides, I find your company restful too."

"You do?" said Slava, astonished. No one had ever said they found her company restful before. Most people were made so nervous by her title that they could hardly even think straight, and those that were able to look past the title were unable to forget her presumed gift, which made them so fidgety they either fled or attacked her. Slava was unused to being welcome to other people.

"Certainly, Tsarinovna," said Dunya, turning back to look at Slava again, and Slava thought she caught sight of the faintest of smiles in the moonlight. "You never quarrel or try to tell me what to do, you just smile pleasantly and stand aside. Even if you can read my thoughts, I have nothing to be ashamed of, and if you did sense something you didn't like, I'm sure you'd forgive me. It's only unkind people who have to fear the kindness of others. But I have no fear of exposure."

"That is good," said Slava cautiously, out of habit still expecting Dunya to turn on her at any moment.

"And perhaps the tundra will do you some good, Tsarinovna," said Dunya. "Some say it has healing powers, if you are strong enough for it."

"Perhaps," said Slava. "What kind of healing powers does it have? Do they describe it in detail?"

But Dunya said those tales had been lost with the people who once lived there, and she didn't know.

The moon and stars were so bright against the snow that night that they illuminated the inside of their tent, keeping them all awake for a long time, or perhaps they had just gone to bed very early—with no sunset, it was difficult to tell. Slava lay on her side long after the others had fallen asleep, looking at the glow and marveling at where she had found herself—and at how glad she would be to return to a place where the need to relieve herself at midnight was a simple matter to take care of. Even the view of the stars she received upon stepping out of the tent was not enough to make up for the piercing chill of the wind that left her shivering well after she had wrapped herself again in her blankets.

She was not aware of falling asleep, but she must have, because someone was calling at her to wake up. She jerked awake, only to discover that Olga and Dunya were still asleep, and decided it must have been a dream. Everything seemed very dark, and she realized that clouds had come in and covered the sky.

Chapter Twelve

The next morning, or at least when everyone got up and ate breakfast, Olga, after consulting with Dunya, announced that they would be making camp there for a little while in order to make short expeditions to the East and West, filling out the map. This was greeted with a mixed reaction: half the men rejoiced at the possibility of resting and treating their blisters, while the other half groaned at the thought of several days' inactivity and boredom in the cold.

"Well, if you're that keen to be out in the wind, you can be part of the exploratory group," Olga told the groaners, grinning at them. "Dmitry Marusyevich will be in command of the group that stays behind, while Dunya and I lead the explorers. So hands up: who wants to go, and who wants to stay?"

This of course caused some confusion and a lengthy argument that went on long after Olga first explained, and then shouted in a way that would have been frightening if she hadn't been grinning as she did so, that what she meant was that those who wanted to go should raise their hands.

Slava started to raise her hand to show that she wanted to go, then thought better of it and lowered it, then thought better of it again and started to raise it, and froze in indecision. She knew she would contribute absolutely nothing to the explorers, that in fact she would hold them back, but she wouldn't be much more useful at the camp, and she was afraid of being bored there, although that was no reason for Olga and Dunya to take her along.

"I think the Tsarinovna should stay behind," said Dunya, making everyone stop arguing and look at her. A rare indecisive expression crossed Olga's face. It was apparent that she agreed with Dunya, but she was afraid of hurting Slava's feelings and so she didn't know how to express her agreement without creating a potential rift in the group.

"Dunya is no doubt right," said Slava hastily, in order to rescue Olga from her uncomfortable position. "I would only slow the others down."

"That's not why I said it," said Dunya, although Slava could see that that was, in fact, the main reason why she had said it. "What I meant was: the tundra is said to have a great effect on those with gifts, like the Tsarinovna."

"It is?" asked Olga and Slava simultaneously. "That's the first I've heard of it," said Olga, looking at Slava once again with the expression of a woman who has just acquired a prize racehorse and wants to see how fast it can run.

"Opportunities to test this are rare," continued Dunya, with the expression of a woman who had said the first thing she could think of, and was now realizing that she had quite unexpectedly said something clever. "Which is why I think, if the Tsarinovna is willing, we should not waste this one. And I think it will be more likely to succeed if she stays here: it will give the stars, or the gods, or whatever else is involved, a better chance."

"You sound as if you're recommending leaving her here like bait in a trap, Dunya," said Dima, frowning.

"No, no, Dmitry Marusyevich, not like bait in a trap, like a flower that must not be moved too often if it is to bloom. And you will be able to watch over her the entire time, of course."

"Yes, but..." Dima shrugged helplessly, "what will I be able to do if something goes wrong?"

"What could go wrong?" asked Dunya.

"Yes, what *could* go wrong?" repeated Slava, trying to smile and make a joke out of it, although she was keenly interested in the answer.

"Nothing, I should think," said Dunya. "Unless nothing happens at all, which is also possible. Perhaps these are just old tales. After all, few people venture out into the tundra, and even fewer return, so who knows? But this is a good opportunity to find out. The Tsarinovna will spend a few days resting at the camp, and will be even more ready when we carry on."

Olga gave Slava a look that said she wanted to agree with Dunya, but was afraid of what Slava would say if she did.

"Dunya is right," said Slava. "I should stay behind. As she said, there is nothing to lose."

"Good," said Olga briskly, glad to leave that painful decision behind. "In that case, Olik, Slanik, Grisha, and Misha will accompany us, while the rest stay here. Dima will be in charge of the base camp. I have proposed, and Dunya agrees, that we should venture out towards the shore, which Dunya says we should be able to reach within half a day. Once we have returned, tonight or tomorrow, I hope, we will decide how to proceed after that."

In order to make as good time as possible, it was decided to take two sleds and leave only one sled and a few dogs at the camp. In very little time, although Slava had no idea what time it actually was, since of course the sun never rose, the scouting party had set off, leaving the camp feeling empty and bereft.

Sitting and waiting in the dark camp was, as Slava had feared, extremely boring. Once the sound of the scouting party had died away, the ones left behind went back to bed in order to try to keep warm. The tent was much colder with just Slava in it, though, and she got very little sleep. She was extremely glad to hear the men stirring around, and jumped up and went out to join them.

It was even colder outside, and so the men decided to go back to their tent and play cards. Dima kindly invited Slava to join them, and, desperate for something to do, she did.

It seemed very strange after weeks of travel to stay in the same place all day, and Slava wondered for a moment if she would be able to stand it once she returned to Krasnograd. Looking back on it, her life there seemed even more intolerably empty and yet pointlessly busy than it had at the time, and she resolved to find some useful way of filling it, although she wasn't sure how.

Her previous scheme to study and catalogue the scrolls on the last invasion by the Hordes still seemed a good one, but also somehow empty. After spending so much time with Olga and her men, Slava thought she would find it dull not to have any friends or confidants. Her sister and her councilors were always suggesting that she take a lover, of course, but Slava shied away from that thought. She decided she would try at least to keep up her newfound strength by taking long rides every day, which would also serve the useful purpose of getting her out of the kremlin and away from everyone's constant demands that she dress up and lend her presence to worthless charades of cruelty masquerading as mercy.

As she was thinking this over, the men were trying to explain the rules of the game, which was called Fool. They were astonished when she admitted she had never played it before, only heard her guards talking about it, but once they got over their astonishment they all tried to explain it to her at once, which only left her more confused than before. Finally she said she would just start playing, and ask for advice as they went along.

"Aren't you afraid we might cheat you, Krasna Tsarina?" asked Zhenya.

"No," said Slava with a smile.

"She'd know if we did, fool," said Vova, elbowing him in the ribs.

"Our first fool of the day, boys!" cried Sasha, pointing at Zhenya and laughing heartily, making everyone else laugh too over his very weak joke. This provoked a great deal of elbowing, although not of Slava, of course, before the game could begin.

The object of the game, Slava discovered after the first hand was dealt, was to be the first to get rid of your cards. Most of the men were very reckless players, which caused them to lose dramatically, a situation that was made worse by the large toasts of vodka (their vodka supplies had been replenished in Naberezhnoye and were still quite ample) they drank after every round. First Vova was the Fool, then Zhenya, and then Sasha, who ended up with fifteen cards and had to drink twice as much vodka as the rest of them as a rewarding punishment for his foolishness. Dima won the first two hands, and Slava, much to her surprise, won the third.

"Ai-da Krasna Tsarina!" shouted all the men when she won. "And you said you'd never played before!"

"I hadn't," Slava said, embarrassed. "I don't know how it happened."

"Native wit, apparently, Tsarinovna," said Dima with a kind smile.

"Sucked in with her mother's milk, no doubt," said Sasha, who was already quite drunk.

Everyone gave Slava a nervous look, but when she took no offense at this familiarity, they all shouted, "A toast to the mother-Tsarina!" and poured another round of vodka.

Once the vodka had been downed, they started reminiscing about the reign of Slava's mother, Tsarina Marislava, even though none of them had known her and the only one of them who had any clear memories of her rule was Dima.

"The good-hearted Empress, that's what we called her in my village," he said.

"You did?" asked Slava. "Was that common? Is that what the people called her?" Slava knew that her mother's councilors liked to *say* that she was called the good-hearted Empress, but her mother's councilors like to *say* many things. Their words and Dima's might not line up at all.

"Your mother was a much-loved ruler, Tsarinovna," he told her. "The people felt she was truly their mother. If you will permit me to say so, there was great mourning when she decided to hand over the rule to your sister and retire to a sanctuary."

"I'm glad," said Slava. "She was often very kind to me, but I thought..."

"Thought what, Tsarinovna?" asked Dima, when Slava trailed off.

"I thought...it always seemed to me that she was very fond of me."

"It is not uncommon for mothers to be fond of their children, Tsarinovna," said Dima, still speaking kindly but smiling slightly as he did so.

"Yes, but I mean..." Slava squirmed and then blurted out one of the many secret worries that had been oppressing her for years, "I sometimes thought...it seemed to me that she...favored me."

"And how could she not, Tsarinovna? What mother doesn't favor her own child?"

"No, I mean...favored me over...over my sister. Although in many ways, especially the most important ones, she certainly favored my sister over me."

"Ah." All the men sighed in sympathetic unison.

"She was never unkind to my sister, not at all," Slava hurried to explain. "Or me either. Well, not often, and not compared to many other mothers. She always treated my sister well, and made sure she was raised to rule. My mother's mother had neglected that duty, and my own mother wanted to be sure her daughter was prepared when her turn came to ascend the Wooden Throne. She undoubtedly spent more time with my sister than she did with me.

"But then—there was a stillborn child, you know. Another daughter who would have been full sister to Vladya—to the Empress. But she died before she took her first breath. Not an uncommon sorrow, I know, but still a deep one. And then my mother's first husband—the Empress's father—died of the Cough. It took him quickly, for a mercy, and my mother was able to take another husband—my father. From the Stepnaya family. Everyone said that he was never really at home in

Krasnograd, and he died when I was very young. A hero's death, they say. The line between heroes and fools is a fine one, they would say, and he often crossed it.

"When I was younger everyone was always waiting for me to cross it too, but I always ran away from it instead, much to their disappointment—which they were so quick to share with me. When I was younger I often puzzled over why everyone was so quick to criticize my father for being a hero, and so quick to criticize me for not being foolish. But then I realized that they merely needed something to criticize, it didn't matter what—but that is neither here nor there. The important thing is that my father died when I was very young—and so was he, I suppose, as well—and I was all my mother had left of him. She never mentioned it as a love-match, but I think she was fond of him, and she was glad to have me to remember him by.

"And I was also all she had to replace the other daughter, the one who was never even named, who was just really a hope of a daughter, nothing more. Sometimes she would tell me so—that the gods had taken away that other daughter, that she had wanted so very, very much, but given me in her place. I don't think, in her heart of hearts, that she considered it a fair trade, even though she always tried to convince me that she saw me as a blessing. I was too troublesome a child for her to see me really as a blessing. Most of the time I know she considered me a burden, maybe even a waste—after all, I was good for so little, as everyone was at pains to point out to me. I was supposed to be my sister's strong right hand, but I wasn't strong in anything, except books and perhaps my own fancy.

"I think my mother saw a lot of herself in me, much more than in Vladya—which was why she admired Vladya and couldn't help but criticize me at times. I know there were times when she wished I were completely different than...how I am. But there was always the feeling—and my sister felt it too—that our mother favored me, even though I didn't deserve it—even though even she didn't think I deserved it. We were more like sisters than Vladya and I ever were. She—my mother—and I often shared an understanding of mind that Vladya could never penetrate, and the more she tried, the more distance there was between us. Kind as she was, my mother could not help but be disappointed in me, or wish she had borne some other daughter, not the one she actually had, but at least I *knew* that. Even when what was in her heart was...not what I wished to see, at least I *saw* it, and she often felt the same for me. While poor Vladya was always on the outside, and could never seem to see how much our mother admired and esteemed her."

Slava paused for a moment, knowing that she should stop, that no one needed to hear all this, and also a little bit afraid that she might start to cry, but before she could gain control of herself, more of the story came pouring out unstoppably, and she found herself saying, even as she knew she should silence herself, "Our mother would speak to my sister as to a valued princess, and then take me in her arms and call me her 'little soul' and 'darling Slavochka,' and I could see the envy burn in my sister's eyes. I was a very fearful and clingy child, but our mother was rarely angry or impatient with me, and I could see how much that enraged my sister. My mother was rarely angry or impatient with her either, but I knew my sister wished to see me punished for my childish behavior.

"And then, after years of everyone assuming I was useless, it was decided that the talents of our family had perhaps manifested themselves a little bit not in her, but in me ...well, it was a cruel blow. To tell the truth, my sister has never really believed that I had been gifted in any way, as far as I could tell, and neither does her council, although they find themselves making use of my council on occasions—providing it is disguised as their own ideas. But when my ability—whatever it is, however strong or weak it might be—to read the hearts of others first made itself known, my mother was so pleased for me, and talked about how finally I had begun to show some promise and take after our foremothers, and how if I could only manage to learn to use my gifts, I would be such an asset to my sister's rule, and she made my sister join her in her pleasure and promise to watch over me like 'the family's most precious jewel,' and it was all more than my sister could bear. She cannot rejoice in the joy of others. It must be a terrible fault to have; I can only imagine how unhappy it makes her.

"But because of all this, I became accustomed to the idea that others did not love my mother nearly so much as I did. I know that I often disappointed her and appeared as a failure in her eyes, and that I was always only her second-favorite in many ways, and that from time to time she would take her disappointment out on me in ways that even I cannot forgive, but she still loved me in her own fashion and we were and are, after all, kindred spirits of a sort, which is more than I can say for almost anyone else, and so I cannot help but think of her as the kindest person I know, because to me she was. But I am aware that not everyone shares my view. Not that that is an unusual occurrence. But I am glad to hear that others counted her kind, as I did."

Despite all the vodka that had already been consumed, the men sat in sober silence when Slava had finished her confession. After a moment, Dima poured another round and proposed a toast to 'Marislava, the good-hearted Tsarina,' which the others joined in enthusiastically.

The vodka revived everyone's spirits, making it as if Slava had never said any of the things she had said, and another hand was dealt. By this time Dima and Slava were the only ones who were anything even resembling sober, and Dima won again. Slava won the next hand, and Sasha and Volodya both lost so spectacularly that a wrestling match broke out over who was a Fool by nature and who was a Fool from vodka. Not wanting to get caught up in the fray, Slava slipped out and went to visit the dogs.

To Slava's amusement, the dogs were wrestling with each other when she came into their tent. They broke off and rushed over to her as soon as they saw her, wagging their tails and panting good-naturedly on her hands, even after they realized she had not brought them any food. Once the initial ecstasy of her arrival had worn off, several of them went back to wrestling each other. The play-fight became so spirited that several times Slava had to jump back to avoid getting knocked over.

"There you are, Krasna Tsarina!" Dima and Vova had stepped into the dark tent and come up behind Slava while she was distracted by the dogs. "We came to exercise the dogs. Do you want to come? If we're lucky, we might see a snow fox or a hare."

"Let's hope so!" said Vova, patting the things hanging off his belt.

Which was how Slava shortly found herself riding in a dogsled that was hurtling at top speed through the darkness, while Vova and even the normally staid Dima skied behind her and whooped like little boys.

"Stars!" shouted Vova, pointing up to a break in the clouds.

"Stars at midday!" Dima shouted back. He started to shout something else, but suddenly the sky turned upside down, and Slava's face filled with snow.

Although Slava couldn't be sure, she didn't think she had actually lost consciousness, but only been so shocked by her sudden plunge into the snow that for a moment she had lost track of everything. Once she had come to senses, she saw that they had all fallen into a hollow of land that had filled with snow and become invisible in the darkness. The dogs were struggling out of the snow with yelps of indignation, and Dima and Vova were calling her name.

"Here I am!" she shouted, trying to use the sled to pull herself upright and only ending up underneath it instead. Being trapped in the snow was a peculiar and frightening sensation, like drowning very slowly, and she had a hard time keeping herself from panicking.

"Tsarinovna!" cried Dima, his voice full of intense relief. "Are you hurt?"

"Just trapped!" she called back.

"Wait there and we'll pull you out, Tsarinovna!"

Slava supposed it was not long at all, although every breath she spent trapped there seemed like a long one, before Dima and Vova came crawling across the snow on their bellies and pulled her out from under the sled and onto solid ground again.

"Are you sure you're not hurt, Tsarinovna?" Dima asked again. His voice sounded strange, and Slava realized he was trying to keep it from shaking. Now that she thought about it, she could see that he had every reason to be afraid—if she had been killed, his life would have been forfeit, and probably Olga's as well.

"I'm perfectly unharmed," she assured him. "Just a little snowy."

"We're very, very sorry, Tsarinovna," said Vova in a small voice.

"For what?" she asked, hoping they could see her smile in the darkness. "A little adventure? If I had wanted to be bored, I could have stayed home."

"True, Tsarinovna," said Dima, starting to smile a little too.

"Are any of the dogs hurt?" she asked, prompting Dima and Vova to get up and look over the dogs. It soon became apparent that everyone had escaped their misadventure with nothing worse than a little snow in their eyes, although Dima said they should return immediately, before they became too cold. As soon as he said that, Slava began to shiver.

"Don't worry, Tsarinovna, we'll be back to the tents before you know it," he told her. "We can't have gone more than a verst or two."

But returning turned out to be more challenging than he had predicted. The dogs set out confidently in what even Slava could see were their own tracks, but, as in the woods where they had met the elk, they traveled much longer than they should have, or so it seemed, and still saw no sign of their destination.

"Have we gone astray somehow, Dmitry Marusyevich?" asked Vova after they had traveled at least three versts.

"We must have, and yet how can we?" said Dima, stopping and looking at the snow, which bore the unmistakable signs of dog tracks. "Unless we've fallen onto someone else's tracks, but how can that be?" He looked anxiously up at the sky, but the clouds had thickened, making it impossible to navigate by the stars.

"Should we turn back, Dmitry Marusyevich?" suggested Vova. "Perhaps if we retrace our steps..."

"Perhaps we've just lost track of time," countered Dima, although less confidently than he was trying to appear. "Who can tell how long we've been going in this endless night? Perhaps we've only gone half a verst, and are confused by the snow and darkness. Let's keep going a little farther."

Vova was unhappy with this plan, but had nothing better to offer, and so they carried on, moving slowly and keeping an anxious eye on the tracks. Slava clutched her arms to her body and tried to convince herself that she was not in danger of freezing to death.

It seemed they had gone on for at least another verst, although as Dima had said, who could tell in the endless night, when Slava suddenly turned her head, she didn't know why, and saw something moving on the edge of her sight.

"Look!" she tried to say through her chattering teeth.

They all came to an abrupt halt. Something white was trotting towards them out of the darkness.

"A snow fox!" exclaimed Vova. "Look at that pelt! My bow!" He started pulling the things off his belt, and Slava realized he had come prepared to hunt.

"What are you doing!" she cried before she could think better of it.

"Hunting, of course, Tsarinovna," said Vova, stringing his bow. "With a few of those pelts I could buy myself a new horse."

The snow fox continued trotting towards them, apparently indifferent to the threat they posed.

"But..." Slava said, trying to come up with a reason for Vova not to shoot the fox and acutely aware that she had a cloak of snow fox fur lying somewhere in a chest back in Krasnograd, a gift from some princess of the North. "If you need money, Vova, I'll give it to you."

"I wasn't asking for your money, Tsarinovna," said Vova, beginning to sound offended. "I can earn it for myself. I'm a dead shot."

"Yes, but..." The fox had stopped and sat down on the snow, and was now watching them with interest. "Just please don't shoot the fox, Vova."

"But why not, Tsarinovna?" asked Vova, giving her an uncomprehending look.

"Just...As a favor to me, please."

"Obey the Tsarinovna, Vova," said Dima. "We have more important things to worry about than hunting right now."

"Oh, very well," said Vova with a heavy sigh. He lowered his bow and looked hungrily at the fox, who looked back at him. After a moment of this staring contest, the fox got back up and, still looking directly at them, trotted past them and over a tiny rise that Slava had not noticed until then in the darkness.

"I could have traded that pelt for new boots, at least," said Vova, too aggrieved at his loss to be respectful to Slava and Dima. He started up the rise after the fox, unwilling to let such a magnificent prize get away from him so easily.

"Vova!" Dima called to him warningly.

"I just want to see where she's going," said Vova. "Maybe there're more over this rise...Dmitry Marusyevich! The camp!"

Dima, Slava, and the dogs followed him to the top of the rise, and sure enough, the camp was just on the other side of it. The fox was nowhere to be seen.

"So it was a lucky fox after all," said Dima, smiling broadly now that they were no longer lost. "And we were lucky to listen to the Tsarinovna; otherwise, who knows what we'd've done if we'd've shot the fox?"

"We'd've kept following our tracks back to the camp," Vova muttered under his breath, but Dima ignored him.

Once they were back at the camp, though, Vova forgot his resentment over his loss and told the others a very thrilling version of their adventures, in which they were led astray by malevolent forces and then guided home by a messenger from the gods in the form of a fox, whom Slava had recognized as such and insisted that they spare. Slava doubted that any of that were true, but the other men were very impressed by the tale and looked at Slava with much greater respect than before.

The rising wind cut off any further discussion, and Slava tried to rid herself of as much snow as possible before hurrying off to her tent. There she spent a while agonizing over whether to change into her other set of clothes. When a trickle of melting snow ran down her collar, she decided she really must change, but with only her in it, the tent was so cold that by the time she was in dry clothes, she was shivering uncontrollably and heartily regretting her decision. She wrapped herself in all the bedding she could find, but still could not get warm. Just when she was contemplating venturing out in order to go sit in the other tent, Dima came into hers.

"I must offer my apologies again, Tsarinovna," he said, looking sincerely sorry. "I don't know what came over me, but it was extremely foolish to take you on such a harebrained outing."

"Think nothing of it," she said, waving her hand dismissively. "I agreed to go, did I not? If something had happened to me, the only fault would be my own."

"Yes, but—forgive me for being so selfish, Tsarinovna—if something had happened to you, you would have not been the only one to suffer. I could have drawn the Empress's displeasure down on Olga Vasilisovna, and I could have never forgiven myself for that."

"You know, Dima," said Slava, smiling at the sudden thought that had come to her, "if something does happen to me, there's no need to tell my sister the truth, you know. You could just as easily lie to her, if it would be to your advantage, and she would never know the difference. In fact, I give you my full permission to lie through your teeth in the event of my death, if necessary."

"Krasna Tsarina!" said Dima, sounding both horrified and amused. "You are a devious one! But I doubt it would do any good: your sister made it perfectly clear that if anything were to happen to you for any reason, even if you laid hands on yourself and we were unable to stop you, our lives would all be forfeit as a consequence. Although," he smiled, "she might not get a chance to do us any harm: Boleslav Vlasiyevich made it even more clear that any of us who allowed even a hair on your head to fall out of place would regret the day he was born. I shudder to think what he'll do to me once he finds out about today's little adventure."

"I'm sorry, Dima," said Slava, feeling remorseful once again over her own selfishness at burdening the rest of them with her company. "I shouldn't have come. All I've done has been to slow you down, and if it weren't for me, none of you would be suffering this trouble over my safety, either."

"Don't worry about it, Krasna Tsarina! It's our pleasure. And besides, if it weren't for you, we'd still be wandering around in the woods down below Vostochnoye Selo, or if we'd ever made it out of there, Vova and I would've frozen to death by now."

"You would have noticed the fox just like I did," said Slava.

"Yes, and shot it, and then blundered off into the snow and never returned. Have you noticed, Krasna Tsarina, how your mercy always comes back to reward you?"

"It does?" asks Slava, startled. Her mercy had always seemed like such a terrible burden to her.

"Krasna Tsarina! Can't you see it? You save the elk, and it leads us back to the path. You save the poachers, and we're welcomed in Naberezhnoye with open arms, which was not, by the way, the reception we were expecting to receive at all—the Severnolesnaya name doesn't command a great deal of goodwill in that part of the world. Now you save the fox, and we make it safely back to camp instead of freezing to death in the snow. If it weren't for your mercy, we'd never have made it to the North. In fact, I doubt we'd've made it out of Krasnograd."

"Why?" asked Slava.

"Krasna Tsarina!" Dima exclaimed again. "Surely you must see that Olga Vasilisovna is not the most favored woman in Zem'. Her own mother, who's been, shall we say, under the Empress's eye for some time now, refused to support her when she asked, and what did she do? Go straight to the Tsarina, who's been looking for a reason to discredit the Severnolesnaya family for years. This would've been the perfect opportunity, except that you, for no reason other than your own noble heart, asked to come with us. At first I didn't understand why your sister agreed, but then I...I overheard some talk in the kremlin, and I realized the Empress's plans. If something happened to you, she'd have the perfect excuse to move against the Severnolesnaya family. No doubt she'd have several of them executed, and claim all their lands as recompense to your heir."

"I don't have an heir," said Slava, blurting out the first thing that came to her, instead of responding to the rest of Dima's statement, which was shocking but, her sinking heart told her, probably true. She had also broken out into a sweat, which would have been welcome under other circumstances, but now only confirmed Dima's words.

"What about the other Tsarinovna—your sister's daughter, I mean?"

"Oh, her," said Slava, and was saddened but not surprised to discover that even in the midst of everything else, she was still able to feel guilty over her neglect of her niece who was also, as Dima had pointed out, her heir. Slava had never really thought about her that way before, because Slava didn't have anything of value to pass down to her. She supposed that in other families her horse and her gowns and her jewels and her books would be considered great riches, but in the Krasnograd kremlin they were completely lost in all the other opulence, and Slava was accustomed to thinking of herself as posses-sionless.

"Yes, her, Tsarinovna. The Tsarina could do a lot against your so-called enemies, and claim it was all for the sake of your heir. Right now she is the richest girl in all of Zem'—heir to both the Tsarina and the Tsarinovna. If you were to die without issue—well, she and your sister would have no shortage of consolation in what they'd gain from your loss. Such were the speculations of your sister's maids and guards, and I have to say I believe them."

"Oh," said Slava again, no longer feeling cold at all as a flush of shame and horror rose up her neck. Part of that, she was mortified to realize, was wounded pride at the thought of how blind she had been. Dima must have understood at least part of what she was feeling, for his next words were: "Don't blame yourself, Tsarinovna! Your sister would hardly've told *you* about her scheming, knowing how much you hate it."

"How do *you* know I hate it?" asked Slava, turning to the minor mysteries in order to avoid facing the major ones.

"Everyone knows, Tsarinovna!" said Dima with a laugh.

"Everyone who? And how?"

"All of Zem', Tsarinovna. And as for the how, why, how many times have you spoken out against it in your sister's court? How many times have you chastised princesses for their greedy, underhanded ways? How many times have you bemoaned their dishonest behavior?"

"I didn't know anyone was listening," said Slava.

"Everyone was listening, Tsarinovna! Everyone always listens, ev-ery time you speak! How can you not know this?" For the first time Dima began to look agitated. The tent was too low to pace back and forth in, so he compromised by wrapping his arms around his knees and rocking back and forth. "Your voice is the most beloved in all of Zem'! How can you not see this?"

"I thought no one ever listened," repeated Slava in a small voice. "I thought I was merely shouting into the wind."

Dima gave her an incredulous look. "Then why did you keep shouting, Tsarinovna?" he demanded. "I always thought—everyone always thought—that you knew what you were doing, and we took comfort from the fact that we had at least one brave voice in Krasnograd. But if you thought no one was listening, why did you do it?"

"Sometimes a person under torture will cry out in agony, even if no one will heed her," said Slava, hugging her knees to her chest too and looking down at the tent floor.

Dima shook his head like a horse shaking off flies. "Then you were not...well, it doesn't matter. You did what you did, no matter why you did it. But the point is, Tsarinovna, that you're a thorn in your sister's side, and she'd be happy to remove you if she could. If she could rid herself of you and any or all of the members of the Severnolesnaya family in one fell swoop, she'd count it a fine day's work and retire to rest that night with joy in her heart. Which is why, Tsarinovna, what I did today was unpardonable. If something had happened to you... well, no one would have made it out of this camp alive, I swear to you."

"Oh," said Slava. "Well, in that case...in that case, I guess I'll try very hard to be careful in the future."

"Agreed, Tsarinovna," said Dima, smiling again, albeit wryly. "And I promise not to endanger you anymore if I can possibly help it, and certainly not through my own stupidity. I don't know what came over me...it must've been this endless midnight. They say it can drive you mad. But it doesn't matter. That's no excuse. Olga Vasilisovna and the boys trust me to watch over you, and that's what I'll do. From now on no more foolishness. Agreed, Tsarinovna?"

"Agreed, Dmitry Marusyevich, although if we are all to be driven mad, I fear nothing can protect us—but that is surely not the case," said Slava, and held out her hand with an answering smile. He took it and kissed it solemnly, before straightening back up and saying with a grin, "And, oh yes, Tsarinovna, supper is ready, which is why I came to you in the first place."

"Supper!" cried Slava. "Will it be warm?"

"It certainly will, Tsarinovna."

"Lead me to it, then!" Slava jumped to her feet. Upsetting as everything Dima had revealed to her— unintentionally, she guessed—had been, the thought that she needed to stay alive in order to spite her sister was immensely encouraging.

A hot supper and a few more hands of Fool did manage to warm Slava up, but most of the heat was sucked away from her by the wind when she crossed back to her tent to go to bed, and she shivered miserably through most of the night, regretting her decision to come. Everything that seemed so terrible about Krasnograd and the comfort that went with it seemed quite tolerable, now that she was shaking with cold in some lonely tent, up above the sunline. Slava knew that this was pathetic faint-heartedness, but it overwhelmed her even so.

As there was nothing to mark the separation between night and day except a faint lightening of the darkness that lay over the land, and that only at noon, Slava lay there until she heard the men stirring around. This seemed like at least two nights' worth of lying in bed, but it was probably, she knew, less than one.

Even though she was tired of lying under her cold covers, she was reluctant to abandon them, and had a hard time convincing herself that she needed to get up and go over to the other tent. When she did, she discovered that she was not the only one in a bad mood: the men were all silent and surly as well. She and Volodya fed the dogs without speaking—even the dogs seemed less than usually exuberant—and trudged back to the main tent, where everyone ate the breakfast Dima and Vova had prepared, breaking the silence only to complain about some aspect of it.

"I don't think it's really morning," Dima said when they were done. "Now that we've been fed, I think we should all go back to bed until we're ready to be cheerful."

There was some grumbling about this, but everyone obeyed, including Slava. She crawled resentfully back under her cold covers, and ordered herself to close her eyes, even though she was sure it wouldn't do any good. She wished that Olga and Dunya would come back, so that she wouldn't be so lonely, or at least the tent would be warmer. She wondered what they were doing right now.

A very clear vision of them setting off in the dogsled appeared in her mind. Despite the cold and dark they were eager to be off. Dunya thought they should be almost to the coast by now, and everyone was keen to reach it, even the dogs, who took off at top speed through the fast-falling snow. Everything seemed strangely soft around the edges, and Slava realized that there was a heavy fog rising up from beyond the low hills towards which they were running.

Watch out! Slava wanted to shout to them. The snow told her that they were even closer to the shore than they thought, and this was dangerous to them. Somehow Dunya didn't seem to realize the danger, but let her dogs run as fast as they wanted, laughing all the while...

Watch out! Slava tried to warn them. For some reason she was looking at them from just above ground level. She turned her head to see where she was, and saw her fluffy white tail.

The snow fox, she thought.

"That's right," said the snow fox with satisfaction. "I thought I would let you run with me for a little while. Perhaps it will toughen you up."

Despite her worry over Olga and the others, Slava took the time to become irritated. *Why does everyone always want to toughen me up?* she demanded. *Why can't you just let me be. Where would you be if I were tougher? Skinned, that's where.*

"Fair enough," agreed the fox amicably. "But I thought you would enjoy riding in my mind for a little while anyway. Are those your friends?"

Yes.

"They should be more careful," said the fox, as the party started racing wildly down a slope.

Why?

"Because at the bottom of that hill is the water," said the fox matter-of-factly.

But it will be frozen, won't it?

"There is a warm spring here," said the fox, still speaking matter-of-factly. "The ice at the water's edge is so thin it would barely support me, let alone all those dogs and humans."

Why are they not stopping? Don't they know this too? asked Slava, horrified at Dunya's carelessness, which seemed so out of character for her.

If the fox had been human, she would have shrugged. "You humans always fill your tent with strange fumes," she said. "Then you act strangely when you come out. You should grow a warm pelt, like me: then you wouldn't have these problems. And, of course, the fumes rising from the warm water can cause craziness too sometimes. That is why I like to hunt here: the little animals become so dazed that they

208

are easy targets." The fox licked her lips at the thought.

A vision of everyone huddling around the tiny stove all night in order to keep warm appeared before Slava's eyes, and she realized that the phrase "crazy as a fume-struck cat" was not just a phrase. The fog hanging in the air took on a sinister quality, and Slava couldn't help but feel that it was burning the back of the fox's throat.

We have to stop them! she cried.

"Oh, very well," said the fox, and dashed off.

Slava was about to scream at it for running away, when she realized that it was trying to cut off Dunya's sled from the water. Much faster than she would have thought possible for such a fluffy creature, it ran diagonally across the slope that Dunya and her dogs were racing so heedlessly down, and cut directly across the path of the lead dog, causing it to shy away from the fox and bring all the others to a crashing halt. There was a lot of yelping as the dogs got tangled in each other's harnesses, and Dunya was plunged face-first into the snow. Misha and Grisha skied right into her and fell over themselves, and Olga's sled avoided them only very nearly.

"What happened!" Olga shouted. "Dunya, Misha, Grisha: are you hurt? What happened?"

"A fox!" cried Dunya, struggling out of the snow. "A fox ran right in front of us and spooked the dogs!"

"Where?" everyone demanded at once.

Dunya pointed at the fox. Several of the men grabbed for their bows, but the fox darted away and was soon out of sight in the white snow, where it settled down to watch the proceedings.

"How unlucky!" Misha was lamenting.

"No, how lucky," Dunya contradicted him. She had gotten back to her feet and was surveying the land ahead of them. "Look: if it hadn't been for the fox, we'd have rushed right into the water without realizing it. I had no idea we were so close to the shore." She shook her head, looking troubled.

Grisha skied down to the bottom of the hill and stepped cautiously onto the flat ground that was really water. It held when he placed one ski on it, but as soon as he moved to place the other ski on it, the ice creaked ominously and he was forced to scramble back.

"There must be a hot spring around here somewhere," he said.

"It is very foggy," Dunya agreed. She sniffed, and wrinkled her nose. "One with evil qualities," she continued.

Olga was helping the other men untangle the dogs from their harnesses. She also looked very troubled.

"I don't see how we could have been so reckless," she said, and yawned widely. "We were running around like fume-struck cats..." She trailed off.

"Because we were," said Dunya. "Fume-struck, that is. Between the stove and the spring, we were poisoned."

Everyone except Olga looked nervous at this pronouncement. "Well, we'll just have to put a warning on the map, then," said Olga. "And now I think we should leave."

"I agree," said Dunya. "Leave, and return to our main camp. Fume-sickness is nothing to play around with."

As soon as the dogs had been disentangled, the whole party set off in the direction from which they had come. A couple of the men turned to look back, as if trying to catch sight of whatever malevolent force had almost caused them to plunge headlong into the water, but the fog continued to hang in the air innocently, and soon they were all out of sight.

"Humans," said the fox to herself.

Won't you be poisoned by the mist from the spring, too? asked Slava.

"Yes, but not nearly so quickly, since I didn't spend the night in a fume-filled tent," answered the fox. "But we should still leave." It jumped back to its feet and began trotting off away from the shore.

Where are we going? asked Slava.

"Hare!" screamed the fox in her mind, stopping dead and pricking its ears.

And indeed, a snow hare was crouched in frozen immobility only a few feet away from them.

Leave it, begged Slava.

"Hare!" the fox screamed again, quivering all over with bloodlust.

It's nearly as big as you are, Slava pointed out. *Taking it on might prove to be more trouble than it's worth.*

"HARE!!!" screamed the fox again, and crouched to spring.

NO!!! screamed Slava, causing the fox to mistime her jump and allowing the hare to bound away to safety.

"What did you do that for?" demanded the fox, once she had regained her balance. "I was hungry!"

I'm sorry, said Slava, feeling both self-righteous and contrite. *I just had to, I don't know why.*

"You let me help you, but you wouldn't let me feed myself," grumbled the fox.

I know, admitted Slava.

"In that case we're quits," said the fox.

"Krasna Tsarina! Krasna Tsarina!"

Slava opened her eyes. She had the sensation that she had been sleeping very deeply for some time.

"Krasna Tsarina!"

Vova was calling her from outside her tent. Groggily, Slava sat up. The cold air that rushed under the covers made her shiver but didn't make her any more alert. Slava began to worry that she was fume-struck, but then saw that her stove had gone out while she was sleeping.

"What is it, Vova?" she called back in a thick voice, as if she were shouting from underwater.

"We're going to eat again, Krasna Tsarina, do you want to join us?"

"In a moment!"

It took Slava what seemed like a long time to get up and put on her boots. Luckily she was already wearing all her other clothing; because of the cold, she hadn't taken it off for days. She stumbled through the snow over to the other tent, which was full of light and warmth, at least comparatively.

"Krasna Tsarina!" cried Volodya when she came into the tent. "Did you sleep? We did!"

"I had a very strange dream," she tried to say, but the words all came out slurred.

"Are you all right, Tsarinovna?" asked Dima, giving her a sharp look.

"Just very tired," she said drowsily, as her eyes closed on their own.

"Maybe she's fume-struck," she heard Volodya say from very far away.

"Let me feel her face." Someone's hand touched her face. "By all the gods, she's cold!"

"It was very cold in her tent," someone said. "I think the stove had gone out."

"Pull her closer to the stove, boys!"

"Are you sure she's not fume-struck?" someone repeated anxiously. The thought of being fume-struck seemed very important to Slava, but she couldn't remember why.

"Vodka!" someone ordered.

The next thing she knew, she was choking on a searing liquid that seemed to burn all the way down to her toes. Soon she began to feel more awake, and after a while she was able to understand that she was in the other tent and that she was being revived after almost freezing to death in her own tent.

"I had the strangest dream," she said again, as Dima spooned soup into her mouth. She couldn't feed herself because Vova had tucked her hands under his armpits. She was beginning to be awake enough to be annoyed by this, but didn't want to cause trouble by yanking her hands away from him.

"What about, Tsarinovna?" asked Dima, although Slava could tell he was only interested in keeping her awake, not in the contents of her dream.

She told the dream to the others, but they did not seem to think it was as important as she did. Dima merely remarked that Dunya and Olga were both wise enough to avoid fume poisoning, and that the dream had probably been a warning to Slava herself that she was in danger of freezing to death. Then he fed her a lot of soup all at once, so that her mouth was too full to talk any more.

Slava managed to stay warm all the rest of the day—if it could be called such, since the sun never rose—and through the night, or at least the time she and the others spent sleeping, and got up the next sunless morning feeling healthy but bored. To her immense relief, Olga and the others returned shortly after breakfast.

"What meal are you eating?" was Olga's first question. "Breakfast? Is it morning, then? I've lost track." She looked tired and irritable in the lanternlight.

"So have I, but we had supper, slept until we were hungry, and now we're eating breakfast," Dima told her. "What did you find? Did you reach the shore?"

"Yes, little good that it did us. We were going up it, heading North, and we set off, it must have been yesterday morning, or what we'll call yesterday morning, anyway, but we must have been fume-struck, because we all just started running around like crazy people until a snow fox ran in front of us and made the sled crash, and then we found out we'd been rushing straight towards the ice, and if we hadn't crashed because of the fox, we'd've plunged right through, because there must have been some kind of hot spring or something that weakened the ice and was also pouring out fumes. So we turned around and came straight back, and here we are." Olga paused, looked around irritably, and then demanded, "Why are you all staring at me like that? I know it was stupid, but it could've happened to anyone."

All the men turned to look at Slava. "Was this as it appeared in your dream, Tsarinovna?" asked Dima.

"What dream?" demanded Olga.

"I had a dream yesterday," Slava explained, feeling self-conscious. "About the events you described."

A good deal of Olga's bad humor disappeared. "Really?" she asked. "Do you think you have started farseeing?"

"I don't know," said Slava. "It wasn't like farseeing as I've heard it described. I was with the fox. In my dream, I mean. I was with her in her head. We could talk to each other, and when she said you were going to plunge into the water, I asked her to stop you, so she did."

An impressed silence followed Slava's words. "Really," said Olga eventually.

"We all heard her recount her dream to us yesterday," said Dima.

"Oh," said Olga.

"It seems that once again we owe a debt of gratitude to the Tsarinovna," said Dima.

"Indeed," said Olga, and shook herself all over, as if trying to wake herself up. There was another silence, while Olga stared at Slava and Slava tried to pretend that no one was staring at her.

"We should put the dogs away," said Dunya, breaking the silence and causing everyone to come out of the immobility that had temporarily chained them.

Slava followed Dunya back to the dogs' tent without being asked, and started feeding them for something to do. The men who had gone with Olga and Dunya unharnessed the dogs and, after a last curious look at Slava, went off to get something to eat. Dunya stayed behind to watch the dogs eat and make sure they had suffered no harm on their latest journey.

"Don't worry about Olga Vasilisovna, Tsarinovna," she suddenly said.

"I'm sorry?" said Slava.

"Don't worry about Olga Vasilisovna," Dunya repeated. "She isn't upset, except with herself. We all feel bad about what happened out there, but it was good that you saved us. It probably bothers Olga Vasilisovna to be saved by you—again, as Dmitry Marusyevich pointed out—but by the end of today she'll be delighted with you."

"I'm surprised, too," said Slava. "I'm not used to being useful."

Dunya almost smiled. "It's not such a bad thing, Tsarinovna. You'll probably get so used to it you won't want to quit."

"If it lasts," said Slava.

"Let's assume it will, Tsarinovna," said Dunya, and went back to watching the dogs.

Chapter Thirteen

As Dunya had predicted, by the end of the sunless non-day Olga had recovered her spirits from her unsuccessful venture to the coast, and was only too ready to question Slava about her dream. She did so for much longer than Slava would have thought possible to draw out the conversation, speculating endlessly on what was happening to Slava, and why.

"You say it's not farseeing or foreseeing," she repeated for the tenth time.

"No, I don't think so," Slava repeated, also for the tenth time. "It's more like I'm inside the minds of these animals—first the elk, and now the fox. Sometimes they talk to me in my dreams as well."

"Really?" asked Olga, looking interested. "Anything useful? Anything about us?"

"No, it's all just mysterious messages about me," Slava told her.

"Like what? My mother always said it was very important to keep a record of your dreams. Things that seemed insignificant at the time could turn out to be crucial. So what did they say to you?"

"I thought you didn't have your mother's faith in dreams," Slava said, unwilling to discuss what the elk and the fox had told her.

"I always thought she was full of nonsense, but now I guess not," said Olga. "I guess I should've listened to her more carefully for once." She laughed at the thought of listening carefully to her mother, but then focused back on Slava. "So what did they tell you? Anything useful?"

"They told me to wake up," Slava admitted, deciding that that, at least, was fairly innocuous.

"And nothing else?" Olga demanded, sounding disappointed at

the lack of wisdom Slava's dream animals had given her.

"Until yesterday, nothing of use," Slava said. Olga looked as if she had guessed that Slava was withholding information from her, but Slava, who very rarely got any real privacy, was determined not to lay out all her thoughts for others, even Olga, to examine. Olga speculated some more on what, exactly, Slava's new abilities were and how they functioned, but eventually had to give up for lack of any further solid proof.

Despite all of Olga's prying, Slava had been glad she had for once been able to do something of use for the party, and had half-hoped, although she knew it was a foolish wish that spoke of nothing more than her own vanity and boredom, that she would be taken more seriously and allowed to go out on scouting missions. Unfortunately, quite the opposite turned out to be the case. Olga declared that Slava's "dreamseeing," as she called it, was potentially much too valuable to risk either her health or her sleep by taking her off exploring. Their current camp would be their base for the rest of their time there, and Slava could stay put and allow whatever was going to happen to her, to happen.

"But what will I do?" asked Slava, trying not to sound like a sulky child.

"Practice your dreaming, of course," Olga told her encouragingly. "Try to contact the fox again. Think what this could mean! If only we knew what caused it. You'll have to speak with sorceresses when we return to the South. My mother has lots." She rolled her eyes. "It seems we won't be able to avoid Lesnograd, no matter what we do. Well, never mind! It's always good for a laugh."

Slava didn't know whether to be amused or concerned at the way that Olga was arranging Slava's future as if she were one of her own men, so she just smiled and acquiesced.

Amusing or not, Olga's decision meant that Slava spent the next several weeks suffering from ever-increasing boredom and discomfort, as she sat around in the dark and cold while the others took turns exploring farther and farther away from the camp.

Being left behind would not have been so bad if Slava's "dreamseeing" had manifested itself again, but it remained stubbornly silent. When she did dream, which was not, most unusually, every night, it was of nothing but the most trivial of banal nightmares, mostly, as the nights wore on, of being weak and helpless. Slava had passed through some dark times in her pampered and cosseted existence, but this, which was miserable *and* uncomfortable, seemed, now that she was experiencing it, to be the worst.

The brief appearance of the sun brightened Slava's existence for a moment, but it disappeared very quickly back below the sunline and she went back to feeling bored and sorry for herself, two characteristics she particularly despised in other people and was appalled to see manifesting so plainly in herself.

Not only that, but with the long days of dark solitude, she had plenty of time to brood over her past behavior and refresh in her memory every incident of selfishness, self-pity, and everything else she could think to accuse herself of. It did not take her long to come to the conviction, fueled by too much inactivity and not enough company, that she was the most despicable person she had ever met, much worse than all the others whom she judged so harshly, and that the best thing for her to do would be to sneak out in the middle of the night—or at least, when everyone else was asleep—and let herself freeze to death.

Her rotating guard, sensing in their dull way—even as she castigated herself for judging others, she found herself judging them ever more mercilessly—that she was unhappy, tried to cheer her up by telling her stories, singing her songs, and teaching her every card game they knew, and she tried to respond to their efforts with the appropriate gratitude. Actually, the men were probably no more dull than most, but her acute irritability made everyone around her seem like the worst kind of blockhead. She chafed at being treated like a child, even though she knew that Olga and Dunya were probably right to leave her behind, and the men were definitely right to try to make her confinement less tedious.

Accordingly, she tried to make herself appear more cheerful around them, but she became so angry with herself over every less-than-pleasant expression that flitted across her face for even half a breath that, despite the fact that she could see that the men thought she was being very good-natured and brave, she ended each day feeling thoroughly disgusted with her behavior.

In an attempt not to be completely helpless, Slava did make a deliberate effort to keep track of the days, and so she knew that it was a week after the first sunrise, and a week and a half after she had first thought that she couldn't bear another day in this accursed camp, that something interesting happened.

Slava and Misha had just spent the time between sunset and when Grisha announced that it was time for supper playing an interminable game of Two Empresses. Misha had rejoiced on Slava's behalf when she had finally taken his empress and won, and it took every grain of self-control she possessed not to scream at him for being so nice to her. Instead she had smiled until she thought her cheeks would crack, and told him in a consoling voice that he would no doubt win next time, as she was a poor card player and her success was, she was sure, mostly due to luck.

"Oh no, Krasna Tsarina, you're a born card player," he told her, apparently sincerely. "Shall we feed the dogs?"

"Let's!" Slava agreed. Feeding and playing with the dogs was the only pleasure she had left to her in the camp. After her ill-fated sled ride, Dima had let be known amongst the men that she was not to be allowed on any more such risky ventures, and now she was not only unable to go sledding, but everyone always found excuses whenever she proposed going skiing as well. In both his initial explanation, and in two subsequent conversations, Dima had made his reasons for keeping her safe so abundantly clear that Slava didn't have the heart to argue with him, especially as she knew he was right, but it only added to her sense of captivity and ill-treatment.

But as she and Misha were walking over to the dogs' tent, a wind suddenly rose from the North, striking them both in the face so hard that Slava involuntarily cried out from the headache it induced.

"Krasna Tsarina!" exclaimed Misha, horrified. "Are you hurt?"

"Just a headache, from the wind," she told him through chattering teeth.

"Let me take you back to the tent," he said anxiously. "You should warm yourself up."

"No, I'm fine," she told him. "Let's feed the dogs."

"Tsarinovna..." he began, clearly unwilling to let her have her way.

"I'm fine," she insisted, "Let's feed the dogs."

Misha's eyes, which were all that she could see of his face under his scarf and hat, crinkled in concern, and she knew that he was afraid something would happen to her if he didn't force her to go back to the tent. A moment later she realized that she didn't care.

"Let's feed the dogs," she repeated for a third time, and headed off in the direction of their tent again. The elation over her own hard-heartedness was so great she had a hard time keeping herself from skipping across the snow as she walked.

"Tsarinovna..." Misha said again, trailing after her unhappily, but she ignored him.

How did it happen? she asked herself. *How did it happen, how did it happen, how did it happen? And will it last any more than it ever has before?* But she shied away from thinking too much on that last question. The freedom from other people's feelings was so delicious that the thought of losing it was as unbearable as it was inevitable.

The dogs seemed to have sensed Slava's new mood, and rushed up to her with even greater eagerness than usual, jumping and barking around her like wild things. Slava laughed in delight.

"You might want to back away from them, Tsarinovna," said Misha, standing in the door of the tent and watching her and the frenzied dogs with trepidation. "They seem wild tonight. They're good dogs, but..."

"They won't hurt me," said Slava with certainty.

"Yes, but Tsarinovna..."

Prygun, the lead dog of the team that had stayed behind, suddenly leaped over the other dogs right into Slava's arms. As he weighed almost as much as she did, she collapsed under him.

"Stop!" screamed Misha.

Prygun stood on Slava's chest and stared into her eyes with his own clear blue ones, so that she couldn't breathe. It felt as if she were drowning in his eyes, and she couldn't even summon up the strength to struggle...

"There you are, human," said the fox.

Slava looked around. She was in the middle of the snowy tundra, with no sign of the camp in sight.

"Where am I?" she asked.

The fox gave the vulpine version of a shrug. "Here," she said.

"Fine." Slava shrugged as well. "Why? What am I supposed to do?"

"Follow me," said the fox, and started trotting across the snow. After a moment, Slava started trotting after her, and discovered that she was able to move as lightly and quickly over the snow as the fox could. She looked down, but she couldn't tell whether her body was its usual self or not.

They went over a small rise and into a hollow. A wind suddenly rose from the North and blew right through Slava, so that it seemed as if even her heart had frozen solid.

"What was that?" she screamed with her frozen lungs.

"Armor, of course," said the fox. "Come." She started trotting off in another direction. After a moment, Slava started trotting after her, and discovered that, despite now being made of ice, she was able to move as lightly and quickly over the snow as the fox could. She looked down, but she couldn't tell whether her body was its usual self or not.

Whether they ran for a long time or a short time she didn't know, but after a while the taiga rose up sharply before her, looming much more suddenly than in real life.

"What's this?" she asked.

"The taiga, of course," the fox told her. "Come." She trotted in under the trees. After a moment, Slava started trotting after her, and discovered that she could slip just as easily between the low branches as it could. She looked down, but she couldn't tell whether her body was its usual self or not.

One of the trees suddenly stepped out in front of her, making her stumble to a halt. Two dark eyes stared into hers.

"You are well come, Krasnoslava," said the tree.

Slava looked around wildly. More and more trees were moving around her, making a tiny glade only large enough for her to stand in.

"Leshiye," she said.

"Indeed, Slava, indeed," said the first tree. "Here to welcome you. We have been watching you ever since you first entered the forest."

"We try to watch over all our little sisters," said another leshaya. "But so many of them gather together in cities, where we cannot reach them. We have been waiting for you for a long time, but we feared you would never come to us, and we would lose you."

"What do you want from me?" asked Slava, as the leshiye all watched her with wide-open eyes. Their look seemed familiar, and then she realized it was the same look she saw every time she glanced in the mirror. It was a look that would reveal anything anyone tried to keep hidden, and Slava felt a moment of pity for anyone who was caught in her gaze.

"We want you to listen to us," said another leshaya. "We want you to become ours."

"And how would I do that?" asked Slava. "What does that even mean?"

220

"Fear not, little woman, you will not lose your face or form!" said another leshaya, stepping forward from behind the others. She had the shape of a fir tree, with two golden eyes staring out from behind her dark boughs. If she had been a human, Slava would have guessed her to be a sorceress. Slava wondered if the leshiye had sorceresses, since they were all, according to the tales, magical. "You will simply be able to speak to us wherever you go," continued the sorceress-leshaya.

"That doesn't sound so bad," said Slava. "But why do you want me to do it? And why me, specifically? Why didn't you just catch Dunya or someone like her? As you said, I rarely venture out into the woods."

"Most women's minds are much too closed for ours to touch them," said the sorceress-leshaya. "But yours was born open. A great magic, much greater than the petty 'magic' your foremothers boasted of."

"If you say so," said Slava doubtfully.

"We do," said the sorceress-leshaya. "Everything is open to the open mind. And soon our minds will be open to yours as well. Just think, Slava: more knowledge, more magic than any woman has ever known before! A most priceless gift!"

"Yes," said Slava, not knowing what else to say. Now that the sorceress-leshaya had mentioned it, it did sound very tempting. Slava wondered if this new knowledge she would acquire would mean greater respect back in her sister's court.

"And once you have gained control of the magic we will give you, you will be able to open the minds of others!" continued the sorceress-leshaya. "You will be able to teach them to see the truth, just as you do!"

"Really?" said Slava. That sounded rather dangerous, but she supposed all magic was dangerous. It might be better than what she currently had, anyway.

"So you agree?" asked the sorceress-leshaya.

"Oh, why not," said Slava, unable to come up with a better response.

"Very good." If the sorceress-leshaya had been human, she would have clapped her hands. "Fox!"

"Here!" cried the fox, moving slowly into the space around Slava. She was moving slowly because she was, Slava saw, dragging something that squeaked and struggled in terror. A snow hare, Slava saw.

"What is that for?" asked Slava, pointing at the hare.

"Blood," said the sorceress-leshaya serenely. "We must seal the connection with blood."

"Surely my own blood would be more effective," Slava objected.

"No, it must be from a sacrifice," said the sorceress-leshaya, beginning to sound annoyed. It had never occurred to Slava that leshiye could be annoyed. It made them seem much less foreign, but also less impressive.

"But I don't want a sacrifice," said Slava.

"But we must have one," said the leshaya, while all the other leshiye nodded in agreement, making a sound like wind in the trees. "To seal the connection. With blood."

"Then I won't do it," said Slava.

"Slava!" cried the leshaya. "How many hares have you fed to your dogs in the past weeks? What is one more or less? Think of all that you could do, if we do this! With its life you will gain your own, a new, better life!"

For a heartbeat the leshaya's logic stood clearly before Slava's eyes, and she could see how right it was, and how easy it would be to agree, and how everyone would tell her she had done the right thing, and how insignificant the hare was in comparison with everything that she and so many others could gain through its death. By protesting, Slava would only be giving into her weakness. She should be strong for once and endure the suffering of others. And it would be so easy. All she had to do was agree.

"No!" she cried. "You can't trade one life for another! You can't replace one life with another! If it is my life, it will be my blood, or no one's!"

The hare made one last desperate attempt to escape the fox's jaws, and then collapsed in despair, panting heavily. It seemed to Slava that he was looking straight into her eyes, and his own eyes had the same expression hers would have had, had she been in his position.

"I won't do it," she repeated.

"We have no time for your squeamishness," said the leshaya. "Fox, rip his throat out."

"NO!" screamed Slava, diving down between the fox and the hare. Something tore through the flesh of her arm, and then she fell into darkness.

222

"Tsarinovna! Tsarinovna! Prygun, get back! Back!"

The weight suddenly lifted off Slava's chest, and she no longer felt like she was drowning. Something warm and wet slid over her face.

"No, Prygun, back!"

She was being licked by a dog, Slava realized. She opened her eyes. Prygun was standing over her, watching her anxiously. Misha was on the other side of her, watching her even more anxiously.

"I'm fine," she said in a weak voice. "I just...fainted or something for a moment, but I'm fine." She tried to sit up, but her head spun. "Help me up," she said.

Misha took her under the arms and lifted her up. Once she was on her feet, she had to hold his arm with one hand and rest the other on Prygun's back in order to keep from collapsing.

"I feel so weak," she said. "I need something to eat."

"Can you make it back to the tent, Tsarinovna?" Misha's eyes were enormous, and she could see the white all the way around the iris.

"Yes, if you both help me."

"You don't want me to go get someone..."

"No, let's just walk slowly."

She, Misha, and Prygun made a solemn procession back to the main tent, where their arrival caused an enormous stir. Volodya and Grisha both dropped everything they were doing to grab her by the shoulders and sit her down, where they plied her with vodka and spoonfuls of honey until they were satisfied she was revived, although it was a long time before Slava stopped shivering. Despite the men's objections, she insisted that Prygun stay curled up against her, which he did with considerable pleasure.

"You're sure you're not hurt, Tsarinovna," Grisha asked for the dozenth time. "You're holding your arm funny."

"I must have twisted it when I fell," said Slava, trying to move her left arm and discovering that it was sore.

"Let me see it, Tsarinovna."

Freeing even a single arm from her warm clothing was extremely difficult and also provoked another bout of shivering.

"It doesn't look broken, Tsarinovna," said Grisha, moving her arm back and forth and frowning at it. "But what did you do to it before?"

"What do you mean, before?" asked Slava, craning her head around to look herself.

"All these scars, Tsarinovna. It looks like you were mauled by dogs."

And indeed, bite marks stood out whitely in the lanternlight, covering Slava's arm from shoulder to elbow.

"Oh, that," said Slava, and started trembling so violently that Grisha covered her back up without any further examination.

Chapter Fourteen

Slava was afraid to go to sleep that night, in case she fell back into whatever place she had been where the leshiye had found her. Up until that moment she had treated everything that she had dreamed, even when it had been proven to be real, to be something that only happened to her dream-self. It had never occurred to her before that anything could affect her physical body.

At one point after the men had gone she freed her arm from her sleeve and examined it again. The bite-marks stood out just as whitely this time as they had the last time.

How am I going to explain this to Olga? Slava wondered. She thought she could probably hide or explain the scars to anyone else, but Olga had seen her bathe recently and there was every chance that they would bathe together again in the near future. Olga would know that she had not had the marks before.

I could just tell her, Slava thought to herself. *After all, she would probably accept it better than most.* But as soon as she thought that, Slava realized that she couldn't bear to do so, at least not yet. Because Olga would want to know exactly how Slava's arm had gotten mauled, and Slava would have to explain how she had dived down to save the hare, and then, she was sure, Olga would refuse to believe her. Not because Olga didn't believe in leshiye—Slava was fairly certain that Olga would be quite willing to believe in them—but because Olga would have a hard time believing that Slava had turned down what the sorceress-leshaya had offered, and all over a stupid hare.

In retrospect, even Slava had a hard time believing it. As the leshaya had pointed out, she fed hare meat to the dogs every day. But when the crucial moment had come, Slava's basic nature had taken over, as it always did, and her basic nature was unable to let her stand by and watch someone else's suffering, even if that someone was a hare. Olga, however, would surely not be able to understand that.

I'll deal with that problem when I come to it, Slava told herself, and tried to make herself sleep. Every time she started to drift off, though, she thought she could see the sorceress-leshaya's golden eyes gleaming at her out of the darkness, and she would jerk back to wakefulness.

She must have fallen asleep eventually, though, for at some point she thought she had heard the hare speaking to her. She couldn't remember how or why or what he had said, but the thought that he, too, had survived the encounter with the leshiye was comforting.

The men were extremely solicitous the next morning, but as they did not bring up the scars on Slava's arm again, she was able to tolerate their hovering with equanimity. In fact, despite her mostly sleepless night and her worries over what had happened, she was in a much better mood than she had been for days. At least she was no longer bored.

She spent the day walking the dogs—she managed to convince Grisha that walking them around the campsite would not be too dangerous or exerting—and playing card games with the men, and her cheerfulness was mostly unfeigned. Nothing alarming happened, and she went to bed that night—the sun had set some time before, of course, so it was impossible to know if it were really night or afternoon, but they declared any time they began to feel sleepy to be night—in a much bolder frame of mind than she had the night before, expecting to sleep soundly.

And sleep soundly she did, at least until the hare appeared before her.

"Thank you again," he said. "I owe you a great debt."

"You're welcome," Slava told him. "Although there was little merit in my actions: I merely did what my heart prompted."

"Then you were able to listen to your better nature, and that is more than most can," said the hare solemnly. Seeing such a white, fluffy animal speak so seriously was incongruous, but Slava listened respectfully. She felt that she and the hare were bound closely now, and had no desire to laugh at him.

"It is especially surprising, given that you were perfectly prepared to heed the leshiye's request," the hare continued. "You had finally started caring more about yourself, or, not to put too fine a point on it, being selfish. For a moment you really were tempted to sacrifice me.

And you were right: it would have been both right and easy."

"Yes," agreed Slava, "but I was unable to carry on with it when it really mattered. It seems I cannot take the easy path, even when I want to. I wish I had not been so tempted, though. I wish I weren't so weak." She thought of what the leshiye had offered her. "It's a shame," she said sadly. "I also wish I could have taken their gifts. I'm especially sorry about the armor."

"Armor?" asked the hare.

Slava told him about the North wind freezing her, and how this was supposed to give her armor.

"Oh, that," said the hare. "Perhaps you will keep that in any case. After all, I have armor against the North wind too." And he scratched himself with a hind paw, showing off his heavy pelt.

"I doubt I'll be able to keep it," said Slava gloomily. "They didn't seem like the type to give things away for free."

"Yes, but once you have been North, you have been North," said the hare, preening himself on the other side. "You earned that on your own, and it is not in anyone's power to take it away from you."

"True," said Slava, cheering up slightly.

"And, of course, I will always be by your side."

Slava didn't see how this would be of much use, but she refrained from saying so. The hare must have read it on her face, though, because he said, "Don't discount my help; it may be more useful than you think."

"Oh, I'm sure it will be very useful," Slava lied quickly.

The hare twitched his nose at her, as if he knew she was lying, and bounded off, his white coat fading into the white snow.

Slava awoke in the darkness. Her conversation with the hare had comforted her, as if he really were watching over her. She still didn't see what good that could do, but it was a nice thought nonetheless.

Olga, Dunya, and the others returned later that day, tired and discouraged. One of the dogs had hurt her paw their first day out. They had stopped, hoping she would recover soon with rest, but after several days they had started running low on supplies and she had still not improved. Eventually they had been forced to put her in the sled and make their way slowly back to the base camp, having wasted time and supplies and not accomplished anything other than injuring a good sled dog.

"We'll have to start heading South soon, and we've still done so little mapping," said Olga dispiritedly, after recounting the story of her failed mission. "How did you fare here at the camp while we were away? Did anything of note happen?"

At that moment it occurred to Slava that there was no need to tell Olga anything about what had happened at all, but before she could put this plan into action, Misha had launched into the story of her collapse and revival, concluding with a description of the injuries to her arm.

Olga livened up considerably at this news, and even Dunya looked excited. Olga insisted on hearing all the details of Slava's adventure, and whenever she thought Slava was holding something back on her, which was often, she insisted on clarification, which was how Slava came to tell the entire group about what had happened to her, omitting not even the slightest detail. When she was done, they all stared at her incredulously.

"Why didn't you take up their offer, Tsarinovna?" asked Misha reproachfully, speaking for the rest of them.

"I don't know," she said. "I just couldn't."

"But Tsarinovna..."

"Enough," said Dima, speaking unusually sharply. "The Tsarinovna made the choice that seemed best to her, and it is not our place to question it. We were not there."

Misha retired in unsatisfied silence, and the others continued staring incredulously at Slava, until Olga broke the silence by demanding to be shown Slava's injured arm. Reluctantly, Slava allowed herself to be led into the tent and her arm exposed. Once again, the scars shone whitely in the lantern light. Several of the others gasped on seeing them, and Slava had to admit that they did look pretty bad. It occurred to her that she was now scarred, and that henceforth, anyone to whom she revealed her arm would react in the same way.

"Impressive," said Olga, once she had recovered from her shock. "And you say they were like this as soon as you woke up?"

"Yes," Slava told her. "I don't even really remember getting them. That is, I knew I was being bitten, but I had no idea I had been bitten so much, and the wounds were never fresh."

Dunya reached over and began feeling Slava's arm. "They feel like normal scars," she said. "I'd never've guessed otherwise, if the Tsarinovna hadn't told me."

"Interesting," said Olga. "I had no idea such things could happen."

"Neither did I," said Slava.

"This is very worrisome," said Olga. Slava couldn't tell how serious she was being. "Before I had always assumed that dreams were just dreams, even if they were true. I had no idea the body could be hurt in them."

"Me neither," said Slava.

"This requires investigation," said Olga, and sat for a while staring at the tent wall, lost in thought. When she had finished thinking, she asked, "Dima, how much longer will our supplies last us?"

"Maybe three weeks, Olga Vasilisovna, if we eat well, or four weeks if we don't mind tightening our belts."

"And to the best of our reckoning, it will take two weeks to return to Naberezhnoye."

"Unless we get lost, of course, Olga Vasilisovna."

"Of course," said Olga. She stared for a while longer at the tent wall, and then said, "Let's set out tomorrow morning. For Lesnograd."

"For Lesnograd?" asked Dima, forgetting in his astonishment—not, Slava thought, that Olga's behavior should astonish him by now—to add "Olga Vasilisovna."

"Yes, let's. So far the Tsarinovna's visions have been the most interesting thing we've discovered here, and I want to consult my mother's sorceresses about them."

"If you are certain, Olga Vasilisovna," said Dima, everything about him radiating uncertainty at such a course. Slava couldn't blame him. Not for the first time, she marveled at Olga's casual planning and her willingness to change her mind in an instant. Of course, she, Slava, also acted that way sometimes—well, often—but she, Slava, was merely a follower, not a leader. No one else's fate was hanging on her decisions. Slava wondered if all journeys were this haphazard.

"Of course I'm certain," snapped Olga, jerking Slava back to the matter at hand. "I'm sick to death of blundering around in this eternal midnight, and we're running low on supplies. If there's anything of interest up here, we're not going to find it. We've got to find something worthwhile up here, and the Tsarinovna's visions are it. But we need interpreters—sorceresses, that is. Severnolesnoye is our only logical destination."

"Of course, Olga Vasilisovna," said Dima. "We'll start packing at once." He and the other men left the tent, their backs radiating profound relief at escaping before a major scene erupted.

"Olga," said Dunya once the men had left. "Olga Vasilisovna," she repeated, raising her voice slightly, when it became obvious that Olga had gone back to staring at the tent wall.

"What?" cried Olga, snapping out of her reverie and giving Dunya a nasty look. For the first time since they had left Krasnograd, it occurred to Slava that a falling out amongst the party was a distinct possibility. The idea made her start to sweat in the cold tent. If the group split up, what would she do? Whom would she follow? She would prefer to go with Dunya, whose quiet certainty was so calm and restful, but would Olga let her?

Slava knew that, despite her supposed higher rank, she was in Olga's power. What would she do if Olga did something she didn't approve of, and she was forced to go against her? Her desperation to escape Krasnograd and her admiration of Olga had blinded her to what had to be the worst danger of the whole expedition, which was Olga's volatility—and the fact that her family was no friend to Slava's. Even if, Slava thought, her heart jumping in her chest, Olga meant her no harm, what about Olga's mother?

"I want to come with you to Severnolesnoye," said Dunya, bringing Slava out of her panicked thoughts and back to the present. She promptly began to feel better. If Dunya were with her, she couldn't possibly come to any harm. Or was this just more blind admiration of someone stronger than herself? She had to stop fretting and start thinking on her own, she told herself severely. Woolgathering at moments such as these was unpardonable.

"You do?" said Olga, looking surprised. "Why?"

"I want to see it for myself. I've heard of it all my life, but never been there."

"How will you get home, then?" asked Olga.

Dunya almost smiled. "I'll manage," she said. "The more important question is what will *you* do, Olga Vasilisovna, once we arrive in Lesnograd. Declare your expedition over and take up permanent residence in your mother's house?"

"By all the gods, no," said Olga, shuddering dramatically. "Not a moment longer than I can help it. If I could think of a better way..."

"Krasnograd?" suggested Dunya. Slava's heart sank at the word.

"There might also be sorceresses there," continued Dunya, "and the Tsarinovna might be happier there, and you too."

"Too far," said Olga. "And besides..." she looked expressively at Slava, and Slava realized she had doubts about the safety of returning Slava to her native city in her current delicate condition. "A few days in Lesnograd won't kill anyone," continued Olga, in the voice of someone trying to convince herself. She rubbed at her right arm, just as she had at Princess Primorskaya's kremlin, but then made herself stop. "And then we'll borrow horses and return to Krasnograd, flushed with triumph and knowledge," she said more cheerfully. "But meanwhile, Lesnograd."

"If we travel due South from here, we should run into the Severnovostochnaya Road," said Dunya. "After that it's a simple matter: if we turn right we'll come to Vostochnoye Selo, and if we turn left, we'll come to Lesnograd. All we have to do is reach the road."

"How long to get there?" asked Olga.

Dunya shrugged. "If we have good luck, a week to ten days at the most. Of course, that is if we have good luck."

"We'll just have to have good luck, then," said Olga. "Especially on the Severnovostochnaya Road. Last I heard, there were still bandits."

"Bandits!" exclaimed Dunya and Slava together, although Slava's voice was, of course, much more shocked and frightened than Dunya's, and kept on talking well after Slava wished it would shut up. "Bandits on the highway! Why has this not been stopped?!"

"My mother claims she doesn't have enough soldiers, and the Empress claims it's not worth sending Imperial troops. That's what they say, anyway."

"Bandits!" repeated Dunya to herself, almost smiling. "I've heard tales of Severnolesnoye, but I didn't know they were true. I look forward to this now."

"Oh, no doubt you'll find plenty to laugh at," said Olga. "I would say: don't believe everything you hear about it, but I'd only say that because the truth is so much worse. But we do have the finest sorceresses in all of Zem', and a sorceress is what we need now."

Slava knew that the steppe princesses also claimed to have the finest sorceresses in all of Zem', but she stopped herself from pointing this out to Olga. The question of which region produced the best sorceresses was a hot point of contention between the steppe and the taiga, although the black-earth riverlanders who lived along the Krasna also claimed that their sorceresses possessed talents not found elsewhere.

The only place that did not brag of its sorceresses was the Eastern mountains, where sorcery was viewed with suspicion and sorceresses were often sent into exile—or worse. The mountainers claimed that sorcery was an abomination and they believed in metal, not magic. Metal was true and would not let you down when you most needed it. Such as when you were facing an attack by the steppe army and their sorceresses, who amongst other things were said to have the skill to steal their enemies' magic and use it against them. Which probably answered the question of who had the strongest magic and best sorceresses.

But Slava kept that thought to herself. The steppe was very far away, and they would have to go through Lesnograd to get to it in any case. And despite the alarming news that bandits were apparently roaming the highway of Severnolesnoye unchecked, Slava was developing a desire to see it, and if Princess Severnolesnaya's sorceresses, weak as they probably were, could tell her something useful, that would also be welcome. Besides, after what had turned into countless days in this dark camp, going anywhere would be a welcome relief, and so Slava seconded Olga's plan to head for Severnolesnoye the next morning. Not, she thought, that her agreement or disagreement would have any real weight in the matter, but it made her feel better to know that she was going along with things willingly.

Although by most reckonings they had very little equipment, and packing up the base camp should therefore have been a quick and simple job, in fact it took all that day and part of the next morning as well, although no one in the group could have explained exactly why. At one point, in answer to Slava's unspoken question, Dunya merely shrugged and said, "That's traveling," which was really all one could say. But it meant that they set off later than they would have liked, inasmuch as anyone could guess the time without the sun, and with the sensation of having left things undone.

Somehow their trip to the Far North had ended with a feeling of failure, and Slava was disturbed to see that she was not the only one who was bothered by it. Everyone felt that, having dragged themselves all the way up there, they should have done more with the time they had had, although what it was they should have done, no one knew. Olga, Slava could tell, was particularly stricken with this feeling, even though it had been her idea to leave, and was trying unusually hard to appear bright and cheerful in order not to betray herself to her men and cause an even greater sapping of spirits.

The dark tundra did nothing to help them, as it concealed many obstacles under its snow. After they had stopped for the second time to pull one of the sleds out of a snow-filled pit, much like the one Slava had fallen into earlier, Olga decreed they had to be more cautious. This meant they were forced to move at a walking pace, checking for hidden dangers.

The midday sunrise found them, by Dunya's calculations, barely three versts from their original camp. Travel was slightly quicker in the daylight, but they went no more than a couple of versts before the sun set again, leaving them in a cold darkness that seemed even colder and darker than before the sun had given them its brief light. Even the dogs seemed to droop under the weight of the wind that rose to their backs, as if reproaching them for abandoning their mission.

In order to cheer everyone up, Olga gave them lavish descriptions of the luxury awaiting them in Lesnograd. The city itself, she admitted, was hardly worth the name, but the Severnolesnaya kremlin really was both a palace and a fortress where even a Tsarinovna could feel at home. Olga told them heartening stories of enormous bathhouses, where the steam was so thick you could barely breathe, feasts where the dishes were crowded so thickly upon the tables, it seemed they would fall off, and feather beds into which you would sink as if into a snowdrift, rising only to open a window and release some of the heat the stove was producing.

These tales produced the desired effect for a time, but then Misha remarked that he was hungry, and asked Dunya how much farther they had traveled since sunset.

"Perhaps three versts," she said.

"Three versts!" he cried indignantly.

"Or less," she said. "Certainly not more, though."

"Three versts!" he repeated. "That means we've only gone eight versts today, and we'll have to stop soon. How will we ever get home at this rate?!!"

"Things will be better tomorrow," said Olga soothingly. "Soon we'll be able to let the dogs run, and then we'll be in the taiga in no time."

"And then we'll be forced to pick our way through trees," Misha grumbled. "I don't suppose there's a road between here and our destination?"

"Roads take you out of your way," said Dunya, by way of an answer.

Misha looked like he had many more objections to make, but fell silent under Dima's disapproving glare. Still, it was clear that he had only voiced what everyone else was thinking, and the last part of their day's journey was completed in a grim silence that grated on Slava's nerves.

Once they stopped, setting up camp took some time, and cooking and eating supper somehow seemed very tiresome and inconvenient. Everyone went to bed in a bad mood, and arose the next morning scarcely any better.

The cloud over the group lifted slightly when Dunya decided that the terrain was safe enough to risk a gentle jog, but by the time they made camp that evening, everyone had fallen back into the same depression with which they had risen that morning.

"We'll never escape this tundra," moaned Misha, whose usual ebullient spirits had sunk even lower than everyone else's.

"Perhaps we're really heading East, not South, and we'll never come to the end of it," suggested Volodya, who had also taken their lack of progress very hard.

"Nonsense! The sun has risen directly in front of us ever since we left camp!" snapped Dima, who was tolerating their slow pace reasonably well, but was finding the moaning of the other men more than he could bear.

"The sun rises in the East!" cried Misha, as if this was a new thought for him.

"Up here it rises in the South," said Dima, who looked very much as if he wanted to tack the words "you ignorant fool!" to the end of his sentence.

"That's impossible," said Misha. "Everyone knows the sun rises in the East."

"But once you pass the sunline it rises in the South," said Dima, giving Misha a hard look.

"But why?" asked Misha, sounding as if the sun's rising in the South above the sunline was a personal affront to his sense of the world, which it probably was.

234

"Because the gods willed it so," said Dima, giving Misha another hard look that was supposed to tell him to accept the will of the gods and stop asking pointless questions.

"But..."

"Go feed the dogs, Misha," said Dima, and Misha set off in bad grace, complaining to himself about the sun's peculiar habits this far North, and also about other things that Slava could not quite catch and hoped that Dima couldn't either, because she thought they might have been things he couldn't have heard without demanding a fight with Misha, or whatever it was men like them did in these cases.

Late the next day, though, scrubby trees started rising up around them.

"The taiga!" Volodya shouted, and all the others broke into cheers.

"That didn't take long," said Misha, sounding disappointed. "I'd forgotten how close the taiga was. We spent hardly any time at all getting here. To tell you the truth, I'm kind of sorry to be leaving the tundra."

As far as Slava could tell, he meant what he said. After a brief internal struggle, she managed to refrain from saying anything. Dima also remained silent, although from the expression on his face, his internal struggle was much fiercer than hers.

The scrubby trees, while a welcome sign of their return to the taiga, also slowed them down even more, and so they made very little distance that day. The lift that was produced in everyone's spirits carried on into the evening, though, and everyone remained cheerful even when they made camp in a thicket of saplings that made it difficult for them to pitch their tents, while providing no shelter from the North wind. Even huddled between Olga and Dunya, Slava spent the night shivering, and found it hard to face the dark morning when it came time to rise. What little sleep she had found had been broken by ominous dreams that disappeared on waking, leaving only a bitter aftertaste in her mind.

No one else seemed affected, though, and they broke camp and set off in an excellent mood. Volodya and Misha even started a song, which the others picked up and sang for several versts. It was a very long song about a little birch tree who had fallen in love with Ruslan Tsarinovich, the youngest son of the Empress. Slava, who still had a hard time keeping up with the others, was concentrating more on her skis than on the song, until the words suddenly caught her attention.

In order to keep the song going, the men were taking turns singing in pairs, and it was Dima and Grisha's turn. As best Slava could remember, the little birch tree had first appeared to Ruslan Tsarinovich in the form of a beautiful maiden, but, having won his love, had shown him her true form, only to have him flee in terror and disgust. The Tsarina, distraught at the loss of her youngest son, had offered his hand in marriage to anyone who brought him back alive.

The little birch tree had set off after him, hoping to win him back and save him from any danger he might stumble into. Having failed to find him in the birch woods and the steppe, the little birch tree had ventured into the taiga and gotten lost, whereupon she had stopped beside a stream to give vent to her tears. A leshaya with glowing golden eyes had come up to her and asked her what her troubles were, and the little birch tree had explained about her lost love. Dima and Grisha were singing the leshaya's reply:

> *Oh birch tree, my little birch tree,*
> *Why are you letting your tears, your crystal tears,*
> *Fall from your eyes so hard?*
> *Your love has been swept up,*
> *Swept up by the North wind.*
> *He has carried him off, off to the Midnight Land,*
> *To live amongst the frost, the never-ending frost,*
> *Where the sun neither rises, rises nor sets,*
> *And the earth is full of magic, powerful magic.*
> *You could say goodbye to him, goodbye to him forever,*
> *And he would be happy, happy there forever,*
> *Held in the embrace, the armored embrace,*
> *Of the frost, the never-ending frost.*
> *But if you wish to bring him back,*
> *Back to your warm embraces,*
> *You must turn him, turn him to face the sun,*
> *And let the sun, the bright burning sun,*
> *Burn off his armor, his frosty armor,*
> *So that his heart will grow warm again for you.*
> *But if you do so, one of you will pass through fire,*
> *Fire and water, burning fire and water,*
> *You will undergo many tests, terrible tests,*
> *Before he will be yours again.*

"Where did you learn that story!" Slava cried.

"It is the story of Ruslan Tsarinovich and the Little Birch Tree, Tsarinovna," said Dima. "Surely you've heard it before?"

"Yes…" said Slava. Her nurse had once told her the story when she had been very small. She had found it terribly frightening, and her nurse had never told it to her again, saying that it did nothing but remind you that the gods could be devious and cruel, and that gifts often came in unwelcome packages. "What happens to them?" she asked, aware that her voice was much too high. "What happens to Ruslan Tsarinovich?"

"Listen and you'll find out, Krasna Tsarina," said Dima, and he and Grisha carried on singing.

It took many more verses to complete the story of Ruslan Tsarinovich and the Little Birch Tree. The need to keep up with the others kept distracting Slava, but as best she could gather, the little birch tree went up into the Midnight Land and found Ruslan Tsarinovich there, only he had been frozen by the North wind and didn't respond to her calls. So she had wrapped her branches around him and carried him back into the woods, where she had warmed him until he unfroze and woke up.

Only he did not rejoice at being awakened, but rather suffered terrible agony as the ice began to leave his limbs. Rather than let her thaw him out completely, he ran away again, and the little birch tree chased after him. In order to escape her, he plunged into the heart of a great fire, and she plunged in after him. His icy armor was still strong enough to protect him, but the little birch tree had none, and was burned all over. Trying to escape the burning, she threw herself through an icehole into a frozen river, and was swept downstream under the ice. When she came out, many versts away, all her leaves were gone and her beautiful white bark had been burnt black, and she was in terrible agony.

Even so, she made her way back to Krasnograd, where she found the Empress had promised Ruslan Tsarinovich to the daughter of a great princess. Many more terrible things happened to the little birch tree, until she finally went to live in the middle of the deep woods, hoping to find the peace of death. However, at this point the gods decided to reward her, and turned Ruslan Tsarinovich into another birch tree and sent him to live with her. So they were finally able to live together, just as the little birch tree had dreamed, only not at all as she had hoped, not at all.

It was, of course, a terrible tale, but what bothered Slava the most about it was that she now realized she had dreamed it the night before. Both the dream itself and the fact that the men had just happened to choose that story to sing seemed to Slava to have a sinister significance, although she didn't know why. She was very glad, though, when a line of tall trees reared up in front of them, cutting off the singing in a burst of cheering.

Slava hoped she would forget about the little birch tree when she went to bed that night, but instead she dreamed of her again. She thought of mentioning it to Olga, but decided against it—she didn't want to sound silly, and she also didn't want Olga to take her seriously and make her even more worried.

Traveling through the trees, which grew ever taller and thicker as the day, such as it was, progressed, was a very slow business, and Slava could see by the set of Dunya and Olga's faces that, although they would never admit it in front of the men and their shaky morale, they were already having doubts about the path they had chosen. With the treetops cutting out the sky, it was difficult to hold to their course even when the clouds cleared, so that Dunya kept calling for a halt in order to refind their way.

Despite long hours of travel, over the next two days they barely made thirty versts. Slava overheard Dunya telling Olga that she had thought they would be moving faster than this, but the size of their group and the quantity of supplies they had to carry was slowing them down.

"Well, at this rate, we'll soon run out of supplies, which will solve that problem," said Olga.

"The snow is deeper than I expected, too," said Dunya. "It's so soft and heavy it's dragging us down. Even the trees seem to be drowning in it."

This was true. They were all floundering through waist-deep snow, the weight of which was also pulling tree limbs down into their path and showering them with cold clumps as they tried to push their way through. By the second day the trees were also crowded so thickly around them that there was no space for them to pitch the tents properly when they stopped for the night, forcing them to set up very makeshift shelters that were completely inadequate for keeping the wind out.

That night Slava awoke with a start from a dream about eyes floating towards her on the wind. She looked out around the tent wildly, but saw no eyes except for those of the dogs, who were piled together under the flimsy shelter of half a tent, strung from a tree branch to the ground. They did not appear to be asleep, but were looking out into the woods, in the direction of the snow, which was being blown towards them in great gusts.

Once Slava became convinced that the only thing watching her was the dogs, she realized how terribly thirsty she was. She felt for her waterskin, and discovered that it had slid out from under her bedding and frozen solid.

She decided to try to warm it with her body, but bringing it back under her blankets let out all her carefully accumulated warmth, making her shiver. She also became acutely aware of a painful need to relieve herself, which was particularly irritating, considering how thirsty she was. She decided to try to ignore it and fall back asleep.

This, unfortunately, proved impossible. She lay there with her eyes closed for quite some time, listening as the wind died down and the snow began falling more and more heavily, so that the air seemed filled with the sliding sound of its descent through the tree branches. After a while she realized that she would have to get up. Without the wind the prospect didn't seem so unappetizing, anyway. She got up and looked out the tent flap.

Two golden eyes were staring back at her from somewhere in the trees, their light diffusing like the glow from a lantern through the thickly falling snow. Slava shrieked and jerked the tent flap closed, setting the dogs to barking and causing everyone else to scramble out of their bedding, shouting, "What is it! What is it!"

"Eyes!" cried Slava, almost sobbing in her shock but unable to stop herself. "Eyes! Over there!" She pointed in the direction of the eyes, but their light had gone out.

"Slava! Tsarinovna! What eyes!" shouted Olga, shaking her by the shoulder.

"There were eyes there!" said Slava wildly. "Big golden eyes, glowing in the snow! I saw them!"

The others exchanged glances. Slava knew they were wondering if she had dreamed it, and if they should take the threat seriously even so.

"I woke up because I had a dream about them," said Slava, her teeth chattering. Tears were coming to her eyes, in spite of her best efforts to suppress them, and she thought she might be sick. She had not realized until that moment how afraid she had become of the sorceress-leshaya. "Then I couldn't go back to sleep, and I lay here for a long time, and then I opened the tent flap, and I saw them! They were right there!"

Dima and Grisha took lanterns and investigated the spot Slava indicated.

"Nothing, Tsarinovna," they said. "Except..."

"Except what!"

Grisha held up his lantern and squinted at the snow. "These *might* be tracks," he said doubtfully.

Dima held up his lantern and squinted at the snow too. "Maybe," he said, even more doubtfully. "Although it looks to me like the marks of branches bent down under the weight of the snow."

"Maybe," said Grisha. "But then how did the snow get knocked off, so that they could spring back up?"

Dima shrugged. "The wind?" he suggested.

"Whatever it was, it's gone now, Krasna Tsarina," Grisha told her.

Now that Slava had roused the entire camp, they decided to pack up and start traveling. The heavy snow made it impossible to guess the time, but no one was keen to go back to sleep. The heavy snow would also, Misha pointed out, make it difficult to find their way, but the rest decided they'd rather be moving through it than sitting under it. At least that way they'd be a little bit warmer.

Packing up was difficult, because the snow was falling so fast it kept getting into everything before they could put it away. And, as Misha had predicted, once they did get underway, they made very little progress. But even so, no one was willing to stop. Even though no one said it, it was clear that Slava's dream had set them all on edge, and they were eager to put as much distance as possible between themselves and whatever she had seen.

They floundered through the soft snow for what seemed like versts and versts. Every now and then Slava would look back, thinking she could feel golden eyes behind her, but she never caught sight of them. Sometimes she also thought she felt them to her left. She tried to ignore the sensation, but she could not help but notice that the others also kept glancing to their left, and the dogs always chose to pass an obstacle on the right rather than the left.

It's nothing, she told herself. *You're imagining things. Everything will be better when the sun rises.*

When the sun finally did rise, they all collapsed as if by prearranged cue, and looked about them miserably. The snow was still falling so heavily they could not actually see the sun, just the warm glow it gave from far away, as if from through a curtain. It was a strange effect, as if there were no actual clouds above them, and the snow was falling from a clear sky. There was, Slava told herself, probably nothing strange about it at all, but it added to the sense of eeriness that had been pursuing her all morning.

"When will it ever stop snowing?" moaned Misha. Slanik, Olik, Vova, and Volodya all looked as if they would like to join in his moan, but were afraid of what the others would think of them if they did.

"At least we'll have the sun to our backs for a little while, warming us," said Vladik, and stopped. A terrible silence filled the air, as everyone realized that the sun should not be to their backs at all, and that they were facing completely the wrong way.

Chapter Fifteen

"How!?!" cried Olga, her voice rising into a shriek. "How did we get turned around!?!"

"I don't know," said Dunya, looking around wildly. "I could have sworn we were traveling South, I could have sworn…"

"So could I," said Grisha, and all the others chimed in in agreement.

"The eyes," said Slava to herself, suddenly realizing the significance of what they had done.

"What did you say, Tsarinovna?" said Dima, who was closest to her.

"The eyes," repeated Slava. "I kept thinking I could see them on my left. I thought it was my imagination, but the dogs kept going right instead of left, too. We must have gone right so many times we ended up going entirely the opposite direction."

"But the compass…" said Dunya, pulling it out of her pocket and consulting it again. Everyone crowded around to look. The needle pointed behind them, showing they were still going South. Dunya and Olga stared at it in horror, and then in the direction of the sun, and then back at the compass.

"Someone else try," said Dunya, and handed the compass to Dima. Her fingers, Slava noticed, were shaking.

Dima cleared the snow off the packs on one of the sleds, and set down the compass. The needle swung around and around before finally stopping. Once again, it was pointing directly at the sun.

"I don't believe it," he said. "Someone else try."

The rest of the group took the compass in turn and tried to get a different reading out of it. Some of them held it in their hands, and some set it down on whatever surface seemed the flattest to them, but in each case, the needle, after swinging around and around as if in confusion, always ended up pointing straight at the rising sun.

"Something must have happened to it," said Dunya, after they had all tried. "It must be broken somehow." The thought that this was only a commonplace occurrence seemed to calm her down slightly, but brought her to an unpleasant conclusion. "We'll only be able to travel during the day," she said. "Only during daylight, I mean. Without the compass, we have only the sun to guide us."

"Unless we can see the stars," said Olga, also calming down a little after hearing this rational explanation for something that had seemed to defy all the laws of reason. "If the stars should come out..."

Dunya looked up at the sky, and got a faceful of snow. "If the stars should come out, and the trees are not too thick to see them," she said. "But meanwhile, I suggest we move as fast as we can while the sun is still out."

They turned around and began moving in the direction of the sun. Misha started to speculate on how far they had gone astray, but Olga told him such thoughts would only make things more difficult, and he fell silent. Soon there was no sound other than the falling snow and the sled runners pushing through it.

Slava tried to keep a watch out for any more sign of the eyes, but saw nothing. The snow was falling so fast she felt completely cut off from everything around her. She could see the shapes of those nearest to her, but they seemed to be on the other side of a veil, and if one of them happened to speak, she could barely make out the words, even if they were so close they could have reached out and held hands. As they walked, trees loomed suddenly out of the snow, giving her the feeling that they were standing still and the forest was moving around them.

I wonder how long it will take us to reach the road now? she thought, and instantly regretted it. If they could only travel during daylight, surely they would run out of supplies long before they came to the road, and it was still a long journey from there to Lesnograd.

Soon the sun began to set, which was also strange and eerie. Slava thought she could see her shadow projected against the falling snow, but told herself it was nonsense. Or even if it were true, there was nothing unnatural about it. But she wished she could see some normal, explicable phenomenon, in order to rid herself of the sensation that she had fallen into some dream world where nothing worked the way it should.

Dunya and Olga were talking about something up ahead of her, but the snow muffled the sound. They came to a halt, and everyone else stumbled to a stop, looking around as if they had just awoken from a heavy sleep, which was how walking through the snow felt.

"We should stop now and make camp, before we lose our way," said Dunya. Her voice seemed to come from very far away.

"How far do you think we've come?" asked Misha. "Two versts? Three? Do you think we've caught up to where we got turned around in the first place?"

"It doesn't matter," said Dunya. "If we keep going in the dark, we'll only get lost again. At least if we stop, we aren't going any farther astray."

They stopped and made camp, considerably hampered by the snow, which filled every pack as soon as they opened it. Snow got into their tents as they set them up, and then melted all over their bedding, and it was, Slava thought in despair, only midafternoon at the latest. Somehow the long night before them in wet bedding made the journey to the road seem insurmountable.

Everyone was too dispirited to play cards, tell stories, or sing songs, and so they sat there in their tents until Olga announced that they should eat. This livened things up briefly, but then the meal was over and there was still nothing to do and nowhere comfortable to sit. Olga said they should all go to bed in order to be as rested as possible for tomorrow's journey. Misha muttered something about "all five versts of it," but the others pretended not to hear.

Slava was afraid that after the afternoon of inactivity she would lie awake all night, but instead she fell into a deep sleep almost immediately.

It was still dark when she awoke, but she could tell that she had slept all night and it was now morning, or would be if they were farther South. She felt much more rested than she had in a very long time.

She slid out of her bedding and stepped out of the tent. The snow had stopped, and a dazzling sky of stars stared down at her through the treetops. She stared back at it, breathing deeply in order to taste the scent of the forest in winter. Everything was completely still, and with her back to the tents, Slava felt as if she were the only person alive in this scene of frozen wonder.

"Beautiful, isn't it?" said a voice to her right.

Slava jumped and looked around, but saw nothing.

"Down here," said the voice.

Slava looked down. A snow hare was sitting at the base of a tree, watching her intently.

"Were you speaking to me?" Slava asked.

"Of course," said the snow hare. Slava realized that his lips were not moving.

"That was something I'd always wondered," said Slava. "Whether animals felt the beauty of nature as people do."

"Even more keenly, because we have fewer thoughts about ourselves to get in the way," said the snow hare.

"Probably true," said Slava.

"You're very calm," said the snow hare. "Do you think you're dreaming again?"

"It doesn't matter," said Slava. "I'm not sure there's a difference."

"Very clever of you," said the snow hare. "Sometimes humans surprise me with their cleverness."

"Am I not dreaming, then?" asked Slava.

The snow hare shrugged. "If any of the others were to wake up and come out here, they would see nothing but a shadow in the snow," he said, "and none of them would hear me. Only you can do that."

"I see," said Slava. "Why?"

The snow hare looked at Slava. "Do you ever feel that your mind is naked?" he asked her.

"All the time," Slava answered.

"You are right. Your mind is naked, like a pool of water in high summer, and so I can dive right in. But their minds are covered with a thick layer of ice, and so I slide across the top, not even leaving a mark."

"I wish that weren't so," said Slava, thinking once again with regret of the armor the leshiye had offered her.

"You lie," said the snow hare.

"I suppose you're right," said Slava. "But I still wish things were different."

"You had a chance to make things different, and you refused it," said the snow hare.

"Yes, but..."

"If you had wanted, truly wanted, things to be different, you would not have done so," he continued.

"I couldn't do it," said Slava.

"Yes, and on behalf of my brother, I am profoundly grateful. But when it came time to choose, you chose to rescue others rather than yourself. You chose not to deny the best part of your true nature."

"And now look where we are," said Slava. "If I had chosen differently, perhaps I could have found help that would have gotten us out of here. Being stuck here is my fault." This thought had not occurred to her until just then, and she was appalled to realize it was true.

"Ah, but Krasnoslava, you have found help. You saved my brother, and now I am going to save you."

"You are?" said Slava doubtfully.

"I am. Follow me, and I will lead you to the road you wish to find."

"You will?" asked Slava, still doubtful.

"Krasnoslava! Why don't you believe me?"

"Why would you do that?" asked Slava.

"Because you rescued my brother, of course. You have done a good deed, and now I am going to do one in return."

"Really?" said Slava.

"Yes, Krasnoslava, really, but you must trust me to do it. Give in to your better nature, just as you have done on so many previous occasions. Wake up the others and tell them you will lead them to safety."

"Why should they believe me?" asked Slava.

"When have you ever led them wrong, Krasnoslava? They have made many mistakes, but you never have."

"That's not true," said Slava, and then stopped. Now that she thought about it, it *was* true. "They won't follow me," she said.

"I think you might be surprised, Krasnoslava," said the snow hare. "Wake them up and find out. Go on, wake them up," it repeated, seeing that Slava was still hesitating. "I will still be here when you get back."

Very slowly, Slava walked back to her tent and went inside. She crouched over Olga for so long that Olga actually woke up from being stared at before Slava could make herself shake her shoulder.

"What is it, Slava?" asked Olga, looking alarmed. "What happened?"

"I..." Slava whispered, and had to clear her throat before she could continue. "I know how to get to the road," she said, in a louder voice.

"So do I," said Olga. "Just go South. If only I had a compass to guide me, the Black God take me."

"No, I mean...I have a guide. We don't need the compass anymore."

"What guide?" asked Olga, sitting up. "Another dream?"

"No...No, I don't think so." Slava could feel herself wringing her hands in anxiety and embarrassment, and forced herself to stop.

"So what is it?"

The conversation had woken Dunya, who was now also sitting upright and listening intently.

"I..." began Slava. "I have a guide," she repeated.

"What kind of guide, Tsarinovna?" asked Dunya.

"A snow hare," said Slava. A blush was rising on her cheeks. Fortunately, she was so covered up that the others couldn't see it, but she was becoming ever more aware of how silly she sounded, and how unlikely it was that the others would believe her.

"A real snow hare, Tsarinovna?" asked Dunya, sounding less dismissive than Slava had expected.

"Yes...I think so...I'm not sure. He said...he said he's here to rescue me, because I rescued his brother," Slava blurted out in a rush, so that she wouldn't be able to hear what she was saying and stop herself before she had said it all.

"Interesting," said both Dunya and Olga together. "Do you trust him?" asked Olga.

"Yes...I think so..."

"Either you do or you don't," said Olga. "Should we follow him, or not?"

"Yes," said Slava. "I think we should follow him."

"Good enough for me," said Olga, crawling out from under the bedclothes and moving towards the tent door. "Let's pack up then and leave! Why stay here any longer than we have to? Dima! Grisha! The Tsarinovna has had a vision, and we're leaving! Everybody up!"

The camp burst into life as the men stuck their heads out of their tent and shouted, "Ai-da Tsarinovna!" which set the dogs to barking. Soon everyone was rushing around in their preparations to take off. Slava put on her skis and sidled out of the way back to the tree where she had first found the snow hare. She half-expected it to be gone, but it was still sitting there patiently.

"I thought you might get frightened by the noise, and run off, or something," Slava said to it.

The snow hare twitched its ears at her. "I won't leave you until you are safe, Krasnoslava," it said.

"All this commotion must be very unpleasant for you," said Slava.

"And yet I will be able to tolerate it for your sake, Krasnoslava," said the snow hare.

"Are you sure?"

"Of course I'm sure, Krasnoslava," said the snow hare. "Stop worrying about it so much. I'm not going to leave you, any more than you left my brother to the leshiye."

"But I didn't know I was going to do that until I did it," objected Slava.

"And there lies the difference between us. You never know what you are going to do until you do it, even though you always do the same thing, while I have made my decision and intend to keep to it."

"But..."

"Just be quiet and be grateful, Krasnoslava," advised the snow hare. "Are you ready to go?"

Slava looked back over their former campsite. Everything was packed up, and the others were watching her expectantly. Slava looked back at the snow hare, hoping for a helpful suggestion.

"Tell them to follow you, Krasnoslava," said the snow hare.

"Aah, follow me, I guess," said Slava, and looked back at the snow hare, hoping it would give her a direction to lead them in. To her relief, instead of criticizing her again, it began to hop slowly through the snow. Slava set off after it, and the others, after cheering loudly, followed her.

Leading the group was less difficult than Slava had expected, mostly because the snow hare hopped very slowly in front of her, making it impossible for her to lose her way. Of course, because she was leading, the group was confined to her skiing pace. At one point she opened her mouth to apologize for that, but the snow hare told her to shut up before she could say anything.

"Can the others see and hear you?" she asked it.

"No, their minds are still frozen over," said the snow hare.

"So they're just following me blindly?" asked Slava. "They can't actually see that I'm not just blundering around on my own?"

"No, for all they know, you became fume-struck and are leading them right into the heart of the forest, never to escape again," said the snow hare.

This thought was so appalling that Slava almost stopped skiing, but the snow hare shouted at her that she had to keep going, so she did.

At some point the sun rose directly in front of them. This confirmation that they were traveling South-East elicited wild cheering and songs. Slava tried not to look as weak-kneed with relief as she felt.

They continued on well after sunset, when the snow hare suddenly announced that it was time for them to make camp for the night. Slava shared the news with the others, who agreed with much congratulatory back-slapping.

"We must have made at least thirty versts today, Tsarinovna," Dima told her over supper. "And all thanks to you!"

"Is that fast enough?" asked Slava anxiously. Despite everyone else's confidence in her, she still felt extremely uncertain that they were doing the right thing, and kept expecting to find out that they had gone astray. Every time such a thought occurred to her, which was often, her stomach hurt. Being a leader was even more nerve-racking than she had imagined. She wished she were back in Krasnograd, hiding in her sister's shadow.

As soon as she thought that, she realized it was a lie, and felt slightly better. "Maybe we could go faster tomorrow," she said. "I'll ask."

"Where is the snow hare, Tsarinovna?" Slanik asked, looking around hopefully. Slava knew that he was very keen to catch a glimpse of the hare, and kept searching for him around her, hoping that this time he would reveal himself.

"Over there," she told him, pointing to where the snow hare was crouching at the base of a tree.

Slanik stared eagerly at the spot she had indicated, but eventually turned away in disappointment. The disappointment was quickly superseded by a new thought, however, which he immediately shared with Slava, wanting to show her that even though he couldn't see the snow hare, he was still interested in his welfare. "Does he need to eat, Tsarinovna?" he asked. "Should we feed him?"

"I don't know," Slava answered, embarrassed that she hadn't

thought of that already. She went over to the snow hare and asked.

"I can forage for food under the snow, Krasnoslava, but thank you for asking," he told her.

"Can we go faster?" she asked him. "How fast can you travel?"

"Very fast, Krasnoslava," he answered. "The question should be: how fast can you travel? Because you are the only one who can see me."

"What if I rode in a sled..."

"Then we could go as fast as the sled could carry you, Krasnosla-va."

Slava returned to the group and relayed the information the hare had given her. Slanik was excited by the news that it could forage for food under the snow, ("Do you think I could see his tracks, then, Tsa-rinovna?" he asked), and Dunya and Grisha promptly began planning how to transport Slava as fast as possible. Everyone went to bed that night in excellent spirits, and several of the men stopped themselves just in time from slapping Slava on the back and kissing her on the cheeks like a brother.

Everyone except Slava awoke in an even better mood than the one they had taken to bed with them the night before, and ate breakfast and packed up in the dark with a great deal of singing and shouting. Dima even had to break up an impromptu snowball fight between Mi-sha, Slanik, and Olik before they could set off, although he was laugh-ing so much it took him several tries. Only Slava was unable to join in the general merriment.

"Normally I always feel whatever anyone around me is feeling, so why not this time?" she complained to the snow hare. "Why am I so worried, when they're not?"

"Because you have a task to perform, Krasnoslava," said the snow hare. "You're worrying about that instead of wallowing in the subtle-ties of everyone's ever-changing moods."

"True," said Slava.

"Are you ready? We have ground to cover today. The sooner we reach the road, the sooner I can go back to my business."

"If this is too much trouble for you..." began Slava.

"Be quiet, Krasnoslava, and let me help you," said the snow hare. "I'm not going to leave you, so the less whining you do, the faster this will go. Get in the sled and tell the others it's time to go." He placed himself conspicuously in front of the first sled. The dogs all sniffed eagerly in his direction, as if they could almost, but not quite, catch his scent.

"Ah," said Slava nervously. "Ah, well, it's time to go, I guess." She had to repeat herself several times before the others heard her, but once they did, they all stopped what they were doing and gathered around the sleds, ready to take off.

It had been decided the night before that Slava would just ride in the first sled, and give the others directions. Slava had wanted to object to that, but had managed to stop herself, knowing that it was the only sensible solution.

"Everyone ready?" asked the snow hare, flicking his ears at her, and then bounded off. It took Slava a moment to remember that she had to tell the others to follow him, but when she did, they all bolted forward with a loud cheer.

The day passed in a blur of tree trunks and snowdrifts for Slava. She was not especially surprised to discover that the snow hare could gallop along for versts and versts, but she was surprised to find out that the others could keep up with him.

How badly did I slow them down? she wondered guiltily, and then remembered the hare's advice to shut up, and decided to follow it. What was done was done.

It was cloudy all day, but the sun was just visible enough to show them that they were still going in the right direction. When they stopped for the night, Dunya announced that they must have gone well over forty, maybe fifty versts, something the snow hare confirmed when Slava asked it.

"We should reach the road in just a few days, if we keep up this pace," Dunya said, eliciting another cheer from the group. The gloom that had overcome them on leaving the base camp had melted away. No one spoke at all any more of exploring the Far North; now everyone was focused on reaching the road and Lesnograd, as if that had been their original and only destination.

It snowed during the night, but once again, this failed to bring down the general mood, and they set off once again with loud cheers.

Everyone seemed to be enjoying themselves tremendously. And when the sun rose that day, Slava's spirits suddenly rose with it, and she joined the others in their cheering.

"I guess I've finally been infected by the others' good spirits," she told the snow hare, when they stopped for the midday meal.

"No, you started leading, Krasnoslava," said the snow hare. "That is what leaders do."

"Ah," said Slava doubtfully. She didn't see how she could be much—any kind, actually—of a leader. But nothing happened all that day to contradict the snow hare's words.

Their good fortune continued the next day, and the day after that, and on the third day, just as the sun was setting, they suddenly burst out of the trees and onto the road. It was such a surprise that for a moment they all stood there, unsure where they were or what they had found.

"Is this the road?" asked Slanik.

"It looks like it," said Misha, scuffing at the snow and giving it a skeptical look.

Olga looked up the straight clear stretch in which they had found themselves, and then turned and looked down the other way. "It has to be the road," she said. "Nothing else would be this straight."

"I think those are old sleigh tracks," said Dima, pointing at faint marks in the snow.

Dunya skied off the road and then skied back on. "It's the road," she announced. "The snow's packed down. Lots of sleighs have passed this way."

Everyone looked back and forth at each other for a moment, and then burst into cheers of "Ura! Uuuura! Ai-da Tsarinovna! The road!"

"Congratulations, Krasnoslava," said the snow hare. "You've become a leader and a hero. Don't forget it." He wrinkled his nose at her, and loped off into the trees. Before Slava could call after him, he had disappeared out of sight.

Now that they were on the road, Dunya decided that they were in no danger of losing their way, and said they should keep going, even without the snow hare. Slava retired to the back of the group, where she felt much more comfortable, and they took off, moving in what Dunya said was indubitably the direction of Lesnograd.

They kept going long after the sun had set and a thin strip of stars became visible between the walls of trees rising up on either side of them. Dunya wanted to find a good place for them to camp off the road, but when the dogs began to flag and they still hadn't found one, Olga convinced her that stopping on the road would be fine, as the likelihood of other travelers coming through at night was extremely low.

It did feel odd camping there, but now that they had left the forest, no one was keen to return to it, even to make camp a few yards from the road. The trees, which had seemed perfectly friendly when they were traveling through them, now stood forbiddingly on either side of the narrow cleared area that was the road, as if guarding secrets.

"I wonder how far it is to Lesnograd," Slava said as they were getting into their bedclothes for the night. Even though she had been surprised at her own ability to sleep on the ground when necessary, the thought of getting into an actual bed instead of a tent in the snow was more seductive than she could have possibly imagined back in Krasnograd.

Olga and Dunya pulled out their maps, and began trying to calculate exactly where they had met the road. The problem, of course, was that they didn't know how far they had gone astray when the compass broke, and whether they had been traveling due South or not when they reached the road.

"I wonder if it can be fixed," said Dunya, taking out the compass and looking at it in disgust. She moved to put it back into the map pouch, but then froze.

"Olga Vasilisovna, which way is our tent facing?" she asked.

"East, most likely," said Olga. "The Severnovostochnaya road runs due East-West most of the way."

"Then..." Dunya set the map pouch on the tent floor, in order to make a flat surface, and laid the compass on it. Olga leaned over and stared at it.

"It's fixed," she said disbelievingly. "It's pointing North."

Slava leaned over it too. The needle was pointing at the North side of the tent. Olga picked up the compass and moved it to the other side of the tent, but it continued to point North.

"It was broken," said Dunya blankly. "It was broken, I could have sworn it..."

"So could I," said Olga. They both turned and looked at Slava.

"It was broken," said Slava, blushing under their fixed stares. "We all checked, and it was broken."

"And now it's not," said Olga, giving Slava a meaningful look.

"No, it's not," repeated Dunya, also giving Slava a meaningful look.

"Yes, it's very mysterious," said Slava, quailing under their meaningful looks and wondering why they seemed to think she had something to do with it.

"Magical, one might say," said Olga.

"I don't see what else it could be," said Dunya.

"But it has nothing to do with me," said Slava, shrinking down even more.

"No?" said Olga, raising her eyebrows.

Dunya had stopped staring at Slava and was staring at the tent wall instead. "The question is," she said, "who changed the compass? The snow hare that led us to the road, or some other force?"

"Yes," said Olga, still looking at Slava out of the corner of her eye. "Was the snow hare rescuing us from someone else's trick, or was it tricking us in order to gain our confidence?"

"Why would it do that?" asked Slava.

"Who knows? I can't pretend to fathom the ways of magical creatures who appear only to the chosen few." Olga's tone was enigmatic. Once again, Slava had the feeling that Olga was looking at her as if she were a racehorse of unknown breeding whom Olga had bought on a whim.

"Well, it doesn't matter anyway," said Dunya. "He led us to the road, and now it's up to us to make it to Lesnograd."

"Without any further magical interference, let's hope," said Olga.

"Let's hope," said Dunya. "Meanwhile, we should rest. Our supplies are low enough that I would like to make it to a town sooner rather than later. If we wander around too much more, it won't matter whether or not the wood-spirits have it in for us, because hunger will do their job for them."

On that sobering note, they went to bed. Slava kept surfacing from sleep with images of spinning compasses in her head, but before she could wake up entirely, she would sink back down into her dreams, which seemed to be trying to say something very important to her.

As best Slava could tell in the winter darkness, they rose and set off very early the next morning. Dunya wanted them to cover as much ground as possible, and also to find a crossroad or village that would tell them where they were on the road and how much farther they had to go to Lesnograd. Everyone was still in excellent spirits, and they covered more than fifteen versts by sunrise.

The sun never actually appeared in the sky that day, only heavy gray clouds that seemed to press down on the treetops, so that they felt as if they were traveling down a narrow dark tunnel through trees and clouds. The sensation of enclosure was so strong that it was a shock when they suddenly encountered a crossroad, just as the sun was setting.

"I wonder where it goes," speculated Misha, as they stood there in the middle of it, looking to see if there were any markers hidden under the snow.

"Do you think it was made by people?" asked Slanik. He was, Slava noticed, standing very close to Grisha. In fact, they were all huddled together, even the dogs. Far from reassuring them, the crossroad seemed to have something ominous about it. Once they had come to the road, the wall of trees on either side of them had seemed to stand against whatever malevolent forces might be dwelling in the forest, but now the crossroad had sliced through that wall, and anything could come through.

"I don't see any markers," Dunya announced, after she and Olga had scuffed through the snow all around the clearing.

"Nor do I," said Olga. "I wonder where it goes."

A cold North wind blew down the crossroad, causing everyone to start shivering. The dogs whined and shifted restlessly.

"I think we should leave," said Dima quietly.

"Right as usual," said Olga. "No point in hanging about in the cold! Let's keep going, everyone. The faster we travel, the sooner we'll be in Lesnograd!"

This elicited a halfhearted cheer, and they took off again. Everyone felt better once they were in motion, but the cold wind kept blowing after them, as if it had found them at the crossroad and was now

255

following them.

The sun set, but they decided to keep going, as it was hard to lose their way on the road, even on such a dark night. From time to time Slava, who was riding on Dunya's sled, would give in to the desire to look back in the direction of the wind. She kept telling herself there was nothing to see, but the wind kept rising, making it sound as if heavy bodies were moving through the woods.

Dunya eventually called another halt, in a slightly wider spot in the road. "I think we should stop," she said. "The dogs are worn out, and so are we. If we go any farther tonight, we won't be able to cover much ground tomorrow."

The dogs were in fact drooping, and seemed grateful for the chance to rest, but as Slava helped Olik and Slanik unharness and feed them, she couldn't help but notice that they kept lifting their heads from their food and looking back in the direction they had come. The wind had risen to the point that tree branches could occasionally be heard crashing to the ground, and no matter how tightly Slava pulled her clothing around her body, the cold air found its way to her skin.

Everyone huddled close as they ate dinner. Dunya, Slava noticed, kept looking up at the sky as if seeking guidance. When she caught Slava watching her, she smiled apologetically, in a very un-Dunya-like fashion, and said, "I can't stop myself from checking our direction."

"And are we still going the right way?" asked Slava.

"Yes, but it's going to be a cold night. Look at the sky!"

Slava looked up. The wind had broken up the clouds, which were rushing across the sky like galloping horses. She felt as though she could hear a distant, high-pitched whistling from their movement, although it must have just been her imagination, because the wind was now so loud in the trees that it would have drowned out any sound from up higher.

They all retired to their tents immediately after supper, but sleep was slow in coming. The wind continued to rise, making the heavy fabric flap vigorously.

"What if a tree gets blown down on us in the night?" Slava heard Misha ask from the neighboring tent.

"You'll have to put your hands over your head, I guess," said Dima. "Now go to sleep!"

Misha fell silent, but Slava had already been infected with his worry, and every time she started to drop off, she saw a tree crashing down on top of them, and jerked back awake.

Despite the noise of the wind and her tree fears, the exhaustion of the day did eventually drag Slava into sleep, where she dreamed of compasses and stars again.

"You're heading straight towards danger, Krasnoslava," someone said to her, and she realized it was the snow hare.

"But danger is following you too," said someone else, and she saw it was the elk.

"You cannot escape us," said a pair of golden eyes, and Slava jerked back awake yet again.

For a moment she lay there in confusion. The tent was no longer flapping against her face, but she could still hear branches crashing in the woods. Branches and something else. Then she realized that the other sound was that of footsteps.

"Olga," she whispered, reaching under the covers and grabbing Olga's sleeve. "Olga, can you hear that?"

"Hmm?" Olga must have been sleeping lightly too, for Slava could feel her jerk awake under her hand. "Hear what?"

"The footsteps."

"What is it?" whispered Dunya, who had also jerked awake and was now sitting up as best she could under the low tent ceiling. "The wind has stopped."

"Yes, but there's something out there," whispered Slava.

"Lots of somethings, by the sound of it," whispered Olga. "Elk, perhaps?"

"It's not elk," whispered Dunya.

There was a particularly loud crash from the woods. The dogs, instead of barking, all whined, and Slava could hear the men scrambling in the other tent to grab their gear and weapons.

"We should get out of here," whispered Dunya. "Whatever it is, we don't want to be trapped in this tent." She pulled something out of her back, which Slava realized was a knife as long as her forearm that she had been keeping tucked under her shirt. Olga fumbled in her bedclothes and retrieved an actual sword. Even under the circumstances, Slava couldn't help blurting out, "Have you been keeping that thing in bed with you the whole time?"

"I didn't want you to know, in case it would worry you," said Olga. "Here." She thrust something into Slava's hands, which turned out to be a knife. It was much smaller than Dunya's, but still much larger than any knife Slava had ever used before.

"What do I do with it?" Slava asked, as they crawled out of the tent.

"Hit anything that looks unfriendly," said Olga. "And Slava?" They came out from behind the tent and saw what had awoken them. "Hit hard."

Chapter Sixteen

At first Slava thought that they had somehow gotten off the road and were back in the forest. Then she realized that the road hadn't gone anywhere, it had just disappeared under all the leshiye that were crowding around their camp.

"What do you want from me?" Slava cried out as soon as she saw them, she wasn't sure why.

Dozens, maybe hundreds, of enormous eyes blinked slowly at her. One pair flashed gold, and stepped to the front of the pack.

"Did you really think you could escape us so easily, Krasnoslava?" it asked.

Around her, Slava dimly knew, half of the group was trying to harness the dogs, who were cringing into the snow, and the other half were trying to form up defensively around her, but they all seemed insubstantial compared to the golden eyes looming in front of her.

"What do you want from me!" she repeated. "Leave me alone!" As she said it, she wondered how many times she had said that phrase, either out loud or in her head, and how many times it had been ignored. No doubt this would be another one of those times.

"Ah, Krasnoslava! If only we could! But I am afraid your gift is too rare for us to let it slip through our fingers, so to speak." And the sorceress-leshaya laughed. None of the other leshiye joined her, Slava noticed. They all seemed to be puzzled by the conversation as much as anything. The sorceress-leshaya, Slava thought, was much more like a person than the others, and could think in multiple directions at once, instead of only in one, like a tree.

"Now, I know you suffer from a certain faintness of heart," the sorceress-leshaya continued, sounding annoyingly like Slava's sister.

"But I will help you overcome that. Wouldn't you like to overcome that, Krasnoslava? Wouldn't you like to be brave? You've already had your first taste of leading—and you liked it. You liked it when the others followed you—admired you—obeyed you, even. You liked it. It runs in your blood to like it. Your foremothers could grow drunk on the mere sight of proud princesses and mighty warriors kneeling at their feet. What we will give you will be like that, only a thousand times better. Wouldn't you like that?"

Olga, Dunya, and the others, Slava noticed, did not seem to be able to hear their conversation. Olga and Dima had taken up defensive positions on either side of her, and were now standing there, their gazes moving back and forth between her and the leshiye in bewilderment. Dunya and Grisha had given up trying to harness the dogs for the moment, and were also standing there, watching her with looks of incomprehension.

"Please leave me alone," said Slava again.

"Krasnoslava! Think of all I could give you! All you have to do is trust me!" The sorceress-leshaya took another step forward and stretched out her branches towards Slava.

"Keep back!" cried Slava.

"For once in your life, Krasnoslava, don't be so fainthearted!" cried the sorceress-leshaya, taking another step forward. Olga and Dima raised their swords, and the others hurried to join them. The leshiye rustled their branches, and clumped together even more closely.

"NO!" screamed Slava. Everyone froze.

"No, Krasnoslava?" asked the sorceress-leshaya. "You won't be brave, not even once? You won't do this one thing, for a lifetime of happiness?"

"NO!" shouted Slava. "I won't! I don't want your courage! The world has too much of it already!"

"Oh come now, Krasnoslava, how many times have you dreamed of being brave? Don't deny it; I've seen inside your head, you know. You can't stop me: it's part of your gift. But is that really what you want? Wouldn't you prefer to be able to have things the other way, so that your thoughts entered other people's heads, instead of their thoughts invading your own?"

"I'm not like them!" shouted Slava. "I won't be like them! I won't be like you!"

"And how are you going to stop me, Krasnoslava?" asked the sorceress-leshaya, taking another step closer. Misha suddenly made a

260

desperate swing at her with his sword, but she knocked him aside effortlessly, throwing him down onto the snow. He lay there groaning, and didn't get back up.

"You can't make me into you!" Slava shouted. "You can't change me!"

The golden eyes smiled condescendingly. "The blood of a hare would have worked," they said. "But the blood of your comrades will be so much better."

Olga and Dima, who had recognized the sorceress-leshaya's intentions even though they could not hear what she said, both stepped towards her. Everyone else moved to follow them.

"NO!" screamed Slava for a third time. "NO, NO, NO!" And, taking the others so much by surprise that they failed even to stretch out a hand to stop her, she darted past them and threw herself into the branches of the sorceress-leshaya.

It clutched her to its trunk convulsively, its branches digging painfully into her back and ribs. "Krasnoslava!" it said in her ear, with the voice of a lover who has finally possessed the object of her desire. "Krasnoslava, I knew you would not fail me!" And Slava realized how desperately badly it had wanted her gift.

"Open your mind to me, Krasnoslava," it whispered, and with the next breath Slava's mind was filled with the golden haze of its eyes. She saw the endless taiga, bordered only by the tundra to the North and the steppe to the South. She could sense all the lives, big and small, animal and vegetable, that filled that vast expanse, and realized that she could speak to them all. Somewhere far to the South—perhaps on the Middle Sea—the sun was already shining down brightly on people who were rising and going about their business with joy in their hearts, but here in her midnight land there was still nothing but stars and darkness.

"Take my gifts, Krasnoslava, in exchange for your own," the sorceress-leshaya whispered to her, and she could feel it running its branches through her thoughts, trying to find something.

"I have nothing to give you," she told it.

"Nonsense, Krasnoslava, your gift is immense," said the sorceress-leshaya.

"No," said Slava. "I see it clearly for the first time. My greatest gift is emptiness. Emptiness and outpouring. You can try to take it if you wish, but how can you take the waterfall? How can you carry off the steppe?"

The sorceress-leshaya held her so tightly that Slava could no longer breathe, and tried again to grasp her essence, but as Slava had told it, it could no more catch her gift than it could hold the wind in its needles. Slava began to feel sorry for it.

"Here," she said, and showed it her pity. "My gift."

"I don't want it!" shouted the sorceress-leshaya, and threw her down onto the snow.

All of a sudden sound returned to Slava's ears, along with breath to her lungs, and she heard how the others were shouting in panic. A pair of arms grabbed her around her sore ribs, and another snatched up her flopping feet.

"Run," she whispered to the arms holding her ribs. "Run while you can."

She had meant for the arms to leave her and save themselves, but instead both sets kept a firm hold on her, and took off running with her dangling between them.

She thumped down on something low to the ground, and then the snow was rushing past her face. "Hold on!" a voice shouted at her. "Hold on to the sled, Tsarinovna!"

Slava clutched at the thing she was lying on, and realized that she was in one of the sleds, and that Dunya was driving her at breakneck speed down the road. She pulled herself slightly more upright, and looked around. Dunya's sled was out in front of the group, but the others were also running, skiing, or driving as fast as they could. Not all of the dogs had been harnessed, and pieces of harness and unharnessed dogs were bouncing and bounding alongside the sleds. The sorceress-leshaya had collapsed onto the ground, and the other leshiye, instead of chasing after Slava and the others, were gathered around their leader.

"I think we're leaving them behind," said Slava.

"Along with the tents," said Dunya grimly, and shouted at the dogs to go faster.

Chapter Seventeen

Dunya drove for at least a couple of versts before stopping abruptly.

"We should wait for the others," she said, getting off the sled to check the dogs.

Slava sat limply on the sled. She felt completely empty, and she was also a little afraid she might throw up. Whatever had happened between her and the sorceress-leshaya had come as a great shock to both of them, and she wondered if it had been hurt. She was also worried she might have broken some ribs.

Olga and Slanik were the first to catch up with them. They had Misha and the second sled, and nothing else.

"The others are coming," Olga announced. "But I wanted to make sure I found you."

"How is he?" asked Dunya, nodding at Misha. The unharnessed dogs, who had refused to leave their packmates, were now crowded around Misha, sniffing him anxiously.

"He'll probably live," said Olga. "And the Tsarinovna?"

Dunya nodded her head towards Slava, and Olga came over to her.

"Are you hurt, Tsarinovna?" she asked.

"No," said Slava, and then winced from the pain in her ribs. "Well, my chest hurts a little," she admitted. "But I'll get better soon."

"What happened there? What did you do?"

"The sorceress-leshaya tried to take my gift, in exchange for her own," said Slava. "But she couldn't. You can't take what isn't there."

Olga gave her a sideways look. "A whole army of leshiye just came for you, Tsarinovna," she said. "You have a gift."

"Yes, but..." Slava realized she didn't feel like explaining everything to Olga, and waved her hand dismissively. "She failed," she said instead. "And I think it hurt her, and we escaped."

"Ah," said Olga, giving Slava another long considering look. Before she could ask any more questions, however, Volodya, Olik, Vova, and Grisha came skiing in.

"Dmitry Marusyevich is bringing up the rear with the rest," Grisha reported. "I don't think they were followed. Is the Tsarinovna safe?"

"I'm fine," said Slava. She thought about standing up in order to prove it, but decided it would be a bad idea. She was starting to feel very hungry, which made her realize that they had, of course, left all their supplies back at the camp, along with the tents.

Dima and the others, along with the last sled, arrived shortly.

"No sign of pursuit," he said. "Whatever the Tsarinovna did, it hurt them so much they didn't even try to come after us."

"Good," said Olga. "Now we just have the tiny problem of being in the middle of the woods in the middle of winter without food or shelter."

"Is that all, Olga Vasilisovna?" said Dima. Everyone laughed, and for a moment, the problem didn't seem so serious.

"The sun will be rising soon," announced Dunya. "We should try to go as far as we can while we can see clearly." Slava realized that among other things, they had also left their lanterns back at the camp. "What is the likelihood of coming across a settlement anytime soon, Olga Vasilisovna?"

Olga shrugged. "Settlements are few and far between in Severnolesnoye," she said. "But there are a few cabins for travelers along the road. If we're lucky, we might find one today or tomorrow. If we keep moving, we should be able to survive for a day or two, even without our tents and supplies. And if we have to, we can always eat the dogs."

Slava's heart lurched at this suggestion, but fortunately there was so much unhappy muttering from the men that Olga was forced to retract it, although she said rather tartly that they might reconsider after a few more hours of hunger and cold.

"In any case, we should get moving," said Dunya, and began catching and harnessing the loose dogs.

They set off again just as the sun was rising. The appearance of light in the sky cheered everyone up, and they all spoke hopefully about coming across some settlement or cabin before too long. Some of them also kept a sharp eye out for any signs of leshiye in the woods, but they saw nothing.

After a few more versts, however, everyone was becoming hungry and tired, and they hadn't seen so much as a crossroad, let alone any signs of food, shelter, or other people. As the sun sank behind the trees, everyone's mood sank with it.

"What will we do if we don't come across shelter soon?" asked Volodya, a whine creeping into his voice.

"Keep going," Grisha told him sharply.

"And then what? We can't go on forever."

"You're welcome to lie down and die, boy, if that's what you want," Grisha said, even more sharply.

"No one's lying down and dying," Dima interjected, in a tone that said the discussion was over. Grisha went back to staring grimly at the snow in front of him, and Volodya fell into a silent sulk.

The wind had been dying all day, and by nightfall—which, Dunya reminded them, was really early afternoon—the air became completely still, and the sky was covered with a thick layer of clouds. With no moon and no stars, it was so dark that they could only make out the road because they could move forward down it without getting caught in the trees.

Slava's ribs had by now become sore enough that every breath was painful, and she lay on the sled feeling sorry for herself. Her self-pity consumed enough of her attention that she didn't understand at first why the group had come to a sudden halt. She had to look around for several moments before she realized that there was more empty space around them than usual, and the reason for that was that they had come to a crossroad.

"Should we keep going or turn?" the others were asking. Everyone looked at Olga for an answer.

"And there's no sign of a marker?" she asked.

Dunya and Dima shook their heads.

"It's not under the snow somewhere?"

They shook their heads again.

"It must be a very minor road, then," said Olga.

"Maybe leading to a cabin?" asked Vova hopefully.

"Maybe," said Olga.

"But which way?" asked Dima, looking up and down the road.

"To the North," said a voice from the woods.

Tired as they were, everyone jumped and looked around wildly.

"Who's there?" called Olga. "Show yourselves!"

"First put your weapons down and your hands up," said the voice from the woods.

Olga started to laugh. The hysterical note in her voice was probably noticeable only to Slava, and maybe Dima. "Bandits!" she said. "Bandits! We've come this far only to be captured by bandits!" She unsheathed her sword, which she had been carrying on her belt ever since they had escaped from the leshiye, put it on the snow, and raised her hands in the air. The others, after hesitating and looking at her in surprise, did the same.

"Now come out of the woods," Olga called.

A rather shabby-looking man, who, as far as Slava could tell in the near dark, was enough like Grisha to be his second-brother, stepped out of the trees, followed by a dozen equally shabby-looking men. Banditry, thought Slava, must be a hard life, especially in Severnolesnoye in the winter.

"I hope you have something of value on you," said the shabby-looking man who appeared to be the leader.

"Absolutely nothing," said Olga cheerfully. "We just escaped with nothing but our lives and our dogs this morning, and have been hoping to come across a rescuer ever since. And here you are."

The shabby-looking leader seemed to be rather taken aback by this greeting, but rallied quickly and said, "Too bad for you, noblewoman. You are a noblewoman, aren't you? You don't have much of a guard to protect you."

"I am," said Olga, still sounding unaccountably cheerful.

"And from what family, noblewoman?"

"Severnolesnaya, in fact."

The bandits all started and exchanged uncertain glances.

"She could be lying, Vas' Marinych," called one of them.

"I'm not, Vasily Marinovich," said Olga. "My name is Olga Vasilisovna Severnolesnaya, and I'm on my way to Lesnograd."

"And what happened to your supplies, noblewoman?" asked Vasily Marinovich, giving Olga a shrewd-but-not-actually-that-shrewd look that showed why he was the leader of a petty group of starving bandits.

"We had to flee for our lives this morning," Olga told him brightly. "Naturally, we were unable to pack up our supplies on our way out."

"And what were you fleeing from, noblewoman?" asked Vasily Marinovich, who appeared to have recovered from the initial shock and was trying to retake the upper hand in the conversation.

"Leshiye," said Olga. "Lots of them."

"Hah!" said Vasily Marinovich. "You'll have to do better than that, noblewoman!"

"You don't believe in leshiye, then?" asked Olga, raising an eyebrow.

"It's not that I don't believe in them, noblewoman," said Vasily Marinovich. "It's just that I don't believe packs of them would be out hunting you. Your leshaya, now, is a shy creature. She doesn't like big crowds of people, especially city folk like you"—Grisha bristled at being called "city folk," but kept silent—"and she won't gather together with others of her kind, like wolves do. She's basically a loner, your leshaya."

"Nevertheless..." began Olga, but the muttering of the bandits agreeing with their leader drowned out her voice.

"Brothers!" cried Grisha, interrupting what was turning into a sticky situation. "Northern brothers! Hear me!"

"And who are you, milksucker?" shouted one of the bandits.

"Grisha, brothers, Grigory Nadezhdovich, from the village of Troyerechnaya, in Severnolesnoye. Aren't some of my Troyerechnaya brothers here? Is that not Vlast' Yevgenich I see there in the back?"

One of the bandits, who had been trying to remain concealed behind the others, shuffled his feet uncomfortably, and the others shouted, "It is, Grish Nadezhdych, it is!"

"And do you really mean to raise your hand against your own brother, Vlast' Yevgenich?"

"Well argued, Grish Nadezhdych!" cried several of the bandits, while Vlastomir Yevgeniyevich continued shuffling his feet, and Vasily Marinovich frowned.

"Enough!" he said. "I make the decisions here. We're taking these noblewomen and their men hostage, and we're demanding a ransom from Lesnogorod for them. That'll sort them out quick enough. If this noblewoman really is the Princess's daughter, we'll get enough money to winter on, and summer too, and if she's lying, we'll get money for catching an imposter."

The bandits, who were clearly a fickle bunch, all cheered loudly at this announcement, and went around smiling broadly and taking everyone's weapons. When Slava said she didn't have a weapon, they gave her a sideways glance, but let her be.

Once everyone had been disarmed, Vasily Marinovich shouted that everyone should follow him, and they set off down the crossroad. Vasily Marinovich had ordered that the sleds were to be driven by his men, and so Slava found herself being driven very clumsily by a lad of no more than sixteen or seventeen, who introduced himself brightly as Mirik.

"Don't worry, noblewoman, you'll be snug as can be while we wait for the Princess to send your ransom," he told her comfortingly. "You have such a sweet look, I'm sure no one will want to raise a hand against you, you know. What village are you from?"

"Krasnograd," Slava told him, having to suppress a smile at his endearing naïveté even under what could only be described as desperate circumstances.

"The Black God take me! Really! Krasnogorod!" exclaimed Mirik, turning to stare at her and almost running the dogs off the road. When he realized his error, he swore with such vigor that Dunya insisted he let her drive. He resisted for a moment, but when she told him that he could always throw her off the sled if he thought she was leading them astray, he agreed, and went back to staring at Slava.

"Krasnogorod!" he exclaimed again, pronouncing the name as if it were the title of some exotic foreign city, perhaps across the Middle Sea. "Why did you leave, then, noblewoman?" he asked, gazing at her with an expression of burning curiosity and awe.

"I wanted to see the North," Slava told him.

"Well, you've come to the right place, that's for sure, noblewoman," said Mirik. "It don't get much more North than this."

"Mmm," said Slava. "Where are you from, Mirik?"

"Malaya Roshcha, noblewoman," Mirik announced, with an expression that told her the name of his obscure village should have some significance for her.

"Yes?" said Slava, hoping for more enlightenment.

Mirik gave her a curious look. "You haven't heard of Malaya Roshcha, noblewoman?" he asked, his voice taking on a tone of superiority.

Slava shook her head.

"Well, perhaps the common folk of Krasnogorod never heard the news," said Mirik, sounding as if this were a new thought for him. "But the Tsarina knows for certain, because we sent her notice of it, only we never heard back, but she must be fearful busy, don't you think, noblewoman?"

"I'm sure of it," said Slava.

"But we sent her notice of it, so the Tsarina knows. Have you ever seen the Tsarina, noblewoman?"

"Yes," said Slava.

Mirik swore again, this time so floridly that Dunya glanced at Slava to see if she would take offense, and, seeing that she had not, had to cough hastily into her glove to hide her laugh.

"They say she's fearful pretty, and very harsh and cruel. Is it true, noblewoman?" asked Mirik, once he had gotten over his shock.

"I suppose," said Slava. "The Tsarina is quite tall, taller than you or I," she told him, struck by a sudden inspiration to gain his trust by telling him what was more or less the truth. "And she has a great long braid of dark hair that she wears as a crown, and her large gray eyes are slanted like a wolf's, and everywhere she goes, women step back in fear and men offer to lay down their lives in her service."

Mirik sighed at this alluring image. "Does she dress very fine, noblewoman?" he asked.

"She has four maids, all white-handed noblewomen themselves, who do nothing but brush her hair and array her in fine gowns and precious gems. Her jewelry is as heavy as a warrior's armor, too heavy for her maids to lift, so she has a trusted guard whose duty it is to dress her in her jewels." All this was, alas, completely true, although Slava, who found her sister's vanity almost as much cause for agonizing embarrassment as her cruelty and selfishness, was not normally in the habit of bragging about it to strangers.

Mirik sighed again and gazed off at the woods for a while at this thought, but then collected himself and turned back to Slava. "They say she has a younger sister, noblewoman, is that true?"

"It is," said Slava.

"They say she is very kind and soft; as kind as the Empress is hard: is that true, noblewoman?"

"I suppose," said Slava.

"They say," said Mirik, gazing ahead with misty eyes at the image in his head, "that she is the most merciful woman in Zem', and will beg for mercy for even the most hardened criminals. They say that she can look into your heart and see all the good in it, even if it is just the most tiny amount, no bigger than a kernel of wheat, and whatever good there is, that is all she will see, and not all the evil surrounding it, and that is why she is so kind, because to her, all people are good. Is that true, noblewoman?"

"I don't know," said Slava, mortified to feel her nose and eyes filling with tears. But Mirik only remarked on how cold the wind was, before continuing, "She must be fearful pretty too, even prettier than her sister, my head for beheading."

"No, not really," said Slava, now having to suppress a smile.

"Oh, but she must be, noblewoman," Mirik argued. "A light of goodness must follow her wherever she goes, and she must have the sweetest face in all of Zem', how could she not?" He sighed again, and gazed dreamily at the trees, clearly lost in some fantasy of the imaginary Slava and her sweet face.

"Really, she just looks a lot like me," said Slava.

"Have you seen her then, noblewoman? As well as the Empress, I mean?"

"Yes," said Slava. "And really, she doesn't look that much different than me. I don't think I've ever heard her described as 'pretty.' Actually, many people find her frightening to look upon: they fear that she can, in fact, see into their hearts, and so they dislike having her look at them."

"I don't believe it," said Mirik. He paused and gave Slava a considering once-over, as if he could see anything under the layers of warm clothing she was wearing. "And you really are quite sweet to look upon yourself, noblewoman. Don't take offense, noblewoman; I meant no harm. You really do remind me of my mother; well, like somebody's mother. You've got a good face: I could spot it right away. You remind me a bit of my sister. Not in the face—no one's face is as fair as Milochka's—but in the softness of your eyes."

"I'm not at all offended," Slava assured him, having to cough into her glove herself in order to conceal a laugh. Mirik no doubt thought he was a real man, now that he was running with a gang of bandits, and that he was talking just as a real man should. Probably in his heart he considered himself secretly noble and above such a life of crime and petty indignities, but was bearing up under it as best he could. "You promised to tell me the tale of Malaya Roshcha," she reminded him, once she had gained control of herself.

"So I did, noblewoman, so I did." Mirik composed himself in thought for a moment, a comical sight in such a young man, and then began grandly:

"Malaya Roshcha is a small village South of Lesnogorod, noblewoman, known for its rich earth, its fertile cows, and its handsome villagers. We were all very handsome, noblewoman, but my older sister was considered the handsomest girl in Malaya Roshcha, so you can imagine how handsome she must have been. Her name was Lyudmila, Lyudmila Krasnoslavovna, and she had hair the color of flame, eyes the color of the summer sky, skin like cream, the figure of a young birch, and the voice of a lark. My mother had her when she was very young, not yet even married, and she claimed that the father was some wood-spirit in human form. And he must have been, to have fathered a maid so fair."

Here Mirik dropped his singsong story voice for a moment to say, "Really, she was fearful pretty, noblewoman; I doubt even the Tsarina could've held a candle to her. Fearful pretty. They say it's not good to be too pretty, sometimes, though, or you'll anger the gods, and I guess that's what happened."

"So they say," said Slava. She tried to tell herself it meant nothing that Lyudmila's mother was also a Krasnoslava. Krasnoslavas had been ten a grosh for the past hundred years, ever since a certain Krasnoslava Tsarina had not only driven back yet another invasion by the Hordes, but had routed them utterly and destroyed that particular clan down to the last suckling babe. For a moment Slava couldn't help but marvel yet again at her descent from such bloodthirsty stock.

Mirik sighed and, picking up his singsong voice again, continued, distracting Slava from her contemplation of her heritage of fire and steel: "All the lads were wild for her, of course, but none of them dared ask their mothers to send the matchmaker to her, and when my mother sent the matchmaker to other families, she was always turned down. 'Too much trouble,' the other mothers would say. 'We want a girl of this earth, not some gift of the gods. Mark our words: she'll come to a bad end, and take our sons down with her. You shouldn't've had her, Krasnoslava, you shouldn't've had her. The daughters of youthful whims rarely turn out well.'

"But my mother loved our Milochka more than anything, and when all the village mothers turned her down, she said, 'You are far too good for them anyway, Milochka. It's time for us to go to Lesnogorod and make a proper match for you. Perhaps some merchant or noblewoman will take a fancy to you for her son, and you'll spend the rest of your life with white hands, instead of ruining your beauty here in Malaya Roshcha.'

"'I care not for his mother's money, so long as his singing is sweet,' said Milochka with a toss of her proud head, for she was proud, noblewoman, very proud. Not of her beauty, but of her spirit and her song. She was always a spirited girl, noblewoman, for all her sweetness. No one could stand against her once she had set her heart on something. To tell the truth, noblewoman, she had let it be known that she cared little for any of the village lads, which may have been why their mothers were so set against her.

"So they set off for Lesnogorod. My father and I stayed behind, to tend to the house and crops. We missed Milochka very much, but we hoped my mother would return without her, but with the news that she had been married to some merchant's son and would spend the rest of her days in silks and satins.

"But it was not to be. One night last spring we were awakened by the sound of someone banging on the door. We opened it, and Milochka fell across the threshold, covered in dirt from the road.

"'Help me, brother, father,' she sobbed. 'Save me!'

"We helped her up, and demanded to know what was the matter and where our mother was.

"'In Lesnogorod,' she sobbed, and for a long time could say nothing more through her tears. But when she was finally able to speak, her tale chilled our blood.

"She told us that prospective brides and grooms come to the main square in Lesnogorod in the evenings, and their mothers stroll here and there, looking for a good match, 'like cattle at the market!' she cried. Her proud heart could hardly bear such humiliation, but for our mother's sake she stood it. And one day she heard a bard singing in the corner, and she went over and sang with him, and soon they decided that they should marry each other and no one else.

"Now, the life of a musician is not overly sweet, and my mother resisted the match. But she could not stop Milochka from running to sing with her sweetheart every evening, and one day some great nobleman, someone from the Princess's family, heard her.

"He asked her to come to the kremlin and sing for him, and she did, and soon his head was turned completely—noblemen have such weak heads sometimes, noblewoman! He approached our mother with a proposition, which she accepted. Milochka refused even to consider the matter, but my mother insisted, and then the nobleman sent guards to take her to his palace, by force if need be, and so she jumped out the window and ran away, and she ran all the way back to Malaya Roshcha.

"At first my father tried to persuade Milochka to take this nobleman's proposition, for by it she would gain riches beyond all our dreams, but she cried so that in the end he promised to hide her if the nobleman or his guards came looking for her. Besides, he said, what kind of life could his daughter have with a man who was so lost to all shame that he would go chasing after young maids. Where, asked our father, was this man's mother, so that she would let him act in so un-seemly a fashion. It was better not to be connected with such a family as that, no matter how rich and nobly born. A man who didn't know his place and his duty was no fit husband for our Milochka, no matter what he could offer.

"But alas, our mother's heart had grown greatly fond of this scheme of hers, and so she led the nobleman straight to our village.

"First he begged, and then he threatened, and so Milochka decid-ed she must leave our house for everyone's safety. She asked all her friends to take her in, but they all refused, saying she should give in to the nobleman, for if she didn't, he would surely destroy the village. When she said he was unpleasing to her eye and her heart, they told her that many a maiden has scruples, but she gets over them soon enough at the sight of her mother-in-law's gold.

"That night Milochka gathered up her things and was preparing to slip out before the nobleman could know that she had gone, when someone knocked at the window.

"'Hide me!' she cried, and went to run out to the barn.

"But then the unknown visitor called through the window, and she heard that it was the voice of her beloved, and let him in and listened to his story.

"At first, he said, he had thought she had thrown him over for the nobleman, but then he had heard rumors of her persecution, and come down to Malaya Roshcha, forsaking his honor and his home, to see if they were true.

"She said she had to run away to Krasnogorod to seek her fortune, free from this Prince's persecution. 'Take me with you!' he cried. And so they grabbed up their sacks, climbed out the window, and were never seen again."

"You mean they're alive!" cried Slava. "They're still alive?"

Mirik sighed heavily. "It's unlikely, noblewoman," he said. "The world is so full of misfortunes..." And he waxed on in that vein for a while, before continuing with his story.

"When the nobleman discovered Milochka's disappearance that night, he was overcome with a fearful rage, and offered a great reward to anyone who could tell him of her whereabouts, and threatened de-struction to anyone who stood in his way. I saw him, noblewoman, and I tell you he truly had the look of a madman. Many a man has lost his head over a woman," here Mirik sighed again, in a world-weary way, as if he personally had lost his head over dozens of women—which,

Slava supposed, might be true—and then continued his narrative, "but his case was something special. He was mad, noblewoman, truly mad, as if the matter were about more than just our Milochka. I swear, noblewoman, he was almost foaming at the mouth, and his eyes were rolling in his head.

"My mother, who has hardly less angered by Milochka's escape than he, told him of her flight with her singer, and he and his men set off after her. And two days later they came back, without her, but with an even greater rage, and they said that she had gotten away from them, and they left in a terrible wrath, and that night the entire village was burned to the ground."

"What!!" screamed Slava, making Dunya jump and almost drive the dogs off the road. Mirik, though, was so caught up in his tale that he didn't even notice, and it only occurred to Slava too late that that could have been a golden opportunity to escape, if she had had the quickness of mind to think of it and enlist Dunya into her scheme. A moment after that realization it occurred to her that they still wouldn't have had any tents or food, and so they most likely were better off because of her slowness of mind.

"Indeed, noblewoman," Mirik was saying, drawing Slava away from her thoughts of fruitless escape, "it was most terrible. We didn't see who set the fire, but it must have been someone from the Prince's retinue, returned to wreak revenge. There is no other explanation. The gods would not have been so cruel for any other reason."

"But what happened to all the people?" asked Slava, giving up all thoughts of fleeing their bandit-rescuers and returning to Mirik's story.

"Two died in the fires, and a great tragedy it was, for they were newly betrothed. Marina Kseniyevna had finally declared that she would set her husband aside in favor of a man who would be less nagging and more faithful, and she and her new beloved were burned in her house that very night. And then many more lost their homes, their crops, and their livestock. The forest was filled that night with the screams of dying animals caught in the flames, and the next morning the entire village was beggared. My parents were forced to hire out as day-workers to a local landowner. I was a day-worker too, for a time, but I couldn't stick it and I ran away to join Vas' Marinych's band, and here I am."

"Oh," said Slava. "I'm sorry," she added.

Mirik shrugged. "Living a life isn't crossing a field, noblewoman," he said. "You have to expect suffering. It's better being gone anyway. All the villagers blamed Milochka for what happened, but since she wasn't there, they blamed me. The other day-workers were always complaining to us about her, telling my father he didn't beat her enough, making threats about if she ever came back, souring our milk, lying to our mistress about us...It's better here. At least here they treat you like human beings."

"I'm sorry," Slava said again. "You said you sent word of it to the Empress?"

"We did, noblewoman, we did."

Slava racked her brains, and eventually came up with a dim memory of her sister laughing with her councilors over a letter from a village in Severnolesnoye, something about some peasant who wanted help getting his daughter back, after she'd run away from some nobleman ...probably that had been Malaya Roshcha, and the peasant had been Mirik's father. "Now that I think on it, the Empress has surely gotten your message. I heard her speak of it with her councilors," she told him.

Mirik's eyes grew round, till they seemed to fill the entire space between his hat pulled down to his brow and the scarf pulled over his nose. "The Empress and her councilors talked about us, noblewoman?" he said wonderingly. "Such an honor for Malaya Roshcha...No doubt, though, they had too many more important matters to send us soldiers."

"No doubt," said Slava.

Everyone fell silent for a while, and Slava became acutely aware that she was hungry, thirsty, and in danger of falling asleep and therefore falling right off the sled as well. "How much farther?" she asked.

"Not too far now, noblewoman," said Mirik comfortingly. "Not too far, and then you'll be snug as can be." He went back to watching the dogs, which had fascinated him from the start. This left Slava free to examine him and wonder if he were really as good-natured as he seemed. If things in the bandit camp began to go badly for them, which seemed all too possible, given the mercurial nature of the bandits, would he try to protect them? Or if Vasily Marinovich ordered his men to rape them, slit their throats, and toss their corpses out onto the snow, would he go along with the others?

Probably, Slava concluded. Probably he would apologize first, and then make excuses to himself afterwards, but he would do it anyway. Given the happy tendency of bands of men like Vasily Marinovich's to rape their youngest members for sport, Slava thought she should not be surprised at all to find out that Mirik had long been a victim of that sort of play, and was already well prepared to turn the tables and inflict the harm that had been done to him on others—Slanik, for example, would be the obvious choice.

Slava tried to shy away from this thought, but she knew that it was the most likely outcome, and that Mirik would no doubt believe he was acting for the best in such a situation. Her heart swelled with pity over his real and imagined wrongs, but she decided not to share either her pity or her concerns with him. She could sense that it was better not to show any fear around him, no more than she would want to around a large dog.

They turned abruptly onto a path so small that Slava would most likely have missed it if she had been traveling on her own. The path was, in fact, so narrow they were having a hard time getting the dogs down it, which caused a great deal of swearing and meant everyone's tempers were strained by the time they arrived at Vasily Marinovich's camp.

To call what the bandits lived in a cabin would have been overly generous, but for want of a better word Slava decided that was what it was. It seemed much too small for everyone to fit in it, and listed noticeably to the right, with a distinct sag to the roof and porch. There was an even smaller and more disreputable-looking shed off to one side, where Vasily Marinovich said they could put the dogs. Dunya looked inside, sighed, and said she supposed it would have to do, although the dogs would be sure to miss their tent. Unfortunately, Vasily Marinovich overheard this, and by the time they had all squeezed into the main cabin, he was in a very surly mood indeed.

"I suppose you'll be wanting food," he said sullenly.

"Food would be welcome, yes, what with our own supplies being left to the leshiye," said Olga. She still seemed unfazed by their sudden capture by bandits, something which Vasily Marinovich had not failed to notice and which was adding to his surliness. He shouted at several of his men to go see what they could find their guests to eat, but warned them not to let the newcomers eat too much. "Eat us out of house and home, I expect," he grumbled. "How can a body make an honest living when you're constantly being overrun by spongers and scroungers, that's what I want to know, it's enough to make you despair..."

Slava saw Olga's eyes light up as they had at some of Princess

Malogornaya's more outrageous pronouncements, but she managed to refrain from laughing outright, which was a good thing. Vasily Marinovich and his men might seem pathetic and silly—in fact, they *were* pathetic and silly—Slava thought, but that didn't make them any less dangerous. Quite the reverse, in fact.

Vasily Marinovich grumbled throughout the meager meal, which they ate standing up and sharing spoons and bowls, and continued to grumble afterwards, when he was faced with the problem of finding a place for everyone to bed down. Slava could see he was regretting his decision to take them hostage, and when someone asked him when he was going to send word to the Princess that he had captured her daughter, he shouted, "By all the gods, these hostages are nothing but trouble! Now I have to send one of my own men all the way to Lesnogorod. You'll worry me to death, you will, worry me to death with your trouble and your nagging..." He gave Olga and the others a very ugly look, and trailed off in a self-pitying whine.

"Give us a day's supplies and point us in the direction of the nearest village, and you'll never see hide nor hair of us again," said Olga. She was, Slava could tell, trying to be diplomatic, but it had been a very long day for her too, and she couldn't keep a note of impatience from creeping into her voice. Slava wanted to warn her to take Vasily Marinovich seriously, stupid as he was, but didn't know how to do so without attracting attention, and doubted it would do much good even if she did. Olga had made it as far as she had by not taking danger seriously, and she was unlikely to change course now.

"Until you come back with the Princess's soldiers," said Vasily Marinovich, curling his lip and looking even uglier and more self-pitying.

"My word as a noblewoman, I will leave you in peace," said Olga. It was clear, at least to Slava, that Olga was growing ever more irritated by Vasily Marinovich's whining foolishness, and could no longer hide her impatience.

Vasily Marinovich and the rest of his men all laughed bitterly. "The word of a noblewoman!" he said. "We're all here because we know what the word of a noblewoman is worth, aren't we, lads?"

The lads all shouted their agreement. A surreptitious shuffling movement was going on in the room, so that Olga and her group were all ending up on one side, and Vasily Marinovich and his men were all on the other. A distinct feeling of hostility was filling the space between them. Slava's heart jumped as she felt it creep over her skin, like dirty fog. Now that the exhaustion and shock of the morning had been dulled somewhat by time and food, she was beginning to realize that the possibility of the bandits raping them, slitting their throats, and tossing their corpses out onto the snow was growing ever more real, and that her great expedition to the Midnight Land and back could end in death, not as she had imagined from cold or magic or hungry wolves, but because people were just as stupid and selfish up here as they were down in Krasnograd. Resentment at this fact rose up in her so strongly that it overwhelmed even her disgust at the scene in front of her.

"How many times have noblewomen broken their word to us, lads?" Vasily Marinovich was shouting.

"Many!" the bandits cheered.

"And how many times have they robbed us, cheated us, used us and discarded us, treated us worse than they treat their horses?" Vasily Marinovich shouted.

"Many!" the bandits cheered.

Looking at the bandits, with their filthy faces and anger-twisted features, Slava couldn't blame their former mistresses for giving preference to their horses, if that had in fact ever happened, but she decided to keep that thought to herself. Even Mirik, she noted without too much disappointment, was joining in the cheering, his face twisted with resentment just like everyone else's.

"And should we trust the word of a noblewoman now, lads?" Vasily Marinovich shouted.

"No! No! No!" the bandits all shouted back.

Slava couldn't tell if the room had actually grown warmer, or if it was just rage that was making her sweat. The anger in the air was making her stomach hurt. She thought she could hear the dogs barking from the shed.

"Let's give them a taste of their own treatment!" someone cried. All the bandits cheered twice as loudly as before. Slava thought she might be sick. More strongly than ever before, she was aware of how unprotected her mind was, and how other people's hate could pour into it unopposed. She tried to take another step back, as if that extra foot of distance would save her.

"What are you running from, noblewoman?" demanded the bandit nearest to her. "Afraid of getting your comeuppance? Come here! I'll teach you to put on airs!" And he reached for her arm.

"NOT THE TSARINOVNA!" screamed everyone in Olga's group. The bandit reaching for Slava froze. Vasily Marinovich laughed in surprise.

"You don't really have a Tsarinovna with you?" he asked. "Her?" He walked over to Slava. "I don't believe it. And they say the Tsarinovna has great magic, anyway. You can't tell me this skinny little noblewoman has any magic to speak of." He grabbed Slava's other arm. She was too trapped in revulsion even to try to shake him off.

"Get back!" Grisha, who was standing closest to Slava, shouted. "Get your filthy hands off the Tsarinovna!"

"Don't insult Vas' Marinych!" the bandits all cried, and suddenly Slava and Vasily Marinovich were surrounded by a mass of pushing and shoving, which transformed into a fistfight before their eyes.

"No!" cried Slava, horrified, but no one heard her. Two bandits tried to grab Dunya, but she snatched up a fork from the table and stabbed the first one in the face, making him scream in a way that even now caused a rush of pity to flow through Slava. Olga had gone one better, arming herself with the knife from the table, and was now holding out in a corner, with Misha, who was still unable to stand, lying on the floor and kicking at anyone who got too near.

Both the bandits and Olga's men were breaking apart the chairs to use the legs as weapons. Everyone's face had been transformed into a snarl, and even as Slava's mind was assaulted by the wolfishness around her, she could feel part of it transforming her as well, as if she, too, were becoming a wolf instead of cowering in a corner like a beaten dog. Her teeth and claws itched.

"You think you can attack me in my own house!" Vasily Marinovich screamed into Slava's face. "I'll teach you!" He shook Slava as hard as he could, and when that failed to satisfy him, he shoved her away from him and hit her in the face.

Slava stumbled backwards until she was caught by the wall. Screams of rage had risen up all around her, and she thought that some of them were on her behalf, but her would-be protectors couldn't free themselves from their own fights in order to save her. She put her hand up to her mouth, and felt wetness. She looked uncomprehendingly at the blood on her fingers.

Vasily Marinovich had caught up with her, and was raising his hand to hit her again. His whole being was concentrated on hurting her as much as possible, in any way he could, as if that would erase all the hurt that others had been forcing on his clumsy, stupid mind his entire life. Slava could see in the cruelty he wanted to deal out to her how much cruelty had been dealt to him, and how he had hidden his clumsy stupidity behind more clumsy stupidity, until it was all he would ever be and all that he had left. He had been broken more times than he could count, and would never be fixed. If he had ever had a soul, she couldn't help but see, he had shed himself of that encumbrance long ago, and now he had nothing to hold himself together other than meanness. Even so, he couldn't help but sense the lack, and could find no better way of filling it than to try to smash other people's souls, as if that would make his own ruined soul less alone. More pity than she thought she could bear filled her chest.

"No," she said softly, catching his hand in both of hers. She could feel her claws slipping back under her skin from the pity, and for a moment her teeth no longer itched with rage. "No, Vasily Marinovich, don't do it."

"Shut up!" screamed Vasily Marinovich, pulling his hands out of her grasp and shaking her so hard her head rattled against the wall. "Shut up, shut up, shut up!" He let go of her shoulders and put his hands around her throat.

Even though it would do no good, Slava placed her hands on his chest. She could feel his heart jumping under his ribcage, racing like the heart of a hunted rabbit. He started to squeeze her throat, and she could feel how a whole lifetime of fear and rage was washing over and into her, so that she thought her mind would burst. There was not enough room inside of her for everything she was feeling...air, there was no air in her lungs...Vasily Marinovich was trying to kill her...so much pity, so much anger...no air...she had to fight back, but she didn't know how...so much pity, so much anger, and all of it hers, there was no room for it in her collapsing lungs...if she didn't get free now, she would die...Vasily Marinovich's face was right in front of hers; if she could breathe, they would be breathing the same air...no air...she had to get free...her fingers were itching again like claws...her mind expanded.

"DON'T!" screamed Vasily Marinovich. "Please, please please!" But it was too late.

For a moment Slava could see into the minds of everyone in the room, as her own thoughts burst free and rushed outwards, pouring uncontrollably into all the fragile empty vessels around her. It was as it had been in the forest, when she had spread out to see the whole world in the blink of an eye. Only there she had been consumed by limitless space. Now it was as if she were trying to force her feet into too-small boots. Vasily Marinovich had let go of her and was writhing on the ground. The others had frozen, expressions of pain and horror wiping away their former expressions of bestial rage. Slava tried to pull her mind back, but couldn't. Like a forest fire, her thoughts had raged out of control and were destroying everything in their path.

"Mercy!" sobbed Vasily Marinovich. "Mercy! I'm sorry! I'm sorry! I'm sorry!"

And Slava saw that she had finally gotten her wish, and that she was forcing others to feel what she could feel, and the horror of her own unforgivable cruelty rose up before her and made her falter, and then somehow the floor was in front of her face, and she stared at it for a long time.

Chapter Eighteen

A pair of dirty boots was blocking her view.

"Is she really a Tsarinovna?" said the boots.

Another pair of boots, which had once been expensive but were now just worn, joined the first pair. "Yes," they said. "The Tsarina's beloved only sister." A face knelt down to join the once-expensive boots, and Dima peered into her eyes. "Tsarinovna?" he asked. "Are you all right?"

Slava tried to assure him that she was, and also to laugh at the idea that she was the Tsarina's beloved sister, when really she was the Tsarina's despised sister, but the only thing that issued from her mouth was a feeble moan. The cheap boots also knelt down to look at her, revealing that they were wearing Mirik's face. "Why, Tsarinovna?" he asked reproachfully. "Why did you attack us? I thought you were kind."

"Which is why you're not dead, you stupid, stupid fool," said Dima, more harshly than Slava had ever heard him speak. "If the Tsarinovna had dealt with you as you deserved, we'd be tossing your body out into the snow right now." He shook Slava's shoulder gently. "Are you hurt, Tsarinovna?" he asked.

This time Slava managed to produce a sound that vaguely resembled "No."

"But..." said Mirik, still aggrieved over Slava's assault.

"You raised your hand against a member of the Imperial Family," said Dima. "For that the punishment is normally death by slow torture. I know the man who'd do it. I would get down on my knees and beg for further mercy, if I were you." He slid an arm under Slava's shoulders. "Do you want to get up, Tsarinovna?" he asked.

Slava tried to shake her head, which made all its contents slosh wildly. "Rest," she murmured. "Just rest."

"You want to rest here, Tsarinovna?"

"Ah," said Slava, but she tried to say it in an affirmative manner. Dima apparently understood, for he sat down beside her and propped her up against him. "Olga Vasilisovna is taking care of everything, Tsarinovna," he told her. "We're safe now, thanks to you. Dunya and Grisha are harnessing the dogs, and we'll be on our way in no time."

The inside of Slava's head seemed to be shrinking back to fit the outside, so that she could think clearly again. "What happened?" she asked.

"Vasily Marinovich attacked you, Tsarinovna"—Dima was so horrified by the thought, he had difficulty even pronouncing the words— "but you performed great magic, and fended him off, making everyone in the room collapse as you did so, but Dunya came to very quickly, and when you released everyone, this gave us the upper hand, and we defeated the bandits, and now we are preparing to leave as soon as we can."

"*I* didn't do anything," said Mirik, returning to what Dima had told him earlier. "*I* didn't attack the Tsarinovna. *I* shouldn't be punished."

"The Empress is unlikely to see it that way," said Dima. "Anyone in this room who lives to see spring will be very lucky indeed."

"That's not fair!" cried Mirik. "But you nobles are all unfair." Slava's clearing vision enabled her to see the resentful anger rising in his face.

"Mirik," she said softly. "Mirik, take my hand."

"Do as the Tsarinovna orders," Dima told him when he hesitated. Mirik reached out a reluctant hand, and took Slava's in his own.

"Mirik," she said. "I thought you were wrong about me, but you were right about one thing. I do see the good in you. But the problem is that I also see all the bad, and I can't ever stop seeing it. I see how it's stronger than the good, so that it is your mistress and you are its slave. But Mirik, it doesn't have to be that way. Let what is best in you overcome what is worst." She squeezed his fingers, and let a little of the pity she felt seep into him. He looked at her for a moment with the stupid sullen face of a many-times victim of injustice, and then the trusting child rose up in him and stared out of his eyes.

"Tsarinovna!" he exclaimed. "Little mother!" He laid his head on Slava's legs, as if she really were his mother, and, she thought, started to cry.

"There now," she said, stroking his head. "There will be no killing. None of you will die, not if I have any say in the matter."

Mirik sobbed in earnest for a moment, before drying his face on Slava's skirt and sitting back up. "You made me feel so bad, little mother," he said. "Like I was evil or something. Why did you do that?"

"So you could stop," Slava told him, amazed at the way the comforting words were rolling off her tongue as if they were true. "So you could shed the evil in you, and embrace the good."

"I'm not evil!" said Mirik indignantly.

"And yet you would have hurt me," Slava reminded him. "Just now. You would have hurt me and my friends, just because someone else told you it was a good idea."

"We didn't mean any harm," protested Mirik. "We just wanted to get some our own back."

"And yet harm would have happened. It is so easy to do evil, Mirik. After all, the nobleman who came after your sister probably meant no harm either. No doubt he just wanted to get some of his own back too. No doubt he was very unhappy, and only wanted to make himself feel better."

"But..."

"And you were no different than him just now, Mirik. Don't forget that." Slava stood up, her strength returning to her much more quickly than she would have ever expected. "Dmitry Marusyevich, how go the preparations for our departure? When will we leave?"

"I'll check, Tsarinovna," said Dima, scrambling to his feet. "If you no longer require my assistance?"

"It seems I am perfectly well, thank you, Dmitry Marusyevich." Slava surveyed the room. A number of the bandits and Olga's men were lying on the floor, groaning in pain. The less-injured ones were trying to help their comrades to their feet, but several of them were in no condition to walk. Slava got up and, to her surprise, strode boldly over to where Olga was watching the scene by the table. For the first time in her life, she felt like a Tsarinovna, and when the others turned to look at her, she took it as her due. An unaccustomed calm had come over her.

Vasily Marinovich was lying on the table where Olga was standing. For a moment Slava thought he was dead, but then he turned his head and gave her a dazed look.

"I am glad to see you are recovered, Tsarinovna," said Olga. She was leaning against the table, and Slava realized it was to keep from reeling where she stood. Her face had taken on an unhealthy greenish tinge.

"Are you sure you are well enough to stand?" Slava asked her.

"I want us to leave as soon as possible," said Olga. She swayed, and caught herself against the table.

"I am sorry," Slava told her. "I didn't mean to hurt anyone."

"I know you didn't, Tsarinovna," said Olga. "We should have defended you better. I just hadn't realized till now what a cruel gift you have."

"I don't mean for it to be cruel," said Slava.

"But it is, Tsarinovna, and for the first time you let us know." Still clutching at the table, Olga gave Slava the look she had given her so many times before—the look of someone who has bought an untried racehorse, and is still waiting to see how she will turn out. Only this time the look suggested that the untried racehorse had beaten all comers by many more lengths than expected, and her mistress was now waiting to see if she would founder from the exertion. But Slava had no intention of foundering. Her strength was rising up in her once again.

"It is a cruel gift," she admitted. "But so is the rest of life. When do we leave?"

"As soon as we can," said Olga. "They," she nodded in the general direction of several bandits, "assure me that we will come to a village no more than fifteen versts from here. I considered staying, as we are tired and several of us are injured, but..."

"There's not enough food for you all, anyway," Vasily Marinovich interrupted weakly. "We used up the last of it for supper."

"Where were you going to get breakfast, then?" demanded Olga.

"We were..." Vasily Marinovich had to catch his breath, "going to kill some of the dogs." He panted for a little while, then asked Slava, "Are you really the Tsarinovna, then? They weren't lying?"

"I really am," Slava told him.

"Oh." He sounded disappointed, and Slava realized he had been clinging to the hope that he had not attacked a real Tsarinovna.

"No harm will come to you," she promised him.

"So you say, Tsarinovna," he said, and closed his eyes.

"Where are you hurt, Vasily Marinovich?" she asked him.

"Everywhere, Tsarinovna," he said, not opening his eyes. "My whole inside...feels...broken." He was sweating heavily from the effort of talking, but kept going. "Like you...broke down...all the little... barriers inside me. I'm broken." And indeed, his coarse, clumsy body and coarse, stupid face did look broken. Slava supposed that thinking must have been especially painful for someone so unaccustomed to it. All the thinking that Vasily Marinovich should have done over the course of a lifetime, had he been one of the lucky few who were taught how to think, had been forced upon him in the space of a single breath, and it was no wonder it had broken him.

Slava thought that perhaps, if he had been given some other life, he could have turned out to be a good man, but the life he had been given had done nothing but beat him down, until he was little more than a savage dog, fit for nothing other than to be finally broken by someone such as Slava. She wished she could either pity or despise him, but lying there he made such a sad, comical, pathetic, awful figure, that Slava's heart couldn't decide between compassion and revulsion, and so wavered over some third, unnamable, feeling instead.

"You'll get better soon," she told him.

"I don't...think so...Tsarinovna. I think...I'll always...be broken... inside."

"He was hit the hardest," said Olga. "And I daresay what he saw was particularly unpleasant. Not that any of us enjoyed the experience very much. Is that really what you think of us?"

"You'll get better if you try," Slava told him. "We all have to live with things we don't like about ourselves."

"And then what will he do?" demanded Olga. "I doubt he'll be able to go back to being a bandit."

For a moment Slava was surprised by Olga's complaint, and then she realized that, of course, Olga was also asking about herself. What would any of them be able to do after seeing themselves through Slava's eyes?

"He'll just have to learn to live in a way that doesn't make him feel ashamed of himself," Slava said.

Vasily Marinovich nodded faintly in assent. "Service..." he whispered. "The gods..."

"You are very wise, Vasily Marinovich," Slava told him. "I'm sure the gods will welcome your service."

"I'm not ashamed of myself," said Olga, her voice rising. "I'm not!"

"Then you have nothing to worry about," said Slava.

Olga looked as if she wanted to continue the argument, but just then Dunya and Grisha came in and reported that the dogs were harnessed and they were ready to set off.

"Mirik...will guide you...back to the road," whispered Vasily Marinovich. He closed his eyes. "Oh, I feel bad," he moaned to himself.

"My insides, my insides..."

Part of Slava wanted to try to comfort him, but, she was pleased to see, she was able to walk away even so. Her sense of guilt, normally so quick to act, was tossing restlessly but had not yet awakened, and she hoped it would keep sleeping for some time. She had, she decided from behind the distance that was still separating her from everything around her, had more than enough guilt for one lifetime. Let the others carry that burden for a little while; she was through.

More than half of Olga's men were injured too badly—Slava didn't know if that was from the bandits or from her, and didn't ask—to carry themselves down the road, and so the others loaded them up onto the sleds, bundling them together like moaning firewood to keep them from falling off. They set off very slowly into the darkness.

"I wonder if it's night or morning," Slava said, looking up at the strip of starry sky visible through the trees.

"Late night, almost morning," said Dunya, who was walking next to her and guiding the lead sled.

"Funny, I know I should be tired, but it's as if I don't really feel it," said Slava.

"Sometimes that happens, when things are desperate," said Dunya.

They walked along together in silence for a little while, their feet squeaking in the snow. The injured men in the sled seemed to have fallen asleep, or perhaps they had just fallen into despair and could no longer be bothered to moan.

"Dunya!" said Slava all of a sudden.

"Yes?" said Dunya, looking back up from the snow.

"What I did in there...did it affect you? Did it hurt you?"

"No," said Dunya. "It didn't hurt me."

"But you felt it?"

"Yes."

"What happened?"

Dunya thought for a moment. "It was as if you suddenly came into my head, Slava," she said eventually. "As if you had suddenly dropped by for a chat. And I saw myself from the outside, maybe through your eyes. Then you left."

"But it didn't hurt you?" Slava asked.

"No more than talking with my mother or sisters, Slava," said Dunya, and laughed. "You don't mind that I call you Slava, do you?" she asked. "Because I feel like we're sisters now."

"Of course not," said Slava. "How are we like sisters?"

"Because now we've shared our thoughts, like sisters do. You saw my thoughts, and I saw yours."

"You did?" exclaimed Slava.

"Of course, Slava, that's what happened," said Dunya, smiling at Slava's surprise. "Don't you remember?"

"It was too painful," said Slava. "Or too...like being terribly, terribly drunk, or caught in some horrible dream. Like being caught up in something stronger than yourself, and unable to stop it or know what will happen next."

"Well, in that case," said Dunya, "you came into my head, and we chatted, just like I said. Not with words, of course—it was our thoughts that chatted."

"But the others..." said Slava.

"Sometimes a chat can be painful," said Dunya. "Sometimes you have to tell your sisters that the man they love is marrying someone else, or you know they stole someone's scarf, or all kinds of things. And all those things are true, but they still don't want to hear them."

"What did I tell you?" asked Slava.

Dunya smiled again. "You told me I keep to myself and make up my mind on my own, which makes some people afraid of me, but I already knew that. And you told me that you were lonely and afraid, but I already knew that too."

Slava could feel tears suddenly well up behind her eyes, threatening to spill out and freeze on her lashes and scarf. "How..." she had to clear her throat, "how did you know?"

"You are not the only one who can see things, Slava," said Dunya gently. "Anyone who took the time to look at you couldn't help but see it. Fear and loneliness are crisscrossed all over you, like tracks in snow."

"I'm sorry," said Slava.

"For what?" asked Dunya. "There's nothing to be sorry for. Hey, Prygun! What are you doing!" And Dunya turned her attention to the dogs, who had gotten distracted by what seemed to be fresh rabbit tracks.

Slava wondered how many others could see in her what Dunya saw. Probably many, even if they didn't realize what they saw. Not with the top part of their thoughts, anyway, Slava thought. But the thoughts underneath—there they could see it. And perhaps that was one of the reasons they were so hurt by her gaze. People don't like feeling that they should feel sorry for other people, thought Slava to herself. It takes away some of the sorry they want to feel for themselves.

Slava stared at Dunya for a moment, and then at the others around them, and wondered if they—they, and all the other people Slava had ever encountered—did, perhaps, feel sorry for her against their will, just as she felt sorry for them against her will. Perhaps they could feel her forcing herself into their minds, not only as she had just now, but all the time, just as she could always feel others forcing themselves into her mind. Perhaps that was one reason why her eyes "made them feel so queer," as she had been told time and again, because she was always, with every glance, as well as every word and every gesture, overcoming them just as they were always overcoming her. Only it was such an unaccustomed sensation, and they had so little awareness of what was happening, that they could only say that she "made them feel so queer," and shun her company.

Despite their slow pace, Slava could feel her heart beating with the exhilaration of a sudden understanding, the wonder of suddenly seeing everything with fresh eyes. There, with the trees rising high on either side of them, and a thin strip of stars drawing close to watch them, she felt something inside her lurch sideways, and all of a sudden it was as if she were watching the world from some far shore, so that everything was the same, but from the opposite direction. Between one breath and the next she had gone in her own mind from the person who needed saving to the person who needed to save others.

She thought of all the times she had seen herself as a beaten dog, and saw that there was no reason for that, no reason at all, and that henceforth she would be neither mistress nor slave, but something free—perhaps the racehorse that Olga always seemed to see her as. Or no, now she was the Empress of her own mind, and no one could take that away from her.

She looked back at Dunya. "Thank you," she said.

"Of course," said Dunya, looking up from the dogs to glance at Slava in uncaring bewilderment before turning her attention back to the more important business at hand. Slava could sense with every sense that Dunya had not the slightest comprehension of what she had said and what she had done to her, Slava, and that for Dunya this moment was just the same as the moment before it, even though for Slava they were as different as the moments before and after stepping off a cliff.

Slava thought she would never be able to express to Dunya how much she loved her right now for pushing her off, and how much she would probably love her for the rest of her life, for those simple words that she had uttered, no doubt, without the slightest intention of them being taken seriously. Just a few words, Slava thought, and yet now my life has been changed, now and forever after.

She looked at the trees and the snow and the stars again. They all seemed very dear to her now, dear and close, and she felt how she was just another creature, like a tree or a star or a snowflake, walking amongst her sisters. She had no protection from them, but she needed none. She brought her gaze down to the people around her. They also seemed very dear to her now. Her nakedness before them no longer bothered her, because they were naked before her too. Everyone was wearing their true form, for what other form could they wear? Slava smiled to herself. The back of her mind wondered how long this happiness would last, but she reminded herself not to doubt it.

"No food, no tents, the dogs completely worn out, and more than half my men too injured to walk," said Olga's voice behind her.

"We'll be in the village by morning," said Dunya.

"Yes, it's not far now, Olga Vasilisovna," said Mirik, who had also come up to them. They were now walking at Slava's side, although paying her very little attention. Slava had the impression that they were trying to ignore her as much as possible. "Only a few more versts."

"The Black God take all bandits, spirits, and other obstacles," said Olga with deep conviction. "This journey has been a failure from one end to the other." She gave Slava the look of a woman in a very foul mood. "I hope Lesnograd is worth it," she said. "But it probably won't be. Lesnograd is always a misery and a catastrophe. How far did you say it was from here?"

"Only five or six days' journey, Olga Vasilisovna," said Mirik.

"Oh," said Olga, and Slava saw that part of her foul mood was the realization that in only five or six days' time she would be back home.

"Olga Vasilisovna!" Mirik burst out.

"What is it now?" demanded Olga.

"Take me to Lesnogorod with you!"

"Why?" asked Olga. "You're a bandit. Why risk going to Lesnograd?"

"You wouldn't turn me in, would you, Olga Vasilisovna?" cried Mirik, surprised and hurt.

"No, but someone might recognize you. What could you possibly want in Lesnograd?"

"My mother, Olga Vasilisovna."

"What's she doing in Lesnograd?" snapped Olga.

And so Mirik recounted the tale of his family's misfortunes once again. Olga listened with increasing thoughtfulness.

"And your sister's father, you never saw him?" she asked when he was done.

"No, Olga Vasilisovna," he answered.

"Or heard what happened to him?"

"No, Olga Vasilisovna."

"I'll look into the matter," said Olga. "It'll give me something to do. Other than knocking some sense into my wayward husband, that is. If it wasn't him who did this, then he had his hand in it somehow, my head for beheading. Apparently my mother is giving him free rein—always a bad idea! If ever a man needed to be kept on a short leash... but no matter. I'll look into it."

"Oh thank you, Olga Vasilisovna!" And Mirik sprang irrepressibly ahead to scout out the road.

They arrived at the village just as its inhabitants were coming out to feed their animals. The appearance of a large party, with sled dogs, caused an enormous stir, and within moments everyone in the village was gathered around them, offering to take them in. Soon the village grandmothers were looking over everyone who had been injured, and Slava was being led to what was, no doubt, the most comfortable bed in the village. That was nothing to brag about, but it was certainly better than the snowy ground.

As she took off her boots, all the tiredness of the past day hit Slava at once, and she swayed onto the bed and pulled the covers over her with difficulty. The bed rocked under her for a dizzying moment, and then there was nothing but blackness.

"Are you really leaving us, Krasnoslava?" asked the golden eyes. They sounded sad.

"No, of course not," Slava assured them. "You'll always be with me."

"I thought you didn't want what I had to offer," said the golden eyes, still sounding sad.

"Only because you tried to force it on me," said Slava.

"And so instead you would steal it, Krasnoslava? And abandon us?"

"I haven't stolen anything," Slava told them. "There was nothing for me to steal. I already had it. And I'm not abandoning you. You made me run away, but I took a bit of you with me."

"Really, Krasnoslava?" And the golden eyes gazed up at her with the hopeful gaze of a lover or a small child.

"Really," Slava assured them. "I'll always have a piece of you with me. It will be the bravest part of me."

"Really, Krasnoslava?" The golden eyes had grown even larger with love and hope, so that Slava felt like she might fall into them and drown. But the thought filled her with no fear. She felt an answering love for the golden eyes rise up in her, even after all they had done to her. She knew now why they had done what they had done, and that she would never let them do it again, and so now the golden eyes were as dear to her as everything else she had recently learned to love.

"Really," said Slava again. "You gave me the courage to do what needs to be done."

"But you wouldn't do it when I asked you, Krasnoslava," said the golden eyes sorrowfully

"Maybe it wasn't what needed to be done," said Slava. "Maybe what I did was what needed to be done. But you are brave, I cannot argue against that, and now a little bit of your bravery has been given to me."

"And a little bit of your kindness has been given to me, Krasnoslava," said the golden eyes. "Although I fear it may be a poisoned gift."

"Sometimes I think so, too," said Slava. "But I hope that is not true."

"Well, I shall have to learn to live with it," said the golden eyes with a sigh. "This was not what I expected from our meeting, Krasnoslava, but it is what I have received."

"Perhaps in time it will turn out to be a real gift," Slava said comfortingly. "In the meantime, I will be with you."

"You will?"

"I promise," said Slava.

"Then I will be with you, too, Krasnoslava," said the golden eyes, cheering up considerably. "Like sisters."

"Like sisters," agreed Slava. "Sisters of the soul."

"Sisters of the soul," repeated the golden eyes, and winked out.

Chapter Nineteen

When Slava awoke, it was still dark. Then she realized that no, it was not still dark, it was dark again, and she had slept right through the brief day. She got out of bed, still feeling dizzy and stiff but not minding, and set off in search of the others. She realized that she had taken little interest in everyone who had been injured, and that she needed to make up for that earlier neglect as quickly as possible.

She found a golden-haired peasant girl with bright blue eyes stirring soup in the kitchen. When she saw Slava enter, the girl set aside her spoon, and, with a smile as bright as her eyes, asked Slava how she was feeling.

"Better," Slava told her. "I must thank you for your hospitality."

"Our pleasure, noblewoman," said the girl. "Are you hungry? You must be hungry. Olga Vasilisovna said you'd lost all your supplies."

"What about the others?" asked Slava.

"All resting comfortably, don't you worry, noblewoman," the girl assured her. "You should eat." She took out a bowl and spoon, her plump hands and body moving deftly around the kitchen. She turned sideways for a moment, and Slava saw that some of the plumpness was because she was with child, and near her time.

"Forgive me for asking, but should I congratulate you?" Slava asked.

The girl laughed. "My thanks, noblewoman—I suppose you should." She put both hands over her stomach. "A child of love," she said, looking both pleased and embarrassed. "It's so close to my time I can speak of it freely. I hope she's as handsome as her father."

"You're handsome enough yourself," said Slava.

"The father was more handsome, even though he must have been twice my age," said the girl. "It was a shame he couldn't stay, but at least he left me a bit of himself with me."

"The child is what matters," agreed Slava.

"Oh certainly, noblewoman, but I hope she has his red hair. It was so pretty." The girl sighed, and then dished up Slava's soup and gave it to her. "My mother scolded me terribly when she found out I'd be giving her a grandchild, and even more when she found out I wouldn't be giving her a son-in-law—what would his mother think! I never met his mother, though—and he was much older than me anyway, like I said. But she's happy about it now—even happier than I am, I think. Even my father has come round. After all, he said, there's nothing wrong with another grandchild. But I hope she has red hair."

"My best wishes," said Slava. "How did you meet the father, if you don't mind me asking?" She tried to arrange her face into a 'we're-all-girls-here' expression, and apparently succeeded, for the girl, with many giggles, related the story of her acquaintance and seduction of the red-haired father of her unborn child. He was, she said, a hunter whom she had met in the woods. Their love had been a bright flame that had burned only briefly, and then he had said he had to go find better hunting grounds, and she had never seen him again.

"They say that some men are like that, noblewoman; that they can never stay with just one woman. Is that true?" asked the girl, her face showing a touching if misplaced trust in Slava's superior knowledge of men.

"Some people say so," said Slava. "But maybe they are just making excuses. Although most will say that it is unnatural for a man to take lovers like a woman—although where we're to get our lovers from, then, I don't know. But whatever they say, it hurts when a man leaves you—hurts most dreadfully."

"He would have been a bad husband anyway," said the girl, staring dreamily at the wall. She did not appear to be suffering too badly from heartbreak. "When I look for a husband, I'll find someone more constant and easier to manage. He was so stubborn and quick-tempered! I never could stand a husband who wouldn't give way to me, I'm sure. But I'm glad I'll have his child to remember him by."

"Yes," said Slava, wishing she could borrow a little of the girl's blithe equanimity in the face of her lover's abandonment.

She was saved from this conversation by the sound of someone coming into the house and taking off her shoes and outer clothes in the entrance room. A moment later, Olga came bursting in, looking as fresh and lively as if attacks by bandits and wood-spirits were something that only happened to other people.

"Awake?" she asked, looking at Slava. For a moment she seemed to flinch away, as if remembering what had happened in the bandits' hut, but then she shook it off with a quick toss of her head, and became her old self again. "You're taking good care of her?" she asked, looking at the girl.

"Oh yes, Olga Vasilisovna," answered the girl, staring at Olga in fascinated wonder.

"What are you staring at?" demanded Olga, making her way to the breadbox and taking out a loaf as if she were mistress of the kitchen. Slava realized she must have been asleep for a long time, long enough to allow hardier people such as Olga to recover from their exhaustion and take command of the situation.

"Forgive me, Olga Vasilisovna, but I hadn't ever seen you before without your hat and outer clothes," said the girl.

"And?" asked Olga, tearing off a chunk of bread and gulping it down in a way that would have made the sled dogs proud.

"I didn't realize...You look just like the father of my child, you know."

"Well, I'm not him," said Olga through her bread. "So don't come to me with any demands or pretensions or attempts to save my honor." She grinned. "I lost the need to make an honorable match a long time ago, and my mother couldn't care less anyway. I think the only thing we'd both thank the gods about is my being a daughter and not a son." She shuddered. "Can you imagine me as a man?"

Actually, Slava could imagine Olga as a man very readily—well, except for the being obedient part—but she thought it might be best not to mention that. If ever there were a woman fitted for rude labor rather than ruling, that woman was Olga. Even Olga's merry temper might not find that comparison a laughing matter, though, so Slava held her tongue.

"No, but..." the girl gave Olga a puzzled look, clearly confused by her glib manner. "You really do look like him, noblewoman," she said, having given up on comprehending the ways of noblewomen. "Are you related?" Slava could see the hope dawning on her face that her lover had been of noble blood.

"I don't have any brothers," said Olga, still grinning. "I don't even have any second-brothers. And I'm certainly not related to anyone from—where are we again?"

"Khladniye Vody, noblewoman."

"I'm certainly not related to anyone from Khladniye Vody. The water's much too cold here to breed, anyway."

It took a moment for the girl to realize that Olga was making a joke about the village's name, and when she did, she laughed very uncertainly. "You look enough like him to be his sister, noblewoman, and you're just as quick and witty. He did like a laugh," she said. "Are you sure you're not related to him? He wasn't from Khladniye Vody, noblewoman; he was a hunter who was just passing through."

"Aren't they all," said Olga. "My own father a hunter who was just passing through, until my mother snared him. But she could only hold him for a little while before he decided to pass right on out of this life and into the next one. The gods alone know what happened to him."

"I'm sorry, noblewoman—I'm sure my man's safe, wherever he is, though," said the girl complacently.

"I'm sure you're right," said Olga, looking sure of no such thing, and also as if she wanted to give the girl a good box on the ear for sheer gullibility. "It's just that...Well, good luck with everything. The Ts...Krasnoslava and I should go check on our men." Olga hustled Slava, who had not finished her soup, out of the kitchen, into her outer clothing, and out onto the snowy street.

"That was odd," said Slava once they were alone.

"Foolish girls with love-children are ten a grosh," said Olga. "I don't see what's odd about it at all."

"No, I mean, red-haired hunter"—Slava nodded back towards the house—"Mirik's mother was with a red-haired hunter, and—red-haired hunter," she finished, nodding towards Olga.

"All fourth-brothers, no doubt," said Olga. "There aren't a lot of families up here, and these boys don't seem shy about keeping the line going."

"No doubt you're right," said Slava. "It just seemed odd to me."

"This is Severnolesnoye," said Olga. "Everything's odd, especially to a Southern city girl like yourself. Don't waste your time worrying about it. We have bigger problems right now."

They turned off the village's one main street and onto a tiny alleyway between two barns. "I don't know when we'll be able to leave," said Olga, going up to the door of what, after a moment, Slava realized was a large but shabby bathhouse that strongly resembled all the barns around it. "Misha, Vova, and Volodya are in a bad way, and Vladik and Zhenya are hardly any better. Even the ones who can walk are limping. And to top it off we have no supplies. The people here have offered us a little food, but they can't spare much, and of course half our clothes are gone. It's only a week to Lesnograd, they say, but a week of strong frost is more than enough to freeze all of us to death." She opened the bathhouse door.

Until that moment Slava had not given much thought to the injuries of the others. Not, she was quick to assure herself, out of hard-heartedness, but she had simply been unwilling to believe that anyone from her group could have been badly hurt, especially under such stupid circumstances. The encounter with the leshiye was fading strangely fast, as if her mind were refusing to accept the existence of something so far from the ordinary, and the encounter with the bandits had been so ridiculously disastrous, that it seemed impossible for any lasting harm to result of it.

In the semi-lit gloom of the bathhouse it took Slava a moment to make out what was going on. Along with the darkness filling her eyes, some kind of moaning was filling her ears and making it hard to focus. Then everything fell into place, and she understood what she was seeing and hearing.

Vova, Volodya, Vladik, Zhenya, and Misha were all lying on the bathhouse benches, and the others were tending to them. Misha and Zhenya were both making the moaning noise, because, Slava realized, they were moaning in pain. Vova, Volodya, and Vladik were all lying still and silent, and she couldn't tell whether that was because they were in less pain than Misha and Zhenya, or because they felt too bad to make any noise at all.

"Ah, there you are, Krasna Tsarina," said Dima, coming over to them. He, too, appeared to be more wary of Slava than he ever had before, but after a moment his native good nature returned, and he asked, with every evidence of sincere concern, "How are you? Did you sleep well? Are you unhurt after all our adventures?"

"I am well," Slava said, ashamed that he would be worrying about her when he should be worrying about the others. Then she remembered that she had no reason to be ashamed over what he happened to think, and that the only thing she could do for the others was show her sympathy, so she said, "I thank you for your concern, Dmitry Marusyevich, but I hardly need it. How are the others?"

Dima frowned. "Difficult to tell, Tsarinovna. The herbwoman is with them," he nodded to a small figure sitting at Misha's side, "but she refuses to give a clear answer one way or another. And perhaps no clear answer can be given, at least for Misha. With the others it's obvious enough: cracked head, cracked ribs, cracked arms and legs—they'll likely heal in a month or two. Or three or four, perhaps, but they'll likely heal. But we don't know what's the matter with Misha. Cracked head, cracked ribs, cracked arms and legs for certain, but there seems to be something else as well."

Slava went over to Misha's bench. The herbwoman was perched by his head. Perched was exactly the right word to use, as, Slava saw as she knelt beside them, the herbwoman had a bright, bird-like face and a tiny little body with a hunch between her shoulders, as if wings were trying to break free. She turned and smiled at Slava, her papery skin crinkling up into a pattern of wrinkles that, Slava couldn't help but think, resembled bird skin.

"You must be the great noblewoman that all the fuss is about," she said.

"I'm sorry?" said Slava.

"All the fuss," repeated the herbwoman. "All your friends have been making a great fuss about your comfort ever since you arrived. I can't tell if they are more afraid some harm will come to you, or that some harm will come from you."

"Oh," said Slava. "How is he?" She reached out to take Misha's arm, then thought better of it, not wanting to hurt him.

"Is it true about the leshiye, noblewoman?" asked the herbwoman. "That he was hurt defending you from leshiye?"

"Yes," said Slava.

"Sometimes people come back from the forest like this, and they say it was leshiye," said the herbwoman. "I had always wondered if it hadn't been bears, though." She gave Slava a very bright look.

"This time it was leshiye," said Slava. "They came after us, dozens, maybe hundreds of them, and Misha thought to stand against them."

"You're a brave lad, I can tell," the herbwoman said to Misha, who had started moaning more restlessly and turning his head from side to side.

"Very brave," agreed Slava.

This seemed to calm Misha down, and he went back to lying still.

"What did they want?" asked the herbwoman.

"Me," said Slava.

"Poor lad," said the herbwoman, stroking Misha's brow with the lightest of touches. "And you thought to stand between them and your mistress? What did they do to you?"

Misha moved his mouth as if trying to say something, but nothing coherent came out.

"They threw him on the ground," said Slava. "But could they have hurt his mind as well?"

The herbwoman's bright eyes gave her a curious look. "Perhaps you know better than I," she said. "Since they were coming after you. Why did they want you?"

"They wanted..." Slava had to clear her throat. "They wanted my... my gifts. My abilities. There was...a sorceress, I guess you'd call her, with golden eyes. She wanted to give me her gifts in exchange for my own."

The herbwoman gave her another bright look. "You must be extraordinary indeed, noblewoman, to attract the attention of the leshiye. Rarely do they interest themselves in the petty doings of the world of women. And did they get what they wanted?"

"They couldn't take it," Slava told her.

"Because you are so strong, noblewoman?"

"Because I am so weak," Slava told her. "They would have had to take the weakness along with everything else, and they couldn't. At least, the sorceress-leshaya couldn't. Because once she had taken my weakness, she would no longer have been able to use my strength as she wished to. But I am afraid she may have done something to Misha, something not just to his body."

"Perhaps, noblewoman," said the herbwoman. "Or perhaps he has done it to himself. It is not uncommon for people's spirits to be broken along with their bodies. Perhaps he cannot live with the thought of failing you."

"But he didn't!" said Slava. "No one asked him to do what he did, and no one could have stood up to the leshiye...the only thing we could do was run away...there's no reason for him to be ashamed..."

"People are often ashamed for no reason, noblewoman," said the herbwoman. "Especially strong young warriors like our Misha. But you could make him feel better."

"How?" asked Slava. "I can't fight their magic..."

"It sounds as if you already did, noblewoman," said the herbwoman with a slight smile. "But in any case you would not have to fight them. All you would have to do is make him feel better."

"I can't make other people feel better," said Slava sadly. "I wish I could."

"Nonsense, noblewoman!" said the herbwoman. "Making people feel better is the easiest thing in the world. All you have to do is tell them what they need to hear."

"But what if it's a lie?" said Slava.

"You have to make it not be a lie, noblewoman," said the herbwoman kindly. "Just tell them the truth, but in a way that will make them feel better, not worse. Try, noblewoman, try on our Misha. It's not hard at all."

Slava looked down at Misha, who had stopped moaning and was looking back up at her with pitiful, desperate eyes. She felt so sorry for him, and so terrible for having been the cause of his suffering, even indirectly, and so helpless to help him. The problem of how to make other people happy spread out before her like an uncrossable river. "Misha," she began.

"I'm sorry," he whispered.

"Why?" she asked. "There's nothing to be sorry for, Misha."

"We shouldn't..." he had to pause to gasp for breath, "we shouldn't have let them take you. And I'm sorry...You showed me so many bad things...bad things about myself...I'm sorry...I don't deserve...not anything..."

"You're not bad, Misha. What I showed you...it was only a little bit true...And you couldn't have stopped them," Slava told him. But then she saw by the grimace on his face that that had been the wrong thing to say. "Because I had to face them on my own," she continued, saying the first words that fell out of her mouth. "Your task was to bring me safely to them, but only I could face them. You were very brave to try to stop them, I will never forget it, but in the end I was the one who had to stand against them."

"Really?" He stopped to pant for a moment. "Really, Krasna Tsarina?"

"Of course," Slava told him. "You did your deed, and then I had to do mine."

"And you did?" he whispered.

"I did," Slava told him.

"I'm glad, Tsa..." he whispered. He closed his eyes before he could finish the sentence, and appeared to drift off to sleep.

"Is that bad?" Slava asked the herbwoman, nodding towards the unconscious Misha.

"No, noblewoman, that's good," the herbwoman said. "You made him feel better, and now he can rest. Was it so difficult?"

"No," Slava told her. "It was easy, and I realized as I was saying it that I was telling the truth, so it made me feel better, too."

"You see, noblewoman, how easy it is to do a good deed," said the herbwoman. "You are from Krasnogorod, are you not, noblewoman?" She gave Slava an especially bright look.

"Yes," Slava admitted.

"And a member of the Imperial family, are you not, noblewoman? Your man just called you 'Krasna Tsarina,' and I don't think that was just a pet name. And you have the eyes."

"Yes," admitted Slava.

"And yet here you are in this distant backwater," said the herbwoman. She gave Slava another bright, curious look.

"Yes," said Slava. "By my own choice," she added, in case the herbwoman thought she had been disgraced and exiled.

"Then why aren't you happier, Tsarina?" asked the herbwoman, who apparently *had* been thinking that she had been disgraced and exiled.

"You can tell I'm unhappy?" exclaimed Slava, sounding much more surprised than she would have liked. "And I'm not the Tsarina," she added hastily.

The herbwoman laughed. "Of course I can tell you're unhappy, Tsarina," she said. "Your shoulders, and your eyes, and your mouth, and even the way you move your hands—everything about you speaks of many years of unhappiness. If you were a dog, I'd say you had a cruel mistress."

"I think I might be getting better," said Slava, to hide the lump that had suddenly appeared in her throat. Just as the herbwoman had said, she was like a dog with a cruel mistress, especially with the way she could be won over with even the tiniest, tiniest show of kindness. "I think...I think my journey to the North, and the encounters with the leshiye, and the bandits, awful as they were—I think they are making me better. Stronger. Funny. People have been wanting to make me stronger my whole life, and failing. I think maybe they could tell I was unhappy too, even if they didn't even know it, and wanted to help me, but they didn't know how. Maybe they didn't even know what it was they were trying to do. And now here I find myself doing it all on my own. And I'm not the Tsarina."

"Perhaps only you could make yourself stronger...Krasna Tsarina," said the herbwoman. "But you had to be given space and time to do it. Few people can manage to do that for others."

The first shock of kindness was past, which enabled Slava to smile and ask, "Are you doing to me what you had me do to Misha? Say things that will make me feel better? Not to mention using my own gift against me. I have met few people who would admit to being able to see what another person is feeling by the set of her shoulders."

"Of course," said the herbwoman. "Healing is most effective when you use your patient's own gifts against her. And just as when you spoke to Misha, my words are true." She smoothed Misha's forehead. "I think he is asleep," she said. "So what will you do now, Krasna Tsarina?"

"Go to Lesnograd, I suppose," said Slava. "And then return to Krasnograd. I wonder how they will receive us there. I know Olga Vasilisovna thinks we have failed in our mission, and my sister may very well, too. We spent very little time above the sunline, after all, and made no great discoveries."

"Is that really true?" asked the herbwoman. "Have you really failed? Have you really made no great discoveries?"

"I have made discoveries," said Slava slowly. "But they were mostly just about me. That doesn't really count."

"Do you think so, Krasna Tsarina?" asked the herbwoman, raising her bright eyes from Misha's face back to Slava's.

"Olga will think so," said Slava. "My sister certainly will."

"Then you will just have to show them they are wrong," said the herbwoman. She leaned in close to Slava. Slava expected her to smell bad, like most peasants, but the only scent she had was that of herbs, as if she were a bundle of plants, not a human at all. "You say you have gifts, Krasna Tsarina," she said. "That is no surprise: everyone in your family has gifts. But like so many of your foremothers, you are squandering them. If the only result of your journey to the Midnight Land is that you stop wasting the gifts the gods gave you, and use them as they were meant to be used, you and everyone who helped you will be rewarded many times over."

"I don't waste my gifts!" said Slava, stung in the vanity she had not known until then that she possessed.

"No, Krasna Tsarina? You claim to be able to read other people's feelings. Very well: I believe you. And yet you also claim that until this moment, you did not know how to make other people happy. So what have you been doing with your gifts, in that case? It sounds to me like all you've been doing has been sitting around feeling sorry for yourself. That is also a favorite activity of your foremothers, so I suppose it is no great surprise that you should indulge in it too, but frankly, Krasnoslava, I would have hoped for better from you. But be that as it may, henceforth you can fix your errors and use your gifts the way they were meant to be used, instead of wallowing in your own feelings day and night, with never a thought for those around you!"

"What...What..." gaped Slava. "I do think about those around me!" she finally managed to say. "That's my problem! I care too much!"

"No you don't!" hissed the herbwoman, her face right in front of Slava's. "If you really cared, you would have done more for them! The only person you've ever really cared about has been you!"

"No..." Slava started to say, but then a great wave of guilt, all the guilt she had been suppressing since the bandits, rose up and told her how right the herbwoman was, and she choked back her objections, shame-faced.

"Not that I blame you too much," said the herbwoman more calmly. "You're right in thinking that you have to look out for yourself, because no one else will. And you were right to think that just watching out for yourself was a difficult task, almost beyond your abilities. Others would like to eat you up, if they could, like wolves in winter. But if you really want to use your gifts as they were meant to be used, if you really want to do good and help others, you will have to start looking out for others as well. Do you think you were given your gifts for your own gratification?"

"I hope not," said Slava. "Because there's precious little gratification in possessing them."

The herbwoman laughed in spite of herself, but then sobered back up and said, "Do you believe in the gods, Slava?"

"Of course," said Slava. "Doesn't everyone?"

"No, not everyone, but do *you* believe that they take a hand in the affairs of ordinary women?"

"Before, I would have said no, but having just fled from a pack of leshiye, I'm more inclined to say yes," Slava told her.

"Good, because they have taken an interest in you," said the herbwoman.

"They have?" Slava realized she sounded much more alarmed than she would have wished, but after all, what woman wanted to hear that the gods had taken a personal interest in her? When that happened in fairy tales, the hero frequently came to a bad end. Even when she didn't end up dead, there was normally a price to be paid for the gods' help.

304

"Ever since you were born, Slava," said the herbwoman, making Slava's heart sink even more.

"Why me?" she demanded, in rather, she had to admit to herself, a whiny tone of voice, as if she were about to start wallowing in her own unhappiness.

"Why not you, Slava?" the herbwoman demanded back. "The gods distribute their gifts unevenly, everyone knows that. Some women are beautiful, and some are clever, and some are long-lived, and some are loved, but rarely is one woman all those things. And it often happens that when one is given more, one has to give back more of the same."

"So what am I supposed to give back?" asked Slava, trying not to sound surly about it.

"What do you think you are, Slava?" said the herbwoman, looking at her intently. Slava thought she caught a flash of something in her eyes that made her uneasy, but it was gone so fast she couldn't even be sure what it was. "What do you think you are meant to do with what you have been given?"

"Perhaps...Perhaps I am supposed to make other people feel what I feel?" she guessed. "Only I can't," she pointed out. "I mean, I used to wish I could, but even then I knew I probably didn't actually mean it, and then the one time I managed it—which is why we are here, by the way, with half our men lying in the bathhouse and being healed by you—the one time I managed it, it turned out just as badly as I had thought it might, and so even if I could, I wouldn't do it again."

"Perhaps that is not the way you are supposed to go about it, Slava," said the herbwoman. "Those who force themselves on others rarely receive much in return. But tell me: when have others been grateful to you? When have you done something that has turned out well for you in the end, even when it seemed unlikely at the beginning?"

"When have I..." Slava tried to think of an example, and suddenly several of them leapt out at her. "When I saved someone," she said. "I saved those poachers from Naberezhnoye, and we got a guide from it...The elk and the hare! Even when I saved animals, I was rewarded, wasn't I? Is that what I'm supposed to do? Save others?"

"Indeed, Slava," said the herbwoman. "There are many ways of saving others, and we expect you to try all of them. You may be astonished to hear this, Krasnoslava, but you were born to be a hero, and you are finally coming into your destiny. No, no, no objections," she said, forestalling Slava, who was in fact about to start objecting. "You are perfectly capable of it, even if it doesn't seem so right now. Just try, and you'll see. You might even find it pleasant. At any rate, you'll feel less guilty than you do now." She leaned forward, putting her face right up against Slava's again, and said, "But you have done your deed for the day, and now I must do mine. Leave me to finish healing these men, and think on what we have said. It will not be the last time you will hear from us, I assure you." Her eyes looked right into Slava's, and for a moment they flashed gold.

"Wha..." Slava's voice was quickly cut off by the herbwoman's finger laid against her lips.

"Go now," she whispered. "But do not forget what you have heard... and seen."

Slava looked around wildly, but no one else seemed to notice anything amiss. She rose on trembling legs, and stumbled out into the snow. The wind had blown away the clouds while she had been inside, and the stars looked down at her hungrily. She ran back to bedroom she had woken up in, and shut the door behind her.

Later she was called out to have supper. She came out of her room cautiously, afraid of finding the herbwoman sitting at the table with the others, but there was no sign of her.

"Misha seems to be doing better since you visited him," said Olga. She was, Slava noted, still studiously avoiding using Slava's name, having apparently decided that her identity needed to be kept a secret. Of course, the herbwoman had found out anyway. Slava remembered that the herbwoman had started out calling her "Krasnoslava," and then switched to "Slava." How had she known? Of course, the names of the Imperial family were no secret, but how had she guessed Slava's identity, and beyond that, how had she dared to use Slava's name? Most people were afraid to, even after being expressly invited. Judging by the flash of gold in her eyes, the herbwoman must be connected to the leshiye somehow, but how? And who was she really? Slava realized that Olga was looking at her expectantly.

"That's good news," she said. "I'm glad Misha is doing better. How are the others?"

"Baba Anya thinks they will all recover fully from their injuries," said Olga. "Unfortunately, it may take some time, although they're already looking better than I would have expected.

"That's good," said Slava, who had only been paying attention to Olga's first sentence. "Who is Baba Anya?"

"Our herbwoman, of course, noblewoman," said the pregnant girl, who was serving them. There was no sign of her mother, which on another day would have occupied Slava's curiosity completely, but today it was no more than a vague background concern. "Baba Anya is the reason many of us in Khladniye Vody are alive. I've never heard of an herbwoman with a skill equal to hers. When I was a child, noblewoman, I caught a terrible fever and almost died, but Baba Anya pulled me through. I've already made her promise to be with me when my time comes"—the girl gestured at her rounded belly—"and I'm sure with her by my side, everything will turn out well. Other women approach their labor knowing they will most likely not survive to see their baby, but here in Khladniye Vody we have no such fear."

"You are very fortunate," said Slava. "Does Baba Anya live here in the village?"

"Oh no, noblewoman, she lives in a hut in the forest, and she spends much of her time out gathering herbs, so you have to leave a sign, like a pile of rocks or flowers, telling her to come, but she always comes very fast, and always to the right family. Some people think she must be some kind of a spirit, not a woman at all, but she always saves us, so I don't care. Don't worry, noblewomen: your men are in good hands with her."

"Thank you, Svetochka," said Olga. "I'm sure you're right."

Svetochka, that is to say, the pregnant girl, bowed as best she could, and, saying she had to go milk the cow, left, taking the lantern with her. Dunya, Olga, and Slava all started eating by the light of the single candle in the middle of the table. As she raised her spoonful of beet soup to her mouth, Slava's mouth started watering like that of a dog looking at a bone, and she realized she was even hungrier than she had thought. In fact, she didn't know how she had made it so far without more food. The beet soup was thin, and accompanied only by coarse black bread, but Slava started gulping it down anyway. She wondered if the lavish meals served at her sister's kremlin would seem even more delicious when she returned, or if they would be too rich for her to stomach.

Dunya, who, probably because of a lifetime spent in the forest, always ate neatly but very quickly, finished first as usual, and immediately asked, "What are your plans, Olga Vasilisovna? Are we to wait for the injured men to heal, or set off without them? It may take days, weeks, or months for them to be fit to serve you again."

"I know," said Olga, shredding a piece of bread. It was tough enough to put up a determined resistance to her assault, but she was upset enough that she tore it to pieces anyway. "If I knew they would be better in a few days, I would say 'wait' without thinking twice about it, but as it is, I don't know...I hate to leave them. I never leave anyone behind."

"They would be the first to tell you to go, if they could," said Dunya. "They wouldn't want to be a burden to you. You can always send for them later."

"I know," said Olga, frowning down at her shredded bread and picking up another piece. "What do you say, Tsarinovna?"

"Who, me?" asked Slava, startled.

Olga and Dunya both laughed. "Of course you, Tsarinovna," said Olga. "Dunya thinks I should leave the injured men behind, and reason tells me I should agree with her. Now I want to know what feeling has to say."

"Well..." began Slava, who until a moment ago had been grateful not to be included in the decision, and who was also trying not to be offended at being called unreasonable, "perhaps you should ask them what they think."

"They'll say I should leave them," said Olga, shredding more bread. "That's not in question. The question is: what should I do, knowing they'll tell me to leave them behind?"

"Perhaps you should, then," said Slava. "Leave them behind, that is."

"You think so?" This time it was Olga's turn to sound startled. "Frankly, I had not expected such an answer from you, Tsarinovna."

"If you stay, they will feel guilty," Slava told her. "And, as Dunya has already pointed out, we have no idea how long it will take for them to heal, and you can always send for them later."

"True," said Olga, still looking rather taken aback. "But it pains me..." Slava could tell that she had been hoping Slava would tell her to stay, and didn't know what to do, now that Slava had told her to go instead.

"Speak to them," Slava urged. "Then make your decision. Of course you don't want to leave them behind. But you must consider more than just what you want."

"Of course," said Olga, who had not ceased to look startled. She dropped the shredded bread into her empty bowl, stood up with the air of a woman about to go do her duty, and left.

"And let us hope we can be out of here by morning," said Dunya, eating the bread bits Olga had left behind. Dunya, Slava had noted before, never asked for extra food or complained of being hungry, but anytime she saw unwanted food, she ate it immediately. Slava supposed it came of spending all her time out in the cold. She imagined that Dunya was, in fact, constantly ravenous, even though she never mentioned it.

"Are you in such a hurry to get to Lesnograd?" Slava asked.

Dunya shrugged. "Right now I can take it or leave it," she said. "I just want to get out of Khladniye Vody. Don't mistake me: I think the men will be perfectly safe here, but I don't like it. There's too much magic here for me to feel comfortable. Trees and animals and sky I can handle, but when it comes to spirits, I prefer to keep my distance. And here the spirits are all around us. Svetochka and her baby on the way, for example. There's something strange about her story. Don't think I haven't missed the similarities between it and the story of Mirik's sister, or Olga herself.

"Not only that, but where are Svetochka's parents? This is their house, but we haven't seen hide nor hair of them since we've arrived, and she hasn't given any kind of reason for their absence. I would feel better if she would just say that they were off visiting her aunt in the next village, or something like that. And Baba Anya: she's not a normal woman, my head for beheading. In fact, I'm not sure we've met any normal people at all since we've arrived here. What do you think, Tsarinovna: is the entire village populated by spirits?"

This rather alarming proposition caused Slava a moment of genuine terror, as she envisioned Baba Anya and Svetochka creeping into her room in the middle of the night and carrying her off to finish what the leshiye had started, but then she pulled herself together.

"When I asked Svetochka about Baba Anya, she said some things that made me think Baba Anya might be a spirit, but Svetochka herself seemed innocent of that sort of thing. In fact, she seems completely innocent of anything; so much so, in fact, that I find it hard to believe she managed to conceive a child," Slava said.

"Maybe she's possessed," said Dunya darkly. "Maybe the spirits have taken over her mind and body and impregnated her."

Slava had hitherto never suspected Dunya of such a fantastic imagination, or of worrying about such things, and stared at her for a moment in fascination, before remembering that she was being rude.

"Or maybe she just let a handsome hunter turn her head," she suggested. "It does happen, you know. How many girls do you know who have borne a love-child?"

"Oh, lots," said Dunya. "But that's not the issue here. The issue is that I think when we escaped from the leshiye, we didn't actually escape from the leshiye. After all, we got away much too easily. I think they're still pursuing us, only now they're using people to do their work. Maybe you think I'm crazy, but in the woods you learn to develop a feeling for things, and my feelings tell me that there's something not right here. Like I said, I think the injured men will be perfectly safe, but that'll be because whatever's following us will keep after us and leave them alone. I doubt we'll lose it just by going to Lesnograd, but at least there we'll have guards and sorceresses to watch our backs, and maybe even fight for us."

"I think you're right," said Slava.

"You do?" Dunya looked surprisingly gratified by Slava's words, reminding Slava that she was, after all, not yet twenty and from a family who could barely write their names. Slava tended to forget that in the face of Dunya's self-assurance, but of course having the Tsarinovna agree with someone like her would not be an honor to be brushed off lightly, not even by Dunya.

"I do," Slava confirmed. She related the story of her encounter with Baba Anya in the bathhouse. Earlier she had been vacillating over whether or not to tell the others about it, but as at least some of Dunya's suspicions matched hers, it seemed only right.

"You think she was a leshaya?" asked Dunya when she was done, looking more alarmed than Slava had expected.

"I don't know," Slava said. "Sometimes I'm not even sure what I saw, and I think I'm going crazy from everything that's happened. But there was certainly something strange about her, and she's unquestionably more than an ordinary village herbwoman. I just don't understand what her purpose was. She didn't seem to want to capture me or force me to do anything right now, she just seemed to want me know that they—whoever 'they' are—would be watching me."

"That's worrisome," said Dunya, still sounding more alarmed than Slava would have expected, which was making Slava alarmed too. "That's worse than if they were just trying to catch you outright. If they were just trying to catch you, you could try to run away from them, but this way...and if we don't know who they are..." She bit her lip and wrung her hands in a very un-Dunya-like way.

Slava could feel Dunya's fear infecting her, and she opened her mouth to beg Dunya to calm herself, so that she, Slava, wouldn't be so afraid, and then it was as if some tide had turned inside of Slava, so that Dunya's fear, instead of flooding into her, flooded back out, leaving nothing but a fierce protective desire in its wake. Instead of being the victim, Slava felt like this time, she was the hero, just as Baba Anya had said she must be, the one standing up for everyone else. More courage than she had ever thought could possibly exist inside of her rose up, and with it came the comforting words that would pour that courage into Dunya, too.

"I do not believe they mean me any harm," Slava said. "They—whoever they are, leshiye, the gods, who knows—they want me, after all. Maybe they want me in order to use me, but they've already failed at that—twice, in fact. And so has everyone else who has tried to use me. I know they think I'm weak, but in the end, I've always been the one who's come out alive and well. Maybe 'they' have finally recognized that, and have decided to use other tactics. But whatever they try, I think I have nothing to fear from them. And if they come after us again, I will stand between them and the others, and stop them from hurting you."

"Like you did before," said Dunya, very quietly.

"I did?" said Slava, unable to remember any particular acts of bravery on her part.

"Tsarinovna! You ran past us and straight into the arms of the leshiye! Not to mention..."

"Oh, of course," said Slava, before Dunya could finish enumerating all her supposed brave acts. She was about to say that there was no particular merit in what she had done, as she had simply been reacting to the unendurable suffering those scenes had caused her, but then she thought that might sound either as though she were bragging of her own compassion, or as if she were crazy, and so she stopped herself.

"And I escaped unscathed," she said instead. "No, Dunya, although you are right to say we should leave this place sooner rather than later, I think that we have little to fear from whatever spirits are pursuing us. No doubt they will keep chasing after us, and probably even catch us eventually, but even so, I think we will escape unharmed once again."

"If you think so, Tsarinovna, then I believe it too," said Dunya, who appeared much calmer than she had earlier. Some other time her faith in Slava would have thrown Slava into a panic, but right now Slava was still sure it was her task to protect others, and so Dunya's trust made her feel braver, not weaker. She wondered when the courage would suddenly ebb back out of her again, and if it would ever return, but knew there was nothing she could do about that except to keep trying to be brave, and so she told herself not to worry about it.

Someone came into the house, making both Slava and Dunya jump, but it was only Olga. "They told me to leave them," she announced.

"That's no surprise," said Dunya. "They're sensible and honorable, so it's the only thing they could say."

"I still don't like it," said Olga.

"But they're right," said Dunya.

"I know they're right, I just still don't like it."

"There's nothing you can do about it," said Dunya, who was starting to sound slightly impatient with Olga's wavering. Of course, Slava reflected, they were not Dunya's men, and so it was much easier for her to leave them behind.

"They're still my men," said Olga, echoing Slava's thoughts disconcertingly. "I still don't like leaving them behind."

"You don't have a choice," said Dunya. "And they'll be safe here. The Tsarinovna and I both agree."

"Even so..."

Dunya and Olga hashed the matter over for a while longer, before Olga, after much hand-wringing, which looked very strange on her, finally admitted to the necessity of leaving the injured men behind, and agreed that they would set off first thing tomorrow.

"I'll go tell them," she said, once the decision had been made, and headed out again into the cold.

"We should go to bed," said Dunya to Slava. "We'll have a long day tomorrow. I'm determined to put as many versts between us and Khladniye Vody as possible."

Slava agreed, and went to the bedroom she had been using. It was only after she had gotten into the bed that it occurred to her that she should have made sure that Dunya had been given suitably comfortable accommodations, and that neither of them were inconveniencing the residents of this house. There was nothing she could do about it now, though, so she ordered herself not to plunge into guilt, as that would only tire her out before their long day tomorrow, and she would hold the others back even more.

Slava was awakened by someone knocking at the door. "Forgive me, noblewoman," a soft voice called. "But Yevdoksiya Anastasiyevna asked me to wake you and tell you they're preparing to leave soon."

"Thank you, Svetochka," Slava called back, and dragged herself out of bed. It was dark enough that she couldn't tell whether it was morning or midnight, and cold enough that the thought of spending the day out of doors suddenly seemed extremely unappetizing. While they had been out in the woods, she had become accustomed enough to the rough life that she no longer experienced it as a terrible inconvenience, but two nights in a real house had reminded her of how pleasant it was to have real food and real shelter.

"Is it cold outside?" she asked Svetochka when she came out into the kitchen.

"There's a terrible strong frost this morning, noblewoman," Svetochka answered cheerfully. "I'm glad I'm not heading out into it, I tell you. And some say there may be a blizzard in a day or two."

"Svetochka, where are your parents?" Slava asked abruptly. "I would like to thank them for the hospitality we have received in Khladniye Vody," she added, coming up with a pretext for her question just in the nick of time.

"In the woods, noblewoman," Svetochka told her.

"In this cold? For so long?" asked Slava.

"They're getting firewood, noblewoman," Svetochka answered. Her round face and blue eyes appeared entirely free of guile. "It isn't uncommon for them to be out for a week or more, when they gather wood. They like living in the woods. They say they feel they're half wood-spirit. It's one reason my mother didn't scold me more than she did when she found out about my...news—she said I must be half wood-spirit too."

"Well, thank them for us when they return," Slava said. "And, for your trouble..." She made to take some coins out of the bag she wore around her neck, but Svetochka stopped her, saying, "Olga Vasilisovna has already repaid me, noblewoman, and extremely generously. We shan't want for anything for the rest of the winter, I dare say."

"And you'll take the best of care of the men who are remaining behind?" said Slava.

"Oh, of course, noblewoman! To tell the truth, it will be fun. It can be awfully boring in the winter sometimes, and right now as you can see I can't go too far, so I'll have nothing better to do than visit them, anyway."

Dunya stuck her head in the kitchen. "Are you ready, Ts...Are you ready?" she asked. "Svetochka's already given us some provisions, so we can breakfast on the way. We need to get started as soon as possible, so that we'll be sure to make it to some kind of shelter tonight."

"I'm ready," said Slava. "Let me just say goodbye to the ones staying behind, and I'll come meet you."

"Very well," said Dunya, and disappeared. Slava bowed to Svetochka, who flushed pink at this honor and bowed back as low as her belly would allow her. Having thanked Svetochka once more, Slava then picked up her bundle of things—which at this point could fit in her pocket—and went out of the house.

She almost got lost in the twisting alleys on her way to the bathhouse, but the light escaping from the crack around the door caught her attention and stopped her from straying too far. She went in, expecting to find no one but the injured men, who would be sleeping, she hoped, but Baba Anya was sitting by Vova's side.

"Come to say your farewells before setting off for Lesnogorod, Tsarinovna?" said Baba Anya, smiling kindly at Slava.

"Yes," said Slava, hesitating by the door, suddenly afraid to come in, despite Baba Anya's friendly face and all her brave words of the night before.

"This one will be glad of any kind words you can give him, poor lad," said Baba Anya, smoothing Vova's forehead. "He's not feeling to well. I fear the wound is turning bad."

"Let me see," said Slava, hurrying over to Vova's side. Only after she was kneeling right next to Baba Anya did she remember her former hesitation, but it was too late to do anything about that now.

Baba Anya pulled back the bandage over a wound on Vova's shoulder, which was, Slava was alarmed to note, red and angry-looking. She reached out and smoothed Vova's forehead too, and noticed how warm his skin was under her hand.

"Does he have a fever?" she asked.

"He does," said Baba Anya.

"What has been done for it?" Slava demanded. "What are you going to do for him?" She was stricken with remorse at the thought that she had spent weeks in Vova's company, and never taken much of an interest in him or found out anything of importance about him. He had never seemed to care much about her one way or the other, except as an object to protect as much as possible from the rigors of the road, and so she had largely ignored him in return, but now he could sicken and die over a trivial, meaningless incident, and she would never even know who would grieve for him back home.

"I have given him herbs and infusions of my own preparation," Baba Anya told her. "They are often helpful against fever and the poisons in wounds, so let us hope they will be this time, too. But other than that, all we can give him is our kindness, and pray that the gods have mercy on him."

"Vova," Slava said to him softly. "Vova, can you hear me?"

Vova, who appeared to have been in some kind of feverish semi-delirium when she had come over to him, calmed for a moment and looked at her with almost-focused eyes.

"Krasna Tsarina," he said thickly. She couldn't tell if he was glad to see her, or afraid.

"That's right, Vova, it's me," said Slava. "I came to say that I am leaving for Lesnograd, but I am sure we will see each other again soon, do you understand? You will heal, and we will see each other soon."

"Yes, Krasna Tsarina," he whispered, raising his head for a moment and then sinking back down onto the pillow, and apparently back into his delirium.

"Isn't there something else you can do?" Slava asked Baba Anya.

"I have done everything in the power of my herbs, my dear," said Baba Anya.

"But isn't there *something else* you could do?" repeated Slava. "Something stronger than herbs?"

"What do you have in mind, Slava?" asked Baba Anya, bringing her face close to Slava's. Once again, Slava was struck by the fact that she smelled only of woods and herbs, not of dirty clothes and unwashed hair, like most peasants.

"Something more than what you have already done," said Slava. She looked Baba Anya in the eyes, and didn't flinch when Baba Anya stared straight back.

"You flatter me, Slava," said Baba Anya.

"I don't think so," said Slava. "I think I see exactly what you are. It is my gift, after all. I am the mirror that reflects only reality. And I think you will save Vova."

"And I think you are right, Slava, but have you considered what I will ask in return?" said Baba Anya.

"Yes," said Slava.

"Yes, you have considered, or yes, you will give it to me?" asked Baba Anya.

"Yes," said Slava.

"You will do this? For him? Without even asking the price?"

"Yes," said Slava for a third time.

"Very well, then," said Baba Anya, and her eyes glowed gold.

Chapter Twenty

"What took you so long?" demanded Dunya, when Slava arrived at her sled. "And what happened to you?" she cried, catching Slava before she stumbled over her own wavering feet and fell down.

"There was something I had to do...in the bathhouse," Slava explained.

"Oh." Dunya gave Slava a long searching look, then said, "In that case, you should ride in the sled. You're in no state to ski. Here, I'll help you."

The others watched with varying degrees of impatience and squeamishness—Slava could tell that the men were still afraid of her, and half-wished she weren't traveling on with them, in case she attacked them again—as Dunya arranged Slava on the sled and found a spare bit of rope and tied her to the sled so that she wouldn't fall out, which, Slava had to admit, was a distinct possibility. She lolled against the front of the sled like a child's doll and stared up at the black starry sky as they took off. Somehow it was hard to focus on anything closer.

She could still feel Baba Anya's firm grip, and the golden rush that had poured from her eyes into Slava's, until Slava could see nothing but images in a golden haze. She had seen leshiye, and animal spirits, and water-spirits, and house-spirits, and in the back of it all, the shimmering figures of what must have been the gods themselves, and they had all turned and stared back at her with hunger in their eyes.

So she had held out her hands to them, and they had all started shouting at once, each trying to tell her something and to beg something of her, and she had promised to give it to them, and then all the bones in her hands had shone through the skin as her flesh wasted away, and then something had hit her hard in the side of the head, and she had found herself on the bathhouse floor, with Baba Anya helping her up and Vova sleeping peacefully.

"What did you promise them, Slava?" Baba Anya had asked.

"Everything," Slava had answered.

"Everything?" Baba Anya had repeated.

"What else could I give them?" Slava had said. "That was what they needed."

And Baba Anya's no-longer-golden eyes had filled with tears, and she had kissed Slava's hands and the hem of her dress before pushing her out into the snow.

At some point Slava must have fallen asleep, because after a while she found herself hanging in a very uncomfortable manner against the ropes Dunya had used to lash her to the sled, looking down at the strange-colored snow that was rushing past. After a moment she realized it was day now, and the snow had changed color because it was reflecting sunlight, not starlight. She struggled back to a sitting position, and looked around. Trees, trees, trees. She looked up. Clouds, clouds, clouds. She remembered the stars of the night before, and realized that snow was coming in, and those who had predicted a blizzard might be right.

Moving around had also made her realize that she was chilled through, hungry and thirsty, and would not have turned down a chance to stop and relieve herself, but all her traveling companions, and all her physical discomforts, still seemed strangely far away, so she only lolled against the front of the sled some more.

She couldn't tell how much farther they had gone, although she thought it might have been quite far, when the sled suddenly jerked to a stop, and she realized that Dunya had called a halt. She tried to unknot the ropes holding her in, but her hands only skittered uselessly over them before falling back to her sides. She had to wait for Dunya to come and release her before she could crawl stiffly out of the sled.

The break was, she thought, quite short, but she couldn't be sure of that either. The others talked about what was ahead of them, how much farther they had to go to reach shelter, and other things of importance, but their words all floated past Slava's ears and were absorbed by the silent trees. At one point she found herself looking deeply into the eyes of a dog she was almost sure was Prygun. He looked deeply back, and Slava sank her gloved fingers into the thick fur around his neck, and for a moment felt completely safe, but then Dunya called for everyone to prepare to set off, and when Slava let go of his fur, the world started spinning again.

At some point the clouds became black, and Slava realized that night must have fallen, and it was now midafternoon. The darkness forced them to slow their pace, which allowed Slava to hear what the others were saying when they spoke. It appeared that they were speaking about her, wondering what was wrong with her. She thought about telling them what had happened, but her mouth couldn't seem to form the words, and the effort of shouting over the sled runners and rising wind was too great anyway.

A while later something cold fell in her eye. It was followed by more cold things sprinkling down on her face. She brushed at them in perplexity until she heard Dunya say, "How much farther now? It's started to snow," and she understood that of course, the cold things were snowflakes, and the snowstorm had started. She turned her head away from them and stared at the sled instead.

A sizable amount of snow had already collected on her hat and scarf, when the sled jerked to a sudden stop. Slava looked around in surprise, and saw that they were standing in front of something bigger than a tree. It was square and constructed-looking, but somehow she couldn't make sense of its outlines.

"Shelter at last!" cried someone.

Dunya came and began to undo the knots holding Slava to the sled. "How do you feel, Tsarinovna?" she asked, examining Slava's face carefully. "You haven't gotten frostbitten, have you?"

Slava tried to say "no," but at first it only came out as "nnnn...."

"No," she finally managed, after clearing her throat and shaking her head. "I don't think so. But I can't tell. I'm numb all over."

"Well, you'll soon be feeling much better, Tsarinovna," said Dunya, but her voice was much cheerier than her face, and she took Slava under the arm and hustled her into the cabin without even stopping to give directions for the care of the dogs, which was most unlike her.

At first it seemed that being inside the cabin differed from being outside only by being even colder and darker, but in what was probably a very short time Dunya and Dima had lit some candles and gotten a fire going, while Olga examined the supplies they had been given in Khladniye Vody and rationed out their supper. Soon the others came in from unharnessing and feeding the dogs, and they all gathered around the rickety table in the middle of the cabin's main room.

Dunya, Slava couldn't help but notice, made sure that Slava was served first, and watched her anxiously as she ate the half-heated pie she had been given. Slava tried to eat it down with greater appetite than she actually felt, which told her that she was starting to recover somewhat, and in fact, after a few bites of the pie and a few swallows of the wine mixed with hot water that they were drinking, she did start to feel hungry. Ravenous, in fact. And along with the hunger came all the other sensations that had been floating somewhere along behind her the whole day, so that she became acutely aware of how cold and tired she was, and how everyone was staring at her with concerned and curious faces.

"You aren't becoming ill, are you, Tsarinovna?" said Olga at one point. "You haven't caught a chill, I hope?"

"Oh no," Slava assured her. "I just...When I went to the bathhouse this morning...I was asked to do something that took all my strength, that's all."

The others glanced back and forth amongst themselves, but couldn't seem to work up the nerve to ask the question, so Slava took pity on them.

"Baba Anya needed my help," she told them. "She needed me to do something so that she could heal Vova. So I did. But it took all my strength. I am afraid I will be useless for several more days now."

"But you're unharmed, Krasna Tsarina?" exclaimed Slanik. "You'll get better, won't you?"

"Of course I will," Slava told him, although she was far from certain about that. Or rather, she was fairly sure she would improve, but she had no certainty that she would recover completely. But Slanik certainly didn't need to hear her doubts about that, so she kept them to herself.

"Don't you worry yourself about it, Tsarinovna," said Grisha. "We'll take care of you all the way to Lesnogorod, and if you're not better by then, the Princess's sorceresses will heal you, sure as sure."

"Where are you hurt, Krasna Tsarina?" asked Slanik, still sounding like a child asking anxiously after his mother. "What did they do to you?"

"They just..." Slava began, before trailing off uncertainly, since she wasn't even sure herself.

"Stop pestering the Tsarinovna with your questions, Slanik," Grisha told him. "No doubt you couldn't understand anyway."

"I'm sorry, Krasna Tsarina," said Slanik, so contritely that Slava felt obliged to say something in return.

"I'm very grateful for your concern," she told him. "It makes me feel better, knowing that you worry about me." As soon as she said it, she began to worry that she had said the wrong thing, sounded too selfish, but her words seemed to bring comfort to Slanik, whose face cleared immediately.

"The Tsarinovna needs to go to bed, and so do the rest of us," announced Olga, rising from the table. "Dmitry Marusyevich, what's the bed situation?"

Dima said something about the beds in the cabin, and soon Slava found herself being escorted into a small, and extremely cold, side room that was almost entirely filled with a musty, lumpy bed.

"I think a mouse died in here," said Dunya, sniffing and wrinkling her nose. "But that was probably some time ago," she continued, shaking dust off the blankets. "No need to worry."

Slava, Dunya, and Olga all crawled into the bed, which was just barely big enough for the three of them. The sensation was, Slava thought as she pulled the blankets over her, not unakin to crawling into a snowbank, but surely the three of them could warm up such a small space quickly enough, especially if they kept shivering as hard as they were shivering now. For a moment she thought of the over-heated rooms back in the Krasnograd kremlin, but then snow drifted over her head, and she sank down into darkness.

She was awakened by something stepping on her legs.

"Oh sorry, Tsarinovna," whispered Dunya. "I was just getting up to feed the dogs."

"Is it morning already?" Slava whispered back.

"Close enough," whispered Dunya. "I wanted to see what the weather was like. I think it's been snowing hard all night."

"What are you two whispering about?" hissed Olga. "What are you trying to plot behind my back?"

"Our escape," said Dunya. "We thought we'd steal a sled and run off together, only coming back when we were sure of your blessing."

"I thought so," said Olga. "Tell me, Dunya: do you think we'll be able to travel today?"

"I'll have to go look at the sky," Dunya told her, finishing her climb out of bed and fumbling around for her boots. There was just enough light from the embers of last night's fire in the next room to make out the vague outlines of things, but not enough for her to be able to tell her own boots from Olga's or Slava's, and so she was trying on each boot she found, in hopes of coming across her own.

"Just don't get any snow in your eye when you do," Olga warned her.

"Don't worry, mother: I'll shield my eyes with my hand like this," said Dunya, putting her hand to her brow as if she were staring into bright sunlight.

Olga burst out laughing. "Get!" she ordered, once she could speak again. "Get out and check the weather, you impudent girl!"

"Yes, mother," said Dunya, with a mock-bow, and left the room with what was decidedly close to a scamper. Slava thought she could hear her laughing to herself as she left, a welcome if decidedly unexpected sound. Slava wondered, not for the first time, what kind of thoughts Dunya thought to herself during her long hours of silence.

"Young women," said Olga, with a sigh of feigned chagrin. "You can't get them to be serious about anything."

"I think she's happy to leave Khladniye Vody," said Slava. "She thought it was a bad place. She thought it was uncanny."

"And she was right," said Olga, also getting up and fumbling for her boots. "After all, look what happened to you." She eventually found two matching boots that fit her feet, and went into the other room to stoke up the fire and prepare the morning tea.

Once she was gone, Slava put on the two remaining boots, which were presumably hers, and followed Olga out into the main room.

"Is it morning yet?" asked Dima, appearing from the second bedroom.

"Probably," Olga told him. "Who can tell in this darkness, though?"

"I'll wake the others," Dima announced, and disappeared back into the second bedroom. There were the sounds of his voice chivying the others out of bed, and the others wanting to know if it was morning yet, and whether it was still snowing, and if they would be able to carry on today.

By the time everyone was up, dressed, and ready for breakfast, Dunya had returned from feeding the dogs. They heard her stamping her feet and brushing herself off on the porch, and when she came inside, there was still lots of snow on her clothes and hair.

"What's it like out there?" everyone asked simultaneously.

"Snowy!" she announced.

"What do you think, should we risk carrying on?" asked Olga.

"It's not a blizzard yet, and we don't have enough supplies to risk staying for too long, either," said Dunya. "But you'll have to see and decide for yourself. It's very snowy."

After they had all eaten, Dunya, Olga, Dima, and Grisha stood on the porch for a long time and watched the snow and discussed whether or not it was safe to set out that morning, while Slava and the others sat inside and waited to hear their fate. Slava could see by their faces that the others felt as she did: unhappy at the prospect of spending more time in this tedious, uncomfortable cabin, with dwindling supplies, but reluctant to abandon its warmth for a long day in the snow, and so unable to make up their minds about what decision they wanted to hear.

"We're leaving," Olga announced, coming back in. "The snow is thick, but we can still see a little bit, and we don't have enough supplies to stay here for long. If we make good time, we should come to a real waystation tonight."

This news cheered everyone up so much that they all dressed and packed with alacrity, and everyone stepped out into the fast-falling snow without a single complaint about leaving their shelter behind.

It had been decided over breakfast that Slava was well enough to take her turn skiing, especially as the snow would slow everyone down to her pace anyway.

At first it was almost fun, skiing through the fast-falling snow. The flakes brushed against her face and settled on her clothes, so that she felt as if nature itself were taking her into its embrace. Everyone else was happy too, with the knowledge that everything they had already been through was behind them and a real waystation, the first since Naberezhnoye, many weeks back, was ahead of them. And when the sky began to lighten through the snow surprisingly early, Grisha declared that it must be drawing in towards spring, and soon they wouldn't have to travel in the dark. Slanik whooped in excitement at this announcement, provoking a chorus of whooping and shouting that soon turned into song.

But after another verst or so the song died away as everyone realized how hard it was to sing with a mouth full of snow. When they tried to halt, they ended up eating almost as much snow as food, and when they set off again, it was unnervingly difficult to free their skis from the snow that had drifted over them during their brief pause.

Mirik, Slanik, and Olik all started making jokes about the snow and getting lost, in voices that showed that the possibility was weighing heavily on their minds, until Sasha, tight-faced, told them to stop fooling around and ski, the Black God take them.

"We can't get lost anyway," said Olga bracingly. "We'd hit the trees if we went off the road."

Grisha, who was skiing next to Slava in a way she was beginning to suspect was protective, looked as if he wanted to contradict that, but he only bit his lip and shook his head.

"What is it, Grisha?" she whispered, when she thought the others were far enough away that the sound of their skis would cover up her voice. Even though everyone was going slowly, she was going even more slowly than the others, and they kept disappearing into the snow ahead. "Do you think we could get lost?"

"You can always get lost in the woods, Krasna Tsarina," he said.

"But the trees..." she objected. "Olga is right: surely we'd notice as soon as we went off the road."

"Krasna Tsarina!" he said reproachfully. "How many times have we been lost already when we shouldn't have? I for one won't tempt the gods with foolish words. Never assume you've made it until you're tucked safe in bed, that's what I say, Krasna Tsarina."

"Very wise, I'm sure, Grisha," Slava told him.

"And keep your eyes open, Krasna Tsarina," he said. "We may need you again."

Slava was about to say, "Need me for what?" but stopped herself and said, "I hope not," instead. Despite Grisha's obvious attempts to go slowly for her sake, every time she spoke she lost ground on him, and had to redouble her efforts not to be left behind.

"Although even leshiye have more sense than to be out in this snow," Grisha added, laughing.

"I wonder if they feel it," said Slava. "Snow, I mean. I wonder how they perceive it." She saw that she had lost another ski length on Grisha, and struggled futilely to regain her place by his side.

"Not like we do, you can bet on that, Krasna Tsarina, but even so, they'd probably rather not trudge through it if they don't have to," he said, looking back at her. Even looking backwards and deliberately trying to go slowly, he still kept drawing farther and farther ahead of her. "Your leshaya is kind of like an animal, and animals know better than to go running about in the snow when they don't have to. Animals know that snow's the time to curl up and keep warm."

"Unlike us," said Slava, and laughed when a large clump of snow fell off a tree branch and landed on her face. She wiped it off and, infected with the good humor that had made Dunya and Olga crack jokes that morning, looked up again in order to shake her fist in mock-anger at the tree, but suddenly realized that she didn't know which of the many trees surrounding her was the culprit.

"Grisha!" she called. "Grisha, why..."

"Tsarinovna!" someone shouted back from far away. "Where are you?"

"Here! Right here! Where are you?" she called, but there was no reply.

Chapter Twenty-One

Slava stood there, she didn't know for how long, waiting for someone to come to her or at least to shout, but it was as if the others had suddenly been swallowed up by the snow, and at last she was forced to admit that Grisha had been right and they, or at least she, had gotten lost *again*, and when it should have been a perfectly straightforward matter to stay on the road. For a moment she considered hurling her ski poles on the ground and screaming like a small child angry with its mother, but after a painful struggle she pulled herself together and refrained. If this was in fact the work of spirits or the gods and not just her own stupidity, then they would not be favorably impressed by sulking or hysterics, the Black God take them.

Slava's first thought was to follow her own tracks back to someplace she was sure was the road, which could only be a few paces away. But when she looked back to where her tracks should have been, they had already disappeared in the fast-falling snow, so that it looked as if she had been dropped there by some enormous bird. This discovery made Slava's heart jump painfully in her chest, but she reminded herself to stay calm, and tried to think of another way to find the road.

"I only just now noticed the trees," she said to herself, speaking out loud for courage. "So there must be some clear path back to the road, or I wouldn't have skied down it. And where did Grisha go?" But that last thought was much too frightening to dwell on, so she shut her mind to it and tried to make out the clearest way through the snow.

After squinting and looking in all directions, she decided that there were no trees behind her, which cheered her up considerably. She must have simply skied into a small clearing by accident, just as she had thought, and so all she had to do was turn around and ski back to the road. Most likely the others were stopped there, waiting, and she couldn't hear them because the snow was muffling their voices. All she had to do was turn around and ski back, and they would be there, waiting for her. All she had to do was turn around.

She started to turn around, but the snow caught on her skis, making her fall to her knees. For a moment she lost sight of the clear space behind her, and the fear rose up in her so strongly she thought she would be sick.

It's right behind you, it's right behind you, it's right behind you, she told herself, and the fear receded enough for her to pull herself back to her feet and finish turning around. Sure enough, the clear space was right in front of her. All she had to do was ski down it, and it would lead her straight to the road.

It was slow going in the heavy snow, especially with her heart beating too quickly, which is why, she told herself, she seemed to be making no progress. The snow was falling even faster now, if such a thing were possible, so that she couldn't tell how far she had gone from where she had stopped, but surely, surely, she must be almost to the road. Just a few more steps, and she would be there, and the others would be waiting for her.

"Slava?" someone called, seemingly from right beside her.

"Grisha?" she shouted, her voice shaking with relief. "Grisha, is that you? Olga! Dunya! Where is everybody?"

"Right here," someone called, she couldn't make out whom. "We're right here, Slava, we're waiting for you."

"I'm coming! I'm coming!" she shouted, and started skiing with redoubled speed in the direction of the voice.

"Stop, Slava!" it suddenly commanded, and her skis came to an abrupt halt in the fresh snow, throwing her to her knees again. When she righted herself, she looked around, and realized she was once more surrounded by trees.

"Grisha!" she screamed. "Olga! Dunya! Anyone! Where are you?"

A figure stepped out of the trees in front of her.

"Grisha!" she cried, almost sobbing with relief. "How did we get lost?"

"It's all right, Krasna Tsarina," said the figure, not with Grisha's voice. "You're safe now."

Slava opened her mouth to ask who the figure was, but what came out was a scream, so ear-splitting it made the hair on the back of Slava's own neck rise, and she had to choke it off by biting down on her tongue. For something like a monstrously large wolf had stepped out of the trees behind the figure of the man. Before Slava could be sure she wouldn't scream again, the wolf-figure—if that was what it was, it was so hard to tell in the snow—was followed by an elk, and then trees, and then what might have been a bear, and all kinds of small creatures too, and Slava knew what had happened.

"You found me," she said. "You tracked me from Khladniye Vody, and lured me off the path, and now you have me."

"We're sorry, Slava," said the elk. "We had to."

"I already gave you everything I could," Slava said in a quavering voice. "In the bathhouse. I gave you everything: all my strength, everything I think and feel, I gave you everything. What more do you want? What more can you possibly ask?"

"Oh Slava," said the elk. "Don't you know that we can always ask for more? Everyone always needs more, including us."

"Who are you?" asked Slava. "Are you the gods?"

"We are those who have taken a little piece of the gods inside of us," said the elk. "We are not gods, but a little of their power resides in us. You were offered the same chance, but you refused."

"And I will again!" cried Slava.

"Of that I have no doubt, Krasnoslava," said the elk, and it sounded to Slava almost as if she were laughing. "And even if you agreed, I doubt it could be done, as my sister," she nodded towards a tree-figure, who gazed on Slava with eyes that seemed to glow golden through the snow, "discovered to her cost. Your gift is not one that is congenial to crueler, weaker powers such as ours, and it leaves little room, anyway."

"So what do you want?" demanded Slava. "Why don't you just leave me alone?"

"Oh Slava, if only we could! But you see, Slava, we need you."

"For what?" asked Slava disbelievingly.

"Do you know what your gift is, Slava?" said the elk.

"Yes," Slava told her.

"Are you sure of that?"

"Yes," said Slava again. "Fairly sure. I've been living with it all my life, after all."

"And as with so many familiar things, you disdain it, underestimate it. Do you remember what you were told back in Khladniye Vody?"

328

"I was told a lot of things," said Slava.

"Among them, that you were born to be a hero. Do you remember that?"

"Yes, but..."

"Gray Wolf!" called the elk sharply. The enormous wolf-figure stalked forward. Slava couldn't be sure through the snow, but it seemed as if he might be grinning.

"Bring me the hare," the elk commanded, and the figure that might have been a man opened a sack and pulled something out of it that might have been a snow hare.

"What are you going to do?" demanded Slava, her voice rising fearfully. "What are you..."

The enormous wolf-figure lunged at the snow hare, which was too disoriented from its time in the sack to do more than squeak in terror.

"NO!" screamed Slava. "No, no, no!" She dived forward and snatched up the snow hare. The wolf knocked her down and pinned her with one of its enormous paws.

"Really, Slava, you should give me the snow hare," he said, grinning at her. "I'm very hungry, after all. Let me have it, and I'll let you go, unharmed. I'll even lead you back to your friends."

"No!" said Slava, clutching the snow hare to her chest.

"I could rip off your arm and take it from you," pointed out the wolf.

"Then that's what you'll have to do!" cried Slava.

"Let her go," said the elk. "You see, Slava," she added. "You were born to be a hero. You can't help yourself."

"How could you!" cried Slava. "Him I understand"—she nodded towards Gray Wolf—"and even him"—she nodded at the man who had opened the sack—"but how could *you*? That could have been *you* they were trying to kill."

The elk snorted. "But it wasn't," she said. "Even elk are more blood-thirsty than you, my little Krasna Tsarina. You can get up now, if you like."

"Don't challenge my bloodlust!" shouted Slava, but she could see that none of the others could or would pay any heed to her warning. She tried to rise, but the skis held her feet in place, and she couldn't get up without letting go of the snow hare, so she knelt there, clutching it to her and glaring at the others defiantly, until the man came over and picked her up. He had, Slava couldn't help but notice, bright red hair peeking out through his scarf.

"Do you know what your gift is, Krasnoslava?" the elk repeated. "Because I don't think you do. Your gift, your true gift, is that you protect the weak. You can't help yourself."

"So?" said Slava. "Why do you care?"

"Because, Slava, we are all weak. We are born weak, and we will die weak. Some of us may be strong for a little while, but strength is a passing thing. And we are so terrible. We are so quick to defend the strong, and even quicker to attack the weak. Except for you, Krasnoslava. You walk against the wind, protecting the weak from the strong. Someday we will all have need of you, or those like you, who are—alas!—all too rare."

"But you said that you had pieces of the gods residing within you..." Slava objected.

"Even the gods can be weak, Slava," said the elk. "Even now the power they have given me is fading, and someday I will be no different from my other forest sisters, and in need of your mercy, just as they did."

"I don't see how I can be much use," Slava argued. "After all, I'm weak myself. Terribly weak. Weaker than anyone else, probably."

"Oh Slava! Heroes are always strong enough, when they have to be. That's why they're heroes. And weakness is your greatest strength. After all, how could you understand the weak without being one of them? No, Slava, you cannot escape this, I'm afraid."

"So why did you have to lure me away to tell me this?" asked Slava. "If it's inescapable, couldn't you just let me go about my business?"

"To warn you, Slava, to tell you to be ready," said the elk. "Ready to help us, that is. To help us and everyone else who needs you, of course. So that you wouldn't lose heart, waiting for your moment to come. Because you were losing heart, weren't you?"

"I've been losing heart my whole life, there's nothing unusual about that," said Slava irritably. "If your plan was to make me feel better about myself, you could have come a lot sooner."

"I'm glad to see that you do have teeth, Slava," said the wolf, with an extra-wide grin that displayed his own magnificent set of fangs. "But I still think I might be a little too big for them, if it comes down to it."

Slava hunched over the snow hare and glowered at the wolf until he burst out laughing.

"Ignore him," said the elk with a snort. "He can't help himself; the gods gave him rather too much of themselves, and now he's completely insufferable, worse than a human being. Even I can hardly stand to be around him. But there will come a day, Slava, when you will take pity on him, and stand up for him when everyone around him—maybe even me—will be clamoring for his blood."

"You're probably right," said Slava gloomily.

"Don't be so downcast, Slava!" said the man. "A glorious fate awaits you!"

"Oh good," said Slava. "I want to go back to my friends now. And I'm taking this with me!" she added, looking down at the snow hare.

"Of course, Slava, we have delivered our message and you are free to go," said the elk, while the wolf grinned his agreement, and all the other creatures looked on with eyes that glowed golden through the snow.

"I'll show you the way," said the man. "It won't take long. It's not far at all, and the snow will stop soon. And I have things to do there. Who knows"—he looked over to Gray Wolf as he said this, as if the two of them had some special knowledge—"how long it will take."

"Not long, no doubt," said Gray Wolf with a grin, but the man did not, as far as Slava could tell under his scarf, return it.

"Until we see each other again, Slava," said the elk. "Don't forget! You cannot escape your heroism."

"I'm so glad," said Slava, but the others had all melted away in the snow before she could get the words out.

"Come, Slava," said the man. "I know you're tired, but it isn't far at all. You can let him go now, you know."

"Who? Oh," said Slava, as the snow hare began to struggle in her arms. She let him go, and he dashed off, quickly disappearing into the trees, which were now standing blackly all around them.

"The snow," said Slava, realizing what this meant. "The snow is slowing. I can see the trees again."

"It will be easier for us to find your friends," said the man.

"Did you cause the snowstorm?" asked Slava. "Did you call it up?"

"I don't have that power, Slava," said the man. "But the gods might have had a hand in it. Snowstorms are not uncommon in winter, though, you know." Slava thought he might have been smiling now, but it was hard to tell behind his scarf. He began walking, and Slava skied after him.

As soon as she set off, her legs started trembling, and she was extremely glad when the man said, "Only a few dozen paces, Slava."

"How do you know who I am?" she asked, in an attempt to distract herself from her weakness, which was spreading from an uncomfortable sensation in her legs to a gnawing pain in her whole body.

"We've been watching you, of course, Slava," said the man. "Ever since you were born, and even more closely since you left Krasnograd."

"Watching a Tsarinovna seems, well...I seem like a very worldly object of interest for, for...people like you. Woodspeople, I guess." Slava didn't know how to ask him more directly what, precisely, he was.

"You mean people who live in the woods, or people who consort with wood-spirits, Slava?" he said, and this time Slava was sure he was smiling.

"Both," she said.

"We're not picky," he told her. "We'll even take a Tsarinovna, if she has gifts."

"What about you?" Slava asked. "What gifts do you have?"

"Me, Slava? Nothing like you, of course. My only gift was that I was a little bit bolder, a little bit wilder than the next man. I loved to hunt, before, and one day I went after game that was a little too big for my teeth, and the next thing I knew, Gray Wolf—you met him just now, you know what he's like—had pinned me down and had his fangs around my throat.

"'Tell me, man,' he said. 'Are you afraid to die?'

"'I'm not afraid to die,' I told him, 'but I've a fine, strong daughter back at home, and I'd hate to leave her. Her mother doesn't love her as she deserves.'" The man stopped and looked off at the trees.

"They didn't let me go back to her, of course," he continued after a while. "But they did let me live, on one condition."

"What was the condition?" asked Slava.

The man seemed to smile again behind his scarf, but this time with sorrow. "All my daughters are fine, strong girls," he said, "and all of them are or will be friendly to magic, friendly to the woods and 'people like me,' as you called us. Such people are all too rare, Slava, as you must see yourself. Good people are rare," he finished, now speaking very sadly, and more to himself than to Slava, "and I fear I was never one of them. But my daughters, perhaps, will be."

"Oh," said Slava. She didn't know whether to feel pity or disgust. Of course, some men—well, most men, if you came right down to it—let themselves be used like that, but it still made Slava a little bit sick to think about it.

"I'm sorry," she said. "Gifts are cruel."

"And yet, if you asked me, I would not give up mine," said the man.

"Gray Wolf and the leshiye took me in, and as you were told, we all carry a little piece of the gods around inside of us. There are compensations for that. I will get to see my daughters and my granddaughters grow to have granddaughters of their own, which is more than most fathers can say. And now," he gave Slava a bright look, "I will get to see my first daughter, the one I bragged of, and started it all." He walked for a moment in silence, and then asked, when it became apparent that Slava was not going to speak, "Did you know?"

"I guessed you were Olga's father as soon as you began your story," Slava confessed. "And you know...We have the brother of another of your daughters with us, too. Although I'm afraid her story is not a happy one."

"Milochka? Her story is happier than you think, or so I've been told. She and her lover made it to Krasnograd. They sing together in taverns there, and everywhere people hear them, a little bit of happiness takes root. That is a great thing, you know: to give people happiness."

"I'm glad," said Slava, and it was true; even though she had never met Milochka at all, the news that she was alive and well filled her with so much joy that for a moment the weakness seemed less painful.

"And Svetochka's daughter will have a great future, too, although," sorrow tinged the man's voice for a moment, "I doubt she will be as happy as Milochka. I am not a foreseer, but you can't consort with the gods without picking up things here and there, and sometimes I catch flashes of my daughters' fates. No, Svetochka's daughter has a hard road ahead of her, and I fear there will come a day, Slava, when she will need your mercy."

"If I can give it, then I will," said Slava.

"I know you will, Slava," said the man, still sounding sad. "That is why we all need you so much."

"You..." Slava started to say, as tears prickled behind her eyes, but she was interrupted by someone saying her name.

"The snow has almost stopped, and if we're lucky, the Tsarinovna won't have gone far," Dima was saying.

"She's a smart woman; she'll know to wait for us," said Grisha.

"But if the leshiye..." Slanik put in anxiously.

"Grisha! Dima! Slanik!" Slava shouted, lunging forward and collapsing into the snow as her knees buckled under her.

"Tsarinovna!" everyone screamed at once. "Where are you?!"

"I'm here!" she called, as her escort helped her back to her feet.

He half-dragged her through a line of trees, and onto the road, where everyone was, just as he had promised, waiting for her.

"We thought we'd lost you!" cried Olga, pushing everyone aside and sweeping Slava up into her arms as if she were a little girl. She kissed Slava several times on the head and face—that is, on her hat and scarf—before letting her go, only for her to be snatched up by Dunya, Dima, and Grisha in turn.

It took some time before everyone's ecstasy had calmed to the point that they noticed Slava's escort.

"Thank you, thank you, thank you!" Olga said, while the men took turns slapping him on the back. "It was so lucky you were there! But how did you stumble on her, and in all that snow?"

"We were watching her," said the man. "We wouldn't have lost her."

It took a moment for his words to settle in, and then everyone drew back from him abruptly.

"Don't worry!" Slava told them. "They meant me no harm, and he did, after all, bring me back. And Olga—you..."

"What are you?" demanded Dima, stepping between the man and Slava, and looking at him with extreme dislike. "Are you a person or a spirit? And why should we trust you?"

"Both, Dmitry Marusyevich," said the man. "That is, I was once a person, just as you are, who became in part a spirit. And you should trust me because I brought the Tsarinovna back to you, and...other reasons as well." He gave Dima a searching look, which did not go unnoticed.

"What are you staring at?" said Dima, glaring at the man with even more dislike. "You act like you know me, but believe me, we've never met before, and we shan't ever meet again, if I have anything to do with it."

"I just wanted to see if you were good enough," said the man.

"Good enough for what?" said Dima, stepping forward and leaning into his face in what was, Slava had to say, an unusually aggressive fashion for someone who was normally so mild-mannered.

"Dima, wait," she said. "He's...It's only natural that he should..."

"There's nothing natural about him!" shouted Dima.

"It's good that you have a bit of fire, sonny," said the man, looking at Dima with amused approval. "I doubt any of those milk-veined princess's sons could satisfy Olga Vasilisovna, but you seem like man enough for the task."

There was an audible intake of breath from all the onlookers, and everyone's heads snapped around to see how Olga would react to this.

"You speak very freely, 'sonny,'" she said. She put her hand to her brow, as if peering at the sun. "But I can't quite make out your features. A truly bold man would match his deeds to his words, and show his face."

"Ah, Olenka," said the man with a sigh. "I see you haven't changed a bit." Slava, who was still standing very close to him, could see how his eyes filled with a sad joy as he looked at her. Dima, who was standing even closer, could also see it, and stared at him in puzzlement. "The gods alone know how hard it was to pass out of this life and into the next one and leave you behind. The gods alone know where I've been, and how much I've thought of you ever since. The gods alone know how much I've missed you. I can't tell you how happy it makes me to hear such bold words come from your mouth. I always knew you would—"

But the rest of his words were drowned by Olga's piercing shriek. Before anyone else could do or say anything, she had flung herself across the distance between them and thrown her arms around his neck. Dima instinctively tried to jump in between them, but Slava grabbed his arm and shook her head, and he stepped back, staring at the scene before him with more and more bewilderment.

"But you died!" Olga exclaimed, once she could speak again. "I thought you were dead...How..." She held him at arms' length and looked at him with one eye and then the other, "You haven't aged... How...They took you! That's what happened, isn't it? They took you! They took you, and let us think you were dead."

"Exactly," said the man.

"Well, not that I blame you for going—I left myself, after all— but I wish you could've dropped by and let me know you were alive, I missed you even though I don't think anyone else did and I—there were times when I wished I could have had you to stand by me, but be that as it may, there were probably times when you wished you had me to stand by you too, it must've been so frightening for you at first, I wish we could've been together, but here we are and I'm so glad you're alive! I'm so glad you're alive!" And Olga burst into tears.

Chapter Twenty-Two

"There there," said the man, patting her back. "You've done a fine job on your own, I can see that."

"Olga Vasilisovna," said Dima, in an uncharacteristically high voice, "who is this man?"

"Oh Dima!" Olga dried off her face, blew her nose into her scarf—this was the kind of thing that only Slava found disgusting; everyone who lived not in a palace found it perfectly normal—and smiled at him. "Dima, this is Oleg Svetoslavovich! My father," she added, when the bewildered expression failed to clear from Dima's face.

"I thought he died when you were a little girl," said Dima, not looking any more enlightened, but looking even more deeply suspicious. "I thought he was killed in a hunting accident many years ago."

"Oh, but..." Olga turned to Oleg Svetoslavovich, her face shining with a childlike expression of trust that seemed even more out of place because she was tall enough to look him in the eye. "Explain to him, papa! Explain how you survived!"

"I was in a hunting accident," said Oleg Svetoslavovich. "But they rescued me, and made me one of them."

"They can do that?" said Dima, eyeing Oleg Svetoslavovich with even more suspicion, if such a thing were possible.

"They can, if you are able to accept their gift," said Oleg Svetoslavovich.

"Is that what they wanted to do to the Tsarinovna?" asked Dima, his lip curling with distaste.

"Yes, but…"

"Well it's a good thing you escaped, Tsarinovna!" said Dima hotly. "And the sooner we're rid of…him," he gave Oleg Svetoslavovich a look of intense dislike, "the better, I say. Who knows what they're plotting?"

Everyone suddenly started speaking at once, with Oleg Svetoslavovich trying to explain to Dima why he was wrong, Dima demanding that Oleg Svetoslavovich be sent back into the forest as soon as possible, Olga telling Dima he was wrong, her father meant them no harm, Sasha wanting to know who "they" were, Grisha shouting that nightfall was coming in and they needed to start moving again, and Dunya shaking her head in disgust and retreating to her sled to calm the dogs, who were getting restless. Slava, after a brief internal debate, went over and joined her.

"Grisha's right," said Dunya. "Night's falling fast, and we're nowhere near shelter. We need to take off as soon as we can."

"Perhaps Oleg Svetoslavovich can help us," said Slava hopefully.

"Perhaps," said Dunya. "But would we take his help?"

"It's better than spending the night in the woods," said Slava. "And I think he is trustworthy, anyway."

"You do, Tsarinovna?" said Dunya, looking surprised.

"Why should I not?" asked Slava. She glanced back in the direction of the arguers, but they were still arguing, with much pointing of fingers and shaking of fists.

"He saved me from the snow, and brought me back to you," said Slava, turning back to Dunya and trying to ignore the argument, which was beginning to annoy her. Not only did being around arguers make her feel sick to her stomach, but, as both Grisha and Dunya had pointed out, they didn't have time to stand around arguing when they should be moving as quickly as they could towards the nearest shelter.

"He's one of them," said Dunya. "Most likely he just wants to turn you into one of them too, like he told us."

"But he can't," said Slava. "They can't. They've tried and tried, and they can't. As he told us, they can only do it if you are able to accept their gift, and I am not."

"I'm not willing to risk it, Tsarinovna," said Dunya.

"It's no risk," Slava told her. "Truly, they can't do anything do me. If they could, they would have done it already."

"I wonder why they can't," said Dunya, and then had to leave to go sort out a quarrel that had erupted between two of the dogs before Slava could answer her.

It is odd, said Slava to herself as everyone quarreled around her. *One would think I would be more able to receive their gift, not less. After all, that is what I do: I receive from others. I am a passive object on which they stamp their passions.*

Oh no, Slava, you're wrong. For a moment Slava thought she had thought that as well, but then she realized she hadn't. Her head snapped around, searching for the other thinker, but of course she saw nothing—thoughts are invisible.

It's me, Slava, the elk, said the voice in her head that wasn't her voice. It had a pleasant, musical sound, like that of a great singer, with a certain husky quality that Slava couldn't help but think was vaguely reminiscent of an elk snorting. *I followed you and Oleg Svetoslavovich, in order to be sure you made it back to your friends safely. And I see you almost did.*

I hope they don't hurt each other, said Slava.

I doubt it will come to that, said the elk. *Sometimes you just have to have a little fight, so you can feel better and carry on.*

I don't have to have a little fight, said Slava. *That certainly wouldn't make ME feel better.*

Ah, but you're Slava, not them, said the elk.

Slava couldn't argue with that, but she couldn't come up with a clever response to it either, and so waited in silence for the elk to say something else.

You were wondering why you couldn't become one of us, said the elk after a pause. *A justified question. I also have thought on this, as have all my sisters and brothers. And I followed you back not only to watch over you, but to share with you the answer, at least as I understand it. We all so desperately desire the opposite. But you see, Slava, you are wrong: you are not passive clay on which others stamp their passions. Despite what you think, your gift is to give, not to receive. You cannot take from others, or at least, not very well. I'm afraid it is we who will have to take from you, and not the other way around. Oh look, I think they have fought it out and settled their differences,* said the elk. *You will be safe now, so I will go.*

I wish I could give something to you, said Slava, who was now very taken with the elk. At their earlier encounter she had formed a fairly unfavorable impression of her, but now that they were just talking, she saw that she and the elk did have a good deal in common, and could, in fact, be friends, just as she would have expected. *I wish you were carrying on with us,* she added.

Well, perhaps we shall see each other again, said the elk, and, with what was unmistakably a snort, she bounded out of Slava's mind and disappeared into the woods.

"Oleg Svetoslavovich will be guiding us to the nearest shelter," announced Olga, as everyone shuffled sheepishly around the sleds. "He says it's not far, only fifteen versts or so, and we should be there by suppertime, but we've got to leave now."

"And it's a real waystation!" cried Slanik.

The reminder of the happiness awaiting them, if only they could pull themselves together and go there, raised a cheer from everyone, and in a remarkably short time, considering how long they had been standing around doing nothing, they were all moving again.

The heavy snow prevented them from traveling as fast as they might have liked, but they were still making better time than they had all day, which kept the mood buoyant as they slogged along. Slava had, of course, been put in a sled in order not to slow down the others. She lay back and watched as the light faded out of the thin strip of sky she could see, slowly bleeding from orange to blue to black, with bright stars that seemed to be watching over her as she looked up at them. She felt as if the whole woods were watching over her as well...eyes were peering out at her from behind the trees...golden eyes...

One star suddenly detached itself from the sky and streaked out of sight in the treetops.

"A shooting star!" Slava cried.

"Ai-da Krasna Tsarina!" everyone shouted in response. "A shooting star!"

"Look, there's another!" cried Slanik, pointing up at the sky with his ski pole.

"And another!" cried Sasha.

"Some nights are full of them," said Oleg Svetoslavovich, also staring up at the sky with wonder. "But we've got to keep going, or we'll freeze."

They took off again, but with one eye cocked to the sky. Slava lay back in the sled again and watched her breath mingle with the shooting stars as her hands and feet grew numb, and a deep cold settled in her stomach, as if she had swallowed a tub of ice.

I'm glad I came, she thought. *I'm so glad I left Krasnograd, and came here. No matter what happens, I'm glad I came. It will all be worth it.*

A flash of movement in the trees distracted her from her thoughts, but when she tried to catch sight of it and puzzle out what it might be, it eluded her, and she returned to her reveries. Once she thought she caught another flash of movement out of the corner of her eye, but it never resolved itself into a solid figure.

After a while a kind of strange drowsiness began to settle over her. *That's odd,* she thought. *I should be too cold to be able to fall asleep. And I don't want to miss the shooting stars!* She sat up and tried to force her eyes to stay open, but somehow her body seemed too distant and clumsy to obey. Her clothing was stiff with her frozen breath, and chafed unpleasantly against her face, but when she tried to rearrange it, her hands skittered away uselessly.

Something moved again in the corner of her eye, and for a moment it seemed as if it were trying to call out a warning to her...to reach her... but then it cried out in shock and pain instead, and disappeared. No one other than Slava seemed to notice, though. She tried to focus her thoughts on the movement in the wood, but they seemed even more distant and clumsy than her body.

I'm freezing, she thought. *I'm freezing and that's why I'm seeing things that aren't there. If I don't get warm soon, I'll die.* But she couldn't seem to do anything about it. She knew she should tell Dunya, but her mouth couldn't form the words.

It doesn't matter anyway, she found herself thinking. *It's so peaceful and pleasant now, it doesn't matter anyway. I'll just sink into it.*

"Lights!" shouted Sasha.

"LIGHTS!!" everyone shouted. "LIGHTS!!!"

What are lights doing in the middle of the forest, Slava thought, and she couldn't understand what was happening when the sled suddenly stopped in front of a blazing building, and people she didn't know came out and spoke to them.

"You should get out now," said Dunya, coming over to her.

Why are we stopping now? Slava asked herself, as she stared up at Dunya uncomprehendingly. She tried to ask Dunya the question out loud, but the only thing that came out was gibberish.

"Help me!" shouted Dunya. "We have to take her to the bathhouse, she's frozen!"

Lots of people, only some of whom Slava knew, rushed over, picked her up, and carried her off to a small building behind the large building. They set her on a bench, and she realized she was in a bathhouse. There was a lot of frantic activity around her, with shouting.

"Her hands," Dunya was saying. "Check her hands and feet for frostbite."

"My hands and feet are fine," Slava tried to say, but no one was listening. She tried to say it again, but the pain that suddenly opened up in them made her cry out instead.

"Krasnoslava! Where are you hurt!" demanded Dunya.

"It-t-t-s-s-s-s j-j-j-just-t-t-t the ch-ch-ch-chill-l-l l-l-leaving-g-g-g," said Slava, through the shivers that had suddenly taken her in their clutches.

"We never should have left you in that sled unattended!" said Dunya, looking much angrier than Slava had ever seen her before. "We were in such a hurry to get here we forgot all about you! A fine thing that would have been, to lose you just when we'd made it to safety!"

"There were sh-sh-shooting s-s-s-stars," said Slava, as if that explained everything.

"Your noblewoman's going to be just fine, Dunechka," said one of the strangers. She had a round, beaten-down face and was wearing an apron over her coarse dress. Her eyes peered out alertly from behind layers of suspicion and sorrow, giving the impression of a foreign soul in her dull, overworked peasant's body. Slava tried to make out the color of those surprising eyes, but it shifted with every flicker of the lanternlight, and she had to give up.

"It was just a little chill, nothing more. She'll be warm as fresh-baked bread in no time, just you wait and see," said the careworn woman, her coarse peasant's voice giving no indication of the bright life in her eyes. She patted Slava on the head in an overly-familiar manner, telling her, "Don't you worry, little dove, you'll be right as rain before you know it."

The agony of life returning to her hands and feet made Slava inclined to disagree, but she held her tongue and retreated into her own private world of pain. The strange-eyed woman quickly slipped into the back of her mind, hidden completely by the sensation that her hands and feet had somehow ended up on blacksmith's anvil.

After what seemed a very long time of not crying out in pain in order not to worry Dunya, but was no doubt really no longer than it took to boil soup, the pain faded away to nothing more than a distant ache, leaving no trace other than a slight redness on her skin.

By then all the strangers had gone off, ordered by the careworn-faced woman to return to their duties, which seemed to be working in the stable and kitchen. They must be, Slava realized once she was able to think clearly again, the waystation servants, and this must be the waystation bathhouse, and they must have made it to the shelter they were striving to reach after all.

"We're back in civilization," said Slava, once she could speak without her teeth chattering uncontrollably.

"Well, I wouldn't exactly call it civilization," said Dunya, who, despite the bathhouse heat, was sitting with her arms folded across her chest and a guarded expression on her face. "It's only a waystation. We'll be back in the woods tomorrow. Olga Vasilisovna and Oleg Svetoslavovich both say that we'll probably go slow because of the snow, but even so we've probably no more than two more nights of staying in cabins, and then two more nights of waystations, and then we'll really be in civilization, if you want to call it that—Lesnograd, anyway. How do you feel?"

"Much better, thank you," said Slava. "It was silly of me to get so chilled. I should have told someone—I was watching the stars, and thinking about other things, and the next thing I knew, I no longer had the sense to do what needed to be done."

"It's our fault, not yours," Dunya told her. She jumped off the bench she had been sitting on, and paced back and forth a few times. Slava tried to watch her without too much overt curiosity, and waited for her to share what was on her mind. With her newly-returned clarity of thought, she couldn't help but notice that Dunya was not only not like her normally calm self, but that she had said "Lesnograd" like a noblewoman or a Southerner, not "Lesnogorod," as the common folk up here did, and that her speech was becoming more and more like Slava's own. This was so interesting that Slava forgot to worry about their present predicament and how she had nearly frozen to death, and began to speculate on why that would be, and how long it would last, and why some people tended to speak like whomever they were speaking to, while others didn't, and whether Dunya was in fact a young woman of naturally refined mind, and what that actually meant...

"Tsarinovna!" said Dunya, breaking into her thoughts. "What do you think of our situation?"

"It's better than it was before, I suppose," said Slava, trying to concentrate on what Dunya was saying rather than how she was saying it. "No leshiye, no bandits—well, other than Mirik, that is—and a roof and four walls to keep us from freezing to death."

"True," said Dunya. "But..."

Slava waited some more in silence, not wanting to say anything that might set off Dunya's apparently overwrought nerves.

"I have a bad feeling, Tsarinovna," said Dunya after some more pacing. "As soon as we drew near the waystation, I got this bad feeling, and it's only been getting worse."

"What kind of bad feeling?" Slava asked her.

"Just...I don't know! I didn't like how curious they were about us when we arrived, for a start."

"They might have reason to be concerned about bandits," Slava pointed out. "One of which we do in fact have in our party."

"Yes, but...I don't know. I just have this bad feeling, like I said. Like they're up to something worse than banditry. Like we're being watched in secret. Like we're being watched right now—like there's something in this bathhouse with us that we can't see, but is watching us."

"Nonsense," said Slava, although as soon as she had heard Dunya's words she had started having the same sensation. She looked all around the bathhouse, but could see nothing. "Nonsense," she repeated, more for herself than for Dunya. "There's nothing here. And if there were, we have nothing to hide."

"I still don't like being watched," said Dunya darkly. "And I don't think anything good awaits us in Lesnograd, either. I wish Oleg Svetoslavovich were continuing on with us."

"Don't let Dima hear you say that," said Slava, smiling at that thought and at the confidence and affection Oleg Svetoslavovich had apparently already inspired in the normally reserved Dunya. He really, she reflected, did have a gift, or so it seemed. She wondered if he—or those who controlled him—had any designs on Dunya, and how much luck they were likely to have.

Dunya smiled faintly in return, although she probably hadn't guessed the real reasons for Slava's amusement. "I think he's warming to Oleg Svetoslavovich," she said. "Once he decided he meant you and Olga no harm, he quite took to him. No doubt they'll end up fast friends."

"No doubt," agreed Slava. "Why would having Oleg Svetoslavovich with us help with whatever is awaiting us in Lesnograd?"

"I just...We're returning to civilization, like we've both already told each other over and over again. But civilization's a dangerous place. Worse than the woods, at least in my opinion. And I just think it would be good to have someone with some of the leshiye's wildness, someone like Oleg Svetoslavovich, with us when we go there. I don't think these Severnolesniye people mean us any good. I think we should watch our backs around them."

"Princess Severnolesnaya is a most troublesome ally," said Slava.

"Yes, and I think all her subjects are just as bad," said Dunya. "They're not like our friendly Pristanogradskiye and Naberezhniye people. Back home they have a bad reputation, and I'm beginning to think it's deserved. Back home we say they're cunning and sly, and I'm beginning to think it's true."

"No doubt," said Slava lightly. "But that may just be because they have a great princess living there. Great princesses are often cunning and sly, and so are their subjects. You may just be used to Naberezhnoye's simple ways, Dunya."

"You know," said Dunya, giving Slava a very un-Dunya-like embarrassed smile, "I'm actually afraid of what's ahead of us! Now that Lesnograd's so close, I'm not sure I want to go there. Have you ever been there, Tsarinovna?" This time when Dunya said Slava's title, it was with a tone of relief at the thought that she had someone with such a grand title to stand between her and all the dangers facing her—also a very un-Dunya-like behavior.

"No, but—" Slava smiled at what she was about to say—"back in Krasnograd we consider Lesnograd a very second-rate sort of city, a real provincial backwater. Of course, everything outside of Krasnograd *is* a provincial backwater, but Lesnograd is supposed to be—well, it is famed for having a certain amount of barbaric splendor, and nothing more. You called it civilization, but anyone who lived anywhere on the Krasna would argue with your description. From what I have gathered, there will be some large buildings, all made entirely of wood, and some large markets, where wood is probably sold in large quantities, and that is about all. I dare say it will be much like Naberezhnoye, only somewhat bigger and with more annoying inhabitants, as they will have been spoiled by serving under a princess. No doubt they will put on airs in front of you, but pay them no attention—they will undoubtedly deserve none."

This description of Lesnograd seemed to cheer Dunya up considerably, so that she took a deep breath, and with her accustomed Dunya-like expression of cool competence, asked Slava if she were ready to leave the bathhouse and have supper.

She did fuss over Slava's outer clothing before allowing her to step back outside, which Slava permitted with good grace, in order to let Dunya regain her courage after their time in the bathhouse, which had spooked her badly. Slava remembered the careworn-faced woman's strangely bright eyes, and began to feel a bit spooked herself, but told herself not to judge anyone before knowing her story, and let

Dunya lead her out into the night. She tried not to pay any attention to the feeling she had of eyes watching her back as she left, eyes that desperately needed her help...It was all nonsense. Slava closed the bathhouse door firmly behind them.

They both instinctively looked up at the sky as they stepped out, and both cried out in wonder as a shooting star, twice as big and bright as any they had seen before, streaked across the darkness and disappeared into the treetops, leaving a brilliant afterglow in Slava's eyes, even when she closed them. She could not rid herself of the impression that the star had made a high-pitched whistling sound as it had burned its way across the sky, even though she knew that must be nonsense.

"Do you think it was a sign?" asked Dunya, once they had recovered their voices.

"Perhaps it was—a sign that there is wonder everywhere," said Slava. "We just have to keep our eyes open for it." This happy thought, having just struck her, seemed so agreeable that she commanded herself not to forget it, especially when she was next bored and miserable.

"You don't think it was an omen?" asked Dunya. "A bad one?"

"Certainly not!" said Slava firmly. "If it was an omen of anything, then it was a good one."

"Well, we'll see," said Dunya, with considerably less confidence than Slava would have liked to hear. Slava thought about demanding where the Dunya who had led them all the way from Naberezhnoye had gone, but was afraid that that would demoralize her even more, and so stopped herself.

After the half-lit bathhouse and the dark path between it and the waystation, the front room of the waystation with its half-a-dozen lamps seemed shockingly bright. Slava stood clutching Dunya's arm and blinking at the threshold for a moment before she could make out what she was looking at, allowing everyone inside to survey them thoroughly.

Aside from their own party, there was a group of what Slava assumed were traders, led by a rough-looking woman staring out from a tangle of gray hair. She grinned a gap-toothed grin at Slava when she caught her eye, with the clear intention of intimidating her. An expression of surprise and annoyance, followed by one of calculation, crossed her face when Slava only looked back at her and then moved on.

Slava told herself to be sure to keep an eye on the gray-haired woman and her shifty followers, who looked to be her daughter and several men who were presumably guards. The guards were all of such disreputable appearance that Slava began to wish they were back with the bandits. Through their greasy locks they watched Slava and Dunya cross the room with openly predatory eyes.

"You are not harmed, Ts—ah, Krasnoslava?" asked Olga as they took their seats. The rest of the group all looked round with interest to hear Slava's answer, but appeared too oppressed by the general level of unsavoriness in the room to speak themselves.

"I am perfectly well," Slava assured her. "It was nothing but a slight chill. I should have taken better care of myself."

"Good, because I plan to be out of here long before first light tomorrow morning," said Olga.

"If the bedbugs don't get us first," muttered Grisha darkly.

"Are there bedbugs?" asked Dunya, her face involuntarily twisting into such an intense look of disgust that Slava almost laughed.

"There must be," said Grisha, even more darkly, but keeping his voice too low for anyone beyond their table to hear them. "This is just the place to find bloodsuckers."

"Which is why we need to leave as soon as we can," said Olga.

"I'll be spending the night here with you," announced Oleg Svetoslavovich. He was sitting next to Dima and, as Dunya had predicted, appeared to be on the friendliest terms with him. He had taken off his hat and scarf, and Slava was surprised to see that he looked no older than Olga. Of course she shouldn't have been surprised, after hearing his story, but it was still a shock to see it with her own two eyes.

He was still a very fine figure of a man, and she could see why Princess Severnolesnaya had chosen him as her second husband, and why Svetochka and the others had taken him as a lover, and why even Dunya seemed to be succumbing to his charms. Handsome, Slava thought to herself, and also something better than handsome—he was just the kind of man one would want to father a child...Dunya had better watch out...Slava quickly turned her thoughts back to the matter at hand, suppressing a grin.

"Now that I've brought you this far, I think I'd better stay with you until I'm sure you're safely away from this place and back in Lesnograd," Oleg Svetoslavovich was saying. This accorded so perfectly with the favorable opinion Slava had already formed of him that she had to suppress yet another grin. The cold must have softened her wits, she thought to herself, trying not to laugh. She could tell that if she ever started laughing, she wouldn't be able to stop until she started to cry—it was that kind of an evening.

She resolved to stay calm and to stop admiring Olga's father so much. The memory of his last words with the wolf-monster suddenly popped into her mind, and she wondered if he had never had any intention of leaving them in the first place. What, she asked herself, was the task he had been set? Should Dunya in fact be watching out for herself, or was someone else the target, or was it something else altogether? Slava told herself she needed to keep a sharp eye on him. Luckily he was such a pleasant sight...she bit her lip to keep from smiling again.

"Thank the gods, and thank you, Oleg Svetoslavovich," said Dima, with, as far as Slava could tell, perfect sincerity. This was a severe tax on Slava's determination to stay calm, and she had to turn away in order to hide her smile. She caught the hungry eyes of the other party all fixed on her. She turned back to her own people, moving calmly, but no longer with any desire to smile.

"Do we know who those people are?" she asked quietly.

"No one good," said Grisha.

"I'll find out," said Dima. "Look, the stationmistress is coming our way."

The worn-faced woman was indeed coming over to them, watching them as she did so with her strangely shifting eyes.

"I hope you're all warmed up now, noblewoman," she said to Slava, patting her on the shoulder once again with an unpleasant familiarity.

"Yes, thank you for asking," Slava told her. As she spoke she became acutely aware of how much her voice differed from the stationmistress's. Slava knew, of course, that she spoke like the noblest of noblewomen, with years of schooling stamped on everything from the modulation of her tone to the words she chose, and normally she thought nothing of it. It was just the way she spoke, and it was only to be expected of her, just as it was only to be expected that she would walk with a certain air of command (not that she did that very well, alas), and smile with a certain grace, and sit down with the expectation that others would pull out her chair for her, and count it an honor to do so. Anything else would have been a gross affront to all the guards and servants and nannies and tutors and maids who had spent years schooling her to be as she was, so that they could have a reason to be as they were.

But now she felt it was drawing even more unneeded attention to her apparently unwelcome high rank. Even Olga, who was quite a noble noblewoman herself, could speak and act in a way that allowed her to pass for a somewhat common person, but not Slava. She wondered if she were about to bring more danger down on the others.

"Well, aren't you an elegant one," said the worn-faced woman, echoing Slava's thoughts unpleasantly. "Tell me: where are you from, noblewoman? Not Krasnogorod, surely?"

Slava tried to catch Olga's eye and see if she should answer truthfully, but Olga didn't seem to have a good answer for that right away, so Slava found herself saying, "Yes, Krasnograd," without being sure that it was the right thing to do.

"Well, isn't that something!" exclaimed the worn-faced woman with a forced jolliness that grated on Slava's real and metaphorical skin. "Krasnogorod, indeed! And tell me, noblewoman: have you lived there all your life?"

"Yes," said Slava, wishing she could send the worn-faced woman away but unsure how to do so. She could tell already from her over-bold, over-ingratiating manner that the woman had been badly beaten down and was now looking to get some of her own back, which made her a figure of such pity and horror that Slava didn't know what do. Show her kindness? But then she might take it as weakness. Brush her off? But not only did that go against Slava's grain to do so, she wasn't sure it would even work. It could end up just provoking the poor woman even more...

"Doesn't your family have some great estate out in the provinces?" asked the worn-faced woman, fixing Slava with an unpleasantly intelligent gaze.

"Yes," said Slava—which was completely true—and then, struck by sudden inspiration, added, "but I was raised in Krasnograd, in order to receive a good education and be near the kremlin."

As this was also completely true, it had a nice ring of truth to it, and the worn-faced woman appeared not only to accept it, but to be impressed by it, and when she asked, "And what family are you from, noblewoman?" her voice held almost as much genuine fear and curiosity as it did calculation.

Even so, Slava saw Olga and the others freeze in horror when she opened her mouth to answer, and so she only said, "my father was of the Stepnaya family,...."

"Marusya Svyatoslavovna, noblewoman," said the worn-faced woman, answering Slava's expectant pause. "The Stepnaya family!

Now there are some great princesses, noblewoman! No wonder they wanted you raised in Krasnogorod. And here you are in our Severnolesnoye! Tell me, noblewoman: what do you think of our forests? Not quite like your steppes, are they?"

"They are most majestic," said Slava. "I am quite pleased to have had the chance to see them."

"The Stepnaya family!" exclaimed Marusya Svyatoslavovna again, loud enough for everyone in the room to hear. "What an honor for us! I'm afraid the rest of us are not so nobly-born, noblewoman: Sanya Serafimyevna over there has her own guards, it's true, but she's certainly no noblewoman, and as for me, I'm just from the commonest of peasant clay." And she fixed Slava with another unpleasantly changeable gaze, waiting for her to react.

"I was never very close to my father's family," said Slava. "And we are all from common clay, in the end. The gods make no distinction between a noblewoman and a peasant."

"Well said, noblewoman, well said!" cried Marusya Svyatoslavovna, clapping Slava rather hard on the shoulder. "Was that not well said, Sanya Serafimyevna?"

"Very well said," said Aleksandra Serafimiyevna, rising and coming over to stand next to Marusya Svyatoslavovna, so that they formed a menacing and frankly rather rank-smelling wall around Slava. "Where did you get such ideas, little noblewoman?"

"The gods speak to anyone who will listen," said Slava.

"But perhaps a little more clearly to those of us who spend our time where they can get to us, instead of locked up in smelly cities, till we get as soft and fat as a hog for slaughter?" said Aleksandra Serafimiyevna, giving Slava a nasty grin that revealed a mouth of missing and rotting teeth. "I think I know what the gods have to say a little better than you do, little noblewoman."

"Don't think you know anything about the gods, old woman," said Oleg Svetoslavovich, speaking up unexpectedly from the far side of the table.

"You should keep your men under better control, my dear," said Aleksandra Serafimiyevna to Olga. "You need to teach them not to speak out of turn."

"My—my second-brother may speak whenever he wishes," said Olga, her face beginning to take on an expression that boded ill for Aleksandra Serafimiyevna.

"We know these 'second-brothers' some women like to take

349

around with them, my dove," said Aleksandra Serafimiyevna, raising her eyebrows so salaciously that Slava had to fight the impulse to gag. "But you should find a better story: you're practically old enough to be his mother yourself, after all."

The expressions of everyone at Olga's table grew so dark that Slava knew she had to do something now or get caught up in yet another fight. Through the revulsion threatening to overwhelm her rose a small sigh: what was this constant need to provoke fights in the people they encountered?

"Aleksandra Serafimiyevna!" she said loudly. "Which direction have you come from? What was the road like?"

"We came from Lesnogorod, where we were trading," said Aleksandra Serafimiyevna, giving Slava a mocking glance that showed she had caught onto her plan but was going to go along with it, for the moment anyway. "And the road gave us no trouble. What about your party, little noblewoman?"

"Snow," said Slava. "We encountered much snow."

"There's often snow in winter," said Aleksandra Serafimiyevna, provoking Marusya Svyatoslavovna to burst into raucous laughter.

"Yes," agreed Slava. "Was your trading successful, Aleksandra Serafimiyevna?"

"So you think you have the right to ask about my trading, little noblewoman?" said Aleksandra Serafimiyevna. "Watch out, little noblewoman: you're so fair-spoken your tongue might turn to gold, and then where'd you be." All her men broke out into sniggers at this, and whispered things to each other that, Slava was sure, did them no credit whatsoever. She would have said that their mothers would have been ashamed of them for even thinking the sorts of things they were obviously thinking, let alone saying them out loud, but she suspected that their mothers were no less coarsely-spoken than they were.

Aleksandra Serafimiyevna, perhaps divining Slava's thoughts, or perhaps merely unhappy with Slava's polished air, gave her a resentful look, but continued, once the malicious laughter from her table had died down, "Good enough, I suppose. We sold all our furs, at any rate. But the Princess closed the market, so we left, and here we are, chatting with you like the oldest of friends."

"Closed the market!" Olga exclaimed.

"Yes, haven't you heard?" The fact that Olga had not, while out in the woods, heard of the latest doings in Lesnograd seemed to fill Aleksandra Serafimiyevna with well-being, and she was visibly more pleased with herself as she continued, "She bought up everything in the market, and shut it down. She's planning something, mark my words, and I'd just as soon be out of Lesnogorod when she starts it. You're heading to Lesnogorod, I take it?"

"Yes," said Olga.

"Well, better you than me," said Aleksandra Serafimiyevna, now grinning with pleasure at the thought of Olga's future misfortune. She clapped both Slava and Marusya Svyatoslavovna on the shoulder. "Let's leave these people to their dinner, Marusenka," she said. "They'll need their strength for what's ahead of them." She and Marusya Svyatoslavovna retreated back to the bar, where they stood talking, occasionally looking in the direction of Olga's party, making no attempt to hide that they were talking about them.

Serving women brought cabbage soup and black bread to the table. It was, Slava thought, possibly the thinnest and least appetizing cabbage soup she had ever put in her mouth, and the bread was burnt on the outside and half-cooked in the middle, but she was so hungry after her day in the cold that she gulped it all down anyway.

Eventually Marusya Svyatoslavovna and Aleksandra Serafimiyevna disappeared into some back room, but their unpleasant atmosphere remained.

"I don't trust them," said Olga, glowering at her soup.

"Nor do I," said Oleg Svetoslavovich, glowering even more. "We should keep watch tonight."

"That we should," agreed Olga. "You men can decide it amongst yourselves. Dunya, I'll take first watch in the women's room, and you can take second."

"Very well," said Dunya, who had one eye on the door through which Marusya Svyatoslavovna and Aleksandra Serafimiyevna had disappeared, as if that would let her know what they were up to.

"What about me?" asked Slava.

"What about you?" said Olga.

"What watch shall I take? I should take a watch too, or otherwise you and Dunya will each be up half the night."

Olga gave Slava such an astonished look that it was hard not to be offended. "You want to take a watch, Ts—ah, you want to take a watch? Are you sure?"

"Of course," said Slava. "I dare say I can watch as well as the next woman, and you and Dunya need your rest even more than I do."

"Are you sure you're strong enough? I mean, after what happened today..."

"If I'm not, I'll wake one of you and let you replace me," Slava promised.

Olga looked like she wanted to make more objections, but Oleg Svetoslavovich said, "Krasnoslava is right: you and Dunya need your rest, and as she said, she can watch as well as the next woman," and Olga gave in.

"I'll take the last watch," said Dunya. "I have to get up early to harness the dogs anyway. And if the Ts—if Krasnoslava is sincere about letting you rest, then she should take the middle watch. Whoever has the middle watch will have the worst night."

"I'll take the middle watch," Slava declared firmly. "After all, I slept in the sled today."

"And almost froze to death!" said Olga.

"Yes, but it was very restful," said Slava.

This provoked a laugh from all the men, and Olga's mouth turned up slightly at the corners.

"Very well," she agreed. "You can have the middle watch, and let's hope it all proves to be for nothing!" She rose from the table. "I'm going to bed now. The rest of you should too."

Everyone else rose obediently and followed her in what Slava supposed was the direction of the bedrooms. Aleksandra Serafimiyevna's men, she noticed, followed them with their eyes all the way across the room and out the door.

Olga, Dunya, and Slava's room was dirty but surprisingly spacious. Dunya peeled back the bedcovers with two fingers and made a face.

"Olga Vasilisovna, can't we go back out into the woods?" she said.

"Alas, I fear we'd hurt Marusya Svyatoslavovna's feelings," said Olga. "She's put so much hard work into welcoming us."

"That would be terrible," agreed Dunya solemnly. "I'd hate to hurt her tender feelings. I'll just have to put up with it, like a grateful guest."

"Look on the bright side," Olga told her. "You'll get to get up extra early in order to take last watch."

"That is something to look forward to," said Dunya, taking off her boots and sliding with extreme reluctance into the bed.

Slava followed suit, while Olga settled herself onto a rickety chair. The bed did have a musty, unpleasant smell, and Slava doubted the bedding had been changed or aired all winter. She began to look forward to getting up in order to take her watch, too.

She had been afraid that the predictions of bedbugs would turn out to be true, but she slept undisturbed until Olga came and shook her on the shoulder.

"It's your turn to take watch," Olga whispered. "Everything's been quiet so far. Here." She handed Slava a musty blanket. "It's chilly, just sitting there. Wake Dunya up when you hear them stoke up the kitchen stove to start the bread—although judging from last night's feast, they don't bother to cook it overmuch." She shook off her boots and crawled into bed. "Civilization," she muttered, sniffing the pillow, and then appeared to drop into an immediate sleep.

The rickety chair was just as uncomfortable as it looked. Slava wrapped the musty blanket around herself, and became immediately aware of all the drafts it let in. She tried to find a more comfortable position, but the chair creaked loudly, and she stopped, afraid of waking the others.

Despite the discomfort, the day's adventures soon began to make themselves felt, and Slava felt herself growing drowsier and drowsier. Pacing, she feared, would also wake Olga and Dunya, as would singing, and even had she something to read—and she doubted there was a single book in the entire waystation; in fact, outside of Lesnograd, there were probably no more than half-a-dozen in all of Severnolesnoye—there was no light by which to read it. There was a dark-lantern on the floor by Slava's chair, but she resisted the urge to open its shade. Instead, she carefully eased the creaking chair over to the window, where a crack in the shutters allowed her to look out onto the yard.

The sky was completely clear, and Slava looked up, hoping to catch another shooting star. This caused her to miss the arrival of someone on the yard until she passed so closely in front of her window that for a moment she blocked out the moonlight.

The figure was, she thought, Aleksandra Serafimiyevna, although she was so bundled up, it was hard to tell. Slava wondered what she could be up to, walking around on the yard in the middle of the night. Nothing good, no doubt.

The person who might have been Aleksandra Serafimiyevna disappeared into the bathhouse. Almost as soon as she had closed the door behind her, another figure made its way across the yard. Slava tried cocking her head and screwing up her eyes, but nothing enabled her to make out who this second figure was, although under its long fur coat she began to suspect it was a man.

The fur coat also disappeared into the bathhouse, and once again, almost as soon as it had closed the door behind it, a third figure appeared on the yard. This one, Slava was certain, was Marusya Svyatoslavovna, even though she could make out no particular features to indicate that it was so. The figure Slava was certain was Marusya Svyatoslavovna also went into the bathhouse, opening and closing the door with the familiarity of long acquaintance.

Slava waited for another figure to appear, but the yard remained empty. After a time a thick stream of smoke began to issue from the bathhouse chimney.

A midnight steam? Slava asked herself, although it seemed so strange. It was Marusya Svyatoslavovna's own waystation, and Aleksandra Serafimiyevna was clearly on close terms with her, so why the need to steam in secret? Unless Slava had been correct in thinking the fur coat had been a man, and they were having some kind of secret tryst in the bathhouse...Slava wrenched her mind away from the vision of Marusya Svyatoslavovna and Aleksandra Serafimiyevna both engaged in the same secret tryst, but not before several repulsive images had risen before her eyes. She wondered who the man was and why he had agreed to such a thing, and whether he was in need of rescue. He had certainly seemed to make his way to the bathhouse of his own free will...

Sparks rose up in the smoke issuing from the bathhouse chimney. Slava waited for them to subside, but they only increased in number, until she began to fear the chimney had caught fire. She was about to wake Dunya and Olga and propose that they go investigate, when the sparks suddenly changed color, from red to blue, so that they looked like stars floating through clouds.

*What could be causing...*Slava thought, but before she could finish thinking, something dark rose out of the chimney.

At first she thought it was just a particularly thick billow of smoke, but then it began to take on form, which slowly resolved itself into that of a small, thick-trunked tree. Slava rubbed her eyes, thinking that they had grown too tired to see properly, but when she took her hands away, two golden spots were staring back at her from the middle of the dark smoke.

I must have fallen asleep, and now I'm dreaming, Slava thought, shaking her head in an attempt to wake herself. But the golden spots, which looked uncomfortably like eyes, were still staring back at her when she had finished.

What is this, Slava asked herself. Somehow it seemed even stranger than everything she had seen before, and she found herself unwilling to believe what was manifestly happening: the spirit of a leshaya had risen out of the chimney and was looking straight at her.

Help me, Slava, said the leshaya. Its golden eyes blinked slowly.

Of course, said Slava. Only after she had said it did she realize that she hadn't asked the all-important question of *how.*

I have to return to the others, said the leshaya. *You can take me there.*

Of course, said Slava. *What happened to you?* she added.

They shot me and brought me back to burn in their rituals, said the leshaya. *They are burning me alive as we speak.*

"By all the gods!" Slava cried out in horror. Dunya and Olga both bolted out of bed so quickly they crashed onto the floor.

"What is it! What is it!" demanded Olga, scrambling frantically for her boots. Dunya, who had hit the ground still wrapped in the blankets, slithered out of them and sprinted towards Slava on her hands and knees. A commotion arose in the next room as the men leaped out of their beds, shouting.

"How could they!" screamed Slava, still staring out the crack in the shutters at the dark form rising from the chimney.

People do horrible things, Slava, said the leshaya. *But if you act quickly, you can save me. I will leave this wood behind, and take on a new body. Unlike you women, we leshiye can do that.*

"Quickly!" cried Slava, stretching out her arms.

"Where?!" shouted Dunya in Slava's ear.

"What is it?!" shouted Olga in Slava's other ear. "What's happening? What must we do?!"

Thank you, Slava, said the leshaya. Its dark form and the two golden eyes rose fully out of the chimney and floated across the yard, like smoke caught in a gust of wind. It stopped for a moment in front of the crack in the shutters, and looked Slava right in the eyes.

Thank you, Slava, it said again, and slipped through the shutters.

Slava instinctively put her arms around it, and felt it settle in her chest. Olga and Dunya were still shouting in her ears, and people were pounding on the door and trying to break in, but all of her attention was focused on this new burden she had just gained.

Hold me close, Slava, whispered the leshaya. *I will have to feed off of your life for a little while, but you will be strong enough for the both of us, and I will be able to let go before it is too late. I hope.*

Let's go, Slava whispered back. Something seemed to hit her hard on the head, and then they were flying away over the treetops.

Chapter Twenty-Three

There, Slava, there, said the leshaya after a little while, and somehow Slava knew that she was supposed to turn towards that particular grove of trees, and then follow that particular stream to their destination.

Although both she and the leshaya did not, as far as she could tell, have bodies, somehow she felt that the sleeping trees turned their faces towards them as they flew past, and the whole forest was aware of their passage. Animals seemed to run beneath them in particularly purposeful ways, and as they dipped lower, trees pulled back their branches.

There, Slava, there, said the leshaya again, and they flew into a very dark grove of firs. There was a thin space between two of the trees, but as soon as they had passed through it, it closed, and they were left in almost total darkness, with only one thin ray of moonlight breaking through the branches.

Slava wanted to ask what had happened and what was going to happen, but as she looked up at the dark trees towering over her, she realized just what a small and pitiful disembodied soul she was, and didn't dare open her nonexistent mouth. If she had been asked about it before, she would have said with thoughtless certainty that of course she would be less afraid in such a situation than if she had had her body with her, because as it was she could just fly away whenever she wanted, but now that she was standing there, bodiless, she felt horribly unprotected and vulnerable, like being naked only a thousand times worse. Before, she had always thought that there was nothing between her and the outside world, but now she knew that her body had, in fact, provided her with a shield, frail and half-useless as it was, and now there truly was nothing between her and everyone else's thoughts and feelings.

A wind suddenly rose up in the trees, and she went to wrap her arms around her chest, only to realize that of course, she had neither arms nor chest. The wind was still cold, though, terribly cold.

Thank you, Slava, said the leshaya. *You have saved me. No one else could have done it.*

Why not? asked Slava.

Because no one else could have brought me here, said the leshaya. *Only someone who wears her body lightly could have flown her soul here all this way, and only you would have brought me along with you.*

What else could I do? said Slava. Another cold wind rose up in the dark trees. *Why is it so cold?* she asked. *I don't even have a body to feel it with.*

They are coming, said the leshaya. *The cold rides before them.*

Who is coming? asked Slava, not liking the sound of that at all.

The gods, of course, said the leshaya. *The forest marked our passage, as you noticed yourself, and informed the gods of it, and now they come to reunite me with my body. Or A body, anyway.*

Slava had many things she wanted to ask, the most important being whether she still had time to escape, although she supposed that escape was useless, as the forest would just mark her passage all over again, but none of her questions would form themselves into orderly sentences, and so she remained silent.

They come! cried the leshaya, as an even colder wind rose up in the trees and blew right through Slava. *Take my hand, sister Slava! We shall meet them together!*

Even though neither of them had hands to take, and the leshaya had not had hands even when she had had a body, Slava had the distinct sensation of a warm, strong hand wrapping around hers, something she had not felt since she had been a little girl and followed her mother around the stable—her mother had always made her hold her hand then. For a moment she wished desperately that her mother were here with her now, but then she saw that even if her mother were there, she, Slava, would still have to be the one to stand in the front and be brave, because she, Slava, was the one who had been given this gift from the gods, and therefore she, Slava, was the one who must face them.

The wind from the trees suddenly gusted up so strongly Slava felt herself stumble in its onslaught, even though she had nothing to stumble with, and then it began to speak.

Our daughters, said the cold wind. *We are pleased to see you before us. But tell us, daughters, what brings you here? We would hear your story in your own words.*

I was following Krasnoslava, began the leshaya. *We leshiye decided we must keep her under guard all the way back to Krasnograd. There are so many dangers on the road, and so many even off the road who would try to use her for their own ends, that we decided we must keep her out of harm's way as much as we could.*

Slava thought it was somewhat amusing that the leshiye had decided (without informing her of it) to offer her their protection from others who might want to hurt or exploit her, but she said nothing. She was even a little touched by it: it was more than many others would have done. She was, she knew, still so starving for kindness that she would grab at even this faint substitute for it.

It was my turn, and I was following her from afar, continued the leshaya, *when I wandered into the territory of Svyatoslav the Sorcerer.*

Ever must our woodland daughters take care when they stray into his territory, said the cold wind.

I am no mean sorceress myself, said the leshaya, *but I was distracted by my concern for Krasnoslava—for I feared she had put herself in danger unwittingly, and that by evening she would freeze to death, so that I was hurrying to warn her of this—and so Svyatoslav came upon me unawares, and shot me with an enspelled arrow.*

He is truly a mighty sorcerer, said the cold wind, and Slava could hear that, however much it might sorrow over its woodland children who fell victim to him, it still admired his ability too much to destroy him.

The leshaya appeared to recognize this as well, for she carried on quickly. *I was immobilized but not killed,* she said, *and it was in this stunned state that Svyatoslav, his sister Marusya Svyatoslavovna, and their accomplice Aleksandra Serafimiyevna dragged me back to their waystation and hid me in their woodpile.*

They are ingenious, even if their actions are so often not for the best, agreed the cold wind.

Krasnoslava and her party arrived shortly after that, continued the leshaya. *As I feared, Krasnoslava had fallen into danger simply through her own innocence.*

Or stupidity, Slava put in.

Oh no, Krasnoslava, you are such an innocent creature, you can hardly be held accountable for your actions in this regard, said the leshaya, before carrying on with her story.

Krasnoslava had, as I had feared, almost frozen, but luckily they arrived in time and brought her straight to the bathhouse, where she was revived. Even in my stunned state I was aware of that, although I could do nothing to free myself.

What sort of spell was in Svyatoslav's arrow, do you know? asked the cold wind, with more curiosity than Slava would have expected from gods.

Some cold-spell, I dare say, said the leshaya. *I was as a tree asleep in the depths of winter, but I could still reason as a leshaya, even though I could not free myself.*

Once the waystation had gone to sleep for the night, Svyatoslav, Marusya Svyatoslavovna, and Aleksandra Serafimiyevna brought me into the bath-house, in order to complete their ritual. I gathered from their words that they had long been planning this, and my arrival in Svyatoslav's territory had been a welcome surprise, finally allowing them to carry out their designs.

What were they planning? asked the cold wind, and this time Slava was sure she heard a distinct note of disapproval in its voice.

They wished to speak with the dead, of course, said the leshaya. *They intended to burn my body, thereby freeing my soul to enter the realm of the dead, and then follow me there.*

They grow too bold, said the cold wind. *There are some things that humans should not meddle with. We are surprised at their temerity.*

The plan was all Svyatoslav's, I am sure, said the leshaya. *He is the only one who hungers for knowledge and power beyond his comprehension. Marusya is too beaten down to try something like this on her own, and San-ya only ever follows Marusya's lead, but Svyatoslav is just clever enough to dream something like this up, without being clever enough to understand why he might not wish to do it.*

You are surely right, agreed the cold wind. *Perhaps it is time we revealed ourselves to Svyatoslav, and took him into our service. He would make a valuable servant, and at the moment he is becoming dangerous as a free person.*

You are surely right, said the leshaya. *He thirsts for knowledge, and would, I am sure, do anything to obtain it, although he will, no doubt, prove a headstrong servant.*

Many do, at the start, said the cold wind. *Carry on.*

They set fire to my body—

HOW HORRIBLE! Slava screamed.

I see the leshiye were right about you, little daughter, said the cold wind.

It IS horrible, said Slava defensively.

Oh, to be sure, but how many would see that it is so? Some, perhaps, have tried, but their voices were so quiet, who would listen to them? Certainly neither Svyatoslav the Sorcerer, nor his sister Marusya Svyatoslavovna, nor their accomplice Aleksandra Serafimiyevna gave a moment's thought to the horror of what they were about to do, nor have many others before them—they were far from the first to attempt to reach the dead in that way. That was how they were certain it would work, after all—others had done it before them. But as soon as you so much as hear the words, you scream in protest.

Someone has to! said Slava.

So true, agreed the cold wind. *And that someone, it seems, is you. For not only will you scream, but there is, perhaps, a faint chance that others will hear you. Perhaps you have been given this task because you might, unlikely as it is, succeed where others have failed. Tell me, little daughter: does it make you happy to be chosen for this honor?*

No, said Slava, *and yet...*

And yet you do it anyway. Why?

I have to, explained Slava. *I can't help myself.*

No, *no doubt you can't,* said the cold wind. *It is your purpose in life, or so it seems. Did you know, little daughter, that everyone—leshiye, the creatures of the forest, even you city-dwelling humans—is born with some skill, some special ability that only they possess? You are all different, after all, and that is why. All of you have a purpose, if only you would realize it. And your purpose, as you have sensed, is to protect others. If we were you, little daughter, and could feel sorry for others, we would feel very sorry for you, very sorry indeed.*

Why? cried Slava. *What awaits me?* She could only assume that the gods had planned or foreseen some terrible event in her future, possibly because of what she had just done, and were, in what she had always imagined to be the nature of gods, watching with detached curiosity to see if it would turn out as they had expected.

Wait, I don't want to know, she said, suddenly sorry that she had asked. *If I'm doomed, I don't want to know about it until it happens.*

But it has already happened, little daughter. It happened the day you were born. You were doomed to be who you are, and you cannot escape it. Because, as you said, you can't help yourself. You must protect others, whether you will it or no. It is, Krasnoslava, a terrible fate, we will not hide that from you. You see, Krasnoslava, your purpose is a particularly cruel one. It is one without which the world cannot get by, but it does not necessarily endear you to the world. Others will, we will not hide from you, want to use you when it will be to their advantage, but they will not love you for your usefulness. Quite the opposite, in fact: all too many of them will turn away from you in dislike after they are done with you. Such is the way of the world, Krasnoslava, said the cold wind, its voice expressing neither disgust nor approval for the state of things, but, Slava thought, despite its earlier words, there was just the tiniest trace of sympathy there.

Not all of them, said Slava. *Not everyone hates me.*

For now, said the cold wind. *Enjoy the friendship of others while you can, but do not put too much store in it. You must learn to rely upon yourself, Krasnoslava, for it is all you have.*

She has us! the leshaya burst in. *Krasnoslava has us!*

*So she does—for **now**,* said the cold wind. *And only after you failed to understand the nature of her gift, and attempted to use her for your own ends. And, no doubt, you will continue to do so. Krasnoslava would do well to consider the price of your help, now and forever. But carry on with your story, daughter, and we will leave Krasnoslava to her fate, for it is the only thing we can do.*

They set fire to my body, continued the leshaya, *hoping to follow my soul to the realm of the dead, but I sensed the presence of Krasnoslava nearby, and so when the bonds with my body loosened, I called upon her to help me, and she did.*

What is happening to my body? Slava asked. Until just then it had not occurred to her to worry about it, but now she was beginning to wonder whether her body was also gone, like the leshaya's. Something she should, perhaps, have thought of earlier, although on the whole she was glad she hadn't: if the answer were to turn out to be unpleasant, she was glad that she had already made her irrevocable decision, and wouldn't have to combat her own cowardice.

You have fallen into a trance, no doubt, said the cold wind. *Let us hope that your friends have realized what has happened, and are keeping guard over it.*

Yes, let's hope, said Slava, her relief making her impertinent.

And now we must come up with a body for your sister, said the cold wind. *The leshiye are so much luckier than you women, in some ways: their souls are so much more loosely linked to their bodies, that they can lose one body and simply take another.*

That is an advantage, agreed Slava. *I wish the same could be done for us women.*

Ah, but you see, their souls are so much more loosely linked to their bodies, said the cold wind. *Imagine being neither of this world or the next, but halfway in between, a soul that had no real body, but could not exist for long without one, either. You women are fully of this world—most of you, anyway; you not so much, Krasnoslava—and that is a great advantage too, you know.*

Are you really so unhappy? Slava asked the leshaya, feeling a great wave of pity well up as she imagined such a half-existence.

We are used to it, of course, said the leshaya. *It is the only life we know. But some of us greatly envy you humans, just as we do the creatures of the forest. What feelings you must know, that are forever inaccessible to us! What a feeling of comfort it must be, to know that you are truly part of everything around you, instead of a soul wearing an earthly body.*

Some of us feel that way too, said Slava. *I think there are many women who feel as if they were no more than a soul wearing an earthly body, and not at all part of everything around them, as you called it. Bodies are a nuisance.*

Then I pity them, said the leshaya.

They muddle on as best they can, said the cold wind, with no particular evidence of sympathy. *But now we have more important concerns. Daughter, how do you feel about becoming a fir tree?*

I don't suppose I have much choice, said the leshaya, and even though it had no eyes to see with, Slava had the distinct sensation that it was looking around the grove they were in and measuring all the fir trees around them for size and quality, like a woman viewing the goods at some second-rate cloth merchant's shop.

Yes, fir is really all we have to offer, said the cold wind. *But there are many good things about becoming a fir tree.*

I did enjoy being a birch, said the leshaya with a sigh. *But you are right, a fir will fit in better, this far North. A fir it is.*

Very good, said the cold wind. *How does this suit you?* The trees in the grove all retreated, Slava could not have said how, leaving a single sapling standing forlornly in the middle of the suddenly empty space.

It is beautiful! said the leshaya, running forward and embracing it as she might a long-lost lover. The tree shivered, shedding snow and needles. The cold wind rose up with a howl, and then seemed to plunge down onto the lonely sapling, with such force that its roots broke free of the earth.

It is done, declared the cold wind. *Take care of your new body, daughter.*

It is beautiful! exclaimed the leshaya again. Her golden eyes blinked open, and she revolved slowly in the snow, her roots leaving strange tracks. *Thank you, thank you, thank you!* She laughed with a kind of delirious ecstasy that must, Slava supposed, be the result of the powerful magic that had joined her soul to this new body.

I am glad you like it, said the cold wind. *Now, Krasnoslava...*

I want to go back to my own body, said Slava quickly, in case it had any other ideas.

And so you shall.

Slava was overcome by such dizziness that, had she still had her body, she would have staggered and fallen down. She had an impression of a million treetops rushing past her, and then her eyes opened, and she was staring up at Dunya's horrified face.

Chapter Twenty-Four

"Krasnoslava! Krasnoslava! Can you hear me! Krasnoslava!"

They're shouting at me, Slava thought to herself. *I need to speak, to reassure them that I'm unhurt.* But it was such a long way from her mind to her mouth that her words got lost on the journey. She tried to move, but her arms and legs went the opposite direction from what she had intended, and she only flopped awkwardly in Dunya's arms.

"She's awake, she's awake, but she's not speaking!" Dunya was shouting at someone else in the room. "What if her mind is gone?"

"Give her a moment to come to," said Grisha.

My mind was gone, but now it's come back, Slava tried to say, but the only thing she produced was an inarticulate moan. She knew she was returning to herself, though, because she was flooded with embarrassment at moaning inarticulately in front of Dunya and Grisha. The embarrassment gave her the strength to coordinate her limbs sufficiently to attempt to sit up. Dunya recognized what she was trying to do, and propped her up on the bed. Slava realized that she must have been moved from the chair to the bed while she was out of her body, and that Dunya and Grisha had been watching over her.

"Where..." she said faintly. Admittedly, it still sounded a lot like a moan, but not quite such an inarticulate one. She tried again. "Where are the others?" she whispered.

"Krasnoslava!" cried Dunya, and Slava saw that she really was crying, with tears running down her face. "We thought we'd lost you! The shadow came, and you had a fit, and we thought we'd lost you!"

"I came back," said Slava weakly. "Where are the others?"

"The bathhouse," Dunya told her. She wiped the tears from her face with her sleeve. Removing the tears seemed to make her feel stronger, and when she spoke again, she sounded much more like the calm Dunya that Slava was used to. "Olga Vasilisovna and the others ran to the bathhouse, to find the source of the shadow and stop it. They sent Sasha in search of a healer or herbwoman, and left me and Grisha to watch over you. I don't know what they found there, but the shadow is gone."

"Go to them and find out what has happened," Slava whispered.

"You're sure? You're sure it's safe to leave you?"

"Grisha will watch over me," Slava told her. "And if it should happen again, there's nothing you could do for me anyway."

"Well…"

"The Tsarinovna's right," put in Grisha. "And we need to know what's happened to the others."

Dunya wavered for another moment, and then dashed off.

"Here, Tsarinovna," said Grisha, offering her a glass of something. Slava sniffed at it. It was clearly homemade vodka of very dubious quality. She drank it all down even so. The coughing seemed to make her body more her own, somehow, and when her head cleared, she felt almost herself again.

"Once again I seem to be causing you so much trouble," she said to Grisha.

"Well, perhaps it's for the best, Tsarinovna," he said. "What was that black shadow?"

Slava told him. As she spoke he stood there shaking his head, although, Slava thought, in astonishment, not disbelief. When she had finished, he stared past her, still shaking his head from time to time, until Slava began to wonder if his mind was suffering from the shock and if she needed to press some vodka on him herself.

A commotion at the entrance brought him to. He looked at Slava questioningly.

"Go find out," she said.

He dashed off. Slava heard him demanding what had happened, and heard Olga shouting, "A healer! Where is that healer!" Slava jumped out of bed and, finding herself fairly steady on her legs, dashed out of the room too. She almost crashed into someone, whom she recognized as one of Aleksandra Serafimiyevna's men. He shoved her out of the way, causing her to crash against the wall. She waited there as the rest of Aleksandra Serafimiyevna's men ran past, and then made her way, now rather less steadily, into the main room.

Olga was supporting Marusya Svyatoslavovna and Aleksandra Serafimiyevna, one on each arm. The others were carrying an unconscious Svyatoslav. As Slava arrived in the main room, they were lifting him onto a table.

"Tsarinovna!" Olga cried on seeing her. "You're awake!"

Marusya, Sanya, and Sanya's men all gave Slava a startled look, and then turned their attention back to Svyatoslav.

"Sasha has gone with a servant for the herbwoman, Olga Vasilisovna, but she lives at least a couple of versts away, and it's the middle of the night—it may take her some time to come," Dunya was saying meanwhile. "And Oleg Svetoslavovich was looking around behind the bathhouse, in case he could find something of use, or so he said."

"It's no use," said Marusya Svyatoslavovna faintly. "They can't do anything for him."

"Come, we must try!" said Olga. "Snow and vodka! Someone fetch me snow and vodka! We have to try to revive him!"

"It's no use," Marusya repeated. "The gods have him now."

"He's not dead yet!" Olga shouted.

"No, I mean..." Marusya whispered, and then gave up, apparently too overcome by weakness to speak. Olga set her down on a bench, where she half-sat, half-lay against the table.

"He's not dying," said Sanya. "But the gods are taking him even now. They're making him their servant, as they have long designed."

"Oh no, they just decided," Slava blurted out. "Because of what he just did."

Everyone stared at her again. Several of them opened their mouths, probably to ask her how she knew, but before they could say anything, Oleg Svetoslavovich interjected, "Then Marusya Svyatoslavovna's right. There's nothing we can do."

Marusya Svyatoslavovna started to cry, a sight that contrasted grotesquely with both her coarse, careworn face, and her too-bright, ever-changing eyes. Everyone shuffled awkwardly, giving her looks that clearly stated that her tears were making them uncomfortable, and as they had no way to help her, they wished she would shut up and stop making them feel bad for her.

"Surely we can at least make him more comfortable," Slava found herself saying. "The gods wish him no permanent harm, I am sure.

Perhaps he will wake up shortly, healthy and well, and it would be better if he were to wake up in a bed, rather than laid out here on this table."

"You think so, noblewoman?" asked Marusya Svyatoslavovna, looking up at her through tear-filled eyes that, even in her sorrow, were sharp with intelligence.

"I do," Slava told her. "Come, let us move him to a bed, at least. And perhaps find some clean clothes for him? His are soaked through with snow."

"He rushed out of the bathhouse, and then collapsed on the ground," Marusya Svyatoslavovna explained. "It was like he'd been struck down by an arrow..." Tears started welling up in her blue-black eyes again.

"The gods are quick to act," Slava said. She had no idea if that were true or not, but somehow it seemed the right thing to say. "Perhaps they will be as quick to leave him, so we must be ready."

"We can bring him to my room," said Marusya Svyatoslavovna, cheering visibly at Slava's words. She straightened up and stepped away from Olga's supporting arm. "This way."

"I'm going to go check..." muttered Olga, and, disentangling herself from Aleksandra Serafimiyevna, dashed out the front door, followed by several of the others. So somehow it happened that it was Aleksandra Serafimiyevna's men who picked up Svyatoslav and carried him after Marusya Svyatoslavovna, and somehow—Slava didn't see anyone making a conscious decision, but somehow it turned out thus—by the time they entered Marusya Svyatoslavovna's room and laid him on the bed, everyone from Olga's group except Slava had disappeared. She supposed that they had no desire to comfort someone they disliked so much in her time of need. Slava tried not to be disappointed in them. She knelt down by the bed and took Svyatoslav's hand as Marusya, Sanya, and the servants bustled around him, changing his clothes and bringing in more blankets.

Svyatoslav's hand was large and coarse, and covered in heavy calluses and scars. The nails, Slava was surprised to see, were bitten to the quick. She had a vision of him biting his dirty nails—they were ringed with dirt—in nervous impatience as he waited for something, perhaps to shoot down a leshaya or some animal, and pity and horror filled her in equal measure.

Svyatoslav suddenly groaned and turned his head towards her. Slava gripped his hand, ready to comfort him if he awoke, but he only went back to his silent stillness. His coarse, heavy face, surrounded by a wild tangle of dirty graying hair, was almost peaceful in its immobility, but Slava thought she could see lines of strain, just under the surface. She wondered what the soul of this large, bearlike, apparently brutal man was like, and how much it was suffering right now, and whether it would be different afterwards.

"Here you are, noblewoman." Marusya Svyatoslavovna was tugging clumsily and too forcefully at her arm. Slava looked round, and saw that she was being offered a chair. Sanya and her men were leaving the room, Sanya giving orders for them to patrol the waystation, just in case.

"Thank you, Marusya Svyatoslavovna," said Slava. She got up off her knees and into the chair. Marusya Svyatoslavovna took her place kneeling by the side of the bed. Slava still had Svyatoslav's hand, and rather than asking her to relinquish it, Marusya Svyatoslavovna began stroking his arm with the same gentle affection one might use on a desperately ill pet. Her position, half-kneeling and half-twisting, made Slava uncomfortable just looking at it.

"Don't you want to sit, Marusya Svyatoslavovna?" she asked, getting back out of the chair.

Marusya Svyatoslavovna glanced up at her, her too-bright eyes surprised and suspicious.

"Who knows how long we'll be here," Slava said. "There's no need for you to be on the floor the whole time. You must be tired after...after everything, too. Won't you take a seat?"

"The others, they called you Tsarinovna," said Marusya Svyatoslavovna abruptly, watching Slava with unblinking attention.

"Yes," said Slava, and then, deciding that there was no point in denying it, continued, "I am the Tsarina's younger sister—Krasnoslava Tsarinovna. I was...well, I am traveling around the country now, and I ended up here."

"You said you were a Stepnaya."

"And so I am, on my father's side. But my mother was the Tsarina Marislava."

"You're really a Tsarinovna," said Marusya Svyatoslavovna, still stroking her brother's arm and staring at Slava as if stunned.

"I'm just a woman like any other, only with a fancy name," Slava told her, trying to smile kindly and put her at her ease. "Won't you take a seat? The floor must be hard and cold."

"You were kneeling on it," Marusya said.

369

"But only for a little while, and I don't like sitting here in comfort while you kneel there," said Slava.

"Are you sure you're a noblewoman?" asked Marusya, frowning in a way that made it hard to tell if she were joking or being serious.

"A Tsarinovna is not a noblewoman," said Slava, remembering something her mother had told her long ago. "A Tsarinovna is selfless duty. Noblewomen may be petty and think of themselves, but a Tsarinovna must always think only of her duty and her people."

"Is that true?" asked Marusya. "Noblewoman—I mean Tsarinovna," she added awkwardly.

"Ideally, yes," said Slava. "Sometimes flesh-and-blood women have a hard time living up to it, though."

"But you offered me your seat, Tsarinovna," said Marusya.

"And I'm still offering it," said Slava. "Come, Marusya Svyatoslavovna!" She took Marusya by the shoulders and tried to lift her to her feet. As Marusya was about twice as big as she was, she didn't succeed in lifting her very far, but Marusya, stung by the shock of it, scrambled the rest of the way up on her own.

"Here, you sit here and hold your brother's hand," Slava commanded her, guiding her into the chair and putting Svyatoslav's hand in hers. "I'll sit on the bed here, and we'll watch over him until he wakes up."

"Why are you being so kind to me, Tsarinovna?" Marusya asked.

"Because you are in need of kindness," Slava told her.

Marusya shook her head. "That can't be it," she said. "You wouldn't be kind to me just for that."

"But I would," Slava insisted.

"They say," said Marusya slowly, "that the Tsarina's younger sister is the kindest woman in our land, and begs for mercy for all, even those that don't deserve it. Is that...are you...?"

"The Tsarina only has one younger sister, and she is sitting right here before you," Slava said. "And it is only those who don't deserve it who are in need of mercy. If they deserved it, it wouldn't be mercy. The gods defend us from only ever getting what we deserve!"

She smiled at Marusya, hoping to make her smile in return, but Marusya appeared sunk in deep and painful thought. Slava looked at her coarse, heavy body, which was now slumped in the chair, clutching desperately at her brother's hand, and thought that she had rarely seen such a beaten-down looking creature. Pity squeezed her heart so sharply she thought tears might well up in her eyes. She thought of all the bad things, ranging from simple rudeness to attempted murder, that Marusya had done in this one night alone, and felt even more pity. What, Slava wondered, was going through her mind that such acts seemed like the right thing to do?

"Are you very close to your brother?" she asked.

"I was married off very young, Tsarinovna," said Marusya.

Slava nodded encouragingly, waiting to see how this seemingly-unconnected beginning would explain Marusya's relationship with her brother. As she had expected, Marusya, after a few deep breaths and stutterings, found Slava's gaze irresistible, and burst out with her tale.

"My mother kept another waystation, one just outside of Lesnogorod. She just had the two of us, just me and Svyatoslav. He was the older of us two—five years older. Already a man when I was still a little girl. After I was born, our father ran off with another woman, a Southerner, from somewhere down the Krasna. Slava says that when he was with us, our mother spent all her time nagging and shouting at him, complaining that he didn't work hard enough and accusing him of spending his time drinking and running after other women whenever they crooked their fingers at him. Slava says she was right. Once he was gone, she spent her time shouting at us, saying she wasn't going to waste her effort raising a couple of lazy good-for-nothings who took after their no-good father.

"When I was fourteen, my mother decided to marry me off to the son of the mistress of this waystation. She dreamed of becoming the overseer of all the waystations on this road, and she thought this was the way to go about it.

"My husband was twice my age, and long hardened in drinking and women. His mother was in despair, thinking she'd never marry him off—the mothers of all the local girls had refused her, saying that they'd sooner see their daughters die unmarried than take such a man into their homes—and then my mother proposed her scheme. I was to marry him and go live with them, and the waystation would pass to our children. My husband had no sisters or brothers to claim any part of it. For once in my life, my mother was pleased with me. 'Syusenka,' she said, 'I thought of kicking you out of the house a hundred times, in order not to waste another crumb of bread on your fat face, but now I see you can be useful after all. Have children, and you might even earn back what I've spent on you over the years.'

"I saw my husband only once before the wedding, and I was so

371

innocent then, I thought him a fine handsome fellow, and counted myself lucky. I would be married, a real woman, and better than that, out of my mother's house, years before I thought it even possible! I thanked the gods for their kindness, and went to the altar with tears of joy in my eyes.

"The next day I had tears in my eyes again, but not of joy. I was so innocent then...My mother had told me to get children, but I had only the vaguest idea of how they were gotten. When...I cried and cried, and my new husband laughed and laughed. Until he got tired of my crying."

Marusya stared at Svyatoslav's hand for a while before continuing. "I was used to being beaten," she said. "I knew how not to cry. I just hadn't expected to have to do that in my new life. But it was even more bitter than my old one. When he wasn't off drinking and dropping his trousers for any woman who would look twice at him, my husband stayed at home and hit me. Sometimes he would forget, and his mother would scold him for his laziness and make him whip me with his belt until his arm got tired.

"'You thought you'd have an easy life with us, didn't you, you ungrateful little bitch,' she'd say. 'You thought you could just sit back and eat us out of house and home, didn't you. I've seen the ungrateful looks you give my son, I have! I'll teach you to be ungrateful! Harder, Pasha, you're barely tapping her! Here, I'll show you, you lazy oaf!'"

Marusya stared down once again at Svyatoslav's hand for a while. "Slava had run away from home and joined a group of wood-hermits and sorcerers," she said abruptly. "My mother had arranged a match with the daughter of another waystation mistress, but he wasn't having any of that. He was always the wild one, and he never seemed to need love like I did. I always wanted to be loved, but he just wanted his own way. He ran away, and one day he came to visit me.

"With one look he measured up my husband and my mother-in-law. He stayed for supper, watching them, and then he left. I was in despair. I'd hoped they'd be too ashamed to beat me while he was there, and I'd have one free day. But that night he came back."

Marusya stopped again.

"Yes?" Slava prompted after a while.

Marusya gave her a look out of the corner of her eye. "They were going to kill me, Tsarinovna," she said. "I had conceived a child, but they had beaten it out of me. I was still so weak I could barely stand when my brother arrived, and they were making me wait on them at the table. They were going to kill me."

"Of that I have no doubt," said Slava, guessing what Marusya was about to tell her. "Your brother must have thought he had to do something. Did your mother know?"

"She did, and all she said was, 'I've gotten you off my hands, and I'm never taking you back.' I had nowhere to turn."

"So your brother decided to step in," said Slava. "To stop them, before they killed his little sister."

"Exactly, Tsarinovna."

"You can't reason with such people," Slava continued. "Nor can you persuade them. And threats never last long with them. They would have started it all up again in a few days, only worse than before."

"Exactly, Tsarinovna, exactly!"

"So he saved you, didn't he? The only person in the world who would stand up for you?"

"He didn't mean to kill them, I don't think, Tsarinovna," Marusya whispered. "He wanted...He wanted to take away their strength, so that they wouldn't be able to hurt me anymore. Only when he came back, Pasha was so drunk that the spell made him collapse, and he... He choked on his own sick. Then my mother-in-law ran at Slava with an axe, so I tripped her, and she tried to...She raised the axe over me, and Slava snatched it from her hands, and...It was over very quick."

"You must have been very frightened," Slava said, when it became apparent that Marusya was not going to say anything more. "You must have been very frightened, and not known how to hide what you'd— what had happened."

"We didn't even try to hide it, Tsarinovna. Slava talked about taking away the bodies and hiding them in the woods, but I said no, I was afraid we would get caught, he should just run back to the woods and I'd tell them what had happened, but he said he'd tell them himself, take all the blame himself, I'd suffered enough, and he'd been the one to kill them anyway. So he went straight away to Bogoveshchensko— the next village over—and told the elder there what had happened, but she told him they'd had it coming to them for a long time and that she wasn't going to turn him in to the Princess, that we should just say they died of sickness and bury them quietly, so we did."

"And then what?" asked Slava. "Did you go back to your mother? You must have still been very young."

"Only fifteen, noblewoman, but even if I'd wanted to go back to our mother, she wouldn't've taken me. No, I was the lawful owner of the waystation, and I took over running it. Running a waystation isn't hard, noblewoman, and I always was a quick study. That was maybe what my mother and mother-in-law hated most about me—they'd have liked me better if I'd only been born stupid. I tried and tried to pretend, noblewoman, I did, but I never could hide it all the way—I'd always give myself up without even knowing how. A fine lady like you wouldn't understand this, noblewoman, you don't know what it's like to be beaten down like I do, but the day Slava killed my husband and mother-in-law—that was the best day of my life. That was day I started to live in truth, instead of just living in fear.

"You probably think I'm a bad person, noblewoman"—Marusya gave Slava a defiant look, her eyes now black and lightless—"you're probably a good person, you think you wouldn't kill no one no matter how much they beat you, but wait till you're in my shoes, and then you'll understand. Tsarinovna. They say you plead for mercy for those who don't deserve it—would you plead for mercy for my husband and mother-in-law? Would you dare?" A sudden flicker of the candle by the bed made Marusya's eyes change from black to blue to gray to green, and back to black again.

"If they were sentenced to death for what they'd done to you, then I would plead for their lives," said Slava. "But I would have taken you away from them, too. I wouldn't have left you there with them, not for anything. And if it came to that, I would have killed them with my own hands, if that's what it took to save you from them. But now... They're gone, and the only one who needs my mercy now is you. Why did you try to kill the leshaya, Marusya? Why were you trying to reach the dead? Were you trying to speak with your mother-in-law, after all these years?"

"A leshaya isn't a person," said Marusya. "Killing it isn't so bad as killing a person."

"It is a person! It's just like killing a person, and you weren't just going to kill it, you were going to burn it alive! Why, Marusya?! How could you do that to someone?"

"A leshaya isn't 'someone,'" said Marusya sullenly. "It's not like we're murderers or anything. We weren't going to hurt anyone. We just wanted...We just wanted to speak with our mother. We wanted to find out...We wanted to find out why. I...After all these years, I never wanted a man to touch me, and then this fall I...It's been long enough now, I guess, and I up and...and got a baby off of one of Sanya's men—she said she didn't mind, and I suddenly started longing for a baby, so I got one. It'll be here in the spring, the gods willing."

A certain amount of Marusya's coarseness of figure suddenly rearranged itself in Slava's vision, showing that, of course, she was expecting a child.

"And you wanted to know why your mother was the way she was," said Slava. "To make sure you don't do the same things."

"What if we're cursed?" whispered Marusya. "What if I shouldn't have this child? I suddenly...I had to know, before it's too late. So I told Slava, and he said he knew how we could do it. All he had to do was find a leshaya. They're hard to find in the winter, though. But lately the woods've been full of them, coming and going, and they haven't been as careful as usual. Slava said they seemed to have some trouble on their minds.

"And so today he got one, and he brought it here. We were going to do it as soon as it got dark—Slava said that would be the best time, it would be easier to follow its soul back to...to wherever we were going to follow it. But then you arrived, and we had to wait until we were sure everyone was asleep, and then we went into the bathhouse, and set fire to the leshaya, and sparks, strange sparks, rose up, and then a great figure, and Slava said it was time, we had to follow it, but then it disappeared, noblewoman! It disappeared, and we couldn't follow it, and it was all in vain! Our only chance was gone! Now I'll never know, I'll never be able to reach my mother and ask her why, why she was so cruel, and maybe I'll be the same, noblewoman, maybe we *are* cursed and I'll be just the same as she was, noblewoman, and I won't know until it happens, and Slava is gone! He's gone, noblewoman, he's left me!"

Marusya started to cry again, an even more horribly incongruous sight than it had been before. Slava had felt simultaneous pity and revulsion many times, but never, she thought, had the contrast been so strong, and so acute. Every time she thought of Marusya's story, she became so angry that she, too, wanted to lash out and hurt someone, preferably Marusya's mother or mother-in-law. She was even surprised at how little the tale of the murders upset her—she would, she thought, most likely have done the same thing, if she had been Svyatoslav.

She wasn't sorry in the slightest that they were dead, even though, if she really thought about it, she felt sorry for them too—how miserable Marusya's mother must have been, and how desperate Marusya's mother-in-law must have been to find a wife for her son, and how much she must have feared that the wife would mistreat or abandon him, and how unhappy Marusya's husband must have been, to do all those things, and how terrible had been the consequences of their unhappiness. And how terrible had been the consequences of Marusya's unhappiness, too. Everyone, Slava thought, must have been dreadfully unhappy, and everyone had done things because of their unhappiness that had only brought more misery into the world.

"Marusya," said Slava.

Marusya raised her tear-stained face to look up at Slava. She really was, Slava thought, an ugly woman. She had most likely never been beautiful, and life—no, not life, it was not some impersonal force that had done this, it was other people, specific, individual people, who had names and faces, who had done this to her—had trampled whatever freshness and joy she might have once possessed right out of her, so that now she was hardly more than a monster.

"Yes, noblewoman?" asked Marusya. Her eyes were gray now. Slava wondered if her own eyes made the same unsettling impression on people. If so, she could, she supposed, understand why others always looked away.

"The gods want Svyatoslav alive, Marusya," Slava told her. "They want a servant, not a victim, and they treat their servants well." Slava had no idea if this were actually true, but Oleg Svetoslavovich seemed to be doing fairly well, so it wasn't a complete lie. "Most likely, he will be returned to you shortly, and even better than he was before. And so you must look to the future now, Marusya, your shining future, and leave the past behind you, where it belongs."

Slava wasn't quite sure what nonsense she had just spouted out, but apparently it didn't seem like nonsense to Marusya, who stopped crying and gave Slava an inquiring look.

"My shining future, noblewoman?" she asked. "What shining future?" Her face attempted to twist into a disbelieving grimace, but a painful, desperate hope took over it instead.

"Why, the shining future you will create for yourself and your child," Slava told her.

"Have...have you seen something, noblewoman—Tsarinovna?" Marusya's voice was trembling with hope now. "They say your family can see things that others cannot—have you seen something of our future? Something wonderful?"

A tiny part of Slava, the part that had been raised in Krasnograd and always did its best to remind her what the grand world of the Krasnograd kremlin would consider normal, couldn't help but be amused that Marusya, who was, without a doubt, one of the dregs of society, didn't even think twice about assuming that a Tsarinovna might not only have visions about her, but would deign to share those visions with their subject, but the rest of Slava was disappointed that she did not, in fact, have any visions to give her.

"I cannot see the future," Slava told her kindly. "But all of us hold our future in our hands. If you want a shining future for yourself and your child, then all you have to do is make it. All you have to do is what is necessary to build one."

"I tried, Tsarinovna, I tried, and look what happened!"

"Perhaps that wasn't what you really needed to do," Slava said, as gently as she could. "After all, killing a leshaya, especially in that fashion—that is a great act of evil. Something like that will haunt you for a long time, the rest of your life even."

"But the curse, Tsarinovna! I have to know about the curse!"

"And if you go about it the way you have been, perhaps you will be bringing a curse down on yourself, even if you weren't cursed before. Perhaps what you need to do is to act as if you weren't cursed at all. Cast it off, Marusya, cast it off! So many curses only have power if their victim gives it to them—think on that! Let go of your curse, and it will let go of you."

Marusya gazed at Slava as if she had just said something very wise, which made Slava want to take back her words and explain that she had only said whatever she thought might make Marusya feel better, and that there was no truth in them, no more than in the wind. But she held her tongue. Perhaps, she thought, Marusya would give meaning to her meaningless words, and something really would come of them.

There was a stirring from the bed.

"Slavik!" Marusya cried. "Are you there? Are you awake?"

Svyatoslav opened his eyes. "Wait," he said hoarsely. "I'll be back soon." And his eyes fell shut again.

"Tsarinovna!" cried Marusya, her face shining. "He awoke! He said he'd come back!"

"He did," agreed Slava.

"You lifted the curse, Tsarinovna! It was you, you lifted it! You told me to let it go, and then he woke up! You lifted our curse!"

"All I did was talk," said Slava.

"But your words are worth more than an ordinary woman's. You lifted the curse, Tsarinovna! How can we ever repay you?" Marusya dropped awkwardly to her knees. "Anything you ask is yours."

"Be kind," said Slava. "The world is sorely in need of more kindness. Especially be kind to the child."

"Of course, Tsarinovna, of course! Oh Tsarinovna! May I name it after you? In your honor, that is? You shouldn't think of names before the child is born, it's bad luck, I know that, but now that you've lifted the curse, I must, I really must. May I name it Krasnoslava? Or Krasnoslav, if it's a boy? But I'm sure it'll be a girl, now that you've lifted the curse."

"If you wish, I would be honored," said Slava. In fact, she felt distinctly uncomfortable at having children named after her, but there didn't seem to be a graceful way to prevent it.

"Oh thank you, Tsarinovna, thank you! Oh this will be a blessed day, I know it!" Marusya looked up at Slava with shining blue eyes, and for a moment she was almost pretty, as she must have been before life had beaten her down. Slava felt a terrible moment of kinship with Marusya Svyatoslavovna: she, too, it seemed to her, had been beaten down until she was no longer the trusting young woman she had once been. She thought of what Marusya Svyatoslavovna would think of Slava's "sufferings" in comparison with her own, and almost laughed at herself. But that didn't change the fact that she had been beaten down.

"Marusya?" Svyatoslav whispered, his eyes fluttering half-open.

"Slavik? Slavik, are you awake? Slavik!"

"I'm here," he whispered, still not opening his eyes fully. He squeezed Marusya's hand. "I'm back, Rusenka."

"Slavik! Where have you been? They said you had been...that the gods..."

"They were right, Rusenka. The gods took me. They wanted me as their servant, and they took me."

"And...?"

"And now I am their servant," said Svyatoslav. He closed his eyes and rested for several breaths, then opened his eyes all the way and looked up at Marusya's stricken face. "It's not so bad as that, Rusenka," he said. "It's even good. There are many advantages to being a servant of the gods."

"Will you have to leave me? But will you have to leave me?" cried Marusya, her voice the same as it must have been when she was fourteen.

"No, Rusenka, I won't. They promised." Svyatoslav paused and

378

rested for a moment, and when he spoke again, his voice was much stronger. "Already I feel my strength coming back to me, twice as strong as before," he said. "There are many good things about serving the gods. No, Rusenka, when I agreed to serve them, it was on the condition that I would never have to abandon you, and they agreed. The gods are not so cruel after all."

"Oh Slavik! We have to make sacrifices, as soon as you're back on your feet! We have to thank them, we have to pay them back!"

"I think they will get their payment, don't you fear, Rusenka," said Svyatoslav. For a moment his eyes, the same shifting color as his sister's, caught Slava's, and she read a much less happy story in them than the one he was telling Marusya. It was almost as if he were suffering pangs of conscience. Just like Marusya's tears, it was a shockingly incongruous sight in his coarse, heavy face and hairy, bestial body. Slava felt pity for him run through her. She thought of the leshaya he had tried to burn to death, but the pity, of course, remained.

"I'll give them anything they ask!" declared Marusya.

"Of you I think they will ask nothing," said Svyatoslav. His eyes returned to Slava. "They tell me that you hate me, or something like that," he said. "They also tell me you are the Tsarinovna. Is it true?"

"I am the Tsarinovna, that is true," said Slava.

"And the hate? They said you were so horrified at what I had done, you screamed out loud, Tsarinovna, even though you had no body to scream with."

"I did," said Slava.

"He had his reasons!" said Marusya defensively. "He had to! He was doing it for me! We had to!"

Slava looked down at her hands, trying to find the strength to say what she knew needed to be said, even though it would hurt Marusya, who had already been hurt so much. When she looked back up, she was so afraid of what she was saying, it felt as if another woman were speaking with her voice.

"You still burned the leshaya," she said. "It doesn't matter why."

"What do you know, Tsarinovna!" said Marusya, her voice rising and rising. "What do you know of suffering! We had to, we had to, we had no choice, you would have done the same, how dare you judge us..."

"It doesn't matter why," Slava repeated, rising from her chair. "Your mother, and your mother-in-law, and your husband—they all had their reasons for what they did too. Sometimes it doesn't matter why you do something, only what it is that you do." She looked straight at Svyatoslav. "And I don't hate you, even so. Didn't they tell you that as well? I can't, no matter how much I might want to. I feel sorry for you. I'm sorry for everything that's happened to you in the past, and for what has happened to you just now, and for what will happen to you in the future. I feel sorry for you, and I always will. But don't burn any more leshiye."

"Don't worry, Tsarinovna," said Svyatoslav. "I'm afraid from now on, what I do won't be decided by me."

"I hope it will turn out well for you," Slava told him. She turned back to Marusya. "My best wishes for the baby. I hope she will grow into a fine strong girl, and I hope she will be happier than you were. My best wishes." She left the room before Marusya and Svyatoslav's misery could draw her back.

Chapter
Twenty-Five

She found Sanya and her men loitering in the main room, looking uncertain. "What news, noblewoman?" asked Sanya as soon as Slava appeared.

"He has awakened," Slava told her.

There was a general cheer at this announcement, and Sanya's men all slapped each other on the back.

"Where are Olga Vasilisovna and the others?" Slava asked.

"Outside, noblewoman," Sanya told her. "Preparing to leave, by all appearances."

"I'll take you to them, noblewoman," said one of the men. Slava remembered that his gaze had been particularly familiar earlier in the evening, over supper, and that he had stared at her much too openly for a respectable man, as if he had been thinking the thoughts that most men would deny even contemplating with shame-filled faces. "It's been a strange night—you don't want to go walking around alone right now."

"Thank you, ..."

"Yura, noblewoman." Yura led her out to the front room and helped her with her outer clothing. He still smiled at her too familiarly through his dirty teeth and greasy hair as he did so, but this time he didn't seem to mean any harm by it—it was just his habit. He led her out onto the porch, gripping her arm too hard, but again, out of thoughtlessness, not malice.

"There you go, noblewoman, your people," he said, pointing to where Olga, Dunya, and the others were gathered around the dogs and sleds. As they were no more than three or four paces from where Slava was standing, she hardly needed him to show her, but she thanked him all the same, hoping that he would read her smile as one of gratitude, not amusement. He gave her a self-satisfied nod and retreated back inside.

"Tsarinovna!" cried Olga. "We were about to come inside and get you! What's happened?"

"Svyatoslav has awakened," Slava told her. "Are you preparing to leave?"

"I think we should—it's not like we're going to get any more sleep here tonight—well, it's practically morning already, anyway—so we might as well get moving. And, well, frankly, after everything that's happened…"

"We've gathered up and packed all your things from your room, Tsarinovna," Dima told her. "Are you dressed? We're ready to set off whenever you are."

"I am ready," said Slava. "But…"

"Yes, Tsarinovna?"

"I was thinking that perhaps Oleg Svetoslavovich should…"

"Stay behind, Tsarinovna?" asked Oleg Svetoslavovich.

"You should do whatever you think best, Oleg Svetoslavovich, of course."

"But Svyatoslav might need someone to stay with him," said Oleg Svetoslavovich. "Someone who knows."

"Whatever you think best, Oleg Svetoslavovich, of course," Slava repeated.

"You are right about Svyatoslav, Tsarinovna, but you and Olga and the others might need me too. It's a dangerous road to Lesnograd, and I've—I may have been charged with…with watching over you. And besides, I'd hate to leave you and have you come to some trouble again—you seem to fall into it wherever you go."

"True," agreed Slava.

"I'll just tell Svyatoslav I'll be back," said Oleg Svetoslavovich, after a moment's hesitation. "I'll come back through here after I've seen you safely to Lesnograd." He went back into the building.

"Is it really such a dangerous road to Lesnograd?" Dunya asked Olga, looking off into the trees with the carefully-composed stance of someone who was asking only for information's sake. "That is, more dangerous than the one we've already traveled? What dangers should we be on the watch for?"

"The gods only know," said Olga, sounding half-amused and half-exasperated. "I've traveled the Severnovostochnaya road more times than I can count, and never had a moment's trouble until now. At this point it wouldn't surprise me if the earth opened up and swallowed us whole. This is the most ill-fated journey I've ever been on."

"You shouldn't even say such things, Olga Vasilisovna," said Sasha reproachfully. "The gods might be listening, and they might take you up on your words."

"Oh, let them," said Olga. "At this point I don't even care."

"Well, let's hope they'll let us arrive in Lesnograd safely," said Dima, with the clear intention of preventing an argument. "No doubt if we all watch out for each other, and with the welcome help of Oleg Svetoslavovich, we'll reach our destination."

"Indeed," said Grisha. "Five days from now we'll be warming ourselves in front of a blazing Lesnogorod fire."

"Oh, I'm sure," said Dunya, still carefully holding herself in the pose of someone who knew what she was doing, and was only looking out for everyone else's best interests. "But caution never goes amiss."

"So true," agreed Dima with careful politeness.

Everyone's strained attempts at not being afraid of what lay ahead were interrupted by the welcome return of Oleg Svetoslavovich, who was followed by a servant carrying a large bundle.

"Svyatoslav is doing well," he reported, "and Marusya Svyatoslavovna has kindly given us these supplies."

"Please, noblewomen," said the servant, handing the bundle to Olga. "With the mistress's compliments."

"Please give her our thanks, and our best wishes for her brother's speedy recovery," said Olga, as if Marusya Svyatoslavovna were a distant acquaintance, and their stay at her waystation had been a mere visit of politeness.

"Of course, noblewoman," said the servant, bowing and retreating to the porch, where she watched with an uncertain expression on her face as they checked the sleds, strapped on their skis, and set off. Clearly the uncertainty that had filled the air since the night's events had affected the servants too, and now no one knew what to do or say. At supper it had been taken for granted by all parties that Marusya had been the untrustworthy waystation mistress, Sanya her shady friend, and Svyatoslav her black-magic-dealing brother, while Olga and her people had been the travelers to be fleeced, and no one had

had to declare themselves openly. Then Olga and Marusya's two sides had been clear enemies for a few hours.

Now it was unclear whether they were allies or enemies, or what Marusya and Svyatoslav had become. Slava wondered how profound the change in them had been, and how long it would last. A day, or a week, or a year from now, what would they do? If Slava were ever to return to this waystation, would Marusya welcome her with open arms, or would she turn away from her, not wanting to be reminded of her moment of weakness, when she had thought her curse had been lifted and a new, better life was beginning? Slava would have liked to think it would be the former, but she knew it was all too likely to be the latter. The thought made her so angry she wanted to run back and shout at Marusya, but she knew it would do no good, and she was falling behind the others, so she forced herself to stop thinking about it and concentrate on her skiing instead.

"You're not tired, Tsarinovna?" asked Grisha, when she caught back up with him—something she was able to do, she realized, because he had been deliberately lingering.

"No," she said, and then immediately realized that was a lie, and had to confess, "Actually, yes. I feel quite weak."

"No surprise there, Tsarinovna—you've been up all night, worn out with the gods know what, and after a long day beforehand too. Do you want the sled?"

"No, I've had enough of the sled for a little while," she said. "I'll wait till I really can't keep up anymore."

"That's the spirit, Tsarinovna! And in the meantime, grab my belt if you need to, and I'll pull you along."

"Thank you, Grisha. Once again, I'm a burden on you all, holding you back, I'm afraid."

"Food is a burden too, Tsarinovna, but you wouldn't get far without it. Don't be shy—grab my belt whenever you need to." Grisha smiled down at Slava, and then, apparently overcome by shyness, looked off into the dark trees.

Slava had told herself she would ski under her own power at least until daybreak, but the first time she had to grab Grisha's belt in order to keep up was well before dawn. She let go after another verst or so of skiing, telling herself she was rested, but within a verst she had to grab hold again, and this time she was unable to let go. Somehow Grisha's skis cut lightly through the snow, never crossing or catching, while Slava's strayed disobediently in every direction, and sometimes stopped completely. Whatever skill in skiing she had acquired over the course of the journey had abandoned her this morning, and she felt as awkward as she had her very first day on skis.

"My mother is an excellent skier," Slava told Grisha ruefully, after one ski had jerked to a halt, making her wobble dangerously and almost go down on one knee. "But that was one of the many qualities I didn't inherit from her."

"And did she practice much, Tsarinovna?" asked Grisha, not even out of breath.

"She skied every day she could, sometimes for versts and versts," Slava admitted. "And rode almost every day, too."

"And you, Tsarinovna?"

"Well...I suppose I have no one to blame but myself. She did teach me, but I was so ashamed of my clumsiness, I kept trying to avoid the lessons, especially as everyone always laughed at me when I tried, and then, well...If only I'd have known how useful it was going to be."

"I don't even remember learning how to ski, Tsarinovna," Grisha told her.

"Really? How old were you when you learned?"

"I don't know, Tsarinovna, I just remember being three or four and skiing after my father as fast as I could, and he would try to outrace me, but somehow I always caught him in the end—he must have been pretending."

"What was your family like?" asked Slava, and to her surprise, the normally reticent Grisha spoke at length about his family and his home village, making her forget about her clumsiness until Olga called a halt in order to rest and eat.

The rest of the day passed for Slava in an ever-increasing struggle with tiredness. For a brief period after their first halt she felt refreshed, and told herself that she was going to be able to keep up with the others for the rest of the day, but within a couple of versts she was clutching Grisha's belt again, letting him drag her along, and after a couple more versts even that was insufficient to prevent her from staggering and stumbling. Grisha claimed she wasn't slowing him down, but it was painfully obvious that that was untrue.

After their midday halt she was put in a sled, with strict instructions to tell Dunya if she became chilled. She promised to do so, but Dunya not only kept making her talk all afternoon, she also kept checking for any sign of freezing by holding her face against Slava's, as if Slava were a small child. At one point she became concerned, and made Slava jump out of the sled and run next to it for as long as she could. This was not very long at all, but it kept Slava warm until well after dark, allowing her to lie propped up against the front of the sled in a blissful state of immobile exhaustion. Travel like this was almost pleasant.

They came to their cabin sooner than Slava had expected. It was a surprisingly large and well-kept building, and showed signs of recent habitation, because, Slava supposed, they were close enough to Lesnograd to have frequent traffic. She was also surprised to see how neat the previous occupants had been—everything had been put in place and swept clean, not what she would have expected from the kind of people who stayed in such wayside cabins. Of course, she was the kind of person who stayed in wayside cabins now, she reminded herself—and then reminded herself that she was not the kind of person who routinely swept up after herself, because the servants always did it for her.

With that thought in mind, she offered to help unpack and prepare things for the night. She was set to putting blankets out on the beds, which somehow turned into a more difficult task than she had been anticipating. There were two bedrooms in the cabin, each filled with bunkbeds, and a closet full of blankets in the corner. She started in the larger of the two bedrooms, which she decided was where the men would stay. First she kept misfiguring the number of men actually in their group now, and made up too few beds, and then too many.

Once she had overcome that difficulty, she moved on to the smaller room. There she had another difficult decision: should she, Olga, and Dunya all sleep in one set of bunks (they were three beds high), or should two of them be in one and one in the other? At first she thought they should all be in one, but when she tried climbing up to the top bunk, she realized it was quite high up, and if it were her sleeping there, she would much prefer to be in the bottom bed of the other set. So she climbed back down, dropping some of her blankets as she did so, and went over to the other bed, where Dunya still found her sitting sometime later.

"Are you all right, Tsarinovna?" Dunya asked her, feeling her cheek.

"I just lapsed into a reverie, I guess," Slava said, trying to shake some life back into her head. "I don't know what's wrong with me. My thoughts keep floating away from me."

"Some food will make you feel better, Tsarinovna," Dunya said comfortingly. "Come, Dima's cooked us something delicious, or at least hot."

Food did make her feel better, but after supper Slava once again found herself sitting there staring into space without seeing what was in front of her, until Dunya came and told her it was time for her to go to bed.

Had Slava been more awake, she would, she knew, be afraid of dreams that night, but as it was she crawled into her bed—the bottom one, with Olga in the other bottom bunk and Dunya swinging lithely up into the middle bunk and saying something about slow old women, while Olga shook her fist at her in mock anger—without any trepidation at all. During the night she thought she felt eyes watching over her through the veil of sleep, but she sensed that they were kind eyes, and sank into their embrace.

The next morning she was awakened by Dunya swinging out of her bunk and pulling on her boots with a decisive yank.

"Just going to feed the dogs," Dunya whispered to her, when she saw Slava's eyes turn her way. "It's still early yet."

"Is it morning?" asked Olga groggily.

"Early morning," said Dunya. "Dog-feeding time."

"Person-feeding time, too, then," said Olga. "We have a long day ahead of us today." She crawled out of her bunk and pulled on her boots with rather less flair than Dunya, and Slava realized that Olga was exhausted, probably even more exhausted than Slava was, and was having a hard time hiding it.

"You stay in bed," Slava told her. "I'll take care of it."

Olga gave her an ill-concealed look of doubt. "You should rest yourself, Tsarinovna," she said. "There's no need for you to be getting up so early."

"Well, I'll ask Dima to take care of it," Slava confessed. "But you should rest as much as you can."

"I can't be lazing around in bed while everyone else is working," argued Olga.

"You can't wear yourself out, either," Slava told her. "We need you to have a clear head—after all, whom else can we trust to make the decisions around here?"

"Good point," said Olga. "I'll just lie here for a bit, I suppose, and gather my strength for the arduous duties that await me as leader. Call me when breakfast is ready, and I'll see if I can deign to join you."

"We could always bring you a tray," said Slava with a grin.

"I guess they're all sufficiently scared of me not to drop the tray or steal my food," Olga said, flopping back down on the bed and propping her feet against the post in order to avoid getting her boots on the blankets. "Probably."

"We could set guards," suggested Slava.

"Is that what you do in the Kremlin?" asked Olga.

"Sort of," said Slava. "Normally anything that has be carried anywhere—anything of importance, that is, such as the Tsarina's food—is accompanied by such a crush of servants that it would be impossible for anyone to steal anything without being turned in by the others immediately."

"I'll have to keep that in mind for the future," said Olga. She gave Slava a stern look. "What are you doing still standing around? Why aren't you preparing my breakfast?!"

"I'm only going to give the order to have it prepared, not actually dirtying my hands with real work," said Slava, backing out of the room with a mock bow.

As she had guessed, Dima and the other men were already up and about, and in fact Dima was already brewing tea, so there was nothing of use for her to do except go through the cupboards until, somewhat to her surprise at discovering such a civilized object so far from civilization, she found a tray. She had intended to carry the food to Olga herself, but before she could so much as put a plate on the tray, Olga herself appeared in the common room.

"It turns out it was really tiring to keep my boots propped off the blankets like that, and I didn't feel like taking them off and then putting them back on," she said. "So I guess I've deigned to join you for breakfast after all."

"You always join us for breakfast, Olga Vasilisovna," said Olik, sounding very puzzled. Olga's lengthy outburst of laughter at his words seemed to hurt his feelings, but when she patted him on the shoulder and told him he was a good boy and she wouldn't trade him for anyone else in the world, his face cleared and he took his place at the table with the expression of a beloved dog who had just had an unexpectedly large dish of food set before her.

Everyone was in excellent spirits when they set off. After her performance yesterday Slava had feared that she would hold the others back yet again, but a night's uninterrupted sleep and a hearty breakfast—Dima had found a large quantity of oats and made a very filling porridge—had poured new strength into her limbs, and she kept up with Grisha, who was as usual holding the rear of the group, without trouble until midday. Most of the time she had the sensation that she was being watched, but it seemed she was being watched by benevolent eyes, and so she neither worried about it nor brought it up to the others.

In the afternoon she began to flag, and was put in a sled. This allowed her to pay more attention to her surroundings, and several times she was sure she saw a tree move just on the edge of her vision, as if she were being stalked by a leshaya. Probably she was, she reflected, and perhaps that was for the best.

It was, as Olga had said, a very long day, and both the men and the dogs were barely dragging along by the time they arrived at the night's waycabin, many hours after dark. Slava was by then the most rested person of the group, and as such offered to feed the dogs.

As she was walking back from the stable where they were being kept, a fir tree suddenly stepped out of the shadows. Slava raised her lantern and waved at it, and after a moment it waved a branch back at her and slowly blinked its big brown eyes, before melting back into the trees around them.

Slava went into the cabin feeling, somewhat to her surprise, comforted. She knew that the leshiye had done many things that should make her wary of them, but now she had done so much for them that she was certain, with a certainty much stronger than reason, that they would now let no harm come to her.

Even so, she decided not to mention it to anyone. No reason to worry them. Although they could still sense that something was out there. That night, as she, Dunya, and Olga were drifting off to sleep, Dunya sat up suddenly.

"What was that?" she demanded.

"What was what?" mumbled Olga, who was still noticeably tired.

"Something just walked past the window, I'm sure of it," hissed Dunya.

Slava, who, at her own insistence, had taken the bed nearest the window, and therefore the coldest, sat up and pulled back the heavy curtain. Snowy moonlight streamed over her, blinding her for an instant. When she could see again, all she could make out were trees, although one had what seemed like a familiar outline.

"I don't see anything," she said.

"It sounded like something big—like a bear," said Dunya. "Are there tracks in the snow?"

Now that Slava looked at it more closely, the snow did appear disturbed, but not, she thought, by a bear. "No," she said.

"You're sure?" demanded Dunya. "I could have sworn…"

"I think some snow just fell off a branch," said Slava. "That was probably what you heard."

"It sounded like footsteps…" said Dunya, but with doubt creeping into her voice.

"We're all still on edge, after everything that has happened," Slava told her. "But I'm sure it was just snow falling off a branch. And even if it was a bear, what danger does it pose us?"

"The dogs…" said Dunya.

"The dogs are locked up snug in the stable," said Slava. "And if something starts bothering them, I'm sure they'll let us know."

"True enough," said Dunya, sounding comforted. "You're right; it must have been snow falling off a branch. I'm just jumpy, like you said." She lay back down and pulled her blankets up around her. Slava lay back down too, but not before taking one final look out the window. Something blinked a long slow blink at her through the trees. She blinked back, and thought she caught sight of a branch raised in greeting, before she closed the curtain.

Everyone was in very high spirits the next morning at the thought of a real waystation waiting for them that night. Their past experiences of staying with others had apparently not dampened their enthusiasm for company, warm beds, and hot food that was brought to them from somebody else's kitchen. Even Slava, who couldn't help but run over in her mind all the bad things that had happened to them by staying with other people, was cheered by the prospect.

As had been the case the day before, she was only able to keep up with the others on skis for the morning, and was put in a sled in the afternoon. The days were now long enough, and they were far enough South—if anything so far North could be so termed—that it was no longer ridiculous to speak of "morning" and "afternoon," and they had begun using the words again without qualification.

So it truly was that afternoon, barely even twilight, when they arrived at the waystation, whose smoke curled cheerily out of its chimney. There were other sleds, both for dogs and for horses, out in front of it, and the snow was all beaten down around it, showing evidence of many busy feet. As they arrived, a head peered out the front door, popped back inside for a moment, and then reappeared, this time wearing a hat and followed by a body that was still putting its arms into its coat sleeves.

"Hello, travelers!" called the serving girl, hurrying down the porch steps to greet them. "Where are you coming from? Have you had a long journey here?"

"Long enough," said Olga in reply.

"It seems funny to stop at sunset, and call that a long day," whispered Sasha to Slava with a grin.

"There were plenty of other long days," whispered Olga, who had overheard him.

"I see you have dogs; so do some others, but lucky for you, we still have a little room left in the stable," said the serving girl, bowing breathlessly and bestowing smiles on all the group, but especially on Olga and the younger and handsomer of the men. "Such a large group! It'll be a merry party in the front room tonight! Vanya here'll take your dogs."

In a moment the serving girl, who introduced herself as Manya, was unloading their sleds, and Vanya was helping Dunya unharness the dogs, and the next thing they knew, they were being led inside. Slava took one final glance into the woods as she went up the porch steps, and thought, as she had several times throughout the day, that something blinked at her. She blinked back, and snow fell off a branch somewhere amongst the trees.

"Come, Slava, what are you holding us up for?" asked Olga, and Slava realized she was still standing on the porch, while all the others were waiting to go in.

"I thought I saw something in the woods," Slava said thoughtlessly.

"Like what?" demanded Olga. "Should we be..." and she trailed off, glancing at the serving girl.

"Probably just a snow hare," said Slava.

"*Just* a snow hare?" asked Olga.

"Oh, we have lots of those here," said Manya brightly. "No doubt you're right and that's what you saw, noblewoman, but let's not linger too long out here, looking at the woods." She shivered a little. "There's not just snow hares out there, you know."

"Yes," agreed Slava. She stamped some of the snow off her boots, and followed the others inside.

With their arrival the waystation was full up with travelers, which delighted the stationmistress, a plump, jolly woman with a tangle of curly red hair that in its day would have challenged Olga's, to no end. Like the serving girl, who turned out to be her daughter, she asked them if they'd come far, but before they could answer her, she burst into such a long stream of chatter that she never heard their reply, which was just as well. She took a great fancy to Olga and Oleg Sve-toslavovich, saying she always loved meeting another redhead, and questioned them at length about their families, although between her chattiness and Olga's silence on the subject, Olga's actual provenance was never revealed.

It was, however, discovered that the stationmistress was, in fact, some kind of third- or fourth-sister to Oleg Svetoslavovich, although the exact nature of the relationship remained unclear, as Oleg Sveto-slavovich was representing himself as his own second-brother once removed, and the stationmistress never could be quiet long enough to hear out his explanations anyway. Despite the distance between them, she kissed him on both cheeks and gave them all a round of vodka on the house, declaring that nothing was dearer than family, and a broth-er was, after all, a brother, no matter how loosely-connected.

The other guests were all of a piece with the stationmistress, and after supper had been served—there was a brief period of silence when the food was put on the table and everyone turned to the serious business of eating after a long day in the cold—the front room became so loud with talk that Slava felt quite stunned. Inasmuch as she had ever thought about what staying at waystations would be like, this was how she had pictured it, but after so many weeks of solitude, punctuated only by the occasional brief encounter with people she would have rather avoided, this much noisy good humor was more than she could tolerate, welcome as she had thought it would be. When Olga said after supper that she wanted to retire for the night, Slava followed her gratefully, in spite of the stationmistress's good-natured protests that the fun was only just beginning.

The stationmistress was, unfortunately, correct, and Slava could hear talking, then singing, then drunken but still good-natured quarreling long into the night, waking her every time she dozed off. It must have been several hours, even though it felt like several nights, after she retired that she fell into anything resembling actual sleep.

She awakened in silence and darkness—probably because of the silence and darkness, she thought to herself. Once again she had insisted on taking the bed by the window, claiming (falsely) to feel the cold less than Dunya and Olga. Something made her draw back the heavy curtain. The cold air coming through the small glass square made her shiver, but she leaned towards it anyway, trying to make out something in the yard through the waviness of the glass's distortion. Sure enough, a tree that she was sure had not been there when they arrived was standing guard by the stable, looking, it seemed her, directly at her window. She waved to it, and it waved back. Comforted, Slava let the curtain fall, blocking off the cold air, and went back to sleep.

In her dreams that night she found herself laughing, something she did not normally associate with dreaming. The forest seemed to be gathered around her, but its eyes were friendly, and its voice made her smile. She smiled and laughed as much as she could, because she knew that this was only a brief respite, and she must take her joy while there was joy for her to take. Something, some great unfriendly wall that kept the leshiye and other spirits out, was looming in front of her, and once she was inside it, there would be pain and fear. Not more than she could take, no, but she would not feel like laughing for a long time. So she let her for-once friendly dreams hold her for as long as they could.

The next morning she woke up before the others, she thought, and looked out the window again. The tree by the stable was just disappearing out of sight.

"What was that?" asked Dunya, who apparently was not as asleep as Slava had thought. "What was by the stable?"

"A leshaya," Slava admitted. "I think they're keeping guard over me, or something."

Dunya shuddered all over. "Or something," she said. "I don't know which is worse: being stalked by leshiye in the woods or people in town. I'm almost hoping that something delays us on our way to Lesnograd, or otherwise we'll be there tomorrow afternoon, they say."

"Do you still fear Lesnograd?" Slava asked.

"Anyone with any sense fears Lesnograd," said Olga, also sitting up. "What's out the window?"

"Leshiye, it seems," Dunya told her. "Watching over our Tsarinovna."

"Well, as long as they're only watching, it will make a pleasant change," said Olga. "I wonder if they'll be able to follow us into the city?"

"I doubt they can go into any city, even a forest city such as Lesnograd," said Slava, remembering her dreams. "I think their protection will end as soon as we pass through its walls."

Olga shuddered all over too. "And just when we'll need it the most," she said. "I tell you what, I wouldn't mind an army of forest spirits backing us up when we go in."

"Is it really so bad there?" asked Dunya. "It was your idea to go there, after all."

"Yes, as usual, I have no one to blame but myself," agreed Olga. "Somehow it didn't seem so bad when we were all freezing our asses off above the sunline. And it is true that my mother's sorceresses will know better than anyone what is going on with our Tsarinovna. The question isn't can they help us, it's will they, or will they do something terrible."

"Do they often?" asked Dunya, sounding so unconcerned that Slava knew she was secretly terrified.

"All my mother's servants do terrible things all the time," said Olga. "Consider the story of Mirik's sister. But perhaps I'm finding trouble where there isn't any. Perhaps it will all turn out well."

Slava almost said she was sure it wouldn't, but stopped herself. Her dreams, which she was certain upon waking were true dreams, would do Dunya and Olga no good, and probably much harm. She doubted the strength they had given her could be shared.

"But we can't stay here, so we might as well get going," continued Olga, crawling out of bed. "And whatever else happens in Lesnograd, we'll probably be warm."

Here in the warm bedroom in the warm waystation that didn't seem so important, but the memory of cold nights in the tundra rose up in Slava's mind and reminded her that being warm was a blessing not to be scorned. She crawled out of bed behind Olga and Dunya and pulled on her boots. Perhaps in Lesnograd they would also be provided with clean clothes, which would also make up for many, many evils. Despite her warning dreams, Slava followed the others down to breakfast and then out into the snow in a cheerful frame of mind.

They set off at sunrise, with clear skies and still air to speed them on their way. There was another group also setting off for Lesnograd that morning, and so for the first few versts they shared the road with a group of traders. By midday, though, Olga began to lose patience with their slow pace, and so they loaded Slava in the sled and took off, leaving the traders behind.

"Not that it matters," admitted Olga. "We'll all be spending the night in the same waystation. But my hands were getting cold."

Nothing happened that day to slow them down: no bad weather, no mysterious encounters, and no losing their way. Even after sunset the road remained smooth and flat, and by the time the stars were shining down on them, they could see the glow of the waystation's windows welcoming them ahead.

This waystation was just as clean and friendly as the previous one, and they dined and went to bed without incident.

"I don't like it," said Olga, once they had all gotten into bed. "Such good fortune makes me nervous, after everything that's happened."

"Or maybe after everything that's happened, we were due a little good fortune," said Dunya, but she sounded as if she didn't believe it. She looked out the window onto the yard. "Have you seen any sign of the leshiye, Tsarinovna?"

"Not since last night," Slava told her. "I think they're there, but with more people around, they're keeping hidden." It did in fact sometimes seem to Slava that she could feel their presence in the back of her mind, and sometimes their eyes on her skin, but she had not caught sight of them all day. She almost wished she would.

The bed was clean and comfortable, the waystation was, while crowded, quiet, and they all slept soundly that night. Once again Slava had warning dreams, telling her that she must gather her strength for the trial ahead, but somehow they were comforting rather than frightening, and she rose the next morning full of cheerful resolve.

The clear skies of the day before had given way to clouds that hung low over their heads, heavy with snow. A surprisingly warm wind was blowing from the East.

"Winter's on the way out," announced Grisha, sniffing the air. "The going will be hard today."

"Well, it's a short day anyway," said Olga. "Only twenty-five versts. No need to hurry."

Somehow they had been slow and inefficient in their morning preparations, and were the last to leave the waystation. Slava could not pinpoint any particular thing that had slowed them down, or any particular sign of dawdling on anyone's part, but nonetheless no one seemed able to move fast that morning, and they did not set out until after sunrise.

Grisha's prediction proved to be true. A warm, wet snow started coming down within a verst of their departure. Today, now that they were so close to their destination, the snow did not seem magical or even threatening; it was just an annoying obstacle to slog through. Slava's knees did not seem to want to stand up on their own, and she found herself yet again stumbling along at the back of the group. She had had a faint hope of skiing the whole day today, as it would be such a short one, but at their first stop she was put in the sled, and she knew that Olga was right to insist on it.

Buildings started appearing beside the road as the day dragged on. At first it was only the occasional isolated cabin, but by early afternoon whole, if small, villages could be made out in small clusters through the trees.

"Hunters and trappers," said Olga laconically, when Slanik asked who lived there. The cabins really were rude affairs, making even the travelers' huts they had been staying in seem sturdy and luxurious in comparison. Slava wondered how anyone could manage to overwinter in them—she would have assumed that they were deserted, if it were not for the smoke rising from their chimneys—and Olga explained that they were not permanent residences, that the hunters would only stay a week or two in them, before returning to Lesnograd.

The road grew wider and wider, until it really was a road and not just a track through the forest. Even so they had to pull over several times to allow large sleighs to pass by. The first few times this happened, the sleigh riders paid them no attention, but then one particularly large sleigh, decked out with a very vocal set of bells, suddenly slid to a stop beside them.

"Olga?" called a voice from inside a mound of furs in the middle of the sleigh. "Olga Vasilisovna? Is that you?"

"Natalya Yevgeniyevna?" asked Olga disbelievingly.

"By all the gods, it is you!" cried the mound of furs. "I half-thought you'd been killed this time! What brings you back to Lesnograd? I thought you were going to the Midnight Land. Did you make it?"

"We're on our way back from there right now," Olga told the voice in the sleigh, which had emerged enough from the furs to reveal a woman of middle years in rich but very warm clothing.

"Didn't you set out with more men?" asked the woman.

"Yes," said Olga.

"I'm sorry," said the woman. "Sometimes the gods are cruel. At least they didn't take our Dima away from you."

"I had to leave some behind in Khladniye Vody," Olga told her. "The gods willing, they will be able to join us in Lesnograd. I won't lie: it's been a hard journey."

"And unlikely to get any easier," said the woman. "Lesnograd isn't a friendly place right now. Why do you think I decided to set off for my summer estates in winter?" She wrapped her furs back around her. "It's a long cold journey, but I decided I'd rather take my chances with the frost than with my sister noblewomen."

"Why?" demanded Olga. "What are they up to? Worse than the usual wrangling?"

"Yes," said the woman. "Much worse. I fear your mother has finally lost her mind, Olga Vasilisovna, and maybe more than that. It's good you're coming home when you are, although I wouldn't want to be in your shoes. Your mother has had some kind of a fit and hasn't been seen for days, and your sister won't do her duty and rule. Your daughter does nothing but moan and complain—it pains me to speak ill of your own flesh and blood, Olga Vasilisovna, but your daughter's been a disgrace to her family since the day she was born, and she hasn't improved in your absence—and so somehow the rule of Lesnograd has fallen to your husband, who is no more fit than the others, just much more greedy and grasping. I'm afraid, Olga Vasilisovna, you're finally going to have to face your birthright. Luck and courage, Olga Vasilisovna, and to you, Dmitry Marusyevich. You'll need it." And with those encouraging words, the woman told her driver to drive on.

"Who was that?" asked Slanik, his eyes big with nervousness at this unnerving encounter.

"Natalya Yevgeniyevna Bogoslavova, a minor Lesnograd noblewoman and also, incidentally, Dmitry Marusyevich's fourth-sister, or something of that sort," said Olga. "Well, I have to say, that meeting did not improve my day." She tried to laugh to show it was a joke, but her throat was too tight and she produced nothing more than a slight choking sound.

"The Bogoslavovy are all a little hysterical, you know that," said Dima.

"*You're* not hysterical, Dmitry Marusyevich," said Olik.

"I'm a Temnolesov," said Dima. "We were never noble, so we all know how to keep a level head on our shoulders. The Bogoslavovy are *very* distant cousins, and all through the male line—barely even family at all."

"And a good thing, too," said Olga. "Well, I suppose there's no help for it: we'll have to keep going. Lesnograd is only a couple of versts away." She squared her shoulders and carried on. Slava suspected that any passer-by would be unable to tell that she had just received word that her mother was ill and the rest of her family was quarreling instead of leading, but Slava could see by the very squareness of her shoulders that she was much more upset by this news than she would care to reveal. Slava hoped that they would not, at least, be too much longer on the road, in order to spare her too much more of the suspense that she must be feeling.

And in fact it seemed like hardly any time at all before a wooden stockade fence was rising up in front of them out of the snow.

Chapter Twenty-Six

Slava's first impression of Lesnograd was that it had not disappointed her in its barbaric, Northern splendor. It was, as had appeared at first glance, surrounded by a stockade fence, just like the forest cabins. The wooden-shingled square domes of important buildings loomed from behind the fence.

There were guards at the main gate, stopping everyone who came in or out and creating a small crush. Their group was waiting behind some fur traders and a peasant woman bringing in cheeses to the market, when the guards caught sight of Olga's face, and ordered them to the front of the line.

"Olga Vasilisovna?" asked the older of the two guards hesitantly.

"As you see," said Olga.

"Thank the gods! Welcome home, Olga Vasilisovna! And not a moment too soon!" cried the older guard, bowing down to his boot tops. The younger guard also bowed, although less enthusiastically. Slava thought she caught him giving their party a suspicious and unwelcoming look. He was the only one, though, as all the peasants and traders around them also started bowing profusely, with shouts of "Olga Vasilisovna! Welcome home, little mother, welcome home!"

"They said you'd gone to Krasnogorod, and they also said you'd gone to the Midnight Land, Olga Vasilisovna," said the older guard, once the commotion had died down.

"They were right," said Olga. "I was in both places."

"I don't know which is more dangerous, Olga Vasilisovna," said the guard, shaking his head.

"Neither are very welcoming, but it wasn't till I got back to Severnolesnoye that I had to leave any of my men behind," said Olga. "We've had a hard journey. Tell me, Denis Mariyevich, how do matters currently stand in Lesnograd? I have heard no good reports."

"I won't lie: matters stand badly in our Lesnogorod now," said Denis Mariyevich. Slava thought that the younger guard's mouth twitched, but he said nothing.

"As you can see by this line, little mother," called the peasant woman selling cheeses. "When have honest traders ever had to beg entrance to Lesnogorod before this? It's a disgrace!"

There was some disgruntled muttering in agreement from the fur traders.

"Yes, why *are* you stopping everyone coming in or out, Denis Mariyevich?" asked Olga. "What does Lesnograd fear from these people?"

"Well, you see, Olga Vasilisovna, it's like this..." began Denis Mariyevich reluctantly, giving his partner a sideways glance.

"We are obeying the orders of Andrey Vladislavovich, your husband, Olga Vasilisovna!" barked out the younger guard. "We are to ensure that no," he gave her a nasty look, "*bad elements* enter the city."

"And does Andrey Vladislavovich rule Lesnograd now?" demanded Olga.

"He does, Olga Vasilisovna!" said the younger guard.

"Oh by all the gods!" cried Olga in exasperation. "A coward like that, in charge of Lesnograd? What *bad elements* could he possibly be fearing? And what of my mother? What of Vasilisa Vasilisovna? Or even Vasilisa Olgovna? Or, by all the gods, Vladislava Vasilisovna? Surely there are better heads for this matter to be found?!"

"No, Olga Vasilisovna!" said the younger guard. "Andrey Vladislavovich has..."

"Olga Vasilisovna," Denis Mariyevich put in, his voice taking on a conciliatory tone. "What our Valya is trying to say is that Lesnogorod is going through a bad spell right now."

"I can see that," said Olga grimly. "If Andrey Vladislavovich is the best ruler Lesnograd can find, then the situation must be truly dire. Well, Denis Mariyevich, I suppose there really is no help for it: let me through, and I'll go in and sort matters out."

"Gladly, Olga Vasilisovna..." began Denis Mariyevich, but the younger guard interrupted him by demanding, his lip curling, "And do you really think your head is best for this matter, Olga Vasilisovna? Do you really think you can sort matters out? You've been doing nothing but run away from Lesnogorod for years! Andrey Vladislavovich has been right here the whole time! What do you know of the needs of the common folk? What do you know of the lot of us guards and soldiers? Andrey Vladislavovich has traveled with us, served with us! He's a man just like the rest of us! He knows how hard our fate is! If anyone deserves to be the ruler, it's him, not you!"

"Since when has Andrey Vladislavovich ever served anyone anywhere?" said Olga. Slava couldn't tell if she was about to laugh or shout. Probably she didn't even know herself. "Since when has he ever been anything other than a cosseted darling? How much did he promise to add to your pay?" Now Slava was sure she was about to laugh.

"That's not the point!" cried the second guard, while shocked muttering rose up from the ever-increasing crowd that was gathering around them. Slava couldn't tell if they were in favor of Olga or the guard. Probably they couldn't tell themselves. Slava wondered if something very, very terrible was about to happen simply because people couldn't make up their minds about what they wanted.

"Walk me over to the kremlin, Valya," ordered Olga.

Everyone stared at her.

"I need to find out what's going on here, and as quickly as possible," she said. "I would hear your take on the situation. You obviously have no fear of telling me what you think is the truth; that's good in a councilor. Walk me over to the kremlin, and tell me what's happening on the way."

"Ai-da Olga Vasilisovna!" shouted several members of the crowd, delighted at this bold and unexpected step. "You'll get us sorted out, sure enough!"

"You heard Olga Vasilisovna, Valya," said Denis Mariyevich, when Valya continued to stand there in shocked silence. "She ordered you to walk her over to the kremlin, so walk her over."

"Yes, Denis Mariyevich," Valya managed to say. Slava thought he might have been thrown and hurt by how quickly the crowd had turned in Olga's favor. He gave Olga and the rest of the party a look of deep suspicion, but said, "This way, please," and led them through the gate. Slava could hear the buzz of speculation rise up behind them as soon as Olga had passed on to the other side of the wall.

"Dunya, Ts...Slava, Dima, to me," Olga commanded, as soon as they were all through. "I want you to hear what Valya has to say."

"Maybe you should hear what your husband has to say," said Valya, with the kind of insolent anger that Slava found very trying, even though she knew it was caused by fear and injustice. She could see him gathering up all his strength and courage to face them, and she wished that he wouldn't, that he could find some other battle to fight, because she could already see that supporting Andrey Vladislavovich was a lost cause, and should probably have never been attempted in the first place. She thought about the fact that those who had the most to lose so often fought the most foolish battles. She wished there were some way to make Valya's lot in life happier for him, and she wished even more that he would be capable of accepting her help, were she to offer it. Little chance of that, though.

"I will, when I arrive at the kremlin," said Olga calmly, cutting through the threat Dima was about to make and returning Slava's thoughts to the present. "But now I want to hear what *you* have to say. Tell me, Valya: what's happened in Lesnograd since I was sent away—and what are your thoughts on the subject?"

"That's right, you were sent away!" said Valya. "The Princess sent you away when she heard of your last scheme, didn't she? She even made a special announcement about it in the town square."

"You see?" said Olga. "That's exactly the sort of news I need to know. What did she say about me?"

"She said," Valya gave Olga an uncertain look, "that..." His insolence was rapidly fading in the face of Olga's refusal to quarrel with him, and he blushed and stuttered over the next words. "She said that you had finally...finally lost all loyalty to your family and your native land, and when she had refused to fund your latest... mad adventure, you had threatened to go to the Tsarina, and that...and that as far as she was concerned, you were no longer her daughter."

"Interesting," said Olga. "Did she disinherit me, do you know? I mean legally. There would have been ceremonies."

"Not that I know of, Olga Vasilisovna," said Valya.

"But you say she is no longer ruling Lesnograd anyway," said Olga. "That it is Andrey Vladislavovich who commands now. How did that happen?"

As they drew closer to the center of the city, their passage was slowed more and more by the crowdedness of the streets. Some of that crowdedness, Slava realized, was caused by their presence, as people kept stopping to stare at them. Many of the starers speculated that Olga Vasilisovna was the tall redhead at the front of the party. Many them sounded hopeful that that was the case. Slava thought she saw someone dispatch a runner in the direction of the kremlin, but she couldn't be certain in the throng and there was nothing she could do about it anyway. Andrey Vladislavovich was bound to find out about their arrival one way or another, and as Olga was clearly determined to confront him, Slava supposed they might as well get it over with as soon as possible.

She wondered what he was like. She had only heard him described by Olga and her men, who in this case were surely not fair and impartial judges. She began to feel a little sorry for him: abandoned by his wife, only to have her return in order to take away his newfound power. She caught sight of Mirik's face, which was setting into an ugly scowl at the very sound of his name, and remembered that Andrey Vladislavovich was probably not a very good person, after all. But unhappy, she thought, probably very unhappy...Why did people always make themselves so unhappy when it could so easily be otherwise... Slava realized she had missed part of Valya's story in her musings, and jerked her attention back to the matter at hand.

"...taken ill," Valya was saying. "Not even her best healers and herb-women could figure out why. And then Vasilisa Vasilisovna said she could not be spared from her duties as caretaker to the old princess, and Vladislava Vasilisovna is too young to rule, and Vasilisa Olgovna... well, she was also very distraught over the old princess's sudden illness, or at least so Andrey Vladislavovich said, and so he was the only one left—there could be no question of Vasilisa Vasilisovna's husband stepping in, you understand."

"I certainly do," said Olga. "But what of Vasilisa Olgovna? She is of age. I cannot believe she was as distraught as you say—that is, so distraught as to be unable to step forward and take control of the city when it was necessary."

"They say she..." began Valya, and then cut himself off abruptly.

"Takes too much after me?" suggested Olga with a short laugh.

"No..." said Valya.

"Oh," said Olga. "Doesn't take after me enough, then, I take it. She never did."

"I have only ever seen her from a distance, Olga Vasilisovna," answered Valya with surprising delicacy. Olga laughed, but then sobered up and said, "Lesnograd square. And look, guards are coming to meet us."

A pair of guards was indeed coming down the street towards them, and there was a sense of openness ahead, which Slava saw was in fact a large square in front of a kremlin wall. A wooden wall, but a kremlin wall nonetheless.

"They say you're bringing us Olga Vasilisovna and her party, Valya," said one of the guards, once he had come up to them. He looked Olga up and down, and added, "And I see it's true."

"Welcome, Olga Vasilisovna," said the other guard, bowing hastily but deeply. "You have been gone too long."

"I can see that, if my reception by Petya here"—Olga nodded towards the first guard—"is any indication. How do you fare, Mikhail Yevpraksich?"

"Better, now that you're here, Olga Vasilisovna," said Mikhail Yevpraksiyevich. "Lesnogorod needs your firm hand."

"So I've heard," said Olga, ignoring Petya's glower. "Are you here to lead me to my needy family?"

"Indeed, Olga Vasilisovna," said Mikhail Yevpraksiyevich.

"She should go back to Krasnogorod or wherever she came from," muttered Petya. He gave Valya a meaningful look, but Valya only looked confused in response. Valya had, Slava knew, found Olga to be much more impressive than he had expected, and didn't know what to do about it.

"You're welcome to set out for Krasnograd or wherever you came from whenever it strikes your fancy, Petya, but I, alas, have a duty here," said Olga, smiling at him in a way that threw him into an even deeper sulk. Mikhail Yevpraksiyevich opened his mouth to reprimand Petya further, but Olga smiled again and forestalled him by saying, "I wish to be taken to my mother and sister as quickly as possible."

"As you command, Olga Vasilisovna," said Mikhail Yevpraksiyevich with another bow. "Valya, go back to your post. I'll take charge from here."

Valya bowed and dashed off. Mikhail Yevpraksiyevich set off in the direction of the kremlin, with the rest of them behind him. Petya took up the rear, but Slava could still feel his glower burning the back of her neck. It seemed that Andrey Vladislavovich had developed quite a following amongst the younger guards, who were loath to see Olga Vasilisovna dispossess him. Slava wondered what he had offered them, aside from money. Slava supposed many of them would enjoy the sight of him putting one over on Olga and Princess Severnolesnaya, as they could not with their own wives and mothers. It was melancholy to think that they were driven by so base a motive, but that, alas, made it no less likely. Slava reminded herself she should spend less time in gloomy reflection, and more looking around.

The square in front of the kremlin was flagged over, but the snow had not been swept away very diligently, and so they had to pick their way carefully over the drifts, while eyes watched them from every street and every guard tower. All of Lesnograd must know by now that Olga Vasilisovna had returned.

As Slava had guessed from her earlier glimpse, the Lesnograd kremlin was a large wooden building inside a wooden stockade, like a miniature version of the town itself, only with higher walls. Calling it a "fortress" seemed undeserved flattery, but as there was nothing made of stone in all of Lesnograd, as far as Slava could tell, she supposed it was as close to a real kremlin as they could get. Square-domed towers rose up above the stockade fence, their eaves decorated with elaborate wood carvings. At least, Slava reflected, it did not disappoint in the matter of barbaric splendor.

"Is Krasnograd much like this?" Dunya whispered as they waited for the gate to open and let them through the stockade fence.

"Not really," Slava whispered back. "Krasnograd is much larger and finer, and the kremlin is made of brick and stone, with golden towers."

"I've never seen such large buildings before," Dunya confessed. "Do people live in those high towers?"

"Perhaps, or perhaps the guards use them to look out of," Slava told her.

"I feel like they're watching us," Dunya continued, still whispering.

"They are," Slava whispered. "I'm sure they have guards watching the square and the gate day and night."

"And sorceresses," whispered Dunya, shivering a little.

"Probably the sorceresses don't do guard duty," said Slava.

"No, but they could still be watching us," said Dunya. "Do you think they're very terrible? I have met many herbwomen and others who dabble in magic, but a sorceress…My mother always told me to keep my distance. No good ever comes from messing with magic."

"I don't know what they'll be like," said Slava. "In Krasnograd we also have minor dabblers in magic, but it is only in the steppe and the great forests that you have true sorceresses. The ones who come to Krasnograd say their gifts weaken when they are there. I am as curious as you are." *Or maybe more*, she thought to herself. The adventures of the journey had pushed their reason for coming to Lesnograd to the back of their minds, but Slava had not forgotten that it was in order to consult with the sorceresses about her changing and, it seemed, ever more terrible gifts.

"Enter," called the guards from the top of the gate, which swung open before them.

The small square inside the stockade fence was also flagged, which turned out to be a bad thing, because the snow had melted— from bonfires, Slava supposed, or from people dumping waterbuckets directly onto the square, as it surely hadn't been warm enough in months for the snow to melt on its own—in places and then refrozen, making them all slip dangerously on the patches of bare ice.

"Why haven't the sweeps chipped away the ice?" demanded Olga, after almost going down for the second time. "You could lose a good horse in here! It could go down and break its leg, and that would be that! What would happen if we were invaded?!"

"Do you think that likely, Olga Vasilisovna?" asked Mikhail Yevpraksiyevich, alarmed.

"No, but I'm sure the rest of my family does," said Olga. "They do love to worry about that sort of thing—or at least they did. And you really could lose a good horse to this ice. Don't think I don't know the barracks are full of guards with nothing better to do than play cards and quarrel. I want to see them out here chipping ice the next time I look out a window."

"You don't give the orders here, Olga Vasilisovna," said Petya, his face even surlier than before.

Olga stopped and faced him. "Petya," she said.

Petya took an involuntary step backwards.

"Don't make my first act on my homecoming be a command to have you flogged on the square," she said. "It wouldn't improve my mood."

"Andrey Vladislavovich won't let that happen!" cried Petya, sounding less certain than he would have liked. "He promised no more floggings for the guards!"

"No wonder things have gone downhill," said Olga.

"Andrey Vladislavovich will stand up for us!" insisted Petya, now sounding positively desperate.

"I wouldn't be too sure of that if I were you," said Olga. "Andrey Vladislavovich is not normally known for his constancy."

"Unlike you, I suppose," said Petya with an even more desperate sneer.

"I may have many flaws," said Olga, "but when I say I'm going to have someone flogged, I have him flogged. Don't tempt me."

"Go get the others and start on the ice, Petya," said Mikhail Yevpraksiyevich, before Petya could doom himself irrevocably. "Olga

Vasilisovna is right: we could lose a good horse to it. And send some-one for the dogs while you're at it."

Petya bowed and ran off.

"I wonder if that did any good," said Olga. "I confess, I had no idea things were so far gone that Lesnograd guards would contradict me to my face." She shook her head, as if clearing it of something unpleas-ant. "I hope I don't have to have anyone flogged in truth. I hope they come to their senses in time."

Slava sincerely hoped so too, because she could see from Olga's face that, unwelcome as marking her homecoming with a public flog-ging would be, she would do it if she felt it necessary, and Slava wanted to see Olga order someone flogged even less than Olga herself wanted to issue the order.

Servants came and took the dogs, and if they were secretly parti-sans of Andrey Vladislavovich, they bowed respectfully enough when Dunya told them to care for the dogs well. More servants opened the doors for them to the kremlin proper, and ushered them inside with more bows. A richly dressed woman, the first Slava had seen since ar-riving in Lesnograd, came up to them in the entrance and said, "Con-gratulations on your return, Olga Vasilisovna! Your family awaits you in the Great Hall."

"Lead me to them, then, Avdotya Vlastoslavovna," said Olga. Sla-va thought that probably she was the only one to notice Olga's bare-ly-suppressed sigh.

The Lesnograd kremlin was, while not particularly fine or well-lit, at least warm, Slava thought as Avdotya Vlastoslavovna led them through several corridors in the direction of the Great Hall, which was apparently on the opposite side to the main entrance. Although they had left their outer clothing at the entrance, they were still dressed for winter travel in the Far North, and after a very short time Slava found herself sweating in her layers of wool.

This made her acutely conscious of the fact that, not only was she coarsely dressed, she was dirty. No doubt she smelled bad, but so did all the others, so she had to hope her own rank odor would simply blend in with that of everyone else. But it was not the way she would have liked to meet the entire Severnolesnaya family for the first time. They were, according to the gossip of the Krasnograd kremlin, proud, hot-tempered, and devious. Plotting, it was said, ran in their blood the way magic supposedly did in Slava's. Magic, it had to be said, ran in the Severnolesnaya blood rather thickly as well, but the Zerkalitsy didn't like to talk too much about the Severnolesnaya magic, in case it diminished their own. Much better to complain about their plotting. Slava reminded herself that half of what her family said about the Severnolesniye was probably pure fabrication, and that she shouldn't be too quick to assume the worst. Keeping that firmly in mind, she followed Olga into the Great Hall.

The Great Hall was a large, high-ceilinged room, as befitted its name. Banners hanging from its walls and ceiling only served to make it seem even larger and emptier.

"Supposedly captured in battle," Olga whispered in Slava's ear, nodding towards the banners. "My family does like to brag. Although I can see, or rather can't see, that they've chosen not to waste money on candles and torches."

"Well, at least it's warm in here," Slava whispered back. What the Severnolesniye had chosen to spare in candles, they had made up with their open hearth, which was large enough to roast a whole ox, or possibly several of them. It was filled with roaring flames that would have been more at home in a forge than a fireplace. Slava passed by it on her way to the raised dais on the far side of the room, where people, presumably Olga's family, were sitting in the shadows, and its unaccustomed heat struck her in the face like a surprise attack. Much as she didn't want to meet Olga's family, she was glad to distance herself from the blazing fire.

There was a wooden throne-like chair in the middle of the dais. It was, Slava saw as they drew closer, occupied by a tall, thin man who needed to comb and cut his hair. Flanking him in smaller chairs were an older, worried-faced woman to his right and a tall young woman with angry eyes to his left. The angry young woman had flaming red hair, and had to be Olga's daughter.

"I see you have deigned to return to us, Olga," said the man once they had come up to the dais. "Just when you are least wanted, of course."

"I missed my sister and daughter," said Olga, sketching the faintest of bows in the direction of the group on the dais.

"Really, Olga?" said the older woman, her voice full of the hope of a person who is often disappointed. The younger woman barked out a disbelieving laugh, but said nothing.

"Really, Vasya," said Olga, her voice softening. "I'm sorry to have left you for so long. I had no idea things would get so bad. How is our mother? The last time I saw her, she was raining curses down on my name, so I supposed she was hale and hearty enough, but I've been told she's been taken ill. Perhaps without me to shed her ire on, she had no one to turn on but herself."

"She is gravely ill, sister," said Vasilisa Vasilisovna, sounding concerned and also a little reproachful. "It is good that you returned when you did. Much later, and..." She trailed off.

"I am very sorry to hear that," said Olga, sounding uncommonly sober and sincere. The young woman who had to be her daughter barked out another disbelieving laugh.

"Be quiet, Lisochka!" cried the man who had to be Andrey Vladislavovich, giving the woman who had to be his daughter a look of intense dislike. "Whom do you have with you?" he demanded, turning to Olga and giving her a look of, if such a thing were possible, even more intense dislike than the one with which he had favored their daughter.

Despite the dimness of the room, Slava could see the deep and permanent expression of anxious dissatisfaction that his face had set into. Slava had met people like him before—lots of them, unfortunately. They so desperately wanted to be clever and important, and they were almost sure that they were, but they were just clever enough to be haunted by a niggling doubt, never clever enough to face the doubt and defeat it, and so they went through life like a terribly vain person with no mirrors—always preening, and always pretending that they weren't checking to see if their clothes were on straight, and never able to rid themselves of the fear that others were laughing at them.

And because of that fear they were cowards, and because of their cowardice they were able to inflict the tyranny of the weak upon the strong, and bully everyone else into catering to their every whim. In other words, the most annoying and difficult kind of person to deal with in the whole world. Slava suppressed a sigh herself. Sorry as she felt for Andrey Vladislavovich's unhappiness, she couldn't blame Olga for leaving him: she hadn't even managed to speak with him yet, and she was already sick of his company.

"Some of my men," said Olga, waving a hand vaguely at her men. "The rest I had to leave in..."

"Which men?" Andrey Vladislavovich demanded. His voice started rising dangerously. "I want them sent away! Who knows what kind of a threat they pose to us! Knowing the kind of company you keep, no doubt there are even bandits amongst the group!"

"Of course not," lied Olga indignantly. "As if I would take bandits into my group!" Slava hoped that the rest of them managed to keep their faces innocent, and to refrain from looking at Mirik.

"Send them away!" shouted Andrey Vladislavovich. "I won't have the kind of filth you like to drag around with you under my roof!"

"Andrey Vladislavovich..." began Vasilisa Vasilisovna, in a conciliatory tone of voice, but the young woman—Vasilisa Olgovna, Slava remembered, her name was Vasilisa Olgovna—interrupted her, saying, "I agree with my father! Send them away!" in a voice that attempted to be firm but came out somewhere between strident and hysterical.

"Be quiet, Lisochka!" cried Andrey Vladislavovich, in what was probably meant to be a commanding shout, but came out as more of a petulant sob. "I don't need your interference here! Let me think!"

"The hospitality of Lesnograd has grown cold since I was last here," said Oleg Svetoslavovich, stepping forward in front of the other men, who were starting to shuffle and mutter threateningly.

"By all the gods!" screamed Vasilisa Vasilisovna. "Oleg Svetoslavovich!"

"It is good to see you, Vasilisa Vasilisovna," said Oleg Svetoslavovich, bowing deeply.

"It *is* you!" she cried. "How are you...And you haven't changed a bit..."

"It is a long story, Vasilisa Vasilisovna," he said.

"Who is this man?" demanded Andrey Vladislavovich, his face twisting into an even uglier frown than before. "Another of my wife's upjumped peasant lovers? One wasn't enough for you, so you had to train up another?"

"No, Andrey, don't..." said Vasilisa Vasilisovna, trailing off feebly. Andrey Vladislavovich brushed aside her protest and continued, "Has she thrown over the one she used to have—I never can remember his name—or does she keep you both simultaneously? Has she taught you to read and write, and act better than you are, all the while meaning to abandon you? I would put nothing past her depravity...her heartlessness...her readiness to ruin the innocent..."

"How did you end up married to this person, Olga?" asked Oleg Svetoslavovich, deliberately turning his back on Andrey Vladislavovich. Everyone on the dais, even Andrey Vladislavovich, froze into silence.

"I was too young to protect myself, and there was no one there to do it for me," said Olga, sounding unaccustomedly sad.

"I'm very sorry," said Oleg Svetoslavovich. "I put much too much faith in your mother's care, I can see."

Olga shrugged. "I got out in the end," she said.

"Why didn't you set him aside years ago?" asked Oleg Svetosla-vovich.

Olga shrugged again, and nodded in the direction of Vasilisa Ol-govna.

"Of course," said Oleg Svetoslavovich, nodding understandingly. "I suppose I can't even blame you for it."

"WHO IS THIS MAN!" screamed Andrey Vladislavovich, finally breaking free of his shocked immobility.

"Your wife's father, my son," said Oleg Svetoslavovich, turning back to him. "Here to teach you some manners, it seems, since your wife never did. Well, I suppose it's my duty, even after all these years. If I'd been around to give you a proper beating like I should have, none of this trouble would have happened, but as it is, I'll just have to make up for lost time. Lucky for me my own wife taught me to read and write and get above my station years ago, so I can spend all my time dealing with you."

"LIAR!" screamed Andrey Vladislavovich. It was hard to tell in the dimness, but Slava thought his face might have gone purple with rage. She tried not to feel too sorry for him, and failed. She wanted to warn him that everything he was saying was only going to come back to hurt him. Then she realized that she could do that, or at least try. She stepped forward.

"I apologize for stepping into your private family business, but it has been a long and tiring journey," she said. "Is there some place I could rest?"

"Be quiet!" shouted Andrey Vladislavovich. "Who are you to speak when I am speaking? Is everyone in your party as insolent as you are, Olga?!"

"I think we should send them all away, father," said Vasilisa Olgov-na, giving Slava a look of malicious triumph at the thought of having them all thrown out of the kremlin.

"By all the gods, stop giving me advice! You're worse than your mother! I'm the one who rules here, not you!" shrieked Andrey Vla-dislavovich, causing Lisochka to retreat half a step in hurt resentment but not to stop gloating over the imminent ejection of her mother and guests from her own kremlin. Slava had seen many horrible interac-tions between parents and children in her time, but she had to admit that this was one of the most horrifying. She began to wish she were back out on the tundra.

"WHAT IS THIS!!" shouted Olga. "IS THIS HOW LESNOGRAD GREETS ITS GUESTS!? Sister," she lowered her voice and turned to Vasilisa Vasilisovna, "as the true head of our family in our mother's illness, and as the only civilized person present, may I present to you my father, Oleg Svetoslavovich, who as you see is not, in fact, dead; my guide, Yevdoksiya Anastasiyevna, of Naberezhnoye; and, with the greatest sensibility of the honor she has bestowed upon us, Krasnosla-va Tsarinovna."

"Oh...!" cried Vasilisa Vasilisovna in a choked voice. She slid off her chair and dropped down on her knees. "A Tsarinovna in truth?" she asked. "The Empress's sister? Here in Lesnograd?"

"I am very glad to be here, in fabled Lesnograd," said Slava. "In Krasnograd we speculate much about it, but rarely is there anyone who can substantiate our fancies with truth. I must say that the re-ports do not do it justice."

"Oh...!" cried Vasilisa Vasilisovna again. She bowed down to the ground. "Tsarinovna! The honor..."

"You don't really believe this...this...*vagabond* is the Tsarinovna, aunt," said Vasilisa Olgovna, giving Slava another malicious look. "This...this...little *nobody*. We all know how my mother loves to tell tall tales. Surely this is just another one. I can't believe that the *Tsarinovna* would ever consent to join her."

"Shut up!" shrieked Andrey Vladislavovich. "Stop butting in where you're unneeded! Vasilisa! Surely you don't believe this nonsense! The Tsarinovna in my wife's company! Who would ever even think of such a thing!"

"Just look at her, you silly man, and get down on your knees if you know what's good for you!" cried Vasilisa Vasilisovna in despair. "You may not know a Zerkalitsa when you see one, but I do! Just look into her eyes!" She bowed down to the ground again. "Truly, this is a day of wonder!" But Andrey Vladislavovich only sneered and looked away.

"I don't..." Vasilisa Olgovna started to say, looking back and forth between her aunt and her father in confusion, but Slava found herself stepping up to her before she could finish her sentence, and looking deeply into her eyes. Vasilisa Olgovna fell silent.

"Dear Vasilisa Olgovna," said Slava, so softly that only Lisochka could hear her. Words that might make her feel better suddenly filled Slava's head, and she found herself saying them, much to her surprise. "Dear Vasilisa Olgovna, I see you have your family's pride, and rightly so. I am so glad finally to meet you, after having heard so much about you. I know you wish to be able to welcome your family and your guests to your home with the graciousness that befits your noble birth, and I thank you for it. I will be most delighted to reaffirm the ties of blood between our two families."

"I don't believe you," said Vasilisa Olgovna, but with the sullenness of unwilling belief. Perhaps Slava's words really had taken effect. Or perhaps not. Some people found words very easy to forget.

"Don't take offense, Tsarinovna!" cried Vasilisa Vasilisovna, still on her knees. "By all the gods, don't take offense!"

"I rarely take offense," said Slava. "But I am who I claim to be."

"How can we know that?" demanded Andrey Vladislavovich, who seemed to be feeling left out of the conversation. "How can we know that you are not just some adventuress, passing yourself off as the Tsarinovna? What proofs do you have?"

"I can vouch for her," said Olga.

"And how do we know you are not part of this scheme to foist this imposter upon us?" said Andrey Vladislavovich, giving Olga a look of deep loathing.

"If she's an imposter, then the entire Krasnograd kremlin is part of the deception," said Olga, starting to sound impatient.

"So you say," said Andrey Vladislavovich.

"Andrey! Please!" said Vasilisa Vasilisovna in a strangled whisper. Slava tried to guess whether the rumors about them were true, and whether they really were lovers, but she couldn't tell. If they were, there was little love lost between them.

"It doesn't matter whether you believe me or not," she said. "And surely you have more pressing matters to discuss anyway. Vasilisa Vasilisovna, please rise: there's no need for you to be on your knees when everyone else is sitting around quarreling."

"Isn't that the truth," Olga muttered under her breath. Vasilisa Vasilisovna rose hesitantly and sat back in her chair, still watching Slava with the air of a dog with an ill-tempered mistress.

"Now that the introductions are over, I would see my mother," said Olga. "Please see to it that my men are properly housed."

Andrey Vladislavovich opened his mouth to refuse her, but Vasilisa Vasilisovna forestalled him by saying quickly, "We cannot turn away guests, especially in winter. Lisochka, please see to the necessary arrangements. And give the Tsarinovna the finest quarters."

Vasilisa Olgovna looked like she wanted to argue with that, but in the end she got out of her chair and set off with bad grace, ordering the men to follow her with a bad-tempered jerk of her head.

"Oh, please, stay, Oleg Svetoslavovich, I'm sure our mother would wish to see you," said Vasilisa Vasilisovna, when he made to follow the others. "And the Tsarinovna, if she is not too tired and would deign to..."

"Of course," said Slava quickly.

"I can't believe you're being taken in by this ridiculous charade, Vasilisa," said Andrey Vladislavovich. Slava winced. She wondered if he would have enough sense to feel embarrassed once he became convinced of her real identity, or if that kind of thing were beyond him. She wondered what kind of thoughts ran through his head in general, and if they could be dignified with the name "thoughts." Vasilisa Vasilisovna only shook her head slightly and stood up from her chair.

"Well, I...I have many matters to attend to," said Andrey Vladislavovich, and stood up from his chair too. He gave Olga and the others another look of deepest loathing, and strode off. Slava could hear him shouting at the guards outside the Great Hall, pouring out all the cruelty he hadn't been able to pour out onto Olga and the rest of them. She wondered how long it would take for him to alienate the guards who were currently eating out of his hand, and drive away his only allies through his own foolishness. Not long, no doubt. Slava supposed that would be better for Olga, but she couldn't help but feel sorry for him anyway, and wish he could be more sensible.

"There are so many things I would know," said Vasilisa Vasilisovna, interrupting Slava's thoughts. She looked from Oleg Svetoslavovich to Slava and back again. "I hardly even know where to start. But I'm sure our mother has been given word of your arrival, Olya, and will wish to see you immediately."

"There are so many things I'd like to know too," said Olga. "Such as how come Andrey Vladislavovich was sitting in the chair that was rightfully yours. How could you, Vasya? Have you no shame! What were you thinking?"

"Oh, Olya, you always judge so harshly," said Vasilisa Vasilisovna, wringing her hands. "You can't imagine how hard it's been..."

"I don't care! How did Andrey Vladislavovich end up making the decisions around here? And Lisochka! Such sulking! I've half a mind to slap her face right here and now! And if I hear any complaints from my men, I will."

"Oh, Olya...How can you talk so...Your own daughter...But I'm sure she'll take good care of your men. Was that not Dima, standing there in the back?"

"It was," said Olga firmly.

"Oh, Olya..." Vasilisa Vasilisovna wrung her hands even more. "Don't you think...It might be better...It's tactless, you know, heartless to make Andrey and Lisochka have him under their roof..."

"It'll be good for them," said Olga.

"Oh, Olya..."

"Vasya!" shouted Olga. "The petty problems of my husband and daughter are not our concern now! I'm sure they feel plenty sorry for themselves without us adding to the burden! Now tell me: how did this happen? How did our mother fall ill? And how, by all the gods, did Andrey of all people end up ruling Lesnograd? I'm ashamed to call you sister, Vasya, sitting there at his side instead of rousting him out of that chair and sending him where he belongs! So explain it to me, Vasya, because I'm having a very hard time understanding it right now! If I didn't know better, I'd think Princess Primorskaya was right, and you've taken your own brother as a husband!"

"Oh Olya..." Vasilisa Vasilisovna wrung her hands yet again, but then composed herself. "Follow me," she said. "I will take you to our mother, and tell you as we go. If that suits you, that is." She gave them all a nervous look.

"Very well. Lead the way, and tell your story," said Olga.

Vasilisa Vasilisovna, stopping herself just in time from even more hand-wringing, led them to the other side of the Great Hall from which they had entered. To Slava's relief, this meant they did not have to pass directly by the great fire again. She was sweating more and more, and wished that she could bathe and put on something clean before meeting Princess Severnolesnaya. Vasilisa Vasilisovna did not seem to be wrinkling up her nose at her, at least, but perhaps she was too afraid of her to do so.

They passed from the Great Hall to a narrow corridor lit by a single candle at each end, which meant that most of it was pitch dark. Olga reached back and took Slava's hand, which was the only thing that prevented her from blundering into the walls.

"There's nothing between me and Andrey," Vasilisa Vasilisovna suddenly blurted out.

"That's too bad," said Olga.

"Oh Olya! How could you! As if either of us would...!"

"I'm speaking seriously," said Olga. "It's too bad. I don't consider

416

him my husband anymore, and your own husband is...well, not a husband. So if you want to...I won't stand in your way. I'd even be glad for you. The gods know, I'm no great advocate of marital fidelity."

"Oh Olya! As if I would ever...act as you have!"

They walked along in the dark for a while, with both Olga and Vasilisa Vasilisovna steaming with indignation at the other, but trying not to scream at each other even so, which must, Slava thought, have been a sore trial for both of them, especially as they both were no doubt lacking in practice at restraining themselves from acrimonious outcries.

"As you know, our mother was...she did not fully support your latest venture," said Vasilisa Vasilisovna's voice from somewhere in the darkness ahead.

"You mean she was pissing herself with rage," said Olga. "She wanted to disinherit me."

"Oh, Olya..."

"Only she was afraid of what would happen to Lesnograd without me for an heir, and I can see why," said Olga.

"Oh Olya, you're so harsh..."

"Enough! Carry on with the story, Vasya."

The candle at the far end of the corridor started to cast a little light in their direction, meaning that Slava no longer had to clutch at Olga's hand in order to keep from falling. Neither of the sisters seemed to have any trouble in the darkness. Slava supposed they had walked that corridor so many times that they no longer even noticed whether it was light or dark there.

"She even threatened to disinherit Lisochka," said Vasilisa Vasilisovna.

"WHAT!" Olga's shout came out even louder than she had expected, and echoed down the corridor. "Sorry," she said. "But WHAT! She wanted to disinherit Lisochka! What was she thinking!"

"She and Lisochka have been at odds of late," said Vasilisa Vasilisovna. "She felt that Lisochka is not...is not the kind of...is not the material from which leaders are made."

"Too right," said Olga. "I'd disinherit her myself if I could. But that doesn't mean I'd let our mother do it. I'm afraid Lisochka is my burden, and I'm the only one who gets to decide how to dispose of her... and the only reason she was born was to provide a spare heir...I can't believe our mother would even think of disinheriting her..."

Olga's voice had grown uncommonly agitated, and Slava could

feel her in the dark, clutching her right arm to her chest as if it pained her. Slava's own arm began to ache in sympathy, and she suddenly saw that, despite all her harsh words, there was some part of Olga that was meant to be a good mother, that could have been a good mother if she had not had Lisochka, but had instead borne some other daughter under some other set of circumstances, but now it was too late, and that that part of Olga had been wasted forever, and that however good a mother she could have been to some other girl, she and Lisochka would never be anything but a torment to each other.

"Oh Olya," said Vasilisa Vasilisovna, interrupting Slava's thoughts before they could become even more gloomy. "Poor Lisochka has been having a very hard time of it, you know, and you do nothing to help her."

"She's old enough to help herself," said Olga. "She doesn't need to be hiding behind my skirts all the time—it only encourages her whining." Slava wondered how she could be so right and yet so wrong, because Lisochka *did* desperately need to be made to stand on her own, but even more than that, Slava could already see, she desperately, desperately needed a mother's love, but that was never going to happen. Slava could not help but hope that Lisochka's manifest lack of charm drove off any and all of her suitors, and that the line stopped with her, because she couldn't see any good at all coming from her producing daughters of her own.

"Oh Olya! Your own little daughter!" Vasilisa Vasilisovna's reproach to Olga made Slava feel even guiltier than she would have already over her thoughts about Lisochka, even though she knew that she was right.

"Yes, well...Oh, never mind," said Olga. Clearly she was more sensible than Slava about this, even though it was her own tragedy, not Slava's. Slava resolved to stop dwelling on it, if she could. "Carry on with your story."

"The next part I don't really know," said Vasilisa Vasilisovna. She came to the end of the corridor, which was now almost light enough for safe walking, and opened the door onto a much larger, finer, and more well-lit corridor. She crossed that and started up a broad set of stairs. She climbed with more agility than Slava would have expected, and turned her head back and talked to them as she climbed without any noticeable effort. For the first time, Slava could see the resemblance between her and Olga.

"There was some kind of a plan, some kind of a scheme," Vasilisa

Vasilisovna continued. "None of us—that is, me, Andrey, and Lisoch-ka—none of us were involved. Our mother would not even admit that there was a plan, but all fall she was meeting with her sorceresses day and night. And then a few days ago a great commotion arose in the dead of night, and when I rushed to her chambers, I discovered her lying on her bed in some kind of a fit, surrounded by her maids and sorceresses. For the first day she could not speak at all. She has regained some of her abilities, but she is still very weak and confused, and I am not sure she will ever recover fully."

"And?" said Olga.

"And what?" demanded Vasilisa Vasilisovna. "That is all I know, as I told you. I don't even know how...what happened, happened. No one will admit to being with her when she collapsed, or being complicit in any of her schemes. Well, except for Vladenka, but...I've forbidden her even to speak of it...A little girl like her...She's troubled enough as it is, poor thing, everyone says she just needs a good beating," Slava could hear the pleasure in her voice at the thought of beating her daughter, "but I won't hear of it," she added hastily and too late, "...I won't hear of it, no matter how she tries my patience, how she tries my patience...Perhaps it was a simple fit that struck our mother, as they claim—after all, our grandmother suffered one too, before she died. I have my doubts, but I cannot prove them, and the city has been in such an uproar ever since the incident that I have had little leisure to investigate."

"Which brings me back to my earlier question," said Olga. "Why was Andrey sitting in our mother's seat? What have you been doing, Vasya, since you obviously haven't been ruling the city. And how could you let some...some incompetent interloper take control of our own Lesnograd, our native city? What were you thinking?!"

"Just because you're ashamed of the way you've treated Andrey and the rest of us is no reason for us to suffer from your bad temper, Olya," said Vasilisa Vasilisovna, coming to an abrupt halt and turning to face Olga.

"My bad temper! Well, I think I have a right to it..."

"Oh stop! You've been singing the same song for twenty years, and it..."

"Girls!" interjected Oleg Svetoslavovich. "Now is not the time or the place for sisterly squabbling! Enough!"

Both Olga and Vasilisa Vasilisovna turned and glared at him with identical glares. He laughed. "Well, at least you can present a united front when you need to," he said.

Olga also laughed heartily at that, and after a moment, even Vasil-isa Vasilisovna smiled a little.

"I'm sorry for shouting at you, Vasya," said Olga, not sounding par-ticularly contrite. "But I still want to know how someone who is not really competent or even of our family ended up taking your rightful place."

"Andrey has had it very hard, you know, Olya," said Vasilisa Vasil-isovna, starting up the stairs again. "He always had dreams of ruling, you know. Princess Primorskaya raised him practically as a daughter, not a son, and he always took pride in his abilities, he always thought he should have been born a woman, he almost was as able as a woman in many ways...Coming here was a heavy blow for him. Had he not married you, he could have inherited Vostochnoye Selo outright— Princess Primorskaya was soft about him and his father that way—but instead he ended up here, and his mother's property will skip over him and go straight to Lisochka.

"He thought at least he would be valued here, you know, the fa-ther for so long of the only granddaughter—oh, how I wish he could learn to love Vladenka! She's done him no injury, no injury at all, but he can't bear her, poor man—he thought he would be given some... some chance to prove his worth, but instead...Abandoned by his wife, a hanger-on for all these years. So now, when the time came, he was so glad to step forward...He had long been riding out into the town and the surrounding countryside, befriending the guards and the servants, giving them money and promising to make their lot better when he got his chance...Our mother was not merciful, you know, and there is much resentment against her in some quarters, so many were happy to listen and support someone...not of our blood...I knew it was...not the best situation, but we needed his popularity...and... and...I have many cares, you know, with Dima and Vladenka, and our mother falling ill...There is no one else to care for the family but me..." They came to the top of the stairs and turned down a corridor towards what were clearly the family quarters. Guards were standing outside one of the doors.

"Well, I suppose I can understand," said Olga. Her face said that she didn't understand, but she had decided to try to stop arguing for the moment.

The guards bowed at Vasilisa Vasilisovna and said, one gladly and one sullenly, "Welcome home, Olga Vasilisovna," before opening the door and letting them into the princess's private chambers. They glanced briefly at Slava and Oleg Svetoslavovich, but without evincing much curiosity—apparently word of their identity had not yet reached the second floor.

Slava had a moment of disorientation on stepping into Princess Severnolesnaya's chambers. Their layout and furnishings were so similar to that of her own chambers at home that for a moment she stood there wondering how she had suddenly arrived back in Krasnograd. Then she remembered that her chambers back home had once been guest quarters, and that some former Princess Severnolesnaya must have stayed in them and decided to furnish her own apartments in a similarly imperial style.

A second look around the room showed Slava all the little signs of tastelessness and barbaric splendor that she would have expected from a Severnolesnaya, such as the heavy gold frame around the mirror and the piles of bearskins in the corner, and this allowed her to remember that she was in Lesnograd and focus back on the matter at hand.

The sitting room had a hearth with an open fire that was blazing fiercely. Two maids were sitting in front of it and embroidering something, but when Vasilisa Vasilisovna and the others came in, they jumped up and bowed, and then bowed again when they recognized Olga, and then gave a third bow to Slava and Oleg Svetoslavovich, apparently for good measure.

"How fares my mother?" asked Vasilisa Vasilisovna.

One of the maids, a pleasant, round-faced woman with a motherly look in her round blue eyes, said, "The same as this morning, Vasilisa Vasilisovna. Vasilisa Lyudmilovna came to briefly while you were downstairs, and called for Vladislava Vasilisovna, who's with her now, but she's lapsed back into dreaming, I'm afraid. Baba Vlastya is sitting with her, along with the little princess."

"But she's not been raving?" asked Vasilisa Vasilisovna anxiously.

"Oh no, Vasilisa Vasilisovna," the pleasant-faced maid assured her. "Lying there quiet as can be. I'm afraid it's been a bit dull for Vladislava Vasilisovna, but she's being a good girl for once, she's been sitting there nice and quiet and stroking her hand from time to time, to give her comfort, you know."

"Well, perhaps we should go in…" said Vasilisa Vasilisovna, looking at the party uncertainly.

"Perhaps Oleg Svetoslavovich and I should wait out here," suggested Slava. "We wouldn't want to over-excite her. Let her get used to Olga's arrival before we spring any more newcomers on her."

"You're very kind to say so, noblewoman, but I dare say she wouldn't notice if you paraded all the handsomest men of Krasnogorod past her," said the pleasant-faced maid, smiling at Oleg Svetoslavovich.

"Even so, the..." Vasilisa Vasilisovna gave Slava another uncertain look, as if she didn't know what to do with her, and her thoughtfulness had taken her by surprise, "the Tsarinovna is right," she finished bravely. "Best not to risk over-exciting her."

The maids' heads whipped round in Slava's direction. "The Tsar..." began the pleasant-faced maid disbelievingly, and then trailed off in shock.

"Please, there's no need to stand on ceremony," said Slava. "Oleg Svetoslavovich and I will wait out here. I'm sure we'll be perfectly comfortable."

"That we will, Tsarinovna," agreed Oleg Svetoslavovich. "Perfectly comfortable, especially...Is that tea there?"

"It is," said the other maid, breaking the silence she had maintained until then. She was much younger than the first maid, still more of a girl than a woman, and her eyes moved back and forth from Slava, whom she seemed to find an object of intense but slightly confused curiosity, to Oleg Svetoslavovich, whom she clearly found an object of intense and not at all confused desire. Slava supposed that the ability to turn young girls' heads was one of the qualities that had recommended him to the gods.

"You're welcome to have some," said the girl. She bowed in Slava's direction. "And the...the Tsarinovna as well, of course," she said. "It's been standing a while, but it's no doubt still fine." She moved towards the tea, then blurted out, "Are you really the Tsarinovna? All the way from Krasnogorod?"

"Really," said both Slava and Oleg Svetoslavovich at the same time. "But she's a very small, sweet Tsarinovna," added Oleg Svetoslavovich with a grin. "She hardly bites at all. Now what about that tea? It sounds tempting—standing a while is just the way I like it." The girl blushed happily and went to get the tea. Olga rolled her eyes before following Vasilisa Vasilisovna into the other room.

"Won't you...Won't you have a seat, Tsarinovna?" asked the older maid nervously.

"That would be most welcome," said Slava, giving her a grateful smile and allowing her to arrange her in front of the too-hot fire and fuss over her. The younger maid fussed over Oleg Svetoslavovich, and soon they were both ensconced in too-soft chairs in front of the too-hot fire and drinking too-strong tea while the maids hovered over them too anxiously. Slava tried to put them at ease by saying a few pleasantries, but only succeeded in frightening them more. Oleg Svetoslavovich soon took the younger maid's mind off her nerves by joking with her, but the older maid continued to watch Slava as if fearing that Slava would either turn and attack her or fall ill for no reason. Slava tried not to let it annoy her.

"This must be a very tedious duty for you, caring for the sick princess," Oleg Svetoslavovich was saying to the younger maid.

"It can be pretty boring when she's asleep, but it's even worse when she's awake and sick in the head," admitted the younger maid candidly, ignoring the older maid's attempts to hush her. "And taking care of sick people is always a chore. But I used to work down in the kitchens, so this is better. Here we get to sit in peace sometimes and sew."

"And very fine sewing you do, too," said Oleg Svetoslavovich, looking over at the work the maid had put down on their entrance. Slava glanced at it too, and decided that he was being generous—the girl was working some kind of very gaudy and unattractive design on the front of a shirt.

"My own design," said the girl proudly.

"Very nice," said Oleg Svetoslavovich. Now Slava was certain, by the way he smiled as he said it, that he was being generous on purpose, for some design of his own. She wondered if he were planning to turn the head of his wife's maid while his wife lay dying in the next chamber. She would have liked to think better of him.

"Do you like to sew?" he asked the maid, leaning forward with every sign of interest.

"Yes, I never got much chance in the kitchens, but I used to do it every chance I got. Then the old princess fell sick and they needed more maids up here, and they knew about my sewing so they called on me because they knew I wouldn't waste my time while I was sitting here—not like a lot of those girls down there that do nothing but moon after the guards every chance they get. It's been three days and I'm already on my second shirt, even though I have to spend time taking care of the old princess—bathing her and taking out her chamber pot and such. It's not very nice work, but it's better than the kitchens, like I said, and I have time for sewing."

"How lucky for you," said Oleg Svetoslavovich, and Slava realized he was gathering information from the girl, and much more adroitly than she could have managed herself, most likely. She was glad he had failed to fulfill her low expectations, and a little chagrined with herself for having them in the first place. Clearly Oleg Svetoslavovich required a sharper eye than she had given him thus far.

"Yes, very lucky," the girl was saying. "I was down in the kitchens, sleeping, you know, when the old princess had her fit, but the commotion was so great it woke us all up and we found out straight away what was going on, well, as much as anyone knew then. Not that we know any more now—it's a great mystery what happened to her. They say it's a fit but we all know some kind of dark magic was involved."

"Ksyusha!" hissed the older maid, but Ksyusha ignored her and chattered on and on about the old princess's meddling in dark magic and drawing the little princess into her schemes against Vasilisa Vasilisovna's will, and all sorts of other gossip, mostly about how Andrey Vladislavovich had been running around with the guards ever since he had gotten back from his journey out to some village, and how a lot of the guards were spoiled completely from all his attention, completely swollen-headed and above their station, or that was the word in the kitchen anyway, until Olga came back out of the bedroom and asked Slava and Oleg to come in.

"She's half-awake and wants to see you both," Olga whispered to them as they entered the room. "I'm not sure if she'll know you when she does see you, though."

"Why are you whispering, Olya?" called a voice that still managed to be ill-tempered despite its weakness. "What secrets are you trying to keep from me?"

"I was just warning them..." Olga began, but then stopped herself and said, "I think you're growing stronger by the minute, mother! How wonderful!" instead.

"Oh, stop your flattery and lies, Olya, it doesn't suit you," said the voice. It was coming from the bed in the middle of the darkened room. As Slava drew closer, she could see that the voice was housed in the skeletal frame of a woman who had once been large and strapping. This, Slava thought, must be Vasilisa Lyudmilovna, the infamous Princess Severnolesnaya.

Vasilisa Lyudmilovna's eyes glittered at them peevishly from the candlelight, and she tried to haul herself up in the bed, but without success, which made her even more peevish. Vasilisa Vasilisovna was standing at the head of the bed and making ineffectual moves to try to keep her mother still. An old woman and a young girl were sitting by the far side of the bed. The girl's eyes fixed hungrily on Olga and Slava for a moment as they drew near the bed, before veiling themselves again and turning back to what was, Slava assumed, her grandmother.

The girl had to be, Slava thought, Vladislava Vasilisovna, heir to Lesnograd. She was, Slava thought, about ten years old, but her face was much more shuttered and composed than the face of a girl of ten should have been. Slava felt sorry for her, and also a little bit afraid, although she couldn't have said why. There was just something indefinably dangerous about her. Even though she was still a child, Slava wasn't entirely sure that she liked her. She remembered what Vasilisa Vasilisovna had said about everyone calling for her to be beaten, and her heart squeezed so painfully for a moment she thought she might be sick. No one, Slava promised herself, would lay a finger on this sharp-faced little girl she wasn't even sure she liked, not as long as she had the strength to prevent it.

"I woke up to see the Tsarinovna, of course, and my dear husband, who has returned from the grave," said Vasilisa Lyudmilovna in a voice that managed to be both weak and harsh at the same time. "I would be surprised, but I don't have the strength, and frankly, my dear Oleg, it's perfectly in character for you. You never were very reliable, and it seems you couldn't even manage to stay dead for long. An enviable problem, really. And of course, who wouldn't expect to find a Tsarinovna snooping around in her business?"

After this long outburst, all delivered in one frantic breath, Vasilisa Lyudmilovna collapsed back on her pillows, and gasped painfully.

"Oh mother..." said Vasilisa Vasilisovna, and then, pausing and visibly forcing herself to sound less irritated, continued, "It is wonderful news about Oleg Svetoslavovich, is it not? And such an honor for us to have a Tsarinovna in our very kremlin!"

Still too weak to talk, Vasilisa Lyudmilovna was forced to limit herself to grunting dismissively and fixing Slava with a mistrustful glare.

"And there is a great tale behind both of them," said Olga. "Strange doings, the likes of which none of us have ever witnessed before! When you are stronger, we must tell you all of it—you and your sorceresses. In truth, that is why we came to Lesnograd, to consult with them..." She trailed off as Vasilisa Lyudmilovna turned her glare towards her, and bit her lip, probably to keep from shouting at her ailing mother.

"Sorceresses..." said Vasilisa Lyudmilovna after a moment. She closed her eyes, gathering her strength, and then finished, "Charlatans, the lot of them. Dismissed..."

Everyone waited for her to say more, but instead she appeared to drift off into whatever dream-state it was that held her in its grip.

"That is all for the day, I would say," said Baba Vlastya, who until then had maintained a solemn silence while the noblewomen spoke. "We won't be hearing from her for another day at least, I would guess."

"What did she mean about the sorceresses?" asked Olga. "Did she really dismiss them all?"

"So it seems," said Vasilisa Vasilisovna. "The kremlin has been talking of nothing else for days, but *I* know little of it—she does not keep *me* apprised of such things, and I do not consort with sorceresses—I have my own cares."

"She did," said Vladislava Vasilisovna. Everyone turned and stared at her in surprise. She stared back, unabashed by being the object of so much adult attention. "As soon as she came to the first time, she called them all to her bed and dismissed them for their failure. I was there."

"Why were you there without me!" cried Vasilisa Vasilisovna, her face twisting up in an angry look at odds with her natural look of incompetence. Baba Vlastya made hushing motions, nodding significantly in the direction of the bed, but no one paid her any attention.

"You never showed an interest in what we were doing," said Vladislava Vasilisovna. "You weren't there when it happened."

"And so my mother just thinks to use my own daughter without consulting me?" demanded Vasilisa Vasilisovna. "What right does she have to drag you into such things? And without even speaking with me about it? I should hope I at least have a voice in the welfare of my own daughter!" Her voice was rising higher and higher, and she presented the ridiculous appearance of a weak-willed person who had snapped and decided to put her foot down, but, being weak-willed and incompetent, didn't even know how to get angry properly.

"Please, Vasya, not here..." said Olga soothingly, while Vladislava Vasilisovna stared at her mother with a level look guaranteed to drive any parent into a frenzy. Of the four potential claimants in the room to the title of Princess Severnolesnaya, Slava could see who had the most right to it. It was a shame she was still so young, although of course time would cure that problem. Slava still wasn't sure she liked Vladislava Vasilisovna very much, but she was undeniably the only person there who was fit to rule Lesnograd.

"You see what it's like, Olya," said Vasilisa Vasilisovna, her voice

426

rising with every word. "You see how they treat me. Not given a say even in the raising of my own daughter! You see how they ignore me! You see now why I couldn't take on the responsibility of ruling the city, don't you? I must be watching constantly or they will act behind my back! My daughter takes all my time and attention, and even that is not enough! How can I turn my energies to anything else? I saw what they did to you, how they took Lisochka away from you, how you were so ready to abandon her, and I swore: not my daughter! That would not happen to me! If I could be nothing else, at least I would be a good mother! At least Vladya would have a good mother, no matter how hard they tried to take her away from me!"

"A good mother would have taught me how to rule, not stood back and wrung her hands," said Vladislava Vasilisovna coolly.

"Now, little princess..." said Baba Vlastya, making placating motions with her hands, but Vladislava Vasilisovna interrupted her by standing up abruptly.

"I have to go," she said. "I am needed elsewhere. Stay here and cry if you like."

Vasilisa Vasilisovna tried to say something, but it came out as more of an angry shriek. A pathetic angry shriek, but an angry shriek nonetheless. She lunged at Vladislava Vasilisovna as she walked by, but Olga restrained her, and, after fixing her mother with a contemptuous stare, Vladislava Vasilisovna walked out of the room unhindered.

"You see..." gasped Vasilisa Vasilisovna. "You see why I must... constantly...They are trying to take her away from me...It must be some spell...She has grown so contrary and difficult...First Lisochka, and now her...I swore it would be different with my own daughter, I swore..."

"Now, now, calm yourself, my dear," said Baba Vlastya. "Daughters are difficult, everyone knows, but I'm sure she loves you..."

"And I'm sure you're behaving like a fool," Olga interrupted her. "No wonder she's being difficult! She's right, you know: a good mother would have taught her how to rule."

Vasilisa Vasilisovna's face started to swell up with another angry shriek. A sharp pain stabbed Slava behind her left eye.

"Excuse me," she said. No one paid her any attention, so she began to back out of the room. No one was still paying her any attention, so she backed right out of the room, past the maids, who gave her curious and startled looks but did nothing to stop her, and right out into the corridor. The guards gave her less curious looks and also did nothing to stop her as she hurried down the corridor after Vladislava Vasilisovna, who was just disappearing around the corner, with an incongruously determined stride for a girl of ten.

"Vladislava!" Slava called after her, breaking into a painful jog. Her legs and stomach immediately began to cramp from too many hours standing in the overheated rooms with no food or water, but she forced herself to keep running. "Vladislava Vasilisovna!"

"What!" Vladislava Vasilisovna turned and faced her with an angry expression that smoothed over slightly when she recognized Slava. "Tsarinovna," she said, with a slight bow. Her bow was awkward and ill-practiced, betraying her lack of experience with noble company other than her family.

"Are you allowed to walk about unaccompanied and unguarded, Vladislava Vasilisovna?" Slava asked her with a smile, trying to pretend that sharp pains were not shooting through her whole body.

"It's my kremlin, Tsarinovna," said Vladislava, giving her a suspicious and haughty look. "Why shouldn't I walk wherever I want to?"

"Where are you going now, Vladislava Vasilisovna?" Slava asked her, still smiling in what she hoped was a soothing fashion. Vladislava gave her another deeply suspicious look. Slava supposed she had her reasons for not trusting well-meaning adults. Now that she was up close to her, Slava, of course, felt sorry for her. She could see that Vladislava was well aware that she was a ruler trapped in a little girl's body, and that her every moment was a struggle to make the adults around her, who so constantly disappointed her, see her for what she was, which was, of course, a doomed enterprise. Adults, especially mothers, aunts, and grandmothers, could be so stupid that way.

"I have things I have to do," said Vladislava impatiently.

"I'm sure you do," said Slava. "You seem like a very capable girl. May I walk with you, Vladislava Vasilisovna?"

"Why?" asked Vladislava, regarding Slava with even more suspicion than she had previously, if such a thing were possible.

"Sisterly squabbles are no place for an outsider," said Slava, she hoped disarmingly. "And I wish to see your kremlin and the people in it. And to become better acquainted with you, Vladislava Vasilisovna."

"Why?" demanded Vladislava again. She started walking once more briskly down the hall.

"Why not?" asked Slava, following her. They came around a corner and stepped into a pool of torchlight, letting Slava examine Vladislava more closely. Her dark eyes stared stubbornly ahead out of her small oval face, and her head was bent down a little, as if she truly were carrying heavy cares. Slava felt even more sorry for her, and also for Vasilisa Vasilisovna.

"Your mother loves you, you know," Slava told her. "All this...All these scenes and so on, it's because she loves you."

"That's what everyone says," said Vladislava coldly. "And then they remind me to be grateful." Her voice started to rise. "Were you going to remind me to be grateful? Because I won't be grateful to someone who treats me so badly, just because she claims she does it out of love. If she truly loved me, she wouldn't act like that."

"Well...yes," agreed Slava. "But she thinks she loves you, and you'll never be able to disabuse her of that notion. And she thinks you should love her back even more."

"That's just stupid," said Vladislava Vasilisovna, but her face was already smoothing from the relief of Slava's words. Slava guessed that Vladislava was used to having everyone disagree with her, and that she was starving for just one person to be able to see what she saw and admit it, instead of pretending that matters were entirely different from how they really were. And the worst thing was that whenever anyone tried to soothe her wounded feelings by telling her that things were better than they really were, it only confirmed her worst surmises, and she felt even more alone and miserable than she had before.

Slava knew this because she had often felt the same way. The pain of being surrounded by well-intentioned liars must have been intense for such a bright girl as Vladislava. "She's the mother," continued Vladislava unsympathetically. "Let her be the one to act like it. And there are other things we should all be worrying about more anyway."

"Such as?" asked Slava.

"Such as Lesnograd," said Vladislava Vasilisovna. She sounded as if she truly meant it, odd as it was to see such a slip of a girl taking an interest in the fate of a city. She started walking again, and Slava hurried after her.

"Are things really so bad, then?" asked Slava.

"That's a stupid question and you know it," said Vladislava Vasilisovna impatiently. "Of course things are really so bad, anyone can see just by looking. Grandmother is sick, Mother is useless, Father is a half-wit, Lisochka is hysterical, Aunty Olya is never around, Andrey Vladislavovich thinks he knows how to rule without actually ruling, the guards are getting out of hand, and the sorceresses have all left the city, leaving behind nothing but threats and curses. Things are much worse than really so bad."

"The sorceresses have left the city!" cried Slava. Her heart sank more than she would have expected at this unwelcome news. Until that moment she had not realized how much she had been counting on their help, although she wasn't sure what they would be able to do for her. "What, all of them?"

"All the ones who could do anything," said Vladislava Vasilisovna. "All the ones that were hired by Grandmother, which means all the ones worth hiring. As soon as she dismissed them, they laid a curse upon this city and left, and no one has seen hide nor hair of them since. As far as I know, anyway. So now I'm going to go see if I can find them, and maybe bring them back."

"What kind of a curse?" asked Slava.

"They said Grandmother would rue the day she raised a hand in magic against her enemies," said Vladislava. "That magic would always serve them rather than her."

"The sorceresses or the enemies?" asked Slava.

"Maybe both." Vladislava shrugged. "Although now the sorceresses are her enemies, too."

"And you think you can find them and change their minds?" asked Slava.

"Maybe." Vladislava started down a flight of stairs, smaller and darker than the one Slava had come up. "They want me, after all."

"They do? Why?"

Vladislava gave her a scornful look. "Why do sorceresses want anybody?"

"They think you can become one of them," said Slava. "Can you?"

Vladislava gave her another scornful look. "The Severnolesnaya family does not rule Lesnograd for nothing, Tsarinovna," she said impatiently. "We have more sorceresses in our bloodline than any other family in Zem', even yours."

"Do you want to be a sorceress?" Slava asked her, trying not to trip on the dark stairs. Zerkalitsa pride she had not even known existed was trying to make her contradict Vladislava's statement, but she hushed it. In the end, the important thing was not how many sorceresses the Severnolesniye might have produced, but whether or not Vladislava wanted to join their ranks.

"Oh yes," said Vladislava, answering Slava's spoken question and also echoing her unspoken thoughts, requiring Slava to make a quick run through what she had and hadn't said out loud. Vladislava hurried along in silence for a few more steps, and then added, "Mother thinks it's too dangerous, and tells me it's my duty to rule Lesnograd, anyway, but since she won't let me rule, I have to do something. And I would be a good sorceress. Do you know what it's like to be good at something, Tsarinovna?" Her last question was no doubt meant to sound as arrogant and impatient as everything else she said, but instead it was full of a tremulous hope that perhaps somewhere in the world there was someone who might understand.

"I know what it is like to have a gift," Slava told her gently. "Is that what you mean, Vladislava Vasilisovna?"

"You have a gift?" Vladislava stopped and looked at Slava for a moment in surprise, suspicion, and a flash of slightly less tremulous hope. "What kind of a gift? What can you do? Are you very good at it?"

"I can feel what others feel," Slava told her. "And I am very good at it."

"That's not a very useful gift, is it?" said Vladislava dismissively, her face falling. "What can you do with a gift like that? It would be better if you could read minds or see across great distances, at least. I thought that's what you Zerkalitsy did."

"Sometimes I can do those things as well," Slava told her. "And sometimes I dream true dreams. But mostly I feel what other people feel. And I used to think it was not a very useful gift, just as you do, but perhaps we were both wrong. Perhaps it is a very useful gift."

"Or perhaps you're just trying to make yourself feel better about your useless gift," said Vladislava, giving her another level look.

"Perhaps," said Slava with a laugh. The more she spoke with Vladislava, the more she liked her, her rudeness notwithstanding. Despite everyone's efforts to put her down she was, Slava could see, painfully honest and very, very clever, which were such refreshing traits to encounter. "How are you planning to find the sorceresses?" Slava asked her. "If they've disappeared, leaving behind only a curse."

"I know some herbwomen," Vladislava told her, hurrying down the steps once more. "You can come with me if you want." They came to a corridor on the ground floor, and Vladislava started down it with a purposeful stride. "You can borrow some of my mother's outer clothing, if you wish," she said. "We'll be going outside, and you'll freeze in what you're wearing now."

"Thank you," Slava said, making sure not to show her smile.

They did in fact soon come to a small vestibule full of cloaks and hats. Slava kept expecting to be stopped by guards and provided with an escort, but they encountered no one. Vladislava told her what clothing to put on, and criticized her method of wrapping herself in her shawl, to Slava's great amusement, which she took pains not to show.

Once she was attired to Vladislava's satisfaction, they stepped outside into a back alley behind the kremlin. Once again no one stopped them, not even when Vladislava opened a small gate in the wall and led Slava out into the city.

"Do the guards not watch the wall?" Slava asked.

"What would there be to watch for back here?" said Vladislava.

"Thieves?" suggested Slava. "Assassins? Princesses sneaking out unescorted?"

Vladislava almost smiled. "Maybe we should be glad they don't watch," she said. "Do you always have guards with you, Tsarinovna?"

"Always," Slava told her. "Before I came here, I'd never been anywhere without at least half-a-dozen maids and guards dogging at my heels."

"You poor thing." Vladislava gave her a pitying look. "Mother's always trying to keep me under her eye, but it's easy enough to slip away from her, and no one else bothers much. Grandmother sometimes tries to assign an escort to me, but it always turns out to be too much trouble, and she gives up. She has more important things to worry about than keeping track of a wayward little girl, she always says."

"Does she pay you much attention?" Slava asked.

"Yes, when she thinks about it," Vladislava told her. "Mostly she's just glad I'm around and she can have a real heir—she doesn't like Lisochka very much, she's always saying that she never should have been born, things like that. But sometimes she tries to teach me things, especially after she realized I could learn—Lisochka doesn't learn very well, she just whines—and I had a gift. She started keeping me around when she was meeting with the sorceresses, although not for the most secret meetings.

"And after her attack, I was the first person she asked for. That's why I was there when she dismissed the sorceresses—well, the ones she hadn't already driven off; she'd been fighting with them all fall. But she doesn't trust my mother or Lisochka very much, so that's why I was there then. She likes Andrey Vladislavovich, but of course she doesn't keep him in her confidence. Mostly she just likes his flattery, I think, and he reminds her of how much she doesn't like Aunty Olya. Sometimes she forgets to be mad at her, but Andrey Vladislavovich always reminds her."

"Oh," said Slava, trying not to sound horrified. "Did she have the sorceresses show you things?" she asked.

"Sometimes, when she didn't have anything better for them to do. Mostly she gave them tasks, but sometimes she would let them teach me things. I think she was sort of proud of my talent, but she always got impatient and told them to stop before I could learn anything. She always had to be there when I was with them, of course, in order to tell everyone what to do, but she never had the patience to watch while they trained me."

Vladislava sounded sad about this, and as if she were—most uncharacteristically for her, Slava could tell—trying not to find fault with her grandmother, much as she deserved it. Slava felt even more sorry for Vladislava than she had before, and also terribly sorry for Lisochka, and angry with Princess Severnolesnaya.

"Did she not trust the sorceresses, then?" Slava asked. "If she always had to be there to watch over you while you were with them."

"Oh, I'm sure she didn't trust them, but that's not why she was there," Vladislava said. "She just likes to control things, you know. She couldn't stand the idea of me learning something without her supervision. That's why she and Aunty Olya fight so much, you know, and why Aunty Olya went away and left Lisochka behind, and why mother won't rule Lesnograd, but only watches over me instead, because she's afraid grandmother will do something with me without her consent. It's very tiring."

"I'm sure," said Slava sympathetically. "Intrigue often is, in my experience."

"Have you known much intrigue, then, Tsarinovna?" Vladislava asked, surprised at the thought that someone other than her would have suffered from the kind of internecine scheming that plagued her family.

"I'm afraid that scheming is a large part of a Tsarinovna's life," said Slava.

"Really?" said Vladislava, giving her a look of disbelief, as if no one so remote as a Tsarinovna could possibly experience something so common in Vladislava's own life as intrigue.

"Do you not enjoy scheming and intrigue, then, Vladislava Vasilisovna?" Slava asked her.

"Sometimes, but sometimes it's very tiresome, especially when people are scheming about me," said Vladislava. "I'd rather scheme about someone else, if there has to be scheming. Grandmother said

I was good at it, almost as good as I was with magic, and that it was a much more useful skill."

"It must have been very flattering to have been taken so much into her confidence that she discussed her intrigues with you," Slava said.

"She didn't just discuss them, she asked my advice," said Vladislava, radiating the arrogant confidence of extreme youth. "She said I gave her better council than Lisochka or even mother. It was my idea to ask the sorceresses to create that spell, you know; grandmother said she'd have never thought of it herself."

"Really," said Slava. She was trying to decide whether another sentence would draw Vladislava out further, and what she dared say, but before she could make up her mind, Vladislava plowed on ahead with the rest of the tale. She had clearly been dying to tell someone about it, and in Slava she had finally found a friendly ear.

"Yes, and I was very proud of the idea too," she said excitedly. "It was after Aunty Olya left this fall, and said she was going to Krasnograd to ask for money from the Tsarina. Grandmother was very angry with Aunty Olya, and she's always hated the Tsarina, too. She thinks she's terribly arrogant, which is funny, don't you think? Since she's so arrogant herself. So she called her sorceresses to her, and asked them what spell they could cast to keep Aunty Olya away, and they said there was no spell, because her blood—Lisochka, you know, well, and all of us, I suppose—was still here, and as long as her blood was here, Aunty Olya could always come back. And then Grandmother got very angry, even more angry than before, and said she wished Aunty Olya would be as much of a curse to the Tsarina as she had been to her, and that's when I had my idea. I said that Aunty Olya was Grandmother's blood, just as we were Aunty Olya's, and that they could use her to carry Grandmother's curse to the Tsarina, and the sorceresses said it was true, they could, so they did."

End of Part I

Dear reader! Thank you for joining Slava on her epic journey. If you would like to continue on with her, **The Midnight Land II: The Gift** *is available on all major retailers.*

From the Author

The Midnight Land was originally meant to be a novella. Ah, well, these things happen.

The inspiration came while I was taking Old Russian Literature for the second time (don't ask) and came across the phrase "The Midnight Land," meaning Russia. "Midnight" was commonly used to mean "North" and "Midday" to mean "South" in older forms of Russian. Obviously I had to use this brilliant phrase. Maybe for a short story...

Although the land of Zem' is a creation of my imagination, it is heavily based on Russian language, culture, and literature. Gray Wolf is a common character in Russian fairy tales, and certain phrasings such as "whether for a long time or a short time" are borrowed directly from Russian fairy tales as well. There are also allusions to works of classical Russian literature: the epigraph is from Aleksandr Pushkin's *Eugene Onegin* and the phrase "somewhere far to the South—perhaps on the Middle Sea" is a reversal of a line from Pushkin's *The Stone Guest*. There are also references to Karolina Pavlova's *A Double Life* and Leo Tolstoy's *Anna Karenina*, and the final lines (spoiler alert!) of the entire mini-series about "the stars looking down on them like wolves" is an allusion to the song "Legends" by the Soviet band Kino. No doubt a close reading would find many more such Easter eggs.

The language itself is essentially Russian, with one important difference: instead of patronymics, characters have matronymics. However, the extensive system of nicknaming is the same.

Distance is measured in versts (pronounced vyorst). 1 verst is approximately 1 kilometer. The gold currency is the chervonets (1 chervonets, 2, 3, 4, chervontsa, 5+ chervontsev—it all makes sense if you speak a Slavic language); each chervonets is worth 200 grosh, which is the coin most commonly in circulation.

There is so much more I could say about the inspiration and writing of *The Midnight Land*, but maybe I should restrain myself (chance would be a fine thing, you might be saying!). If you'd like to find out more, I'm always happy to chat with readers at epclark@epclarkauthor.net. You can also grab a free copy of the short story collection *Winter of the Gods and Other Stories* on my website epclarkauthor.net and, if you're feeling like it, sign up for my newsletter, where I share my inspiration and backstory in depth. And of course, reviews are always deeply appreciated! They really help authors out, and even a short review can make our day.

If you're curious about the typefaces used in this edition, the titles are in Luminari and the main body text is in Athelas. Luminari is based on High Middle Ages ornate religious texts. Athelas is inspired by classical British literature and is named after the healing herb used by Aragorn in *The Lord of the Rings*

Happy reading!
E.P.

About the Author

E.P. Clark's first story was about a ghost in the bushes back in her native Kentucky. Fortunately for all concerned, it has not survived. Since then diverse adventures have happened, many of them unexpectedly involving Russia. Having, much to her surprise, gained the ability to speak Russian, she then went on to complete her Ph.D. in the subject. When she is not writing, she teaches Russian and contemplates the mysteries of literary form. She is the author of multiple short stories; this her first novel in what turned out to be a massive, multi-volume series. Her website is http://epclarkauthor.net. She loves to hear from her readers, and can be reached by email at epclark@epclarkauthor.net, on Pinterest at http://www.pinterest.com/EPClark-Author/, on Facebook at https://www.facebook.com/epclarkauthor/ or on Twitter at https://twitter.com/EPClarkauthor.

Also by the Author

The Zemnian Series: Slava's Story
The Midnight Land I: The Flight
The Midnight Land II: The Gift

The Zemnian Series: Dasha's Story
The Breathing Sea I: Burning
The Breathing Sea II: Drowning

The Zemnian Series: Valya's Story
The Dreaming Land I: The Challenge
The Dreaming Land II: The Journey
The Dreaming Land III: The Sacrifice

Giaco & Luca
The Shadowy Man: A Renaissance Fantasy Thriller
Half a Dream: A Renaissance Fantasy Thriller
The City of Shadows: A Renaissance Fantasy Thriller
Giaco & Luca Complete Trilogy